# The E Ticket

A Novel

## Lawler Kang

Purpose at Work Publishing

Manchester-by-the-Sea, MA

Purpose at Work Publishing is an imprint and division of
Passion at Work Partners, LLC

Purpose at Work Publishing
7 Butler Ave
Manchester-by-the-Sea, MA 01944

Book cover design by Dawn Greene.

Printed in the United States of America.

For more regarding The E Ticket, please visit: www.TheETicket.com
Library of Congress Cataloging-in-Publication Data
Kang, Lawler
The E Ticket : a novel / Lawler Kang
pages cm
Summary: "A case for accelerating women's rise to power."–Provided by the publisher.
Includes bibliographical and research sources.
ISBN 978-0-9974349-0-3
eBook ISBN 978-0-9974349-1-0
Library of Congress Control Number: 2016936629

1. Female empowerment–Fiction. 2. Suspense thriller–Fiction. 3. Global issues-
Controversial literature. 4. Stem cell therapy–Fiction. 5. II. Title

# Preliminary Praise for *The E Ticket*

"Lawler Kang's *The E-Ticket* is a thrilling, global ride through the issues that define our time and heralds the need for an elevated and magnified feminist movement. You will think, read and emote more voraciously than you thought possible as he masterfully crafts a 'what if' scenario that raises simple yet fundamental questions about how and why we live in today's world–and how it could be so much better. You won't just digest this book–you'll devour and savor it for the rest of your life."

Alyssa Dver, CEO, American Confidence Institute
Author, "Kickass Confidence: Own Your Brain. Up Your Game."
& "Ms. Informed: Wake Up Wisdom for Women"

# Gratitudes

Showers of thanks to all those who contributed to and supported me through this purest release of my life's work. Specifically:

My sister Cambria, without whose fellow finishing school's influences this concept may never have come to light.

My parental units, for whose support I am eternally grateful.

Debbie Merrill, soul sister and college counselor, who advocated the Vassar experience, which has made all the difference (I wish *everyone* could go through it…Thank you Debbie!)

Jerry Martin, for his curse of good grades in English.

My content editor, Marissa Colón-Margolies, for her holistic and dedicated perspectives.

My three kids, for their thoughtful and oblivious contributions and inspiration; may this work help clear your paths.

My wife, Dawn, whose feedback, patience, strength, and sustenance throughout this process—and my life—has been instrumental to the evolution of both.

Finally, supreme recognition to all the women around the world who have had to endure systems not of their making, or nature, every minute of their lives.

May these words provide you strength and resolve to rise above.

Your future is now.

# About the author

## Finite Loops

I wish you could
see the world with my blind spot,
touch it with my one working hand.
Be hindered by my limp
and liberated
by the clip of metal
in my brain
and scars of staples and tubes
on my stomach.

You'd see a world of absurd walls
of Schrödinger's cats
blithely waiting for the hammer to fall.
A world where what matters
is not what you possess,
but with whom to share
what you have.
Of purpose over profit,
meaning over mundane.

A world of ignored next years
(and maybe months)
where seizing the present
of the present
my present
is tantamount.

A world where risk is relative
Of Zen attachments
Not fearing lack of control
For I understand
I am my end.

# Contents

"If all men are born free,
why are women born Slaves?"

-Mary Astell, *Some Reflections on Marriage*, 1706

# 1

## The Captain

### Present Day Minus Four Months

Downtown Poughkeepsie, or "Po'town," as locals lovingly called it, had been a shithole for as long as Captain Jablowski could remember. Even when he was a child back in the 60s, it was a sketchy place to hang. It was also the last stop on the Metro North train line that hugged the Hudson River out of NYC which, when combined with its cheap rents and pervasive, slum-like demeanor, made it an immaculate hothouse for drugs and related vices. Dealers would come up and camp out in boarded up houses and commercial buildings within walking distance of the train station, the word of their arrival spreading faster than the outbound trains. A park near the station on the river had a reputation for all sorts of illicit dealings and was to be avoided during the day. Murders weren't common but they also weren't unheard of.

A local boy, after surviving high school and a needed stint in the

Marines, Jablowski had returned, joined the local police department, and risen through the ranks. These days, nothing happened without his say so.

Today, as he quietly savored a glass of Chardonnay at The River Station restaurant overlooking both the park and the majestic Hudson, he gazed at the powerful pull of the river and a mental stupor overtook him. Images of the transformations that had graced these sleepy, post-industrial environs slid past his glazing eyes with the tempo and pull of the waterway's flow.

All in all, things were looking good, and even great. The town had survived decades-long declines in jobs and average incomes, and its fortunes were reversing. Vassar College, one of the larger employers, was firmly nestled into the top-tier liberal arts ranks and was actively revitalizing commercial real estate near its campus. Along Route 9, the main north-south thoroughfare, business was booming—a BMW dealership had arrived, and young families faced with the skyrocketing costs and the space constraints of raising their kids in NYC were now considering Poughkeepsie as a potential suburb. And, most importantly, the major thorn in the side of the city seemed to be dying on its vine…

For years Jablowski had focused on the supply side of the drug problem. Squad cars and a noisy helicopter routinely scoured the downtown with searchlights, generating fear, anxiety and fatigue within the mixed-race community. "Stop and frisk" was in full force. He acquired the latest flak jackets, black trench-warfare helmets with Plexiglas visors, and wicked-looking automatic rifles for Marine-inspired assaults on the garrisons. He attended conferences in Los Angeles and Phoenix to learn the latest techniques for dealing with gangs and how to read the graffiti. He even positioned officers at the train station with dogs to try and curb the flow of drugs as the dealers got off the train. Not surprisingly, the demographics of arrest rates by his predominantly Caucasian police force were the inverse of the racial makeup of the town's residents.

The issue was that no matter how many dealers or users Jablowski busted, no matter how many houses he took down, more would pop up and take their place, seemingly in a matter of days. The local jail became a way station for junkies. And no matter how hard he tried to instill the Semper Fi ("Always Loyal") attitude in his officers, going out on patrol for months on end in a hostile and potentially deadly environment had taken its toll; his attrition rate was significantly higher than most of the state. It was like trying to stop the current of the 315-mile-long Hudson with an inflatable water chair from Walmart.

Most disconcerting was the posture his officers had developed toward the people they had pledged to serve and protect. Well, at least those who didn't look like them. He realized his officers showed a deeply held bias, based on the perception that 'all black people,' 'all Hispanics' and most recently 'all Asians' were the same. Blocks of humanity, with vastly different histories behind each profile, were considered already guilty no matter the charge. A few years ago, one of his newer Caucasian officers was filmed beating an unarmed, middle-aged, black construction worker to death with his billy stick for no apparent reason. The case against the officer, instead of going through the normal channels, was deferred to a grand jury that decided not to press charges for murder.[1] Animosities and divides were flaring into full-scale confrontations. At a subconscious level, Jablowski knew his role as leader set the standard, the 'dos,' the 'don'ts' and 'what passes' for his entire force. They were extensions of him.

Then, about a year ago, something changed. Something profound. Something inexplicable and, as it turned out, extraordinarily positive. It was more than a mere shift in Jablowski's skills; it was a transformation in mindset, his overall perspective as to how he wanted to interact with the world. And while this catharsis was driven to some degree by the immense guilt he suddenly felt for the adversarial culture he had enabled and its deadly downwind impacts, there seemed to be deeper drivers at play. It was like someone had opened a door to a radically new realm of emotion and perspective, which dramatically altered and swelled his capabilities to deal with these seemingly intractable issues.[2]

The surprise of an empty glass broke his transfixion, bringing his focus momentarily back to The River Station. He motioned the bar for another and quickly returned to the spread of his memories.

Jablowski decided to join forces with other local nonprofits, which he disparagingly referred to as "do gooders," and work on the demand side of the drug equation. In the past, he and his more muscle-bound, crew-cut officers had made the yearly middle and high school rounds to deliver the "this is your brain on drugs" lecture. These interactions were done in full uniform replete with bulging 45 caliber pistols protruding

---

[1] http://www.newyorker.com/news/news-desk/use-grand-jury. In 2015, California became the first state to ban grand juries in police shooting cases.

[2] http://www.policechiefmagazine.org/magazine/index.cfm?article_id=1000&fuseaction=display See section titled Police woman are less likely to use excessive force

from thick, black polished leather holsters. Videos produced and scripted by the Department of Homeland Security sternly spouted off the "government's line" on drug use. Looking back, if he had been forced to sit through one of these presentations when he was in high school, he would have needed a nice fat joint afterwards to calm himself down from the anxiety generated by the strong-armed performances. And he had gone on to the Marines...

Now, he and mostly female officers would show up to the schools on a regular basis, decked out in polos or T-shirts embroidered with a small local police logo, with nothing but perhaps a mobile phone on their belts. Gone were the 'obedience by fear' tactics, the statements linking drugs to terrorists and speeches about how getting high was not patriotic. Instead, they would get into conversations with the kids (with the assurance that what they shared would not get them in trouble), get to know them as humans, as citizens, listen to them, respect them and learn from them. And what they learned was fascinating. As it turned out, only a very small percentage actually wanted to get into the hard stuff: the meth, the coke, the smack. The most influential driver of usage was whether the kids felt that their parents loved them, regardless of marital status.

The officers would take notes on potential problems and, a few days later, would pass by those student's homes to check in with their parents, just to see if there were any services they might need to know about. The majority of the time, they found themselves referring parents (and families) to counseling of various scopes.

But "community outreach," a term he had once pooh-poohed, didn't stop there. With the assistance of several support agencies, a grant from a local housing authority, and some philanthropic donations, he established a trust through which he negotiated the purchase of former drug houses (at rock bottom prices), which were refurbished and rented out to needy families. What were once houses of hopelessness became homes of hope.

There was one exception: a stately, fourteen-room Victorian was converted into a homeless shelter with an Al-Anon, Alcoholics and Narcotics Anonymous meeting hall, where sessions were held three times a day. Instead of taking customers of drug busts straight to jail, they were transported directly to the next meetings with a plain-clothed police representative on site to accompany them until the end of the session. From that day on, if the perpetrator missed two consecutive meeting, the arrest warrant for that bust would be issued. Jablowski instituted this policy because he realized addiction was a physical condition, a biochemical disease, not a crime that required punishment, but an affliction requiring therapy and support.

Of course this protocol did not eradicate the problem completely. But in combination with other initiatives, the number of drug-related felonies dropped dramatically over time. In fact, the number of all felonies committed in his hometown dropped dramatically. He recognized that skin color, hairstyles, clothing, musical tastes and accents were all superficial accouterments covering a common underlying humanity. It is, he observed, a small world after all and everyone, even the junkies and hustlers, needed to be treated with dignity if they were going to ever be open to changing their ways. "How do you respond to hostility?" he would ask his officers in morning roll call sessions as he unveiled his new philosophy. "Do you think the people outside of this building are any different than you?"

Stop and frisk was stopped in its tracks. All officers were given extensive communication and negotiation training. He publicly apologized and took responsibility for the construction worker's death, calling it a "personal failure;" the officer involved was fired. Jablowski hired more women to his force, with the conviction they were better at resolving conflict without the use of force. He also hired more bilingual officers from different racial backgrounds, preferably from the same parts of town as their communities.

He put all his assault gear—weapons, outfits, helmets, shields, etc.—into storage as intuitively confrontations escalate when police act in a confrontational manner. He canceled the pending order for an assault vehicle (the reduction in national military spending had shifted the sales efforts of those manufacturers to the local levels), and made it a rule that force of any kind should only occur after a minimum of ten minutes of discussions with a suspect.

Other local captains were generally "intrigued" by Jablowski's "interesting tactics" but privately snickered, calling him a "softie" and were counting the days before he would be asked to retire. This was until evidence of his efforts started coming in. The significant drops in charges reduced the prison population and thus recidivism. Drops in hospital visits by both officers and perpetrators had a systemic impact on health care costs, days off, and morale. High school graduation rates spurred school rankings, and thus, housing values. Fewer "wrongful" claims significantly reduced legal costs. Attrition rates declined sharply as his officers were happier and less stressed by their work.

Best of all though, was the shift in his community's perception of the police from "enforcers" and "thugs" to "supporters" and "protectors." Intuitively, he knew that once he had the public and his officers on his side, he would have the higher ground, and could make gains prosecuting offenses of all sorts, including crimes like domestic violence. Where could you go, and why would you report something if you don't believe the police were there for you?

Perhaps the most amazing aspect of this transformation was that *he believed in what he was doing*. He had uncovered a source of purpose and passion, one that focused on understanding and working with the entire system of constituents rather than decimating a particular piece of the problem. A completely new side of him had been birthed.

His second glass finished, his eyes tracked back up the river and then to the once-feared park. It was teeming with children of all backgrounds, playing and chasing each other on structures of various shapes, a few blowing bubbles into the wind.

He smiled.

# 2

## Roger Lusted

### Present Day Minus Two Months

"Yes, I fully understand The Street will be quite surprised…and yes the stock in your comp packages as Board Members, and mine as CEO, will most certainly take a hit. That said, this is the course we absolutely must take. There is no other way. This is the right thing to do and we will do it!"

Somehow this quote from a recent Board of Directors meeting had found its way to media channels. *The Wall Street Journal* picked it up first, showing up on Roger's phone as a *breaking news* story. The leak probably came from Jeff Blanche, a Board Member with an impeccable pedigree who, Roger felt, was likely a sociopath. The only thing Jeff didn't like to see damaged more than his net worth was his frail, male ego. Jeff also had little regard for legal protocols, and the leaked quote could be the final straw facilitating his departure from the Board. A *to do* item, but

Roger had more pressing things with which to deal.

Roger had spent the last 22 years of his life at General Motors, starting as an electrical engineer, then moving into Product Management, Supply Chain functions, Quality and Human Resources, with a couple of positions in Europe and China thrown in for global leadership measure. During his tenure, he acquired an executive MBA from The Wharton School of Business at UPenn. He was a company man through and through, and had not rocked many boats. He was a superior performer and, in the opinion of the Board, a very safe candidate for the position of CEO, which he filled about six months ago. His plate was packed from the start.

Foreign competition, fuel economy, union issues and a perception from the global investment community that GM had lost its capability to compete were all brightly blinking targets on his radar screen. He was ready to take them all on, of course. Then something really novel happened: his management style and actions, and the verve with which he was executing both, had taken on a completely new persona. He couldn't put his finger on what exactly had changed, or what could have caused "the shift," as he called it.

He tripled R&D spending to dramatically increase his vehicles' mileage above all global requirements, with a strict 'minimal-to-zero' emissions standard. "The world cannot survive on a petrochemical platform," he found himself saying. He mothballed product lines that lacked compelling designs. "Women buy, or influence, a large part of our higher-margin models… If we can't aesthetically please them, we are doomed," he exhorted his product managers. He rolled out a campaign called "Quality at All Costs," and staffed the program primarily with thought leaders he lured away from certain German and Japanese competitors. He was making unprecedented investments in efforts to reduce traffic congestion, because it was "a global health issue of climate changing proportions."[3] These included driverless cars, battery stations, and radically new concepts to shift the public's mindset from "who has the biggest engine" to simply getting to a destination safely and soundly.

He also wanted to change cars' effects on his customers' health, such as obesity. He recently signed a joint venture with Illumina, a leader in human computing devices to support initiatives such as tracking drivers' vital signs (weight, pulse, blood pressure, etc.) via the car seat. The data

---

[3] Search 'Milan, New Delhi, Beijing red alert'

would upload to a personal health platform that could be accessed by a health professional.

But the "shift" didn't stop with what GM was producing. Within GM, benefits such as yoga and meditation breaks were offered to both office and factory workers. Instead of giving nonsensical annual performance reviews, managers now engaged reports in quarterly growth-related conversations. "We have to treat everyone in the company with dignity and respect, and to focus on developing them, not continually assessing them." The results—increased engagement scores and productivity—raised eyebrows in the offices of financial analysts and competitors.

His most heartfelt initiative, the one he believed in the most, took the Board, the world, and himself completely by surprise. For over ten years General Motors management had been aware of a lethal defect in some models.[4] If the brake and gas were applied at the same time, the engine could simply shut down due to a programming error. It had led to 13 confirmed deaths and hundreds of injuries. GM had steadfastly refuted that these interruptions of life were linked to its product. For years Roger supported the company's position; a blend of rationalized, spreadsheet-driven, quasi-denial and deflection.

Now, he unequivocally had to get GM to do the right thing in dealing with and supporting the people whose lives had been forever altered by this error. The fabrications GM's attorneys and PR spin-doctors had developed to mislead claimants, and the public at large, would not sit well with his sense of integrity and justice.

Call him a Trojan horse, but the first mandate he undertook upon taking on the role was to recall more than seven million cars to replace their defective processors. He also held a press conference publicly accepting responsibility for the deaths, and established a fund to pay all claimants for their losses, starting at a $1,000,000 each. Total compensation could be much more, depending on the condition of the claimants (some were paraplegic) and past and future health care costs. There was no limit on what the company would pay. The total projected hit to GM's bottom line would exceed $2 billion, and it was $2 billion he wanted to spend. He refused to put profits and near-term earnings ahead of his morals.

"We are taking responsibility for what has happened by treating them [claimants] with compassion, decency and fairness,"[5] was the statement

---

[4]  Search for 'GM CEO Mary Barra ignition recall'

[5]  http://www.latimes.com/business/autos/la-fi-hy-gm-feinberg-compensation-fund-20140630-story.html

he made publicly when he announced the fund.

The upheaval to GM's pervasive mindset was matched by the response from consumers. GM's brand, though definitely tarnished, was on the rebound. People, especially women, had faith that the company would stand behind both its products and its customers, and would do the right thing should something fail. Roger realized intuitively that trust was a critical element in the buying decision, and he was out to regain it.

On reflection, maybe the board meeting leak was a good thing after all.

# 3

## The Invite

### TODAY

On the surface, it seemed like just another invitation to speak at a two-day corporate event.

Well, there were a few anomalies.

It came in a dark purple, thick cardboard box that smelled of lavender.

The invite was actually a professionally produced HD video of the corporate chieftain, Heidi Delisle, graciously requesting attendance on a tragically stylish screen that automatically started to play when the box was opened.

A complimentary private jet would be the preferred mode of transportation to and from Biarritz, France, where the event was scheduled to take place. A quick tap on the screen revealed Biarritz was located in the southwest corner of France, on the coast, very close to the Spanish border.

The speaking fees were more than a bit extravagant.

And, finally, this event was being hosted by Illumina, a leading global manufacturer and distributor of award-winning, user-embracing computing devices and applications, which could explain both the excess and the rather boring title of the pow wow, "Women at the Crossroads of Culture and Technology."

*Great, I already have a presentation ready to go!*

Ok, there were a few notable elements, but nothing that would raise an eyebrow higher than a pair of overly fashionable reading glasses…

Except for the content of the video. There were a few oddities that might not seem to make complete sense. Though, then again, these corporate gigs could get a little funky.

*No need to review my presentation prior to the show? In fact, I can present about whatever I want? A bit unusual. And what about that slightly cryptic reference to "you will be joined by other presenters with similar stories," but no names. Is this mystery intended?*

A quick Internet search conjured up only one hit: a plain page on the Illumina site that merely reflected the title, date and location: *Women at the Crossroads of Culture and Technology*, 9:30am on Tuesday, September 24th, at *La Rotonde* in the *Hotel du Palais*.

*A bit odd to be paying this much and not have more marketing. Maybe this is a "by invite only" event.*

All this noted, the most unusual and, frankly, most compelling aspect of the invite was the aura that Heidi Delisle, the Founder and CEO of Illumina, brought with her. With slightly wavy, long pewter hair, charming smile, glittering blue eyes and naturally attractive face that required very little makeup, she could easily sell a clunker to a used car salesman at a premium price.

But beneath this genteel demeanor you could sense a woman of courage, of strength, of purpose. A woman whose convictions had been repeatedly tested in late night board meetings as she changed the landscape of global technology and manufacturing. Whose ingenuity and care for her employees paved the way for the highest paid, non-union workforce—and suppliers—in her industry with stratospheric loyalty levels. And the largest profit margins the sector had ever seen.

In her brief two-minute appearance, Heidi's essence transcended perceptions of her as an inspiration, given her position at Illumina, to a true image of power and leadership. She was the breathing manifestation of a woman who had defied the odds, shattered stereotypes, eschewed ceilings and had triumphed on her terms, using her femininity, not the male map, as her guide. And quite possibly, on a subconscious level, she denoted destiny.

At the end of the video, Heidi made an upbeat and direct, but not forceful, ask, "Will we see you there? And oh, by the way," she closed with a childish grin that conveyed empathy versus intrusion, "this date was specifically selected not to coincide with your birthday." Then her face stopped speaking and simply stayed there, smiling, eyes patiently waiting for an answer.

The whole package, from the presentation and player, to the topic and sponsor, to the logistics and the fees, was so tastefully and expertly done, who wouldn't make time on their calendar to attend?

With less than two seconds reflection, five women's lips, whose shapes and colors could have been highlighted in a Benetton 'We Are the World' campaign, eagerly replied to the player as if they had been having a personal conversation with Heidi.

*YES!*

At this point, with no break in the video flow, Heidi confirmed with unbridled enthusiasm, "Fantastic, we look forward to seeing you!"

The video stopped and was replaced by a screen displaying a personalized itinerary, starting with the date and time that participant would be picked up to meet Heidi's corporate jet, with a little note at the bottom about the weather in Biarritz at that time of the year, empathetically reminding them not to forget their passports.

...

The five Gulfstream G280s converged on Biarritz with impressively timed precision given their airports of origin: Islamabad, Shanghai, Qatar, Tel Aviv and Sao Paulo. Predictably, as the event drew closer and the session's themes had been designated "speaker's choice," each participant had scrapped their standard content and had been furiously working on their "next big thing" en route. Given the sponsor, there was a good possibility other deep pockets would be present.

Upon arrival, five slightly frazzled women were shuttled down the fanciful, sun-washed streets of Biarritz in a sleek white, tinted-windowed van, and through the ornate 19th century iron gates enclosing the resplendently-coiffed grounds of the stunning *Hotel du Palais*. A few recognized each other, as they operated in similar circles, though none had ever been formally introduced. Pleasantries were exchanged in the van, and the group was in good spirits, though this being the final leg of their trip, they all just wanted to get to the hotel, relax and maybe catch some setting rays by the pool.

At check-in, the group made inquiries about any specific details regarding the "Women at the Crossroads of Culture and Technology" event. They were assured with a courteous and warm south-of-France smile that everything was ready to commence the next morning promptly at 9:30 in *La Rotonde*. The desk manager then conveyed how honored the hotel was to be hosting such a "globally impressive and accomplished cadre of guests."

Upon hearing this characterization, the group's anxiety again rose dramatically, and triggered another round of presentation edits that left the night shift wondering why an influx of patrons were requesting both cappuccinos at 11 p.m., and wake up calls at 6:30 the next morning.

...

*La Rotonde* was an expansive, glass-enclosed hall overlooking the sea. It was where the majority of the hotel's meals were served. Other guests, having been informed it was required for a very private event, had been directed to other venues on the property or were encouraged to enjoy room service which would be taken care of by the event sponsor to offset any inconvenience.

By 9:20, five visibly caffeinated and sharply dressed women had gathered at the French doors to the entrance of *La Rotonde*. They all looked surprisingly relaxed as they all had just received a thank you text message notifying them their presentations, due by 9:15, had been successfully uploaded to www.illumina.com/eventprep. Outside the closed doors sat a 2' x 3' sign on a polished wood easel heralding the event in dark purple modern font on lily-white background, but nothing more.

Morning salutations flowed, though the presenters began to feel slightly puzzled as 9:30 quickly approached and it seemed they were the only ones present.

*Maybe the audience has already arrived and Ms. Delisle is briefing them inside?*

Somewhere in the hotel, a grandfather clock's half hour chimes kicked in and just as one of the presenters, an older woman with short, muddled hair, started making movements to knock, the doors were confidently pulled open by none other than Heidi Delisle.

Heidi, who couldn't be more than five foot five, was wearing a pair of white linen capris, an un-tucked light blue cotton blouse, some slightly funky dangling earrings and a chic pair of slightly worn, open-toed leather sandals. Her lustrous silver hair framed a sweet face that, while having seen many a summer, had not wrinkled nearly as much as one might expect. Set inside her heart-shaped visage was a pair of sparkling sapphire-colored eyes. The only element that looked a bit off kilter was an aging silver necklace that looked like it had been found at a 1970s-era thrift store.

"Welcome, welcome all…Please, come in!" she implored buoyantly, motioning the women into the center of the room, where a round table clothed in purple skirt was waiting. Blank posters mounted on easels had also been placed a few feet behind each seat. "Coffee or tea?" she asked cheerfully, motioning to a nearby station.

The speakers followed her lead. As they made their way to the table, they saw that the room could easily accommodate 20 times their current numbers, but no one else was there. Not even wait staff. Eyebrows first raised in surprise and then furrowed in speculation.

Heidi smiled and shook hands, her blue eyes benevolently trying to connect with their souls. She was obviously ecstatic. "And you must be Shalala…It is such a distinct honor to finally meet you in person."

Two women briefly dispensed themselves coffee and then joined the rest of the group that was now seated and eyeing Heidi with a polite mix of curiosity and inquiry. Heidi finished her individual salutations and then turned and expanded her attention to the entire table.

"I just love Biarritz! Isn't this place fabulous? We can explore a bit during our time here. But first, I'll bet you all are wondering just what it is you are doing here. Am I right?"

"Yes," replied five voices, whose anxieties were becoming incrementally more relaxed with each passing word.

*Perhaps she isn't too crazy…*

"Well, as you can probably tell, there isn't much of an audience here," she laughed, sweeping an arm around the room. "And I am sorry if any of you went a little overboard with coming up with new content for your presentations. I was just reviewing all your decks and I am truly stunned by the potential in this room."

*OK, now I am a bit upset… I really would have liked to have gone for a walk on the beach last night.*

Heidi continued, "So, there won't be any formal presentations today per se, though I fervently hope we all get to know each other—our stories and our work—a lot better over the next day. I'd really like to include you all in something extraordinarily special, if you are up for it."

All eyes were riveted on Heidi.

*She spent how much on this event just to have us get to know each other? Isn't she in technology? Hasn't she heard of online meetings?*

A dark skinned woman spoke first, her firm French-Congolese accent blending skepticism and interest. "So Heidi, this event, is it a hoax?"

"Ha-ha! Well, yes it is, in the strictest definition. Make no mistake though, we will be discussing women at the crossroads of culture and technology in some pretty meaningful ways." Heidi's confidence in her yet-to-be-released agenda and palpable glee at getting to be in their company once more put the group more at ease. Several women nestled into their seats in slightly more relaxed positions.

"Again, I am so sorry this whole thing has been a bit of a mystery. It needed to be, and you will understand why as the day goes on."

Heidi then rose from her chair and started to slowly circle the table as she spoke. It was obvious she had put a great deal of thought, and probably practice, into what she said next. Her voice suddenly became intently sober.

"The reason we are here is because I believe the state of the world needs some major re-aligning…Wouldn't you all agree?" she asked with the positive, honed experience of getting people to "yes." Heads nodded slightly.

"Our oceans," she said, waving one hand toward the water and using the other to touch a Latin woman's shoulder, "are becoming acid baths with plastic bubbles as climate change is reaching an irreversible point of inflection." She continued, "The amount we spend, as a species, on ways to destroy each other dwarfs what we spend on ways to grow each other." She gently cupped the shoulder of a woman in a headscarf as she passed her. "Wars just keep happening and the world still does not understand that women's rights are human rights." Her voice had gone from serious to serrated.

She paused both her monologue and movement and then asked with utmost frankness, "The question is why? Why are we in this mess? Why does 80% of our global population—5.6 billion people—try to live on under $10 per day, and half attempt to survive on less than $2.50[6], while their male rulers squirrel away billions? Why is it that a woman in Pakistan can be court ordered to be gang-raped by six men for a sexual offense her 12-year-old brother allegedly committed?[7] And when financial restitution from the state finally comes in recompense for this crime, the leader of that nation belittles the trauma by publicly stating that to be a millionaire all you need to do is to be raped?"[8] This time, her hand fell on the dark-skinned woman's visibly tensing shoulder, which remained taut after Heidi had passed. Heads again nodded a bit with a degree of anxious stiffness; even though their lives had been irrevocably altered by these dynamics, the group was not expecting this particular kind of discussion at 9:40 am in *La Rotonde* at the *Hotel du Palais*.

"By the way, apologies if my examples bring back too many memories. I will share some of mine, I promise. I have found that denying or repressing our past does not allow us to befriend it and draw on it for strength, rather than letting it hold us back." Heads dipped with an empathetic torpor that conveyed the fact none of them had been fully able to put their respective pasts to bed. "So the question is why? Why are we in this mess?"

She stopped and let the silence prompt responses.

The woman wearing a hijab replied first, with a light British accent, "Education, it is all about educating people and giving them the knowledge, tools and confidence to both improve their lives and understand others."

"Yes, yes, Shalala, education is a critical part of the equation!" Heidi fervently echoed, instinctively picking up a purple sharpie and writing EDUCATION in all caps on the nearest poster. "Ignorance of whatever sort is one of the world's greatest problems…What else?"

A woman in her mid-50s with fierce yet gracious grey-blue eyes and short black hair was next. "Religion. When used for political means and not for peace and helping others. If one looks at the historical and current state of the world, an unimaginable amount of suffering has happened when religious dogma tramples common dignity."

"Brilliant, Gilat," Heidi responded and wrote RELIGION on the poster under EDUCATION. "Absolutely brilliant."

---

[6] https://www.dosomething.org/facts/11-facts-about-global-poverty

[7] http://en.wikipedia.org/wiki/Mukht%C4%81r_M%C4%81%27%C4%AB

[8] http://www.theguardian.com/world/2005/sep/17/pakistan.randeepramesh

"As a follow-on to religion, a need for personal power and control with no regard for its consequences," an unassuming woman with oriental features observed in well-practiced English. "Essentially, looking out for yourself, rather than those you are leading and, by extension, other nations as well. This has happened throughout history and across the globe...and there does not seem to be any stopping it, regardless of the type of government in power."

"Yes, Qin. I believe you are spot on. A rapacious need for power that can often bring religion into the equation is undeniable...and tragic," Heidi replied.

POWER AND CONTROL appeared on the pad.

"One thing that gets me daily," the Latina-looking woman shared, "is the vain self-centeredness that can both cause and inflame problems, at the expense of the larger group. Climate change is an excellent example. The U.S., no offense Heidi, hasn't even signed the Kyoto Protocol."

"None taken, Elena," Heidi quickly replied. "I couldn't agree more with your observation."

The dark-skinned woman was last. "From my perspective, a central cause of this mess is simply a lack of caring for others around us... Treating others as objects that can be ignored, or worse, versus treating others as fellow humans with feelings and dreams."

"Oh Divine!" Heidi exclaimed, tears welling in her eyes. She nodded her head, bent over and gave her a light hug from behind her chair.

She returned to the poster, filled out the last entry and then stood back and mentally reviewed it.

EDUCATION
RELIGION
NEED FOR POWER/CONTROL
SELF VERSUS GROUP INTERESTS
OBJECTS VERSUS HUMANS

"This is an excellent start...By no means complete, but it will serve our purposes nicely." She paused a moment, perhaps for effect. "Now ladies, I ask you: Is there is a common thread that weaves this pattern together?"

The women sat there for a bit, synapses on fire, though no one responded.

Heidi smiled and said, "The answer to this question, from my perspective, is much simpler than your beautiful minds are probably looking for." She continued, "Let me share some of my story with you. I grew up in the height of the Cold War. I can remember being trained in school to duck under my desk in case of a nuclear attack. And the threats back then were very real. When the U.S. discovered Russian missiles were en route to Cuba—in response to our planting some in Turkey mind you—the initial solution from the U.S. military leaders was to actually drop a nuclear bomb on Cuba. If it weren't for President Kennedy, and his focus on how that might impact children around the world, there is a very good chance that today would be dramatically different."[9]

She let her words sink in a bit and then finished her story with a humorous and personal flair that was all about connecting with her listener's experiences on a personal level. "And my father would have made McCarthy look like Mother Theresa." For the first time that morning, laughter, partially emanating from empathy, showered the room. If the guests hadn't had the experience themselves of living with an oppressive parent, they could surely imagine it. Heidi let the laughter subside naturally as she too felt the need to release some anxiety, though before the smiles had faded, she again took control.

"Now, do any of you see any patterns here? What is at the center of all of these issues?" she inquired, with a slight flourish of her hand at the words in purple on the poster.

Her audience was silent for a few more moments as they incorporated Heidi's story into the mix.

It was Divine who spoke, with barely noticeable but still pronounced verbal and visual hints of disgust. "Men. Men are at the center of the problem. They force their will on the world, through governments, armies, religions, customs and their sheer physical strength. They compete when they don't need to and their need for power and control blinds them to the needs of the many."

"YES, YES, YES," a giddy Heidi confirmed, doing a little happy dance. "In fact I would say they aren't at the center of the problem; they ARE the problem."

"That isn't to say our gender is perfect either," she added quickly. "As I'm sure we've all experienced, women can be vicious, petty and super critical at times. Some have committed atrocious acts against humanity."

"Women have been conditioned and socialized to accept a state of

---

[9]  http://en.wikipedia.org/wiki/Cuban_Missile_Crisis

learned helplessness.[10] We've been taught to allow, and actually take part in, some extraordinarily heinous things. This said, I would argue that when these horrible things happen, on the whole we are considerably more at odds with ourselves—our nature—than men are with theirs."

Heidi again paused and let her words hover in the air.

She continued, "So what is it about men that gives them this power? Yes, they are stronger, but they are also more aggressive and, as Divine points out, far more power hungry than we are."

Qin who had been relatively quiet, piped up. "It's just how they are. Like you said, it is their nature to want to…to need to be…in control. To dominate. To do things that challenge, at least, my sense of ethics."

"And what drives their nature?" replied Heidi who seemed to have some background in the Socratic method. "Evolution? God?"

"Well, first our brains are different," Divine replied with a confidence that belied she had experience with this topic. "The sizes of the parts of our brains that temper feelings, process gut feelings and recall emotional moments are all larger and more active in women.[11] Men's brains are more focused on problem solving, fight or flight reactions and sexual pursuits. What I must note is that women's capability to problem solve is just as good as men's. It just requires us a little longer usually since we use different, more inclusive and whole brained mental circuits."[12]

"What else?" Heidi inquired, egging them on.

Divine continued, "Secondly, the hormones that control our brains are different. While there are many hormones, and each has a different impact on men and women's hormones, the big ones are testosterone and estrogen. We all have both in us, just in different proportions."

"Could you be more specific?" Heidi inquired.

"Yes, human males have roughly eight times the amount of testosterone in them as females. During the day they can produce more than 20 times the amount we do."

Heidi waited a bit to let the audience digest these facts.

"And Divine—you are the expert—what effect does testosterone have on human behavior?"

"Well," she said, using a slightly clinical tone, "it serves multiple

---

[10] http://www.newyorker.com/science/maria-konnikova/theory-psychology-justified-torture. Another relevant article: http://ieet.org/index.php/IEET/more/7417

[11] Louann Brizendine, M.D., *The Female Brain*, (Three Rivers Press, 2007). page xiii

[12] http://www.theatlantic.com/health/archive/2013/12/male-and-female-brains-really-are-built-differently/281962/

purposes, many of which are critical to overall physical and reproductive development in both sexes. This said, it is a fact that testosterone has been linked to aggression, criminality and competition, particularly in males post-puberty to early 40s. It is not surprising that there is a significantly higher degree of rule-breaking—from illegal activities to armed conflict—in those regions where there is a preponderance of unemployed young men."

As Divine's summary of scientific facts ended, and her mental focus shifted from the factual left brain to the emotional right, her facial expression transformed from that of an objective researcher to a mother of a son fathered by rape and lost in childbirth.

"Thank you…very much…Divine," Heidi noted solemnly, observing the change had proliferated the group's consciousness. It would have been obvious to even a blind male.

After letting everyone inhale and exhale a few times, she proceeded with the calm yet commanding CEO comportment she had perfected over the last three decades of growing Illumina.

"This brings me to my main question ladies: what is the role of testosterone in a civilized society? Yes, it was needed way back to hunt and kill the daily catch, and it was helpful in defending one's tribe, if you believe such acts are necessary."

"What do you mean by 'if…necessary'?" queried Gilat with a degree of skepticism.

"From my experiences, women are much more open to welcoming and nurturing strangers as *people*…versus anonymous *objects* that are not understood, should not be trusted and should probably be disposed of," Heidi replied. "Yes, people may have different skin colors, languages, religious beliefs, sexual preferences, etc. But, so long as the strangers don't pose a threat to your well-being, why would we need to randomly and proactively kill them? Why would we need to manufacture nuclear missiles?" She paused.

"Female biochemistry has evolved to nurture ALL life, from plants to puppies to people. Men often have relatively little issue destroying it. And I know I am speaking in relative absolutes here. Most men aren't bad… they have dreams, they care for their kids, they can love animals, not just like us, but in their own special and different ways. Again, testosterone versus estrogen. In fact, there are many men who have seen the civilized light."

"This noted," she continued, slowing down her speech a bit to relax her audience as she set up a punchy line, "I believe there are much better, more productive ways of channeling testosterone than its historical, aggressive applications. Yes, many men have been able to refocus their competitive urges in the business arena but even there the results, from my perspective, are quite archaic. The Lord-peasant dynamic of 1,500 years ago is still alive and well in the corporate domain, both in terms of relative pay scales and simply treating colleagues with dignity and respect. Not to mention the ravenous greed, loop holing and outright illegal and immoral practices many men in my sphere fall victim to every day. Just to see who has the bigger penis."

Heidi's levity was predictably well-timed and whatever vestiges of disempowerment that lingered after Divine's statements were lost in the ensuing brief fit of hilarity.

"So, what are you suggesting?" Qin asked, with a faint, hovering smile. "Mass castration?" This response, particularly coming from Qin, who seemed so stolid on the surface, incited another squall of laughter amongst the group.

"No, but that was an option I considered," she replied with enough seriousness to remind the group that something real was in the works. "And I am also not suggesting the despicable chemical castration that was done to Alan Turing, without whose utter brilliance Illumina most certainly would not exist."[13]

"You see, I believe the future of our planet, and our species, rests on reducing the amount of testosterone in males, particularly in men who enjoy enormous global power. Imagine the impact of flipping defense spending with education spending. Of focusing, as a planet, on our environment. Of investing in infrastructure, health care, economic development and research of all sorts instead of wantonly wasting our resources on war, the threat of war, the production of war. Of tracking Gross National Happiness and birthrates instead of Gross National Product and the number of missiles one has as leading indicators of a country's strength. Of working together, as humans, to solve problems rather than letting self-interest shrouded as dogma create impasses."

Heidi's oration had risen in both volume and conviction, and to avoid any perceptions that she was completely off her rocker, she decided to finish the list, which could go on for hours, with some topics she knew were close to home for all of them.

---

[13] http://en.wikipedia.org/wiki/Alan_Turing

"What if women simply had equal rights? In society at large, in religions, in the workplace, in what we earn, and in our homes? What if women could report abuse of whatever sort knowing that they would receive a fair and transparent response from the police and prosecutors, who wouldn't shame the woman and her family literally to death?[14] What amazing global impacts could the 700 million women alive today who were robbed of their childhood and future prospects by forced marriage have had?"[15]

She hesitated a bit to let her closing statements linger in the ears of her audience. Then she continued. "Ultimately, I believe we need a predominance of women in positions of power, at all levels throughout the global system. Women managing governments, corporations, non-profits, and universities. This is my long-term objective. It will happen. It is inevitable that women gain power, but if left to develop by itself, this change will take far too long and, as I'm sure you have all experienced, there will be a high degree of pushback as the transition happens. We will be upsetting a status quo that has existed from the beginning of "so-called" civilization, and there are many entrenched players who do not want to lose control—especially to women."

"We need to accelerate the process, dramatically. Time is our greatest enemy. And judging from the recent U.N. report on climate change, we may already be too late."[16]

"So, what are you suggesting...men be killed?" Elena asked, with a healthy dose of curiosity. "I couldn't agree with you more that men have done a great job messing things up, but to take out an entire gender seems a bit extreme...and besides," she said, without changing her tone, "who will fix my car?" Heidi was a bit surprised to note she couldn't tell which scenario was more troublesome to Elena.

"Ha-ha! No mass castration or genocide...and in fact, I don't believe we necessarily need to go after more than a few targets, at least initially," Heidi responded with a laugh and a wave that brought immediate relief to the entire table. "We may be rebels," with a mischievous grin that unconsciously started to bring the group together, "but we aren't men. What is key is what we do, and when we do it. Timing is absolutely critical for reasons I will address later in the day."

---

[14] http://en.wikipedia.org/wiki/Rape_statistics

[15] http://www.girlsnotbrides.org/where-does-it-happen/

[16] http://www.nytimes.com/2014/11/03/world/europe/global-warming-un-intergovernmental-panel-on-climate-change.html

"So what are we going to do? Lap dance these men into submission?" Gilat asked with a tone that was more mocking than humorous. "While I am enjoying this conversation, I have no idea why I am here and why you are sharing these ideas with us. Seriously, what can just six women do against the global male machine? This is not a Disney plot with rainbows…"

Gilat's question, which Heidi had predicted would come from her, yanked the conversation back down to earth. Heidi was ready for it.

"First, let me broach why I brought you all here today. Each of you," she said, her eyes panning the table, "has experienced the despicable horror and stark grimness of the realities men have created, lorded over the world and defended with all their might for millennia. And each of you has overcome stigmas and isolation by your societies, and even by your own families. You have not let your stories be buried. Your power lies in your speaking out, in using your experiences as gifts, finding purpose in them and making them into movements that have gained global recognition and awareness. I can think of no one better equipped for the challenge I am going to present."

She didn't include the fact they were all, herself included, single and without children or, in the case of Gilat, in a "complicated" relationship. This was important to Heidi, as she didn't want them risking anyone else's future, and potentially life, other than their own, depending on where this venture led.

"I also want to note how the grit each of you has accumulated due to your experiences has freed you from most of the terribly alluring mundane and trifling distractions of life. Purpose trumps pettiness, for you. I'm quite certain none of you really care about 'what she did to her'," Heidi said, making a put-on dramatic face. "That stuff just doesn't matter to us, does it? We have far more important things to focus the time of our lives on…yes?"

The entire group gave her an affirmative nod, and Gilat sat back in her chair, still visibly unconvinced, but intrigued by Heidi's process and psychoanalytical prowess. She was right so far.

"Now I really hope you don't find this to be too strange but I've been tracking each of you for a few years now. There were more… many more like you when I started and most fell out of contention; their scars simply hadn't healed enough yet. And I'll have you know they all received the same counseling each of you received from the International Verve Fund, my favorite non-profit." She knew that the fact they had all been through similar experiences, and had come out the other side not unscathed but unbroken, would subconsciously bring the group's togetherness to a new level. "But there is more. I believe you all went through some screening as part of the due diligence required for your foundations to receive funds from your sponsors, yes? You see, I had to be sure you were psychologically ready for what lies in store. I needed to know I could trust you…And you all passed the tests with flying colors." Heidi finished her revelation on an enthused note.

"So let me get this straight," Elena said, her slightly stunned reaction reflected in the faces of all present. "Those tests and interviews we went through were actually to see if we had what it takes to battle the testosterone hordes? And the monies we received came from you?"

Every ear, eye, and possibly nose was focused on Heidi's response. "Yes, Elena, that is correct," Heidi confessed with an expression that communicated she knew she had been sneaky, but she had done what she had done for the right reasons, at least from her perspective.

"And why do you think we will trust you now?" Shalala asked objectively.

"Aside from the fact you all did marvelously well in your screenings, I believe we all share a very common purpose, which we will get to in a bit, and it is this shared purpose that above all is the most important underpinning to the task at hand. This said, going forward, if for ANY reason you want out, just say the words and you won't hear from me again…and all pledges of financial support from the International Verve Fund will stay intact and will most certainly continue."

It was at this point that Divine's eyes suddenly lit up. "Oh my goodness…Oh my goodness! Heidi, you are brilliant…You are absolutely brilliant! Yes, this can work! This can work!" She leaped up and gave Heidi a huge and heartfelt hug.

"Actually Divine, *you* who are the brilliant one. I'm merely the facilitator," Heidi beamed.

"Would someone tell us what is going on?" Gilat and Qin interjected, their interest palpably peaked.

Heidi gave the virtual podium over to Divine and headed for a cup of tea.

In an excited voice that belied submission, Divine started, "So… where to begin…OK…I will never forget the morning after the attack, I woke up and saw a pair of swallows in a mating ritual. I was fascinated by the sheer beauty of their act, which was the diametric opposite to the horror I had just experienced. I became entranced, partially to momentarily escape the world of hurt I would need to deal with but also because I realized this was a passion, to understand the joy and splendor of nature's most precious gift. I was in high school then, though the money that was available for a science curriculum afforded just two battered books on biology and chemistry, both of which I subsequently devoured. My hopes for continuing my studies started to wane, but then, miraculously, boxes of Illumina tablets, a Wi-Fi router, a satellite dish and solar panels showed up. And now, I think I know who they came from," she surmised, giving Heidi a look of unabashed gratitude. "Oh Heidi."

Heidi just stood there, cup of tea in hand, with a smile of liberated resolve.

"Though we had to share the tablets, I used my time soaking up whatever online content I could. Late into the night, I would immerse myself in expanding my knowledge. Khan Academy, in particular, was an absolute lifesaver. Before I knew it, I found myself with a full, anonymous," she gave Heidi another glance, "scholarship to Columbia University, where I majored in bio-chemistry. I then pursued doctoral work at Stanford where I have to say, Heidi, the Lord-scullery-girl dynamic is still embedded into the university fabric. At Stanford, I studied stem cells and their applications on hormones. Currently, I head up a team of scientists who have expanded this research into real world applications, one of which essentially regulates testosterone and estrogen production. We have been able to turn the most ferocious male rat mercenaries into cuddly team players." Her closing laugh was a characteristic mix of self-deprecation and pride in her accomplishments.

"And where are you currently working?" Gilat asked, her curiosity even more pronounced.

"In Qatar," Divine replied. "The Evangelical lobby in Congress has done a very good job at curtailing investment in science, which is a bit funny given their purported religious aim is to help others. Like many other programs, we needed to go elsewhere for funds." She shot Heidi a look, "Though something tells me there are other reasons in our specific case."

"You're quite right Divine. Qatar has a relatively stable government, excellent facilities and qualified female talent that is eager to learn. And it is far away from the biotech hullabaloo of California and Boston. Nobody really knows you exist. We're just a bunch of quiet and unassuming women with minimal ego in white lab coats, doing something techie."

Divine nodded again with appreciation and awe at Heidi's careful and patient planning.

"I am curious to know how far along you are in terms of bringing these stem cells to market?" Shalala inquired.

"Well, in normal circumstances, I'd have to ask you all to sign Non-Disclosure Agreements though I believe, given that we are at the 'crossroads of humanity,' they won't be necessary," Divine responded with a grin and a glance at Heidi, more out of courtesy and respect than for her consent.

Heidi confirmed and added, "I will be asking you all for your commitment in time, but for you to understand your specific roles in this venture you need to understand the technology…" Heidi was extremely pleased. The group was coming together brilliantly as evidenced by the openly shared humor amongst them, the ease of questioning, and the overall direction of the conversation. This might be an easier close than she had previously projected.

Divine continued, "So, we have made tremendous strides forward, much greater than I ever imagined possible in such a short period of time. Given our work set up, I should not be so surprised." She smiled and then almost as an afterthought added, "Essentially, we've been able to create stem cells that can realign the production of testosterone/estrogen levels in male rats to mirror, to precise degrees, those of females. Now this gets tricky in a few respects. All mammals evolved by being able to self-regulate their respective hormone's levels. Having too much of either hormone in the bloodstream can have undesirable physical and mental health effects. On the surface, it seemed like an impossible task to raise male estrogen levels in balance with their production of testosterone."

"Given this symbiotic relationship between the hormones, we decided not to go after testosterone production outright, but rather explore how we might mask its effects using different types of estrogen whose appearance in male plasma may not trigger unhealthy downstream effects. You see, there are actually four types of estrogen whose relative amounts change at different stages of a female's life and one, Estetrol or E4 for short, only appears during pregnancy. Coincidentally, this particular class of estrogen has particular effects on gene expression, including increased nurturing, giving, working together and reductions in aggression. Obviously, E4 hasn't historically made many appearances in male bodies, however through some novel stem cell modifications, we have been able to introduce it to males with no harmful side effects…

well, at least from our perspective."

"Why did you choose stem cells? Why not just inject targets with this E4?" Shalala asked.

"Good question, Shalala. Injections only last so long. Stem cells, once introduced, will just keep pumping away. For our purposes, they should be considered to be irreversible."

"And how are these stem cells introduced into the rats? Do they need to be injected or inserted during an operation?" Shalala was thorough.

"Here is another really novel achievement. To date, stem cell therapies have had very specific targets: liver, ear, skin, etc. These applications have required injections into the specific organ. This is not the case, or at least is not as pronounced, in our particular usage. We only need to get the cells into the bloodstream and the body's circulation will do the rest. Thus, our cells can be ingested or inhaled. There are certain restrictions about how long they can be out of a temperature-controlled environment. They don't survive long in very warm surroundings outside the body."

Shalala was about to ask another question but was trumped by a familiar, deep male voice coming out of Heidi's watch, whose screen suddenly flashed a talking (and grinning) face.

"Heidi, this is George. It is 11:55. Time for lunch with your crew at the *Hippocampe*. Enjoy and stay in trouble for me."

"Thank you George," Heidi replied with a bit of urgency as if Clooney was beckoning her to join him from the French doors of the entryway. "Apologies ladies. I have to respond within 5 seconds or it will repeat itself." She continued, "Shalala and everyone, I look forward to answering any and all questions so please hold on to them for the time being. It looks like an absolutely lovely day outside. Anyone hungry?"

Yes, the group was hungry…and they needed a break. The morning's topic had been intense. And not exactly what they had expected.

Heidi provided the segue. "So, do you like the watch? In the commercial version you will be able to select from over 20 celebrities for different kinds of appointments. You will also be able to customize it with your own people." And with a laugh that echoed amongst all present, "I must admit, I am not looking forward to my Dad asking to be included…for any type of appointment."

As the women stood and gathered up their things, Heidi tore off the poster with the list on it, folded it into eighths, and slipped it in her purse.

Her plan was now officially in motion.

# 4

## The Whys

### Qin: 1977

Qin was so happy to be returning to Shanghai, her hometown. Though memories were few and fuzzy—she was only nine when she had left—it felt rejuvenating to merely be back in a city, especially one with the scale and history of Shanghai. She was particularly looking forward to seeing the Bund, one of the few icons of the West she heard had not been destroyed. She still possessed a now-tattered and fatigued postcard of its European-influenced architecture, the only enduring artifact of her life she had been able to quickly stash in her satchel when the Red Guards arrived at midnight to take her away as part of the Down to The Countryside Movement during the height of the "insurrection."

The Great Proletariat Cultural Revolution was the brainchild of Mao Zedong whose efforts to strengthen his control of the Chinese military and government led to the torture, rape, random imprisonment, public humiliation, property seizure and prolonged harassment (to the point of suicide) of millions of Chinese citizens for no other reason than they came from families that had a little money or land. This was in addition to the outright mass purges of senior governmental officials and the educated. More than 20 million people were killed. Millions more suffered terribly because of this one man's paranoia and deranged desires for power.[17]

Qin's family was one of the countless that were destroyed in the chaos that started in 1966 and would last a decade. Her father, an anthropology professor, was accused of harboring an affinity for a particular ethnic group within China and was beaten to death using a metal rod right in front of his family. Her mother was summarily raped while their house was being confiscated, and she eventually went mad. Though her mother's death was ruled an accident, Qin believed her stepping in front of a heaving truck laden with soldiers was neither uncalculated nor unplanned.

After being shipped, via a four-day train ride, from Shanghai into the central plain of China, Qin's life for the next nine years was nothing short of wretched. Coming from Shanghai and being the daughter of a teacher, she was supposedly an "educated youth" whose role was to learn how manual farm labor operated and in turn would receive state subsidies.[18] The reality was a bit different. The local farmers derided her. Whatever financial assistance that came from the state required bribes of various sorts to pocket, and when the crops suffered, which happened frequently, she suffered right along with the farmers.

The only thing that kept her alive during those years was the gift of literacy. She read anything she could get her hands on, even Mao's Little Red Book, which she would mentally reword into silly and contrarian meanings. She could also recite every line of Sun Tzu's *The Art of War* which, given its historical significance, was one of the only things worth reading that was not banned. Eventually she would teach the farmers and their families how to read.

It was 1977, the Gang of Four had been arrested, Mao had died and the country was starting to take an exact account of what had happened. It was then when an uncle, who Qin had presumed dead, tracked her down and invited her back to Shanghai. Somehow he had been able to

---

[17] Search "Mao Cultural Revolution"

[18] Search "Mao down to the countryside"

survive the purges and had become an influential public administrator. She arrived at his doorstep with nothing but a small suitcase, her postcard and a huge, yet slightly anxious, smile.

After a lengthy hug and before their tears had dried, she said with the resolve of a battle-hardened warrior, "Uncle, I don't care what I have to do. I must go back to school."

## Shalala: 1983

The attack had been swift and organized, much like the other recent assaults on schools teaching girls in the Swot valley of Northern Pakistan. There had been more than 400 bombings in the last two years. Others had been killed and wounded, however those casualties had been coincidences, not deliberate.

Today's was different. Today the men were after a specific target, a diminutive girl in the seventh grade named Shalala, who would not cede to the notion that humans of her gender should not receive the same education as boys. That they should be able to dance and sing. That they not need to cover their faces in public for fear of being shot.[19] That they could serve more capacities than cooking and bearing children for a husband. That their testimony in court cases had equal—not half—the credibility of a man. That to prosecute cases of rape, they need not find four men to corroborate the rape, otherwise the rape victim's family would need to make amends, sometimes including marrying another daughter to the rapist's family, while the victim was at times stoned to death or committed suicide in shame.[20]

The men had stopped her bus en route to school, climbed aboard, located her and opened fire point blank with pistols. Three girls, including Shalala, were hit.

Shalala opened her innocent, dark brown eyes slowly, uncertain at first if her surroundings were real. A slightly blurred vision of her father confirmed that the setting was true, unless he had been silenced as well and had joined her in death. No, that irrationality was dispelled by the muffled hum of monitoring devices combined with a feeling that head movement would be painful. Her voice was calm and matter-of-fact.

"Father, I don't remember what happened."

"You were the target of an assassination by the Taliban," he said.

---

[19] Search "Gilgit dancing girls shot stepbrothers"

[20] http://en.wikipedia.org/wiki/Rape_in_Pakistan

"How many times was I shot?"

"Three times."

"Where was I hit?"

"Once in your head and twice in your shoulder."

"Will I live?"

"Yes, miraculously, the doctors say you have a very good chance, though some of your functions may be impaired. The most important thing is that you are alive."

Though the un-bandaged side of Shalala's face showed no emotion (her left facial nerve had been severed by a bullet so that side would not function anyway until a reconstructive surgery was done), her eyes flickered with a complex series of emotions in their rawest state: rage, joy, sadness, frustration and, eventually, conviction.

"Idiots, Father. They are such idiots."

## Divine: 1986

The rebels had claimed victory the night before in nearby Goma, in the Democratic Republic of Congo and the news that the defeated government forces were heading their way had put the entire village on edge. Though death was a common occurrence—the civil war had claimed over five million lives in true genocidal fashion—the fact that many men with heavy weapons were in the vicinity was not heartwarming. From experience, it didn't matter to the villagers if the men with guns were the winners or losers.

From the moment the troops arrived, Divine sensed something very bad was going to happen. Yes, there were the customary "payments" of food, but when the roadside offerings were tipped over and bypassed by soldiers who started entering houses to claim whatever they could find, she started to run. She wasn't fast enough.

Divine woke the next morning at dawn face down in a nearby, unworked field. Her dress had been partially ripped from her body, her cheeks were swollen from being slapped, her pelvis was so badly bruised she could hardly move, and there was a bloody gash above her temple where she had been knocked unconscious by the butt of a pistol. She lay there for a while, watching the sun make its daily ascent into a dusty, smoke-enveloped sky. The chirping of a pair of mating swallows momentarily silenced the horrors of the night before, and she painfully rolled over to watch their timeless ritual as they merrily flitted around a Kapok tree.

Then suddenly, they were gone. And with them, Divine's ephemeral diversion.

She started to cry despondently. As her widening eyes encountered the surrounding destruction of burning buildings and broken bodies, and moans from other victims eviscerated the sanctity of the morning, the scale of the atrocity forced itself on her consciousness. Her sobs turned to wails as she uprooted whatever shards of plant life were within reach and flung them at the sun.

A total of 130 women, 33 of them girls, had been raped and beaten. Homes were looted and burned. Citizens of both sexes were murdered. The lives of over 1,000 people were irreconcilably altered in the 'incident' at Minova.[21] In what the United Nations termed a stunning travesty of justice, military tribunals convicted only two soldiers of the crimes.

## Elena: 1998

The noise could be heard a mile away. At first it sounded like a flock of enraged mosquitos zipping in for the kill. As the din grew closer, more nuances became discernible. The buzz became lower and more menacing, the sporadic metal chinks became linked, like bony steel snakes lazily slithering on the ground. The skyline would then quiver, shake and abruptly dissipate, the unmistakable Morse code of machine flatulence bursting into the sky. Haphazard tremors in the earth had become a constant throb as the steel pincers and teeth gouged, ripped and masticated anything in their path.

Elena had been born outside of Quito, Ecuador. Her family owned some land on which they grew coffee, cacao beans and bananas. Ever since she was young, her mother had taught her the land and people were one; if the land suffers, she said, so eventually will the people. She would point out how other farmers who didn't treat their soil with respect, who didn't diligently rotate their crops and who tried to extract every last ounce of production from each acre might prosper in the short term, but would experience devastating long-term effects. "The earth does not forget what you do to it," she would say.

From an early age, Elena became entranced by her mother's philosophy. She started picking up news feeds from around the world that supported her thesis. She learned of an amazing woman in Kenya named Wangari Maathai, who sparked a movement by women to plant

---

[21]  Search: "2012 Minova mass rape"

20 million trees in deforested areas of their country to conserve the environment and enable the return of local farming.[22] Summoning her courage, she sent a letter to Kenya, and miraculously received a response from Wangari herself! A long-standing relationship ensued.

Elena had grown increasing frustrated with what was happening on her continent. Huge sections of Brazil's rain forest—the size of the entire country of Iceland—were being destroyed to make way for cattle ranches. A trifecta of politicians, government officials and businessmen were profiting handsomely from this arrangement.[23]

As the pillaging of the earth continued unabated, Elena became increasingly furious with the shortsighted and "me-first" model in which these men had locked themselves. She thought of Kenya, and what happened to the earth when the forests were taken away. Over time the land became barren, lifeless and unusable. Drinking water was scarce as the soil, no longer anchored by trees, ran off the land and into waterways. People's health declined as they could no longer grow their own food and raise livestock, but had to buy expensive foods poor in nutritional value.

Elena's letter-writing and in-person efforts to stop the aggression were either brusquely rebuffed or simply not acknowledged.

Finally, in an act of desperation, she and a small band of other concerned women she had converted travelled to the front lines of the battle and, wearing t-shirts that read "*a terra e as pessoas são aquela*" (the land and people are one) lashed themselves to trees in the path of the oncoming chain saws and bulldozers.

She had also convinced a local camera crew to appear for the festivities. The video went viral.

## Gilat: 2000

Gilat had always played by the rules, or at least had tried to. Growing up in Jerusalem was no small feat. From a child's perspective, there were simply so many rules to follow. There are rules the Christians follow, rules the Arabs follow, rules the Palestinians need to follow, rules the blacks and others from around the world must follow and specific rules for each flavor of Judaism, of which there were many.

She had been raised to treat other's rules with respect, though growing

---

[22]   Search "Wangari Maathai"

[23]   Search "Brazilian deforestation"

up with things blowing up around you made this arguably difficult. Nonetheless she tried, if for no other reason than to survive. She saw what happened to those who started violently disagreeing with rules, regardless of belief. Inevitably, they would either kill or be killed and she viewed both paths with distinct derision; she was determined to avoid either fate. How she ended up married to a man who would become one of Israel's top generals was beyond her. Though, on reflection, respecting rules can go a long way in political circles.

Gilat had been blessed with twins, Amram and Nissim. They were the moon and stars to her. Handsome, bright, and strong, she looked forward to seeing them married and fathering her grandchildren. They, like her, preferred to not get involved in the extreme political ideologies that could easily vacuum up the idealism and life of youth.

It was the violence that followed Ariel Sharon's visit to the Temple Mount, in Gilat's hometown of all places, that killed her children.[24] They were 23, had recently finished their service duty and were going to university. Amram was studying to be an accountant and Nissim was getting lost, happily, in computer science.

A suicide bomber on a motorcycle, decked out with enough plastic explosives to take down a five-story building and accompanied by an overcoat of ball bearings[25], decided to detonate himself in a busy outdoor marketplace in Tel Aviv. 18 people died, and 45 were injured, with many suffering irreversible and crippling damage.

For days Gilat didn't want to see sunshine. She drank heavily and her husband had their house monitored for a potential suicide. It was in this state of total emotional despair that Gilat realized that following rules makes you a slave to someone else. In this case, the rules were religion. It didn't matter whose religion, she felt they were all to blame.

And who created religion? Who had ruled for thousands of years, and had exploited religion to their own sick and controlling ends? Men. She realized that women had been crushed by the canons of almost every major religious system. This fact struck her with such force that she couldn't stop crying for days. What left her most wrecked was the question of *why*.

Eventually, she cried so much that crying lost its power of release. The rage and anger stayed with her though. And the realization that one

---

[24] Search "Sharon Temple Mount"

[25] Search "Israel-Palestine conflict suicide bombers"

should follow only those rules in which he or she believes would not go away. She did not want these feelings to dissipate. They had become part of her identity, and she was happy, in fact exuberant, about this transformation. Her purpose was back, and her sons remained at its core.

She started to write.

## Lexie: 2008

Lexie had been sure he was the one. Taller than she by a hand, handsome in an endearing way with thick black hair, a lean face Michelangelo would have given his marbles to imitate, incandescent blue eyes, a wry smile and a body sculpted by his affection for rowing, he wasn't a real catch; he was THE catch. Rory filled in many other checkboxes as well: brilliant, ambitious, yet seemingly humble. He had interned for a leading Boston consulting firm for two years, though he hoped to get into venture capital. His smooth personality and intelligence made securing interviews a snap.

Most importantly, he made her laugh—at herself, at the world, at him, at professors she didn't like, at his parents and at the most asinine and trivial aspects of life. His humor reminded her of Seinfeld's, though they also shared the kind of all-consuming sex that transcended reality between jokes. His humor was also instrumental in keeping her from slipping back into a particularly anguished grief cycle that she struggled with after her father's murder in the 9/11 attacks. He had been a technology executive on UA Flight 175 bound for Los Angeles on that fateful day.

Lexie and Rory met while in their sophomore year at MIT, at the Middle East, a local bar and nightclub in Central Square, Cambridge. They were both there to see a local punk band, The Dropkick Murphys, expel their Celtic-suffused sound. Lexie was a struggling pre-med student, and Rory a carefree philosophy major. It was a little like *Good Will Hunting*, though he hailed from a rather highbrow family of distinguished pedigree that went back for generations. Born and raised in San Francisco, he wanted to return to Northern California for work, which was fine with Lexie. She was looking forward to escaping the seemingly interminable cold of her Northeast stomping grounds for the permanently temperate climate of Portola Valley, right down the road from the VC capital of the world in Palo Alto. She had busted her butt to get into Stanford Medical School and their future was rosier than her cheeks post-orgasm.

It was then, as commencement festivities overtook the graduating class, that she made the discovery. At first she thought it was nothing.

Rory got home a bit late from a department send-off fête, and though he seemed a bit distracted, who wasn't? His parents were coming to town in a few days, half of their stuff was in boxes and they were in the middle of a major transition moment on the birth-school-work-death continuum. She let his tardiness pass, though later that evening, while taking an uncommon shower before coming to bed, his phone vibrated with a text from a number she didn't recognize. She idly decided to give it a look, perhaps to use the message and its contents to play a trick on him.

The trick was on her.

> So sad you are leaving.
> It has been a blast.
> Thanks again for the last
> hurrah. It was wonderful
> as always. Let me know
> if you are ever on this
> coast.

In fact, there were many tricks to come. After yanking Rory out of the shower and confronting him about this 857 prefix number (who turned out to be Vicki, the women's crew coach, with whom he'd had relations for over three years before he started seeing, and then living with, Lexie), the conversation inevitably turned to "others;" and there were a few. He confessed he had been with some women on and off for a few months over time, and then shared that he had had a couple of one-night stands as well. At this point however, Lexie didn't know if she could trust a word he said, and her need to be able to believe, no matter how damaging the information, overwhelmed her. They continued to talk in the feeble glow of a 20-watt reading light until the sun rose and he went to sleep.

Lexie finally collapsed that morning around 10, after combing through three years of email, text messages, Tweets and Facebook threads, looking for infidelity Yeses and Nos in a sea of Maybes. Her nerves, and her dreams, her plans, her future—their future—had shattered before her eyes. She left him that afternoon, upon waking, never wanting to speak with him again. She fled home to metro Boston's North Shore where she simply lay, curled up in a ball in her childhood chamber, with instructions to let anyone who called know, "Yes, she is alive. And, no, she'd prefer not to speak with you right now." Her phone and laptop stayed off for weeks. She missed the glorious celebration of graduation, missed goodbyes and missed her father.

A week later, her mom showed at the apartment Lexie and Rory had shared, packed up all her things and promptly donated them to charity. Lexie needed to make a fresh start. In July, she withdrew from Stanford and enrolled in a Masters Program at MIT in Neuropsychology. She wanted to understand, in the minutest of detail, the mind that could have done this to her.

## Heidi: 1969

Heidi couldn't wait to get the hell away from home, back to school and hopefully get some use from her birth control prescription...Vassar was going coed that year. Her father was driving her up the wall. How could anyone support the war in Vietnam? Not support abortion? And his steadfast belief in Nixon as the savior of the country made her want to puke.

She knew she should feel sorry for him. His life had not been the easiest, his health was starting to leave him and not too far under his fading leathery skin resided an irretrievably vain, yet frail, ego.

But the way he sank into the saggy contours of his beat-up crimson leather chair, snarling at the TV with an omnipresent whiskey in hand, making either racial slurs or not-so-hidden allusions to affairs he wished he was having was just too much for any sane person to bear—including Heidi's mom, who joined him in drinking until they both passed out. But her mother's 'guilty by association' tactic was not enough to avoid his frequent physical abuse. He would slap her around until Heidi and her brother, Dale, had enough and would call the police before throwing themselves in the path of his incoming fists. Heidi was concerned by what would happen when Dale started college the next year and could no longer protect their mom.

Her overriding anxieties however, were centered on the future of the planet...and the human species itself, perhaps because it was easier focusing on 4 billion humans than four family members. Why do we need underground radiation shelters, those wailing sirens testing our readiness at random times and stockpiles of supplies in case of attack? [26] Had the world truly gone mad?

She felt there had to be a better, safer and more humane way to

---

[26] Search "Cold War, Cuban Missile Crisis"

run the world than two masculine giants duking it out via proxy wars waged on other nations' soil as an excuse to spend exorbitant amounts of resources on fighting capabilities while schools needed bake sales to augment their budgets.

She knew there had to be a better way.

# 5

## Morgan Stanley Equity Research

**Company Profile:** Illumina
**Stock Ticker:** LUMI    **Exchange:** NASDAQ
**2015 Revenues:** $174.2 billion
**2015 EBITDA:** $65.8 billion
**Current share price:** $329.50
**52 Week Low/High:** $289.25/349.75
**Market Capitalization:** $624 billion
No dividend policy

**History of Firm:** Illumina was founded in 1981 by Ms. Heidi Delisle out of a loft in West Philadelphia. The Company subsequently moved its headquarters to Cupertino, CA, and went public in 1993. With a promise to make computing intuitive, easy and fun, Illumina has introduced numerous industry-leading software and hardware products including desktops, laptops, tablets, and operating systems. The company also singlehandedly created the "intelliphone" market. Unlike many of her competitors, Ms. Delisle quietly persevered for years before getting her first product—a portable desktop computer—to market and unveiled it only when it worked infallibly. This strategy proved very effective, as her competitors were caught completely off guard by the superior design, ease of use and rock-solid performance. Almost overnight she created and dominated a new multi-billion-dollar category. Subsequently, Illumina has rolled out complimentary products with significant penetration into the markets of education, consumer, government, design, enterprise, and small & medium-sized business.

**Competitive Differentiators:** Ms. Delisle has publicly stated that engaging and trusting her employees (she calls them 'colleagues' or 'Illuminaries') to "do the right thing" is her most important task. Bucking a century of "patriarchal corporate mentality," she relies on Illumina's values and purpose statement, "Add meaning to life," as the guiding principles for decision-making at all levels and functions of the organization. From her perspective, trust and respect are critical to unlocking the innovation, empowerment and initiative Illumina needs to compete, and these elements are vastly more difficult to engender in policy-based cultures. "Why do we need rules if we trust you?" she says.

Her investment in her employees—spanning from best-in-class skills training, to physical and mental support for their entire family as needed, to tools and workshops that help with life—"because it's all life" —has had a pronounced and quantifiable impact on productivity, engagement and retention. Illumina has the highest female to male ratio of all firms based in Silicon Valley, in all functions and levels of management, including software development, which Ms. Delisle says is a main driver of the company's success. She has also created a novel algorithm, which can be downloaded off her website, that removes gender identifiers from résumés, objectively presenting candidates' skills, experiences and managerial aptitude so that offers of work and compensation achieve gender parity.[27] The calculations also give mothers returning to work full credit because, from Ms. Delisle's perspective, their ability to multi-task, and manage budgets, projects and people are all enhanced by the experience. She has also done away with performance reviews and stacked/bell curve rankings, choosing instead to concentrate on her employees' growth with a novel career manager program designed to "nurture versus knock."

Finally, Ms. Delisle is a champion for the environment and women/human rights, and has undertaken bold initiatives in both of these spheres. To support her initiatives, she has famously scheduled board meetings at landfills, coal-fired power plants, on a glass-bottomed boat in the Caribbean to review the state of coral, and women's clinics in Asia.

**Forecast:** Though the competitive field is large and invariably becoming commoditized, Illumina's business and people strategies continue to produce cutting-edge products rapidly with higher-than-average margins, enabling ongoing R&D and employee-related investments. Based on third-party data, Illumina's installed base is incredibly loyal and will continue to grow. We remain quite bullish on Illumina's medium to long-term prospects. We rate Illumina a **Strong Buy** with a 52-week share price target of $400.

---

[27] http://en.wikipedia.org/wiki/Gender_pay_gap_in_the_United_States

# 6

## Two Questions

Biarritz has a long and storied history that stretched back centuries. However, it really rose in fame when, in 1854, Empress Eugenie, wife of Napoleon III, built herself a seaside palace, which eventually became the *Hotel du Palais*. The hotel became a favorite of the royal coterie at the time. The Parisian elite quickly followed...and never left.

Biarritz is also known as the surfing capital of Europe, and it is not uncommon to see beach-blond, board-toting wave riders hanging out in front of Hermès and Gucci retail storefronts. Maps of Heidi's favorite shops, a couple of spectacular walks and a chocolate house were waiting on the speaker's plates as they were seated at the outdoor eating venue called *La Hippocampe*, which "contrary to how it sounds, means seahorse, not a camp for hippos," Heidi happily shared. "I haven't had the heart to let them know why women whose primary language is English may have a slight aversion to eating here, not to mention *La Rotunde*."

The women were joined by a striking young woman, who introduced herself as Lexie Seekay. Tall and slim, with a wild Eurasian look, accentuated by greenish hazel eyes, her long dark hair was tucked behind a pair of fun-loving sunglasses. Lexie managed the various corporate and philanthropic endeavors with which Heidi was involved. Lexie greeted everyone with a passionate hug. It was clear to the invitees that she had an in-depth understanding of each woman's background, as she congratulated each of them on their specific achievements. "Lexie also has a story which she will share with us in time," Heidi said with a smile.

The *Hippocampe* overlooked *La Grande Plage* (the main beach) of Biarritz. The seriousness of the morning's discussion was quickly replaced by amusing anecdotes of serving their respective organizations' constituencies, while the group dined on smoked salmon salad, and sampling the delicious local Pyrenees cheeses. Always smart to let people unwind before you drop another bomb, Heidi reflected. The women were really bonding, and Heidi actually waved off the dessert order twice to let conversations continue.

Eventually, the proceedings reached a lull. Orders were placed for waffles with poached apricots, almonds and anise ice cream. Espressos queued atop the bar.

"So let me share a bit of Lexie's background with you all," Heidi said. "I met Lexie while at a conference at the Yale School of Forestry and it was she who convinced me that zero-landfill facilities were not only possible, but profitable. Now the funny thing is that Lexie wasn't even enrolled at the School of Forestry. She was actually there on behalf of a joint program between MIT and Yale that focused on Big Data's analytical impacts on clinical research methods. Her real passion is therapeutic development. She just happened to be up on zero-landfill stuff for her own giggles."

"Now, in addition to being my proxy in a variety of contexts, Lexie is also intimately involved with Divine's efforts in Qatar. Lexie, would you care to elaborate?"

"Sure thing Heidi," Lexie responded. "First, I'd like to underscore the tremendous progress Divine and her team have made with their stem cell work. We," she said glancing at Heidi, "have been following her advancements with tremendous enthusiasm and attention. Now, unbeknownst to Divine, and Divine, you'll have to forgive us here," Lexie shot Divine a sheepish grin, "I've been working with a small, top-secret team to bring your therapy to humans and…we are there! We've been able to figure out dosage levels, by age, that make men collaborative problem-solvers versus egocentric problem-creators. It even seems to work on sociopaths!" she closed with a palpable degree of researcher pride for her therapy trials on all potential (and probable) populations.

Desserts and espressos arrived to the table that had suddenly gone from boisterous to noiseless. They had gone into lunch with the knowledge that it was *possible* to cause tsunami-like transformations throughout the global structure and systems of power. But the details were still fuzzy and the actual timetable for implementation had to be a few years away. Now, within the space of two minutes, the possibility had become a reality, an inevitability. The timeline to change—and to commit—had gone from 'TBD' to 'later this afternoon.'

Heidi had learned from experience, primarily watching men futilely trying to force their agendas on others, that once you drop a bomb it is always best to let the recipients react first. Simply shut up, listen to their concerns, and make whatever concessions might be needed, if they are required at all. More often than not, people just like to know their FUDS (fears, uncertainties, and doubts) have been heard.

The silence wasn't all that awkward, given the circumstances.

Gilat broke it with gusto, "Fantastic! I have been waiting for this day for the last 16 years. When do we start?"

One down, five to go, Heidi reflected happily. It's usually those who seem to be the most skeptical at the onset who become your greatest evangelists. "Thank you, Gilat. We'll get to the plan in a bit but first I'd like to hear what others are thinking."

The mudslide started. Lexie and Heidi were prepared and patient. Five Illumina tablets appeared out of Lexie's satchel. They were loaded with all necessary background, technical and research information, intuitively presented with click-through content organized to meet each woman's individual learning style. Even Divine was impressed with the quality and scope of the data.

*Qin: "How does it work exactly?"*

Heidi: "We create stem cells from a sample of the target's blood that triggers the production of E4 in their livers. The E4 is then carried to the brain by the target's blood circulation. So long as the recipient's heart is working, the flow of E4 will continue unabated and indefinitely. We will get into more detail about how it works when we show you the production device."

*Shalala: "How much blood do you need?"*

Lexie: "For humans, we only need about 3 milliliters, about as much as fits in a mascara bottle."

*Elena: "How long does it take to kick in?"*

Lexie: "Very good question. Initial signs start to appear in roughly three to four days, with full-fledged conversion within two weeks. Conversion can be accelerated a bit with a stronger dose, however our test results reveal only so much E4 can be produced by a normally functioning liver over time. There is a ceiling beyond which a dosage's effectiveness declines dramatically."

*Shalala: "How do you know how much needs to be produced?"*

Divine: "Three primary drivers here. One is age and this information is very easy to obtain. Two is the recipient's weight, which doesn't need to be precise. A good estimate is all we need. The third is the relative amount of testosterone in the recipient's system that the E4 needs to contend with. This percentage is gleaned from the target's blood. With this information, production amounts are automatically calculated by the production device."

*Gilat: "You say the E4 will be produced by the recipient's liver. What if the liver is not functioning normally?"*

Divine: "Another good question. As you probably know, there are many things that can impact livers: alcohol, acetaminophen, viruses like hepatitis, etc. Fortunately, most of the major use cases can be diagnosed by blood using the same mechanism to assess testosterone levels and dosage amounts can be adjusted accordingly. Alcohol, which can have detrimental effects on some types of stem cells, does not seem to impact these."

*Qin: "When will we see this production device?"*

Lexie: "There's not one with us presently. Presuming things fall into place, you will see one in a few months when we next meet."

*Elena: "How do you get the stem cells back in the targets?"*

Divine: "As long as the stem cells can get into the blood stream somehow, they will do their thing and trigger a response in the liver."

*Qin: "How do you know it is safe? How was it tested?"*

Heidi: "Using computer simulations at first. Illumina's machines and software, which have been built primarily for consumer and standard business uses, weren't up to this challenge. So we purchased quantum computers from a company called D-Wave, whose processing power is simply mind-blowing. Additionally, we've run all testing and related procedures in-house to minimize the risk of somebody getting curious with our information. We've even purchased a completely redundant system, located off-site, that backs up instantaneously in case anything should happen at our facility in Qatar."

She continued, "Once we accounted for most use cases, many of which we just discussed, we then experimented on insects and then primates, and finally conducted a few human studies. Full confession, we did break some FDA regulations in testing on humans, though this was a risk we decided we simply had to take. Given the state of the world, the 10 to 14 years required to get things through the clinical trials process and the fact that the research would be public, were major influencers in this decision. We were very concerned about what could happen if those currently in power found out about our direction. The brilliant and controversial way the birth control pill was presented to the FDA, tested, and subsequently marketed wouldn't pass muster today."[28]

*Shalala: "Are there any side effects?"*

Lexie: "So long as the dosage is correct, there've been no detrimental physical or mental side effects…with one notable and unanticipated result…I just love the law of unforeseen consequences. Can anyone guess what it is?"

If Heidi had placed a bet on who would have figured it out, she would have been correct. Gilat piped up, "So, if a man is thinking about more than himself, and is more nurturing, and caring…he will give much more pleasure in bed! Is that it?"

The table gushed with giggles. "Yes, Gilat. That is it!" said Heidi, "Additionally, per our test reports, if men are nicer, more civilized humans, their partners are more apt to *want* to have sex with them. What's great about this is that the hormones that are released during sex—oxytocin and dopamine—trigger happiness, which incites a self-fulfilling cycle. Men do good, and their sex life improves."

*Shalala: "You mentioned human trials. Can you share more here?"*

Lexie: "Absolutely and, by the way, full reports on our three human trials—Captain Jablowski, Roger Lusted, and the Smoky Mountain Group Experiment—are available on your tablets."

*Elena: "Wait, you mean Lusted, the CEO of General Motors, who came out about that quality issue that was killing people?"*

Lexie: "Yes, he was our second trial. Improbable that a man would have done that yes?"

*Elena: "WOW! This stuff REALLY works…Who is Jablowski?"*

---

[28] For more on this fascinating topic, refer to "The Birth of the Pill" by Jonathan Eig and http://www.pbs.org/wgbh/amex/pill/peopleevents/e_puertorico.html

Lexie: "Captain Jablowski was our first human trial. We wanted to give our product a good test so we chose a former Marine turned policeman. The results were so encouraging, we decided to immediately go after a much bigger fish. Hence, Mr. Lusted."

*Qin: "Tell us about this Smoky Mountain group experiment. Sounds intriguing."*

Lexie: "Absolutely. We started thinking long and hard about the impact our medication could have on systems, more specifically balances of powers that exist within governments and between nations. The effect testosterone exerts in both spheres of the brain are profound and we needed to think through and test what happens to groups of men when, for example, some have been dosed and others haven't. Would there be a rush for power if men sensed other men were no longer alpha dogs? Would new factions form to upset the existing structures?"

She continued, "Likewise, in foreign policy, where force or the appearance of force can dictate winners and losers, a perceived softening at the top can have immense repercussions on how nations perceive and deal with each other. Let's say you are Country A and you've had a long and unpleasant history with Country B." Lexie snagged two water glasses for effect. "You both have 'weaponed up,' have beaten your nationalistic drums hard, maybe drawn on religious themes and have characterized each other in dehumanizing terms." Lexie followed the narrative by furiously adding sugar cubes to both glasses, madly salting one and peppering the other and ending by pouring the dregs of her espresso over both. "What if, all of a sudden, Country A starts making moves for peace, for expanded economic cooperation, and publicly announces even a small reprioritization of public and private investment away from defense spending to, say, education. What might Country B or, expanding a bit, Countries C, D, and E, do?" Lexie pulled in other random glasses.

"They might say, 'Oh Country A is going soft. Something must be up there. Maybe their economy is collapsing. Maybe they have lost the will to fight us.' And given the blatantly male aphorism 'the best defense is a good offense,' there is a good chance Country A might find itself under attack of some sort—militarily, economically and/or politically—as the circling sharks smell blood. Net sum, there is a group dynamic here that is very important for you all to understand as it will have profound impacts on our strategy in terms of who we go after and when we try."

Heidi: "We needed to find a suitable group to really test both our dosage levels and our predictions as to what kinds of individual and system-wide behavioral changes we could achieve. As it turns out, we needed to look no further than my family. My cousin, Jeremiah, had for years been on the wrong side of the law. He was part of a Hell's Angels kind of outfit out of the Smoky Mountains, which are located primarily in the state of Tennessee. We discovered he was involved in producing and distributing a highly addictive drug called methamphetamine, also known as crystal meth."

She sensed that perhaps something she had just said hadn't registered with the group. Backtracking, she said, "Hell's Angels are a motorcycle gang…"

"*Sons of Anarchy*," the group chimed in in unison, "*meets Breaking Bad.*"

Heidi's espresso narrowly missed her lap. Lexie laughed while Heidi quickly regained her composure. "You all know these shows?" she asked incredulously.

"Of course we know them," Shalala gleefully replied. "My government *wants* us to see them as they represent everything that is wrong with Western infidel culture…though my brothers all now aspire to get tattoos and wear denim vests. Does anyone here think the guy who plays Jesse Pinkman is cute?" Gilat and Elena shared a slightly subversive look with Shalala.

"Well, you are right on," Lexie said. "Classic white trash setting complete with empty bottles and cans and filled ashtrays on *every* available surface." Her shoulders quivered as she recalled the putrid state of their standard of living. "Boy, were they surprised when Heidi showed up with me, at the gate of their compound in a sleek new RV saying she was touring the state on vacation and how she thought she'd like to see what Jeremiah was up to. We brought cases of bourbon and beer as gifts, which we used to sedate our targets so we could draw the blood, produce the stem cells and deliver the doses. We had to make sure each target got the right bottle. We also had a control group—not dosed—for comparison."

She continued, "Now, it wasn't as if their houses suddenly became a setting for a Better Homes and Gardens photo shoot, but the changes were significant and quick. In a few days, we observed those who had received the therapy became markedly non-violent. Weapons of all sorts were locked up." Lexie's background as a scientific researcher had kicked in and was reflected by both her tone and presentation style. "We also noted that the men started taking better care of themselves and the property. Finally, the meth production stopped abruptly and the men started looking for legal work. Jeremiah, who was dosed, is actually now employed by a local addiction center doing outreach work."

The women's amazement at the Smoky Mountain crew's results was unmistakable and Heidi sensed each was internalizing the potential impacts the therapy could have on certain targets, and their downstream effects.

"Lexie," Qin observed with her curious and deferential aura. "You said this is what happened to those who received the therapy. What happened to those who did *not* receive it? How did they interact with those who did?"

"Excellent question, Qin. A few fascinating dynamics emerged that will influence our direction going forward. There was notable dissonance between the 'dosed' and the 'un-dosed.' Because the 'un-dosed' had no idea where the 'dosed' were coming from, and their way of life was being *seriously* altered, they pushed back on changes with increasing force and eventually banded together to try and stage a little coup. This may happen with our plans and we should be ready to deal with the consequences."

"That's predictable," Gilat said with a slight intimation of sarcasm.

"Yes, very," Lexie agreed. "So we learned it's vital to identify the *real* leader of the group, and make sure he gets dosed. This is critical as oftentimes there can be those without a big title or position but whose impact on group decisions can be profound. They're the puppeteer, if you will. If this person does not get the therapy, he may either seek out or install himself as the presumed leader of the next 'government.' In the Smoky Mountain case, we missed a key person——the person who ran their books. This person led the rebellion."

"This case also confirmed a classic human behavior: *the leadership and the follower* paradox. When Jeremiah's leadership team, if you can call them that, overcame the rebellion and the coup was dissipated, most members of the rebellion went along nicely with the new direction, even though it was as different as night and day. Many people will allow someone else to dictate their lives to avoid making decisions themselves. This said, there were a small but significant number of members who, realizing their game was up, melted away."

"Question here," Gilat interjected, the gravitas of her personal experience rearing within her. "Going back to your Country A example, I presume there must have been other competing outfits in the area, yes? What happened when they found out that Jeremiah was no longer in business? Did they come after them? I can't imagine Jeremiah was able to carve out his territory without force and even killing others…like in

*Breaking Bad."*

Heidi handled this one, perhaps because the question had to do with her kin, but also because it echoed business strategy to various degrees. "Great question, Gilat. We had very similar concerns. What ended up happening was this: Jeremiah met the leaders of two competing outfits and told them he was quitting the business. He then offered each group an equitable portion of his production equipment, raw materials, and distribution channels for free. No payoffs or fees that could make things messy down the road. In exchange for this, the other groups promised they wouldn't come after Jeremiah or his members, for anything they had done. To this day, things have been peaceful in his compound."

...

After roughly another half hour of strenuous questions and answers, the group suddenly fell silent, their intellectual energy depleted, though Heidi sensed their overall interest was collectively strong. To add a little humor to the conversation she proffered another fact with her trademark smiling eyes leading the way. "And—though I'm not sure why any woman would want to have sex with the particular men we are targeting—rest assured their machinery will still work, though they might need a testosterone patch for a long session." The laughter that followed, while a bit fatigued, was very real.

Heidi continued, "You ladies have predictably asked some very good questions wouldn't you say?" gesturing to Lexie and Divine who nodded in agreement.

"Now there are two more questions you probably have been wanting to ask but may not have felt comfortable asking. The first is the moral question. Does administering this therapy—and I consider it a therapy and we can debate this if you'd like—constitute a breach of your personal ethics? Aside from any legal guidelines, the vast majority of which have been constructed by men," she added, with emphasis, "how do you *feel?* What does your inner self say about the overarching context of the problem and our proposed solution? Your actions could have immense impact on the world in both incredibly good and bad ways, depending on what happens. I'd really like you all to give this your most serious thought because if you have any flags of whatever color here, you won't be able to give us your full commitment."

Heidi had chosen these words very carefully. She fervently believed that in order to take on huge challenges, and potentially put your life and freedom on the line, you must fully believe what you are doing is right. And these women might very well be putting their futures in jeopardy. She also wanted to underscore that the future of her program did not hinge on their involvement.

The sun was starting to wane in the sky, and the afternoon shadows were starting to elongate. It was going to be a gorgeous sunset.

"So, I suggest we all take some time to reflect, meditate and discuss this question amongst yourselves as you'd like. We will reconvene at *La Rotonde*."

Heidi checked her watch, pushed a button on its side and said, "Gloria, *La Rotonde*, 3:15." She and Lexie then stood and without another word, left the table and started walking toward some nearby stairs. "To the beach, Lexie?"

. . .

"Heidi," Ms. Steinem's voice resonated with a slightly taunting tone, "it is ten past three. Please be a good girl and don't be late to *La Rotonde*. Ta ta."

. . .

Heidi glanced at her watch, which read 3:17. She and Lexie had enjoyed a delightful walk on the beach. They both had slipped off their sandals and had let the warm fine sand and the slightly cooler Atlantic water squish between their toes. As they walked, they debriefed on the day's events thus far. Lexie had been following the entire morning's conversation via Heidi's watch. She had taken copious notes which were added to each woman's file, already catalogued with their test scores, prior interview assessments, psychological determinations and every piece of information available that wasn't covered by some sort of privilege. Heidi was quite sure she had better intelligence on them than the C.I.A. There had been other women they considered for the project…but these women were the best. Lexie and Heidi agreed that these five women were keenly interested, though the most uncertain part of the whole process, the part where women would most likely drop out, was upon them.

They reached *La Rotonde* expecting to hear the women's vivacious voices clamoring over the clatter of cups.

They were greeted with silence. The women weren't there.

None of them.

Heidi didn't seem fazed, though Lexie could sense she was a bit anxious. The way she dug her toes into the rug (though they had rinsed off their feet before re-entering the building, Heidi had elected to not put her sandals back on) was a dead giveaway.

Lexie herself was in a minor internal panic. What if even one or two of them decided to leave and happened to mention to someone, anyone, what Heidi was up to? Lexie had been in charge of the data gathering, had personally reviewed each woman's interviews and had spoken with their colleagues. She reassured herself that all signs triangulated on "Minimal Risk," including divulging information.

From experience though, she knew there were always things that one could miss, that were outside the realm of what could be known about others. Things people might not want to be known about them. Most fascinating and frightening were the things they (or others) didn't even know about themselves. Lexie had often visualized a wintry representation of a person's conscious knowledge of him or herself. A good size snowball is what people want others to know about them, at least in a casual context. A snowman (or woman in this context) represents what people know about themselves but would prefer to keep to themselves. An avalanche exemplifies everything people don't want others to know about themselves, are in denial about, or simply are unaware. Getting caught in an avalanche with the current stakes in play could be devastating, requiring more than a few distress flares.

3:20 snuck by, and then 3:30 arrived with chimes. A concerned glance from Lexie conveyed the most likely scenario was there were one or two holdouts that the group was still convincing. Though two in this case would mean 40%. The last consideration was the possibility that Heidi and Lexie would never see these women again. Ball, snow-woman, avalanche….

At 3:40, Lexie was about to inquire with the front desk to see if any of the Illumina guests had checked out, while Heidi was ringing food service to order up a pitcher of Cosmopolitans, when suddenly the French doors burst open and the five women somberly strode in. Heidi and Lexie, eyes fixed on them, hurriedly breathed, "*Il faut m'excuser*" (You must excuse me) into their phones and hung up simultaneously.

Heidi was not caught off guard; she knew how to appear professional even in the midst of such a situation. She had been through too many male-induced games of brinksmanship to concede defeat before at least negotiating another round.

"So ladies, I hope your break time has been productive," she started with her usual calm coolness, though a glance under the table would reveal all ten toes were firmly curled in the carpet.

Gilat started to speak, which immediately took Heidi and Lexie's anxiety to a whole new level. Of the five, she was the farthest along, as far they were concerned, and here she was, seemingly leading the resistance.

"So Heidi, Lexie," she said, making eye contact with each individually, "first, we all want to thank you for the absolutely splendid treatment you have shown us today, and over time as it turns out," *as it turns out* with a hint of *I-can't-believe-you-have-been-stalking-me* sentiment. "We are all forever in your debt."

Lexie, whose face had lost whatever color was left in it, shot Heidi a look of terror, which Heidi ignored. She was sizing up Gilat to look for any signs of disagreement with the group's presumed "no go" stance. If Gilat was the spokesperson, turning her around could have a ripple effect.

"This said, we have come to the conclusion that—" her words were interrupted diplomatically by Heidi, who wanted to derail the reason before it could be voiced. There would be a better chance of a changed outcome if the conclusion was not verbally presented.

"Before you share your reasoning, I just want to understand that you all agree the world is facing some critical issues." This was a classic tactic Heidi had used many times before. Start again with the problem and then logically lead people down your path.

"Oh yes," Gilat replied quickly, shutting Heidi down, "we fully understand the nature, depth, and massive scope of the problem…and we agree men, and more specifically testosterone, are the main issue." Listening to the cadence of Gilat's words, Heidi knew that a conditional statement would follow.

"And we do not believe there are any ethical issues with your divinely brilliant plan," Gilat concluded with a beaming smile of confidence.

For once in her life, with a couple of hallucinogenic exceptions in college and her first Burning Man experience, Heidi's reality made no sense. Lexie had frozen as well, the knots in her stomach impeding her ability to breathe, her face showing profound cognitive dissonance.

Heidi's eyes, which had been locked with Gilat's non-emotive stare, widened their gaze to the other women around her and mentally registered the fact that almost all of them were *smiling*. In fact, they seemed to be stifling *laughter*.

"I'm sorry Gilat. What don't you believe again?" Heidi pointedly and quizzically asked, her mind rebounding with the sub-surface notion that everything just might be groovy.

"We don't believe there are any ethical issues with your divinely brilliant plan," Gilat repeated, emphasizing "divine-ly" to underscore the double-entendre of Divine's contributions to the plan. "In fact, we aren't sure why you went through all the trouble to come up with your whole 'crossroads event' thing. You could have just sent us invites saying, 'I am putting together a small band of women to take down global male domination' and we all would have showed…in coach class, on our own dimes if need be." Gilat's smile, hardened by life, had suddenly become ebullient, like the sun's late afternoon rays as they bounced off the ocean and lit up the walls of *La Rotonde*.

Heidi and Lexie went from supremely stupefied to supremely stoked in about two seconds.

"YES, YES, YES," Heidi and Lexie cried as they threw themselves into the open arms of the group. "YES!!!" they all screamed at the top of their lungs.

A few patrons of the Hotel became curious to know what on earth those crazy Americans were doing in *La Rotonde*. One couple, obviously from Paris, looked downright irritated.

It was at this point that several open bottles of wine appeared from behind a few backs. "We sat down and discussed your question for about five minutes, and then we decided it would be better debated over wine. I hope you don't mind a few bottles will show on the bill," Divine giggled, obviously having already consumed a glass or two. She continued with a huge smile, "We also started sharing our personal stories as we sensed we have a lot in common. It was then we decided to play a little trick on you, in part to see how you would react, but more so as a form of admittedly sick revenge for your scheming to date. We do have a little testosterone in us, after all."

Heidi immediately seized a bottle of wine and, not locating an appropriately sized glass in the vicinity, grabbed a water glass and poured herself a very full serving, which she almost downed in one unladylike gulp. Lexie, remembering she could breath, quickly followed suit.

Well, Heidi reflected, the most important threshold has been crossed but we aren't completely there yet. She knew the second question had to be broached or *her* personal ethics would be violated. And what better way to address issues of life, liberty and the pursuit of happiness than to discuss them with wine? Bottles of local red and white and proper glasses were delivered within minutes.

"Well, thank you all again so much for your support," Heidi merrily toasted the table as soon as everyone's glass had been filled, "and the well-deserved surprise. Well done!"

"Now, before I share the details of my plan, there is the second question I must ask you to contemplate. This one is equal in seriousness to the first one and I must bring this up or *I* will not be at peace as we move forward." Heidi was in "sell mode" again, though the emotional roller coaster she had just experienced combined with a hearty slug of vino on a near empty stomach revealed that her "happy self" and her "sales self" were virtually identical.

"Men don't particularly like seeing their power going away. Per our Smoky Mountain experiment, they are going to be scared because they don't know what, how or why their worlds are suddenly changing and, what's more, the change is beyond their control."

"Welcome to our world," Shalala interjected, her eyes glistening with a sparkle similar to the light sashaying in her drink. The entire table, Lexie and Heidi included, laughed empathetically.

"And we all know what happens when men get scared," Heidi held up both hands with fingers signaling an alarm flashing on and off. "Physical and mental lockdowns ensue, and the possibility for crackdowns… and violence of a multitude of sorts and scales…rises with their blood pressure. Think McCarthy or any other crackdowns." What these women were signing up for could imprison or even kill them.

"Or Mao," Qin chuckled, whose silk-white cheeks glowed red as wine. Her smile was undeterred by Heidi's warnings.

Qin continued, "Yes Heidi, these concerns also came up during our discussions." Heidi got the sense Qin was the real ringleader of the hoodwink. "We all fully understand the dangers and risks to our freedom and longevity if we get involved with you. And we are all, completely, unconditionally, 110% in. Aren't we ladies?"

While the wine certainly had an influence, it was the power of knowing they were embarking together on a somewhat absurd mission that could change the course of history, that fueled an impassioned "YES!" For the second time in 15 minutes, no one within one-hundred yards did not turn to track the noise.

# 7

## Everything Change[29]

The drought in California had been dragging on for over five years, leaving in its cracked and dusty wake billions of dollars in losses from food that couldn't grow, associated labor losses throughout the supply chain, and most distressingly to some, golf courses that needed to cease operations. Everything was being impacted, from smog levels, to wine, rice and dairy production, to craft beer manufacturers fleeing the second-largest state in the contiguous union. Over half of California was in 'exceptional drought (the highest level), while another 30% was in 'extreme drought."[30] NASA estimated California would require 11 trillion gallons of water to replenish the losses.[31]

The state had responded by taking drastic measures, including a statewide ban on washing cars and watering lawns, punishable by up

---

[29]   A term coined by Margaret Atwood, author and environmentalist

[30]   "California's Drought: Getting grimmer, say experts', Mark Koba, CNBC, October 20, 2014

[31]   https://www.nasa.gov/press/2014/december/nasa-analysis-11-trillion-gallons-to-replenish-california-drought-losses

to $500 per infraction.[32] Voters also approved a $7.2 billion bond issue to provide water storage and delivery to drought-stricken communities and farms,[33] and pretty much whatever parts of the state weren't desert already.

Things were looking ever grimmer as the winter approached. Predictions of an El Niño effect had been toned down and experts were hoping for even just a repeat of the year prior which had approached 60% of normal precipitation.[34] "It's already very ugly and looking to get a whole lot worse," a seasoned forecaster glumly envisioned.

Coincidentally, 2014 was the warmest year—globally—in the 135 years since temperatures had been recorded. The top ten runner-ups had all been since 1998.[35]

Coincidentally, the drought was not confined to California, but had extended to two-thirds of the continental U.S.: Arizona, New Mexico, Texas and up to the breadbasket states—those being roasted the hottest. For the past century in Lubbock, Texas, the number of 100+ degree-days had jumped from nine or ten days on average to almost 50 days in 2011.[36] The increasing temperatures would only further dry out the soil, solidifying the drought condition. This trend was predicted to continue, and to increase over time. Its impacts on food production—feed, meats, grains, fruits and other produce—and the local economies that depended on them, were sure to be enormous. Entire towns and communities began shutting down, with folks moving to cities to find work because their historical sources of income had literally dried up.

Coincidentally, the transition of farmers to cities had been pinpointed as the primary driver of the Syrian revolution. An unprecedented drought of four years had driven more than a million farmers and their families to the cities in search of income and food. The male government's response to their pleas for help ranged from indifference to derision. Citizens were actually imprisoned for months for speaking out. "Starving will make you do anything," a Syrian freedom commander observed. "This is a revolution of freedom and a revolution of hungry people."[37] The scarcity of water in Syria was part of a larger, Mediterranean-wide drought

---

[32] Ibid.

[33] Search "California Proposition 1 Water Bond"

[34] "California's Drought: Getting…", Ibid.

[35] NOAA/NCDC

[36] Dr. Katharine Hayho, Years of Living Dangerously, Showtime

[37] Abu Khalil, commander Syrian revolutionary force, Ibid.

stretching from Morocco, Portugal, Albania and Greece, to Syria and Iraq. Even northern Italy and the Ukrainian breadbasket, which supplies a significant amount of European, Russian, and Chinese staples, felt the impact of dramatically reduced rainfall.

Coincidentally, ocean temperatures chronologically paralleled the air, with more thaw occurring at the poles during the last 20 years than over the last 10,000 combined. The melting was only the tip of the iceberg. In addition to rising sea levels, more heat was trapped by the icecaps' dark water holes rather than being reflected back into space, thereby accelerating the defrosting.

Coincidentally, ocean currents, which drive weather patterns, were being altered by the large quantities of fresh water from melted ice being introduced to the sea.[38]

Coincidentally, warmer temperatures hastened and intensified evaporation, which increased precipitation. Models (and recent history) predicted a decrease in the number of overall storms, but an increase in the number and intensity of extreme events.

This raised probabilities of flooding,[39] droughts, erosion and wildfires.[40] Essentially, the dynamic created a scenario where wet areas get wetter and dry areas get drier.[41]

Coincidentally, these shifts in air and water temperatures were having pronounced global impacts on food supply and animal, bird and marine life. Polar bears balanced on the tips of rapidly disappearing icebergs. Spruce Beetle infestations were having serious implications on the future of forests and everything in them.[42] Coral reefs—the rainforest of the ocean—were being savaged twofold: by warmer waters and by acidity as carbon dioxide from growing levels of greenhouse gas were being absorbed into the oceans.[43] It was predicted that by 2050, *all* the world's reefs—and the life (ours included) they support—would be in danger.[44]

---

[38] "Polar ice sheets melting faster than ever," DW, Irene Quaile, 4/2/2013

[39] Data suggests that from 1984 to 2007, the number of flood events per year rose by 500%, and killed approximately 500,000 humans. Doocy S, Daniels A, Murray S, Kirsch TD. *The Human Impact of Floods: a Historical Review of Events 1980-2009 and Systematic Literature Review.* PLOS Currents Disasters. 2013 Apr 16. Edition 1.

[40] Intergovernmental Panel on Climate Change (IPCC)

[41] http://www.climatehotmap.org/global-warming-effects/drought.html

[42] Andrew Nikiforuk, *Empire of the Beetle: How Human Folly and a Tiny Bug Are Killing North America's Great Forests* (David Suzuki Foundation Series, 2011)

[43] http://coralreef.noaa.gov/threats/climate/

[44] http://www.theguardian.com/environment/2011/feb/23/coral-reef-report-dying-danger

The oceans were of extraordinary concern as they housed huge deposits of methane, the other greenhouse gas. The EPA deemed methane responsible for twenty times the climate change impacts than its evil twin, carbon dioxide, over the last one-hundred years. To further the concern, the EPA found that global volumes of methane increased 50% since the industrial revolution. And recently, plumes of methane trapped in the Arctic Ocean floor had been released, possibly due to melting ice at deeper levels. If even a small portion of this Arctic methane were to be released into the atmosphere, its degrading impacts would accelerate the cycle of climate change destruction and potentially push us past a point of no return. Per a leading climatologist, "We're f'd."[45]

Coincidentally, when the earth's intractable, interconnected levers that have evolved over the course of millions of years get played with, *everything changes*. Not just a few things. Everything. In ways our puny minds have a sadly myopic ability to fathom.

Coincidentally, believing, through delusional hubris or perhaps with the assistance of a god or two, that humans can control (or deny) the changes and predict and pre-empt the lever's impacts, will undoubtedly create results much worse than expected…and potentially catastrophic.

Coincidentally, it is dangerous to ignore that more conflicts like Syria, potentially on a much larger scale, will spawn when climate change propagates water scarcity, poverty, and hunger.

Coincidentally, when profits and national self-interests are placed ahead of the environment, *everyone*—regardless of location, income level, religion, country club and political persuasion—will be in the crosshairs of forces way beyond their control. No one will be exempt. Everything is changing.

Coincidentally, thermometers are neither political nor religious.

---

[45] http://www.natureworldnews.com/articles/8401/20140805/fd-methane-plumes-seep-frozen-ocean-floors.htm#ixzz3Iy8ldxgR

# 8

## Common Threads

Heidi awoke to the sound of waves on rocks. She also woke up topless, face down, perpendicular on the bed, comforter over her with a pillow carefully tucked under her head. She remembered leaving the French doors to her balcony open the night before to let some air in. She also vaguely remembered belting out 10,000 Maniacs songs from the balcony though she wasn't sure with whom, if anyone, she had been singing or what, if anything, she had been wearing. She fumbled around for her phone, found it under an ornamental pillow, and rang Lexie.

"Hi Lexie, good morning!" Heidi started enthusiastically, forgetting her impending hangover.

Lexie was not nearly as far along as Heidi in getting going that morning, or dealing with the prior night's excesses. A barely audible and slightly annoyed monotone creaked from Heidi's watch.

"Oh, I'm so sorry Lexie…Is it still that early? I must be jet lagging. OK, I'll let you get back to sleep for a bit. Will see you at 9:00."

"Oh, and by the way," Heidi continued, "was I singing last night?…With…*everyone*?…And my blouse?" Heidi's eyes widened in horror, "Really…AGAIN? You MUST stop me next time."

Heidi hung up and flopped over on her back, eyes locking on the impressive crystal chandelier set into the 15-foot ceiling above. A flood of thoughts started racing through her mind, starting with the chandelier but quickly moving on. When was it made? By whom? What was his name? Where did he live? What was his life like? Did he have kids? What dreams did he have that went unfulfilled? How did he die? Did he beat his wife?

*Why*, she thought, *do all my thought threads eventually lead me to this last question?*

Heidi knew why, of course, and she had shared this reason last night over dinner when Shalala had innocently asked her about her necklace. The group, having given its verbal commitment (which was all she needed), was done with any serious discussions for the rest of the day. Heidi had led them all down the beach and then into town to a little local bar she liked to frequent, Bar Basque Biarritz, for some local cuisine, more wine and more bonding.

The mood was incredibly festive and though Heidi didn't want to spoil it, she also didn't want to avoid the question about her necklace. It explained her decision to take the road less traveled and let nothing stop her—to attend the Wharton School of Business, to be turned down by 32 investors when she was trying to raise her first round of funding for Illumina, to compete with and defeat the male power paradigm on her terms, to prove to the world that women's time had come.

"It was my mom's favorite necklace. I don't know where she got it and frankly it's quite dated, isn't it?" Heidi started in her usual poised and upbeat voice and then quickly added, "She was wearing it when my father shot her in the head from behind, point blank, as she sat watching TV one night. From how they found her, it was apparent she had no idea it was coming."

Imbedded sadness seeped into her voice as decades-old memories momentarily took center stage. To surmise the pain would eventually leave completely would be to deny her of her humanity.

"And then my father shot and killed himself." With that final fact shared, and with a wistful smile, Heidi politely asked Elena to pass her a piece of cheese.

The table froze and Shalala's eyes bulged, her face and body recoiling in a mix of horror as to what her innocuous question had unearthed and the sadness of identifying with her own life experience. Heidi was ready for the reaction. She had dealt with it before.

"Oh Shalala, please don't worry," Heidi comforted. "You've done nothing wrong in asking. I wear it for a reason. If I didn't want people to ask about it, I ordinarily wouldn't wear it. And I wanted, very badly, you all to know."

Heidi was well-versed in this particular dialect, the vernacular of vulnerability. She knew the most important aspect of leadership was to be open about your idiosyncrasies, your liabilities and your sorrows. You have to connect as humans. Once that bond has been made, trust, commitment, creativity, and empowerment flow effortlessly, not forcibly. The deeper you go, the quicker you will connect and the greater the potential commitment from others.

She continued, "We all carry scars, some visible, others hidden. I just choose not to hide mine any more. They have become sources of my strength."

With that she stood up, gave Shalala a nurturing hug and moved her head scarf a bit to expose the residual effects of her bullet wound which had been conveniently covered. "Not that I want you to renounce your culture, but you might enjoy taking this off every once in a while," Heidi exclaimed with effervescent respect. "If anyone *ever* has *any* questions about the necklace, please don't hesitate to ask," she finished with a serious but now emboldened nuance. "I want to be an open book for you all."

...

Heidi smiled as her recollection of the dinner started to fade back to the chandelier hanging above her. Aside from providing the group with her deepest motivation, she had also created a space of safety, of openness, of love that all those who were present could use to share their deepest secrets, emotions, feedback and what motivated them to sign up for her objectively cracked undertaking. She already knew what drove each of them. Their pasts were the reason they were here with her. And while they may have known bits and pieces of each other's backgrounds, particularly Shalala's whose book had garnered international notoriety, for the most part they were still fairly unacquainted.

Glancing at the clock, she hurriedly slipped into a red one-piece bathing suit and an official white *Palais* Turkish robe, but no shoes. Not even sandals. She wanted to go for a quick plunge in the late September ocean before breakfast, to experience the freedom of the water and rinse her head of its alcohol aftermath. And she wanted to experience every grade of texture, from plush rugs, to smooth tiles, to coarse footpaths, to the slightly gritty beach, with her bare feet.

The weather had turned overnight. The scattered, foamy clouds of yesterday had been replaced by a sky that resounded with the dank warmth and bland color of the grey cement retaining wall that protected the Hotel's ocean-facing perimeter. An on-shore fall breeze had also appeared, slightly stinging any exposed skin with whatever sand it could acquire. The gentle sets of translucent blue rollers had become a mildly boisterous mishmash of mud-colored undulations. A storm was coming.

Without the sun, first the wind, and then the water, had become cold. Colder than they appeared and for a moment, after dropping the robe near the waterline and gingerly dipping a toe, Heidi considered bagging the idea. The sky's ominous vibe, the thrashing, unpredictable sea, the unknown of what lurked beneath the water's surface and the physical masochism of entering and submerging oneself in the chill were enough to redirect any 'sane' person back to the pampered, soothing glow of the *Hotel du Palais*.

"But I am not sane," Heidi reminded herself with a conviction and courage inseminated by purpose. "I can't be sane in an insane world. I must join the fracas, without permission, without regret, without shame, and without fear. Then, and only then, will I have the ability to deal with, and heal, the insanity."

With open arms, she fearlessly strode into the frenzied sea.

And laughed.

...

The group met at 9:00 a.m., back in *La Rotonde* for a delightful *petit-déjuner* (breakfast). Everyone had had a tremendous time the night prior, including (Heidi now recalled) taking turns singing a meaningful song of their culture from Heidi's balcony. Heidi still wasn't sure how her clothes had come off but it had happened before. Even Lexie, whose tolerance for alcohol was still relatively low, seemed incredibly refreshed when she showed at 9:02, hair still wet.

The easels and posters were still there behind each seat. But today, they were blank, except for the title "Life to Date." Heidi absolutely loved this tool. It was an incredibly easy and stress-free way to share with anyone—from random strangers to 10-year team veterans—whatever you'd like from your existence to date. Simply draw out your life, however you'd like, and then share your masterpiece with the rest of the group. Heidi usually gave each participant ten minutes to draw and five minutes to explain. Today, she gave the women twenty minutes to create and unlimited time to expound. This was mission-critical stuff.

...

While Qin's depiction of her Life to Date wasn't all that complex or intriguing, the backstory most certainly was. She had gone back to school knowing that education was key to improving both herself and her country. She finished high school, graduating at the top of her class, and then studied Political Science, a rather new subject, at Beijing University. Beijing Law School came next, as by this time Qin realized what her purpose was: to bring China into the 20th century: politically, economically and, most importantly, socially. She knew the task would be much like a female Sisyphus trying to push the weight of patriarchy ensconced in a ball up the steps of the Forbidden City, flanked by every cocksure government official sniggering at her madness. Nonetheless, if for no other reason than familial honor, she would try. She had no other choice than to take on the challenge. "What," she had thought, "do I have to lose?"

She joined the Communist Party and was able, through her Beijing Law School connections and her uncle, to eke out a position in the Judicial Branch of the government as an aide to a lower court judge. Though the position was menial, she was happy; her foot was in the door. She felt it was much wiser to understand how the machine worked internally, in order to change it from its insides than to futilely brandish banners. She had seen what happened to those brave and idealistic souls who protested. And though she immensely respected from afar, she realized her biochemistry was different than theirs.

This philosophy was challenged with the Tiananmen Square incident which caught her, China, and the rest of the world by surprise. The massive outpouring of bottled up revulsion against a male-conceived and run institution that essentially did not treat people as humans struck her at her core. She almost joined the protest, during which several friends from Beijing Law were killed. But at the last moment, she decided to watch from the sidelines. There were too many cameras in the area and she didn't want her "ghost in the machine" status compromised. Not yet.

Slowly, inexorably, she started to grasp the levers of power. Not by self-importance, there were too many men to compete with who had that attitude. Besides, it simply wasn't who she was. She rose through sheer hard work, humility (which was expected as a woman), and focusing on results and her vision. Being able to compromise, to find solutions unconstrained by ego or personal self-interest, was a pronounced advantage. In the eyes of many, she represented the idealism and virtues of the system, versus its dark, conceited and fat underbelly.

She was promoted from aide to Lower Court Judge, where she dealt with all sorts of offenses—from trespassing to murder—with a fair and humane hand. As she established herself in this position, her sentences occasionally raised some eyebrows. She would oftentimes order defendants convicted of lower crimes to undertake "forced education", a sort of court-sanctioned study hall, instead of jail time. She would personally follow up to ensure they were obeying her decision and at times, she would lead the classes. She could justify these rulings were not emotionally driven, but were based on proven outcomes revealing a reason why people (primarily men) steal is because they lack education and thus job prospects.

China was changing dramatically in relative terms and by 1996 it was clear that the country's economic ascendancy was linked to foreign investment and exports. "They who have the money have the power," Qin thought, ironically echoing Mao's thesis. She had heard of an opening in the Foreign Affairs Department. Through quiet persistence, rational arguments and unobtrusively making herself known to everyone in the department, she landed the spot. Her knowledge of China's political system was soon matched by her prowess at international finance, capital markets and supply chain dynamics.

Her responsibilities shifted from applying policy to creating policy, supporting "foreign aid" (a.k.a., payoffs to foreign governments for access to their natural resources—the purchasing of the shipping docks in Long Beach, California was one of her deals), and tackling the issue of human rights in China's export-focused factories. Qin was fond of this last area, as women were becoming an increasingly large and valuable component of China's economy…and she felt they should be treated as such.

There were two additional and incredibly useful benefits to this position. First was her need to study English, at which she became exceedingly proficient, spending late nights with a male tutor who hailed from Boston, whose "wicked ahesome" accent she learned to mimic with a degree of credulity. The second was watching foreign television (CNN and the BBC specifically) and having access to many websites ordinary citizens could not, though she knew quite well whatever roaming she did in either of these mediums was being inscrutably monitored.

Qin was an active member in the Party during this time, which was controlled by the Politburo Standing Committee, a club of four to nine old men whose power over matters of state and military dwarfed those of the US Congress. Her countless nights of introductions, meetings and satiating men's egos (nothing sex-related, though many inferences needed to be discretely and sometimes physically quashed) eventually paid off. She was promoted to Secretary of the Central International Liaison Department (CILD) where she briefed members of the Politburo on matters of foreign trade relations, a wide swath of policies and, eventually, China's foreign policy itself.

Qin met Heidi during one of her visits to a supplier's factory outside of Shanghai and immediately felt a very strong attachment to her. Heidi was there to not only tour her supplier's facilities to make certain they met Illumina's zero-tolerance requirements for worker's benefits and zero-landfill standards, but to also explore how, with Illumina's support and sharing of information, the workers could be paid *more*. Qin was beside herself.

It was at a dinner that night, at a venue coincidentally named "Lost Heaven," that Qin shared with Heidi her founding of a non-profit[46] that focused on one of China's many dark secrets: girls who were abandoned because of the "one-child" policy and the prevailing preference for boys. Qin underscored this absurdity, given women made the highest value-adding products. Girls who were abandoned were often picked up by gangs and used for begging. The lucky ones got into orphanages, which were often severely under-funded and under-staffed.

To mask her identity and transfer funds, Qin ran this operation out of the U.K., using her knowledge of how the Chinese banking system works to her advantage. After about four months, and interviews and test-taking while on a trip to Africa, that COCOA received its largest

---

[46] http://www.cocoa.org.uk

donation from a non-profit venture called the International Verve Fund.

...

Gilat Feynman was next. A passion for the truth led Gilat to establish her Foundation for Good Reason, whose purpose was to provide education to families around the world about the slippery slope of religious beliefs and the power of scientific inquiry. Her first interaction with the International Verve Fund was about two and a half years ago.

Something sane had to be done to combat the religious-based violence that had killed her sons. She had known the odds were against her but, "I frankly couldn't give a fuck," she said, in a deep, resonant voice that conveyed both immense conviction and immense sorrow. Something radically different. Something radically profound. Something that at least roughly half the population of the world might understand: we are all human and we all share very similar dreams and purposes. And sustainable change starts with how children are raised.

After her sons' deaths, she left Tel Aviv and holed up in a little flat in Haifa that was owned by a relative. Located on the border of Eli Cohen Garden, it overlooked the sea and provided Gilat with the tranquility, access to nature and a view of the setting sun she needed to re-form (and reform) her scattered soul, focus her thoughts and plan out her next moves.

Though her husband understood she needed space, he was always quick to judge. He wanted her to be by his side as he intentionally revved up hatred for the foes of Zion by using his son's deaths as a pulpit to publicly call for the extermination of the Palestinian state. In his male skin, he could not see past the twisted reference in the Torah to an "eye for an eye," to which Gilat would call on Gandhi's observation, "An eye for an eye makes the whole world blind." This sentiment, expressed during every telephone rant session, would send her husband into an unrestrained fury. He would bestow her with some rather crass descriptions, Gilat's favorite being a "Gaza whore," to which she'd typically end the conversation by casually sharing how she'd just been texted a request for a blow job by Hamza[47] (who lived up to his name). Gilat's marriage was on the brink of divorce.

Her healing started by journaling. Whatever, whenever, wherever.

---

[47] Hamza is a given masculine name in Muslim circles that means strong or steadfast in Arabic

First in a light brown, leather-bound notebook and later on her laptop. Eventually she purchased a tablet, coincidentally manufactured by Illumina. "I loved the brand, what the company stood for and how easy it was to use!" she told Heidi later. She named it *Neshama*, "my soul mate" in Hebrew, and it would accompany her wherever she went. When she introduced her blog, *Notes from the Front*, *Neshama* provided the vital conduit between Gilat's observations on the state of Israeli-Palestinian relations (eventually expanding to world events) and an exploding global audience of readers of both sexes, though predominantly female.

Her signature topic was what she lovingly called the "military-religious complex." Men need power, thus, religion was created by men to control others. This control could come in the form of commandments, required belief in interpretations of certain books, and as a reason for genocide. Regardless of cultural backdrop, she knew that historically, women got screwed by religion. They were, at best, second-class citizens and, more likely, treated as a mere means for reproduction or objects onto which the most odious sins were blamed, "just because some old man who deservedly hadn't gotten laid in decades says so." Gilat required very little prompting to share exactly how she saw the world.

It was this no-holds-barred, call-it-like-I-see-it attitude that catapulted Gilat's writings into a bankable brand. She was mentioned on South Park and became a regular on *The Daily Show with Jon Stewart*, who compared the ferocity, timeliness and poignant nature of her work with that of Sylvia Plath's "Daddy." The only difference, he said, was that the swastikas had been replaced by world flags. Gilat fearlessly followed his lead by underscoring the power fathers have on their children.

She also delivered an impressively researched TED talk on the military-religious complex that ended with a call for "hardcore activism" against organized religion, for "Militaries cannot survive long without an excuse to bash someone else." No religion was safe from the ease with which she could dismember it like using, for example, just one scientific fact: the age of our earth. If the earth was divinely created ten thousand years ago, how is it that dinosaur fossils date back over 200 million years?

"Inevitably," she reservedly yet proudly admitted to the group in *La Rotonde*, "my journey of healing took me to atheism and science for answers." On her *Life to Date* poster, she drew the Jewish flag with the Star of David replaced by a cell nucleus.

...

Shalala's story began with her attempted murder. She had been quickly shuttled out of Pakistan to nearby Singapore more for safety purposes than better treatment. There were those in Pakistan who were furious that she had survived the brutal and unprovoked attack. In fact, in the years that followed, Shalala would not return to her home for fear of lethal reprisals. After a few days in Singapore, she was moved to London where the arduous process of facial plastic surgeries and physical therapy to help her walk without assistance, and move her arms again, kept her under wraps for a few months. But when her catharsis was complete, out popped a stunning and resilient butterfly that was willing and able to take on the world.

She was a hero, an international inspiration to girls of someone who simply would not let archaic and patriarchal mores dictate her life. Her calm, objective and mature persona was an instant hit with the media, who gobbled up every word she said. Radio and TV talk shows on all continents, a book that eventually led to the Nobel Peace Prize, and a striking appearance at the United Nations in New York City raised extravagant amounts of awareness, and funds, for the simple purpose of educating the female gender. She set up a foundation and got to work while finishing high school, eventually receiving a degree in Women's Studies from Oxford University.

An adamant view emerging from her studies was the observation that the central role of any government was to educate its citizenry, and that having women versed in business and management training was, per a report from Goldman Sachs and the World Bank:

> A key source of long-term economic growth…Female education can lead not only to increased revenues and job creation, but also to healthier, better educated families and, ultimately, more prosperous communities and nations. Put more simply, by helping to transform the lives of promising women entrepreneurs, we in turn transform the lives of those around them.[48]

Looking at the state of just elementary school education for girls across the map of developing nations meant that men running those

---

[48]  Search "Goldman Sachs 10,000 Women"

countries were more concerned with generating power through military means (expenditures) than developing their respective economies. Indeed, the military-religious complex at the heart of Gilat's work had a significant degree of credibility for Shalala. The physical and societal manifestations were abundant: at the extreme end, being required to wear clothes that covered from head to toe, not being able to drive or vote, genital mutilation, forced illiteracy, dismal work prospects and being stoned to death for owning a cell phone or for "allowing yourself" to be raped.[49]

Shalala's *raison d'être* (reason for being) rapidly expanded from women's education to women's rights. Not only was her foundation funding schools for girls in some of the poorest regions of the world, the schools were being used at night, sometimes in secret, to provide a place of learning for all women. She produced seminars on how to start and run your own business (replete with a guide to micro-finance), sales skills, communication and team building, accounting, and the value of marketing.

And, with a generous donation from the International Verve Fund a few years ago, each school found itself with a LED TV, high-speed satellite Internet access and wireless routers, and Illumina tablets and laptops (similar to the crate that arrived at Divine's school), all powered by a combination of solar panels on school's roofs and a nifty, washing-machine sized box that turned animal dung into electricity.

. . .

Elena was ready to go. Her poster started with her incident as well. Heidi would later reflect that she might want to retitle the poster from 'Life to Date' to 'Life *after* Date,' as one might start to really exist only after a life-changing event.

Elena and crew's confrontation with the forest killers changed her life. The video and audio footage of men with powered metal, noisily barreling toward young women strapped to gorgeous, mature trees was metaphorically priceless. CNN picked up the story (which was noted by a particular corporate chieftess who was immediately attracted to the leader of the 'gang').

The moment was pivotal for Elena for she learned that a few

---

[49] Search for "Women stoned to death in Pakistan"

committed individuals could really make a BIG difference. She had experienced firsthand what Wangari had in Kenya: the power of a grassroots environmental movement.

Elena seized the opportunity of the media circus and her "the land and the people are one" campaign was born. It would eventually evolve to "the planet and its people are one," incorporating a host of interconnected issues on land, air, and water into her overall mission. Her special interest, the state of the oceans, introduced her to the work of marine biologist Sylvia Earle, with whom she also eventually developed a correspondence.

Regardless of the issue, everywhere she looked she saw the same consortium of business and political ignorance, indifference and denial of the tenuous balance our species and environment need to maintain. She knew that if humans did not maintain this balance, "all hell" would break loose. And it was already starting.

The leaders within these colluding interest groups were all men, or "motherfuckers" as Elena would cheerfully refer to them in her spicy Ecuadorian accent. There were women Elena had encountered who were part of the system, typically at medium to lower levels. She could sense they wanted to do something, they just didn't know what or how to do it. They felt powerless to stop the testosterone juggernaut. Most importantly, they needed permission to walk the path less travelled— permission that Elena emphatically granted.

Elena, like Qin, realized two things: that outright confrontation of the powers that be would only increase those powers' focus on thwarting her efforts, and that education opens many, many doors one could spend decades banging their head against. On a lark, she applied to Cornell University for its famed Natural Resources Department. With her application, she sent a copy of the video and the actual shirt she wore during its filming. She got in on a full scholarship from an "anonymous donor," she said, smiling gratefully at Heidi. While at Cornell, she spent a semester at Smith College whose avant-guard campus sustainability program would become a very useful model for her later work.

Once out of college, armed with the confidence, knowledge and idealism education can instill, Elena returned to Brazil and started up a little non-profit that provided women in managerial positions with the education, resources and self-confidence to discretely change any conversation related to the environment. Through human resources departments ("which were predominantly run by women," she said with a conspiratorial smile) of large multi-nationals, governments, and political parties, women were encouraged to reach for quantum goals, not just incremental change. To dare to build skyscrapers and not just lay bricks, she would pontificate.[50] The International Verve Fund had made a substantial gift about two years ago and had been instrumental in helping to raise other monies to endow the program for growth.

"Thank you, thank you," Elena said to Heidi, her eyes again watering with the newfound recognition of what Heidi had done for her, and the other women at the breakfast table. "We are going to teach those motherfuckers a lesson!"

"No, no…Thank YOU," Heidi replied, accepting Elena's hug with open arms. "And yes, I hope we do."

...

Heidi glowed with small bursts of pride as everyone's story had a reference to the International Verve Fund whose name, when fashioned into an acronym "wasn't a bad option," she comically shared. Though her humor was met with laughter, it was tinged with slight tones of sadness, frustration and anxiety, depending on the woman, her history and age.

The time it took for the women to share their stories had far exceeded Heidi's schedule…and she was fine with it.

"In the interest of time, we need to push on. I believe we all got a good understanding of Divine's life yesterday and Divine, if you'd like we can give you some time later." Divine graciously nodded.

Heidi flipped to the next poster on her easel which had a pyramid on it. "This is called a Passion Pyramid and it will help us identify our personal *purposes* and *passions*." She asked the group, "When was the last time anyone asked you what your purpose was and gave you a tool to help you figure it out?"

"During the screenings for IVF funding," said Shalala in the midst of nodding heads. Heidi had momentarily forgotten about that part of IVF's protocols. "Ha-ha, you are quite right. What about the second part of the question…anyone ever give you a workable process to help you figure it out?" All heads shook, *no*.

"I'm not surprised at all," Heidi continued, "Taking you through this process will help you clarify your purposes *and* help us come together as

---

[50]   Thanks to Mark Burrell, awesome human, for this reference

a team."

"The man who introduced me to this process reports that in his work with some of the largest and most powerful organizations in their industries, nine times out of ten no one has ever, in the length of their career, been asked the first question and much less been supported by the second. From his perspective, identifying these purposes and passions and then aligning them with your work, and the efforts of your organization, can have extraordinary impacts on not just performance, but also on happiness, health, and relationships.[51] He likes to say "It's *all* life." Identifying your purpose is essentially the difference between, using Elena's metaphor, "building skyscrapers and laying bricks," though I personally like to frame it as "growing gardens versus turning soil." Skyscrapers are a bit phallic, don't you think?" The laughter from the day before, which hadn't really gone away, re-awoke with relish.

Heidi proceeded to walk the women through the pyramid process and then busily got to work on hers. Forty minutes later, the group took a collective step back from their posters and, at Heidi's suggestion, looked for patterns across their entries. Themes became patently obvious. The women were passionate about making a difference, not being held back and improving the lives of others. Purpose statements reflected each woman's personal experiences, though one overarching word rose to the pinnacle of everyone's pyramid: *peace*.

Gilat, with a hint of surprise, was the first one to call out this consistency. "Wow!" she exclaimed. "This is fascinating…though we all come from different backgrounds and life experiences, we all share similar values…and making peace happen is at the top of the list."

Heidi, who had run all her management teams through this process, was prepared for this observation. "Yes Gilat. What I love about this tool is that it reveals we are all human at a very basic level and men, especially, cannot be forgotten in this context. We all have very similar passions, purposes and dreams as it turns out."

She continued, "I'll be sharing the outlines of a plan this afternoon, a plan with which I will be asking you to become irreversibly involved." Her voice slowed a bit to impart the seriousness of her next statement. "Now, I'm sure you are aware what we will be doing could be hazardous to your health…" she said with a wry smile. She knew humor always helped in these situations. "…and could test your already-tested cores."

---

[51] Lawler Kang, *Passion at Work* (Pearson Prentice Hall, 2005)

Instinctually, she paused again. "Should this ever happen, I'd like you all to think back to what has been done here today, and the feelings each of you are experiencing right now. Our power as individuals is stunning…as a collective we are unstoppable. Draw on this for additional strength you may need to reach our shared goal…of peace."

Heidi was right. The outputs said it all. Seven spines shivered with a rush of adrenaline and the entire group started hugging each other. Eyes teared up. Tears of joy, of strength, of a camaraderie they all had been longing for their entire lives that now had come together, a union with the power to create change on a global scale. Heidi wrote "PEACE" in large purple letters on a blank poster for a backdrop. With the assistance of her voice activated-tablet camera, she captured that pivotal moment in the lives of all present. The picture, which had been automatically retouched using the *festive* setting, was texted to each woman's phone.

"May it serve you well, should you ever need it," Heidi whispered to herself.

# 9

## Putin: Round 1

B y all accounts, Vladimir Putin had a tough road in front of him but he was used to difficult situations. In fact, he really didn't care. It was all a game to him. Friends and trading partners, adversaries and enemy states all blurred into chess pieces that he could move, remove, disempower or simply jump over (trampling isn't possible in chess) as he oversaw the largest stockpile of nuclear weapons in the world.

The child of detached parents, his career was one of cunning, ambition, and, most of all, a polished veneer of controlled ruthlessness that some said indicated a lack of conscience. The persona of the 17-year KGB veteran was supported and extolled by the Russian media. Russia's economy, fueled by soaring oil and natural gas prices, grew tremendously in the first decade of this century. Earnings of the average Russian citizen almost doubled from US$8,706 in 2000 to US$14,299 in 2010. The middle class rose dramatically to 60% of the population over the same time frame.[52] It was during this period when Putin held a variety of Russia's top posts, and increasingly cracked down on freedoms (of speech, media, etc.) and democratic advances at all levels.

The majority of the Russian populace didn't mind. They had been oppressed for centuries and finally they could see (and taste and touch) a hopeful future. Life was good enough. And then the slowdown began. Oil prices, though spiking in 2010 and 2012, started to fall just as Putin was elected for a six-year presidential term. Spot prices on the global market for natural gas (which was heavily subsidized by the state) favored U.S. suppliers for the first time ever.

Facing these challenges, Putin needed a way to maintain his power and his net worth, estimated by *Forbes* at $70 billion. Like most Russian billionaires, it was amassed by securing ownership of Russia's natural resources through, coincidentally, oil and natural gas. "Humbly serving" the Russian populace on a yearly salary of US$187,000, his ownership of 58 aircraft, a $340 million palace on the Black Sea, a $44 million yacht and a $500,000 timepiece collection was facilitated by shell companies, front men, and back-room deals with his privileged inner circle.[53] And, having the majority of the Russian population in his back pocket, Putin could beat whatever nationalistic drums were at his disposal to restore Russian pride in the new global order with little fear of internal reprisals. After all, he was the savior of Russia.

At the center of this strategy, like virtually all others from past failed empires, was armament or, in this case, the re-armament of Russia. Starting in 2010, Putin called for expenditures of $730 billion over a 10-year period.[54] These monies would fund 100 new warships, 8 missile-carrying submarines, 600 warplanes, 1,000 attack helicopters and an additional 400,000 troops to bring the total strength of the Russian army to 1.2 million. The rationale behind these expenditures was not about re-freezing the Cold War, but rather to manage near-shore conflicts with Russia's former republics where Russia and Putin felt the need to re-assert dominance. Surprisingly, none of these former republics, having relatively tiny economies and military expenditures, were clamoring for war.

The spending surge was the basis for Putin's win in the 2012 elections

---

[52] http://www.globalsecurity.org/military/world/russia/economy.htm

[53] http://heavy.com/news/2014/07/vladimir-putin-wealth-forbes-net-worth/

[54] Russian Defense Ministry

through job and wage growth. His pitch for international redemption furthered his popularity with the people, many of whom could still remember the "good old days" of Russian global hegemony. Political contributions from self-interested allies sealed an easy victory.

The trouble with boys and guns is that if you give a boy a gun, it is likely he will want to use it on somebody. In 2008, Russia became involved in the Georgian affair, perhaps as a test to see how domestic public opinion would be affected (it wasn't) by the project of reclaiming former territories of the Russian empire. The global consensus was that Russia, which subsequently occupied parts of Georgia, was the aggressor. But all Moscow received was a diplomatic wrist slap from the international community and a threat of retaliation from neighboring U.S. states if Putin was to invade them as well.

Then in 2014, during its hosting of the Winter Olympics, Russia essentially invaded Ukraine—the Crimean peninsula specifically—to "liberate Russian-speaking citizens who were being disenfranchised by a brutally racist regime." The move drew global condemnation and a flood of sanctions from the U.S. and other N.A.T.O. allies which had, and continue to have, a pronounced effect on the Russian populace. Predictably, Putin used this discontent to fuel "non-Cold War" Cold War rhetoric and blamed the West for the plight of the Russian economy, which was faltering in all respects due to precipitous declines in oil and natural gas prices.

Subsequent actions accelerated a revival of the East-versus-West crusade:[55]

- The mysterious downing of a Malaysian airliner over Ukrainian air space, with missiles only Russia had access to
- An unidentified submarine smelling of borscht was tracked but not confirmed to be Russian by Sweden in its waters
- Russia blatantly supported Ukrainian rebel activity
- Russia ordered super-bomber practice flights near Alaska, and over the Caribbean and the Gulf of Mexico

These actions elicited frenzied media attention in the West, and sparked right-wing fervor in the U.S. Many partisan pundits, particularly from countries surrounding Georgia, called for greater increases in military spending in order to match Russia's, and, for counter-moves, reviving the Reagan-era "Star Wars" program. Others even called for the

---

[55] Search all relevant terms, except for the borscht reference

impeachment of the U.S. President "to show those Commie-bastards who's boss," ignoring the fact that Russia was no longer a communist country.

An *Economist* story on the state of Russia described the current situation perfectly:

> As Putin, whose ferociousness has been compared to that of a Bengal tiger, grows more frustrated and economically caged by the impacts of falling resource prices on his country's and personal fortunes, there is a good probability his actions will become more erratic, less long-term focused, and more deadly. For while it is unclear if tigers have souls, Mr. Putin's possession of such an asset, amidst his vast acquisitions, does not seem remotely likely.

# 10

## The Plan

The morning had gone extremely well. "Not surprising," Heidi reflected with a smile. Passion and purpose were obvious. One could perceive an increase in the urgency of their steps, an internal glow of optimism and possibility bubbling through confident eyes, as well as the resolve of a mission backlighting their bodies. Heidi had encountered this shift many times prior when building and engaging teams, and she delighted in the speculation from outsiders that she had slipped Prozac into her colleagues' coffee.

No matter how hard she had tried to remove compensation from the offer when signing folks up, it was always there, dangling in the breezy background of personal commitments, and the ever-present calculus of "could I get a better deal someplace else?"

But this group was different. The women had committed to the venture for no other reason than to tap their evolutionary bio-chemical dispositions. Indeed, while the project would have no direct impact on their personal net worths, Heidi sensed they were the most engaged team on the planet, ready to courageously and instinctively give life and limb for their cause. An image of Navy Seals, fully masked and flippered, in purple wetsuits with white floral designs on their chests, wearing Illumina watches and carrying small, silver shock-proof briefcases containing the vials of cells, superimposed itself as she watched them chat, while waiting to be seated for lunch. They had one final task to do as a unit, Heidi reminded herself, though she wanted the imperative to come from them.

...

On her way back from her chilly daybreak dip, Heidi had decided another lunch at the *Hippocampe* would not be the best idea. *Le dejuner* (lunch) and the subsequent session would be better suited for the *Salon Edouard VII*, a stately yet cozy chamber at the end of the west wing of the hotel. The décor was a bit masculine, mirroring the room's namesake. But there were minimal opportunities for disruption, which was preferable as the program this afternoon would focus on an attempted reworking of the entire global political-religious economy and supporting militaries. Secrecy would be a necessary new norm.

Lexie had already done a sweep of the room (using a small attachment to her Illumina tablet) and had located an aging Soviet-era transmitter in the grating enclosing the radiator. Major kudos to its design team, she thought, as it seemed to still be working though the receiving end had long since been disabled.

The women were seated for lunch, while Le Cordon-Bleu-trained staff precisely placed the easels and posters once again behind each seat. The conversation focused primarily on what else the women had learned about themselves and each other, from the tools, strengths and weaknesses, to key experiences, values and motivations. The correlations and synergies were prolific. Once again, the repast exceeded all expectations and the wine flowed.

As soon as the dessert plates had been thoroughly scraped, they, along with the staff, retreated through the only door in the salon. Satisfied that there was an ample coffee and tea supply at a station located next to the door, Heidi produced a device no larger than a deck of cards and set it next to her tablet while a screen silently dropped from the ceiling.

"I am ecstatic," she said as her device automatically synched with the projector and promptly displayed a map of the world behind her, "to see this team come together, as one. And I want to applaud you all, in advance, for your involvement in what is coming next." She paused briefly, as if concerned she was going to divulge potentially upsetting information but then smiled and continued. "Each of you was selected for multiple reasons, many of which we have learned about over the past two days. But there was another filter we used to select you, the filter of reality, and a concept at the heart of my business which I call 'Tipping the Gorilla.'[56] Has anyone heard of this concept?" she inquired.

"Yes," Qin replied, with a hint of a grin. She continued in slightly professorial tone. "I learned about it during my studies of high-technology manufacturing. I believe the syndrome you are describing occurs when something radically new is introduced to the market. There are people who absolutely have to have a product, no matter what the cost. These folks, called 'Early Adopters' typically make up roughly 8 to 15% of the market. Many products fail to break out of this demographic and leverage the advantages of scale production and marketing. To do this, you must get more than the just 'Early Adopters', you must get the 'Early Majority' to buy in. This demographic comprises around a third of the market, with the 'Late Majority' and 'Laggards' making up the remainder."

Qin stood up during her semi-rote recall of this dynamic. She drew a bell curve with the relevant demarcations on her next blank poster.

"From research, we see that whoever can get to roughly 20 to 25% of market share first can become the Gorilla, the largest animal in the ecosystem of apes, or competing products and firms. Being the Gorilla is preferred because you are more than likely to have the lowest production costs, and you also have a brand that consumers identify with and respect. As a matter of course, you can spend more on marketing to build your brand because of the combination of revenue and higher margins. Essentially, 20 to 25% market share is the tipping point. Whoever can get to this penetration first is likely to win." Even Heidi was impressed with Qin's synopsis.

"The key, and where most firms fail, is how they make the jump from Early Adopter to Early Majority." Qin depicted this movement with a purple arrow going up the curve.

"Now, I'm smiling because Heidi has had great success in bringing

---

[56] Search "Geoffrey Moore Crossing Chasm"

new products to market—in fact creating new markets—while going up against much larger and more financially powerful competitors. She has tipped many Gorillas from their lofty trees…and I believe," she said, giving Heidi a friendly yet suspicious glance, "she has a similar plan for our project."

"Ha-ha! Well done, Qin. You are quite right in all contexts," Heidi responded with the satisfaction of a hiring manager who knows her hard fought selection of a candidate was the right choice. "I believe, if we can provide therapy to some specific areas of the world, we can dramatically slow down, possibly neutralize, and maybe even roll back the malevolent impacts of testy testosterone." She paused for effect. "If we can penetrate our target market quickly with the right sequencing, we can tip the Gorilla."

Sprinkles of laughter sprang from around the table but they petered out quickly as it was clear the group had questions. Questions Heidi wanted to answer. "So gals, before we get down to specific assignments, what kind of questions can I answer?"

Qin, who still had the metaphorical microphone, went first. "From my experiences there are gorilla states, like the US, my country, Russia, etc., and there are 'chimps,' if I may call them that. Smaller countries whose intricate and delicate histories and accords with both other chimps and gorillas still have a large influence, especially in numbers. Your Smoky Mountain example provides some intelligence on this dynamic, however it would seem the actual world order is much more complex…even though they are both inherently male-based."

Shalala quickly interjected. "So we are able maybe to get these cells into a few Prime Ministers' drinks. What effect can just a few countries have?"

"And what will happen if just a few countries start playing sane?" Gilat followed on closely. "Won't they be sitting ducks? I agree with Qin…The world is much more complex than a crystal meth compound."

Heidi was ready, "Apologies all. You are quite right. I wasn't clear enough. We aren't going after merely the gorillas. We will most certainly need to take down more than a few chimps as well." She grinned, "Actually, not take down per se…more like 'gently dose.'"

After a brief pause for effect, she continued, "I agree that one random government alone, or even a few, probably won't do much, and could actually lead to some potentially bloody internal and/or external conflicts. Being the only one with a knife at a gun fight can be problematic." Heidi's word choice underscored the seriousness of what they were planning. They all knew the plan could have material, in fact potentially deadly, impacts on people's lives. Though this fact had existed from the get-go, hearing it framed in the context of "We will be responsible," introduced a chill into the room that took a while to dissipate.

"What is absolutely key is coordination and timing. If we can get some key players on board, again with strategic sequencing and timing, I believe the possibility that we hit our tipping point will increase dramatically. If, for example, India and Pakistan's leaders become civilized at roughly the same time, the potentiality for Gilat's scenario of one nation seizing the moment to invade another drops dramatically. We just need to figure out who these players are, and when and how we can dose them."

Though this response made perfect sense, Heidi intuited she was only partway there in restoring warm feelings about the plan to the room. She decided to broach the heart of the matter, which was risky but, hell, they would have to get there eventually anyway.

"Yes, there is a chance people, in fact many people, could lose… lose their work, lose their homes, lose their way of life and even lose their lives," she candidly and softly admitted, projecting the pain from personal loss on a much wider canvas. After what seemed to be a moment of mourning for what might happen, she returned with force, slowly circling the table, hands moving from chair back to chair back, eyes moving from one pair to the next.

"Two future states to consider, ladies: What happens if we *don't* do anything and we let the status quo carry on? Do we want women to be unable to control their reproduction and all the consequent issues? Do we want women to keep being circumcised?[57] To have acid thrown in their faces merely for upsetting boys?[58] To see war, and all its glories—the disease, the refugees, the rapes and the killing, all the senseless killing, not to mention the asinine expenditures and nuclear and chemical threats—continue? Do we want our animals and food supply, from branch, soil and sea, to be irrevocably altered by the changing of our climate?[59] Do we want 842 *MILLION* of our fellow humans to continue going to bed hungry every night?[60] Do we want millions more people, many of them

---

[57] Search "Female genital circumcision"

[58] Search "Women acid thrown in face"

[59] Search "Climate change impact food supply"

[60] Search "Global hunger"

children, to be sold for sex?[61] Do we?"

She stopped to catch her breath and let the stakes sink in.

"Or do we want to at least give it a shot, because *if* we win, if we do pull this off, the *entire* planet will win. Not just a few countries or a few tigers. *Our* whole beautiful, wonderful world—oceans, creatures, people, environments, and future generations—will win." Heidi stopped and made an earth-like circle above her head with her arms. "I am willing to take that risk…and responsibility."

She didn't need to ask the women for their commitment. She had them after the second or third, "Do we?" Heads nodded solemnly, empathetically.

While she had their attention, there was one other issue she needed to bring up. "Now, I know I can come off as a hippie, a flower child of sorts, and my Northern Californian roots can be difficult to understand, particularly as all of you, save Lexie, come from other corners of the globe." She gestured around the table.

"Even though I may appear to be invincible because of the success of Illumina, I am not perfect…not even close. You'll have to trust I don't get a little drunk, undressed and sing-songy for no good reason." Heidi, and the rest of the table, couldn't help but notice Lexie's simultaneous eyebrow raise and lower lip drop when she heard this confession. "Oh come on Lexie…we had just won Product of the Year." Lexie, who realized she maybe should have tried to hide her reaction a little better, gave a meek shoulder and face shrug, and leaned back in her seat, implicitly giving Heidi center stage again.

"As I was saying," Heidi chided though with a "in jest there is truth" tone, "I am not perfect…and I never will be though, like you all, I have been able to harness many of my imperfections and struggles, and turn them into sources of strength. From my experience, there is immense value in suffering, not that I would wish it on anyone, but suffering can quickly wash us clean of materialism and can replace frivolous needs with something infinitely more powerful…purpose and urgency. While I do believe change is possible and powerful, we have to deal with and play the cards we have been dealt and have accumulated over time. What is critical to understand is no matter what happens, we control how we respond to whatever situation faces us. Those who have an understanding

---

[61] Search "Global sex traffic"

of their *why* no matter what happens can survive almost any *how*."[62]

She continued, still lightheartedly, though she was facing an increasingly serious audience, "And I look forward to learning as much as I can about myself from each of you going forward." She reflected for a moment if she should close the whole event with a feedback session or a listening circle. That could be a very good idea.

"I don't believe you will find a sponsor who is more committed to your particular causes," she began. The statement was completely true; IVF was the largest contributor to each of the attendee's efforts. "I am completely committed to seeing this effort, which I have been nurturing for the last five years, through to whatever lies in store. So, if I offended any of your sensibilities, I am sorry. I promise you, the next time you see me like last night will be the day the U.S. Senate is run by more estrogen than testosterone!" Heidi completed her mea culpa with clasped, apologetic hands and a hearty laugh, which was (thankfully) echoed by all.

"You know Heidi," Shalala started with an atypical grin, her English accent pronouncedly slicing up the air, "last night, after we put you to bed, we had a little chat."

Heidi's demeanor didn't notably change though a look of concern instinctively shrouded her eyes as she waited for Shalala's next sentence.

"What some people might consider 'weaknesses,' we consider to be merely idiosyncrasies. We all have them…and we are so thankful you are so comfortable being so open with yours. We see your vulnerability as one of your most powerful strengths."

Heidi's face went from "ready to be chastised" to "ready to saint all present."

"Thank you."

. . .

The next two hours were spent reviewing global hot spots and topics of concern with the group. Heidi already had a good idea as to which woman would take on which conflict, though she wanted them to be committed to their particular targets, to own them…and owning them required that the they choose their challenges.

There were obviously many more targets than the group of women

---

[62] Viktor Frankl, *Man's Search for Meaning*

could handle, even working overtime. This noted, if things worked out, hitting the mid-level targets would be much easier and possibly not even necessary depending on how hard, fast and far the gorillas could be parted from their prominence. What was amazing, Heidi noted, was how a few key men's personalities and politics could have huge reverberations on the global order; if we can knock them off, the whole house of cards might fall a whole lot easier…and quickly.

The process required research and the women had pulled out their new tablets and easily figured out how to select their "personal assistant" from a list of celebrities, though unfortunately "we only have licensed Westerners to date," Heidi sheepishly admitted. No matter, *Salon Edouard VII* quickly filled with a chorus of voices ranging from Clark Gable (Divine?), Pierce Brosnan (Gilat), Antonio Banderas (Elena), to Will Smith (wait, that's Shalala?) eagerly fulfilling requests.

Most of the women, Lexie included, stayed at the table or used their posters for notes. The only outlier of this group was Qin, who had drifted off, seemingly deep in thought, speaking softly to her tablet as she stared out the curved main windows of the room that overlooked *les jardins*. Her volume was lowered. Heidi unobtrusively cruised by and overheard a woman's voice helping Qin. It didn't take more than a few words for Heidi to recognize the headstrong and gifted speech of Jodie Foster.

Heidi was surprised this woman who had been raised in a country where, until recently, no western media had been allowed, would know of Jodie. She waited for Qin to pause and then politely inquired, "Qin, excuse my curiosity, do you know who this is?"

Qin hadn't noticed Heidi behind her and jumped a little when Heidi's voice suddenly appeared over her shoulder. "Oh Heidi, I didn't know you were there," she started. Then, quickly regaining her composure, she continued, "Yes, I know Jodie Foster's work well. I am a huge fan of hers. It is an advantage of my position to be able to access foreign media." Qin finished her answer with a smile, though Heidi sensed there was something else at play here but she didn't have a clue what it could be.

"Well, I like her work too! Did you know she speaks French fluently?" Heidi replied conversationally, the fact they were in France potentially driving this question.

"Yes, she studied French in high school in Los Angeles," Qin softly reported, "she can also understand some German and Spanish…and like Gilat, she is an atheist."

"Wow Qin, you certainly are a fan!" Heidi exclaimed. "I look forward to comparing notes sometime…How goes your research?"

"I think I'm on to something," Qin responded, with an unmistakable mix of courage and fear in her voice.

"Great," said Heidi, not wanting to push. "Let's see how the others are doing."

# 11

## ISIS

"Hello, this is Fareed Zakaria hosting a special CNN segment, 'The Radical Sunni Threat' on the rise of ultra-conservative Islamic groups, their impact on the global terror landscape, and the U.S. response to date."

"The death of Mohammed in year 632 triggered a power struggle between two sects of Islam—the Sunnis and the Shia—that continues to this day. Over time, geographic factions emerged primarily in the Sunni camp, which have complicated things significantly. The Wahhabi sect of the Sunnis is of particular note as it gestated the terror group Al Qaeda, which was responsible for the World Trade Center attack of 9/11. The degree of enmity between the Sunnis and Shia may be best exemplified by the observation that Saudi Arabian schools teach their Sunni students that Shia beliefs are heretical and are far worse than Judaism and Christianity. You can think of it as a little like Northern Ireland, though on a much larger geographic scale."

"Numerically, Sunnis vastly outnumber Shia, by a 9 to 1 ratio, and most countries where Islam is the main religion are dominated by Sunnis, with the exception of Iran, where the ratio is reversed. This is important to understand since a major prong of U.S. foreign policy in the Middle East under President Bush was arming Iran's Sunni neighbors in an attempt to contain Iran's influence in that region's politics."

"This policy was arguably short-sighted. Controlling who exactly receives and eventually uses these weapons is near impossible and the U.S. has been justifiably criticized for possibly even bolstering the power and capabilities of Sunni extremist groups such as the Taliban, Al Qaeda, Boko Haram and the Islamic State, also known as ISIS, which has seen a dramatic rise of late."

"ISIS has been aggressively taking over large amounts of land and natural resources in Syria and Northern Iraq, most particularly oil-related territories, which are providing them large amounts of cash—by some reports $3 million per day—to fund their operations. They have also been brazenly brutal with videotaped beheadings of Western civilians, mass executions, mutilation and torture of those who do not subscribe to the Wahhabi version of Sunni Islam. They are also reportedly enslaving and raping women, an act that is allowed by their interpretation of the Qu'ran. They are headed up by Abu Bakr al-Baghdadi, a 42-year-old PhD graduate of Islamic Studies from the Islamic University in Baghdad. Al-Baghdadi has been the mastermind of many attacks against Shia in Afghanistan and is so extreme in his views and goals that Al Qaeda, a former ally, recently renounced any ties with ISIS."

"With me today to discuss the radical Sunni threat is former Secretary of State under George W. Bush and Chairman of the Joint Chiefs of Staff, retired four-star general Colin Powell. Welcome Secretary Powell."

Powell: "Great to be here as always, Fareed."

Fareed: "So Secretary Powell you, recently made the point that since WWII the U.S. has been involved in five wars, yet in only one have we reached our stated objective. You also are advocating for military action against ISIS with very defined objectives, which is understandable given our record to date. My question is, given our current administration's focus on 'boots on the ground' military intervention do you see us getting into another war we can't win?"

Powell: "President Bush initiated military actions which increased our national debt by four trillion dollars thus far, and these figures do not take into account two important additional costs: ongoing expenditures due to the regional change in the structure of power resultant of his actions, and the costs of caring for our veterans, which will continue for decades. While I do believe we need to take military action to take out these fanatics, I am firmly against putting our soldiers on the battlefield again. It is too expensive and trying to replicate post-war Germany and Japan isn't likely if we look at the failure of our efforts in Iraq and Afghanistan. Having worked for the Bush Administration, looking back, they seemed to be more focused on winning for the sheer pleasure of saying 'We are still the biggest boys in the sandbox.' They did not seem to understand the very complex histories of that region or the medium- to long-term impacts of such actions—be they financial, structural in regards to our regional and global allies, or in terms of how the world perceived America."

Fareed: "Secretary Powell, you have also recently responded to questions about the role and proliferation of nuclear weapons in the Middle East. While you seemed confident they would not be used by states who currently have them in the next five years, you are fearful that the use of nuclear weapons could be triggered by a group, more than likely religious, that believes this kind of destruction would lead to some sort of salvation. Would you care to expand on this?"

Powell: "Yes, Farheed. From my experience, and I include all religions in this statement, whenever people believe in something so fervently they will blow themselves up for it, or believe an apocalypse is on the horizon, their perceptions of reality become distorted to a degree where their basic humanity is lost. This holds true for those who justify violence with the Bible, Qu'ran, Torah or any other holy texts. They actually believe they are carrying out God's will by starting the apocalypse and, in so doing, they believe they will secure some kind of self-inflated importance in history. It is a very frightening scenario because the role of religion in global politics, the U.S. being a major player and example, is extremely self-evident. It haunts me."

Fareed: "On this note, I have seen reports that when ISIS captured Mosul a few months ago, nuclear materials were seized from the university, materials that Iraq's U.N. Ambassador Mohamed Ali Alhakim reported to U.N. Secretary-General Ban Ki-moon could be used to make a potential weapon. Do you believe ISIS could be building a bomb?"

Powell: "While I believe it is highly unlikely ISIS could make a device, and though the International Atomic Energy Agency purports the materials are too low grade to present a real threat, this is a situation where we cannot be too careful. Even though the odds may be very small, the possibility that they are able to use a bomb either for leverage or actual deployment is not worth ignoring."

Fareed: "Thank you, as always, Secretary Powell for your time."

Powell: "Thank you, Fareed."

# 12

## *À La Prochaine Fois*

### (Until next time)

The rest of the afternoon unfolded as effortlessly as a cashmere sweater coming off a shelf at Bloomingdales. The women made excellent progress identifying issues and targets, and Heidi called for a much-needed break. After all, this was only the first of a few meetings the group would be having. And besides, from experience, Heidi realized their brains would undoubtedly keep working on this task, even when they were sleeping, and breakthroughs would penetrate their consciousness, probably when they least expected it.

A pitcher of Cosmopolitans was delivered to the Salon and the women toasted their bond. It was obviously Shalala's first taste of that particular mixed drink and her eyes merrily reflected her tongue's delight. "WOW, this is DELICIOUS!"

From Heidi's perspective, the real celebration was recognizing that they had an extraordinary opportunity, the permission, the courage, and the plan to fundamentally improve the lives of billions of their fellow humans. That was indeed a reason to celebrate, though not like what she had done the night before, she reminded herself. A knowing and sharp glance from Lexie when Heidi started to pour her second drink reinforced the need to be self-aware of her consumption. These women are putting everything they hold dear to themselves on the line for someone else's crazy mission, Heidi reminded herself. Though, at this point, having gone through the pyramid exercise, she believed each woman had internalized and accepted the project as an extension of their own life's work.

Heidi's watch prompted her of the group's next commitment. Lexie hastily gathered up all the poster notes and dashed upstairs to her room. She planned to take pictures of the notes on her flight that night and electronically distribute them to the group upon landing. She shoved a nondescript black object the size of a large necklace box into her purse. Then, with suitcase in tow, she hurried back downstairs so as to not hold things up. Meanwhile, Heidi led the group out to the lobby where the van with tinted windows was waiting. Twenty minutes later, they found themselves exploring the enchanting cobblestone *rues* of St. Jean de Luz, a seaside town roughly two-thirds of the way from Biarritz to the Spanish border. Heidi off-handedly mentioned how she would have loved to take the girls to San Sebastian, the first town on the other side of the border, but the last time she was there a Basque independence riot had broken out. The women could easily imagine Heidi joining the throng.

It was over dinner in a private chamber at *Le Brouillarta* that the last topic Heidi wanted to cover was broached, though she was surprised at who brought it up.

"So," Shalala started with an unusually mischievous grin, "I think we need a name. My brothers were always big into super heroes and fantasy stuff, like Lord of Ring Fellowships…"

"We could be the Horsewomen of the Apocalypse," Gilat ventured merrily, and then quickly added as she sensed Heidi's confusion, "yeah, I used to read the New Testament to put myself to sleep."

"Or The Gang of Seven," Qin contributed contentedly, building on Gilat's irony, her lapse of group engagement of a few hours ago had apparently either been internally resolved or swept under a convenient mental rug.

"What about The Magnificent Seven?" Elena joined in, "I am certainly feeling very magnificent right now!"

"You know, *The Magnificent Seven* is the American re-make of *The Seven Samurai*, by Akira Kurosawa," Qin added. "I love that movie! And you know what? We are very much like the Seven Samurai, only in Japan women couldn't be samurais."

"Well then, it fits us perfectly," Divine exclaimed with a laugh. "You know something, if my memory is correct, I believe the samurai had a major influence on helping Japan transition from their feudal state to becoming a world power."[63]

"You're quite correct, Divine," Qin said with unusual excitement. "It was utterly amazing how powerful, and dangerous, they became so quickly. Maybe we too can become as powerful, but much more humane!"

Cheshire cat grins wafted around the table.

"Done!" Gilat happily confirmed, "unless there are any objections?" The group smiled at her in agreement.

"A toast to The Magnificent Seven!" Elena extolled. "Or TM7 for short," with a sexy Latin wink.

The glee of simply being there, with a newly christened official name, outshone the boisterous jangle of glasses.

...

Heidi was extremely pleased. She didn't need to be involved in the naming process as the group had done it themselves. It was a superb sign that they were coming together in a very accelerated time frame, taking control of their future paths, as both individual contributors and as a unit. A mentor had once told Heidi, "Your job as a leader is to get the best possible people on your team, point them in the right direction, let them go and then follow them from behind to make sure that if their navigation or health suffers, you are there to support them." The non-trivial investment of time and resources she had focused on these women over the last few years was paying off. Though the odds were small that these magnificent six other women would transform the world's despots and misogynists, they were the best and most meaning-driven team on the planet for the job.

Heidi needed to address one final key point. As soon as dessert was ordered, Heidi filled the women in on next steps, "My Magnificent

---

[63] Search "Bushido and the rise of modern Japan"

Seven," she started and then needed to pause while her audience cheered a bit. "I am so grateful to be here, right now, with you all. History has been made already over the last 48 hours, and I can't underscore the pleasure of getting to know you all better as collaborators…and sisters."

"Your flights leave tomorrow morning. We will meet again, as a group, in early December, in Qatar at our lab. Qin, though you are the most difficult one to schedule around, I believe you will be there working on negotiations for China's access to natural gas, yes?" Qin seemed pleased, versus freaked, by Heidi's knowledge of her whereabouts. "That's correct Heidi."

"Great!" Heidi exclaimed, an obvious part of her wanting to make sure everything was a go with Qin.

"So ladies, first the assignment and then the enablement. You all made great headway today taking an initial swipe at targets. When we meet in December, I'd like you all to present your plan of attack for review and feedback. Focus on targets and timing. Who needs it worst and where can we most easily get to them, preferably in as few places as possible? And for the moment, don't worry about how we will get their blood. Concentrate on the who and when. I will leave it to you to come up with your respective To-Dos."

Again, Heidi didn't want, or need, to dictate next steps. She knew implicitly that these women didn't need those parameters defined in written, black and white terms, and If they had questions they would ask for help. She was confident the team, now empowered with the controls, would come up with a very solid and probably excellent plan, more likely leaps and bounds better than those she had been mentally constructing. It was a classic case of simply letting many powerful minds loose or, as Laszlo Bock, Senior VP of People for Google, observed, teams with consistent leadership perform much better when the members have relatively free reign to do what they like, within defined boundaries, versus teams with little freedom, who suffer because they don't know when they might step on a land mine.[64]

"Can we do this, my Magnificent Seven?" Heidi extorted, volume rising.

"Yes!" came the mildly thunderous, united response. Coincidentally, the middle-aged Parisian couple from the *Hotel du Palais*, apparently wanting to escape the noise in Biarritz, happened to be waiting for a table

---

[64] http://blog.idonethis.com/google-most-important-leadership-trait/

at *Le Broillarta*. Having endured the group's optimistic outburst the day prior, they immediately chose to dine elsewhere, muttering something about how distressingly American the Pays-Basque region had become.

Heidi rang a bell and dessert appeared. Small talk about the selections ensued until the waitress had left the room, at which point Heidi took the meeting's reins.

"Ok, great! Now the fun part." Heidi motioned to Lexie, who was waiting with the black box from her purse. Lexie opened it up and passed out small black rectangles about the size of a pack of cigarettes. "These are my beta-babies," Heidi proclaimed. "Please don't use them in public. If an analyst should see even a Snap Chat of this device, I will have a LOT of explaining to do."

"Lexie, why don't you show the group how they work? You're much better at this than I am," Heidi admitted.

"Sure thing Heidi," Lexie replied, eyes glistening with a delight that conveyed she had been personally involved in designing the feature set and overall experience. "They work like this."

Essentially, this little black box projected an interactive interface above it that could range from 10 to 26 inches diagonally, with the same clarity and color palettes as the most up-to-date, retinal-enhanced laptop screens. It also had a sexy touchscreen that lit up and performed by verbal commands based on the owner's voice. Any kind of document, including spreadsheets, could be created by hand, verbally or in combination. Video, text, email, and of course phone chats, were also voice controlled. Conference video calls had the same resolution as a Cisco Telepresence machine and everything could be recorded for playback. It had a voice-controlled, 60 MB camera with a digitally driven zoom which could go from 35 to 200mm. It was waterproof to 200 meters and held a charge (delivered via a wireless plug) for more than 18 hours from any power source. Security was a combination of a hidden fingerprint reader on the side of the device and a snippet of each woman's voice saying something of their creation. And a personal avatar was at their disposal to find anything they needed, including very polite directions that could key off landmarks, in consideration of a common female preference. Elena immediately christened them 'MoPhones', pronounced like the inferred profanity, as "they're way more than just another phone—they're the mother of all phones!"

Heidi resumed control in a soft tone that shifted the focus of the conversation from the ephemeral glee of new playthings to the long-term seriousness of their mission. She knew they understood the meat of what was coming, and she felt it was vital to make sure the small details were understood.

"So ladies, I don't need to tell you how vitally important it is to the success of TM7 to keep this device secret. It will be our only means of communication when we are not together going forward, other than random corporate announcements that you will receive because you are on our email list and, as I'm sure you are aware, you can't respond to those." Everyone grinned, partly at the humor, but more as a brief release of anxiety due to the topic of conversation. "All communications are channeled anonymously through a super-strong network that cannot be cracked.[65] The device is set to vibrate when an incoming message is received. This can be changed, though I ask you to use your utmost discretion in switching it to ring. If anyone should ever find it, simply say it was a throw away from your speaking gig with Illumina. And please throw it away if you have to. Through its GPS, I will know where it is, if it's heading to a landfill, or if it falls off the grid because it was destroyed. I can always get you another one."

"And if you are ever discovered, or for whatever reason decide you don't want to continue, please *try* not to give the rest of us away. If you must share a name, share mine. That way all the others will be safe." She paused to make sure none of the devices were on. "Simply say 'Flotsam' if you want out, and 'Jetsam' if you are discovered. The device has been programmed to melt its insides so that no trace of manufacture can be identified, and the group will be notified immediately with instructions on what to do next.

The group was as silent and unwavering as the poised statue of Saint-Jean-Baptiste on horseback they had passed on their drive to the restaurant. Yes, they too had forgiven many sins in their lives, but this forgiveness had been forced on them by the need to move on and not allow someone else to control them. What they were about to embark on could be considered forgiving both past and future sins on a massive scale.

"Again ladies, no worries at all if you need to quit for whatever reason. You all know what you've signed up for, yet *you* don't know what you don't know, yet. This could get hairy and I presume your target research and presentations will be framed around the least risky course of action

---

[65] Search 'Tor'

to you personally."

With that final request, Heidi glanced at her watch, and then at Lexie who nodded, lifted her now-lightened purse and stood to leave. The group followed suit. "*À la prochaine fois*, until next time, my fabulous femmes," Heidi gushed as she and Lexie showered the group with hugs. "I have a deal in San Francisco I need to close tomorrow. I must be on my way. Until next time…"

And with that, Heidi and Lexie hopped into a waiting cab and were off to the airport.

…

Lexie had captured the posters with her device, and had already proofread the auto-transcript of all the conversations that transpired over the last two days. Everything was in queue to be sent out, she just needed to wait until they hit U.S. airspace for Internet access to kick in. TM7 would wake up the next morning to a vibrating beta box.

She was just about ready to turn in when Heidi, dressed in a lavender bunny onesie pajama, emerged from the plane's meeting room. Lexie, unfazed, had obviously seen her in it before.

"Well, that went relatively well, don't you think?" she asked Lexie.

"Yeah, it was awesome," Lexie echoed. "All of it…you were right about all the tests by the way. They were invaluable."

"Yes they were, though I was surprised a few times by who initiated certain topics. I was certain Gilat was going to take more of the lead…"

"Yeah, I suppose it just means that no matter how well we think we know someone, there are aspects to everyone that will always surprise us."

"Quite right, Lexie," Heidi reflected. "On this topic, something happened with Qin this afternoon…and I can't for the life of me, figure out what it was. I was just reviewing her files again and can find nothing that would presumably cause her to withdraw like she did, even just for those few moments."

"That was a bit odd," Lexie confirmed.

"My sense is there is something under the surface there that Qin wants…perhaps needs, to keep to herself. I suppose when she is ready, she will let us know what it is…Good night and Lexie, great job!"

# 13

## In One Month's Time

Heidi loved data. Looking at it. Analyzing it. Playing with it. And, perhaps most importantly, presenting it. Her product launches had become legendary. She would prepare in a slightly OCD-manner by spending two days painstakingly iterating her presentation, as well as the perfected mélange of timed and crafted voiceovers, images, video and text she used to accompany her speech. It was as if she was selling something directly to you, something that met your distinct, unmet needs.

But it was more than merely *what* she sold, it was the *why* behind it that was so powerful, that connected with your core. Illumina was out to improve the world and enrich the lives of its employees, not merely create returns for shareholders.

She had contemplated putting together a similar product presentation for TM7 though she realized she didn't need to sell them on this particular *why*. They got it, just like every other woman on the planet gets it. This *why* had irrevocably physically, mentally and spiritually damaged their souls, leaving scars that would never heal completely, but would become stronger and more resilient than the original skin. They each used this strength to overcome, to rise above the absurd and petty issues that plague their species and to understand what really matters. And they had each experienced the happiness that came from putting everything on the line to work for a better world.

For Heidi it was addictive. Her happiness came from working to serve something much greater than one's own needs. It obviated the tragic tendency to seek out and cling to society's pre-programmed, spurious and oftentimes materialistic norms. It liberated you, it engaged you, it engulfed you. Perhaps most of all it provided meaning to your suffering and, inevitably, the suffering of others. It made you feel alive…in the time of your life.

This was the *why* behind their magnificence.

Heidi also liked dashboards to display her data, as long as the data was correct and what was being measured aligned with her respective goals. Her Illumina dashboard was very simple. Three key performance indicators were all she tracked. Everything else fell into place depending on the health of these numbers: colleague engagement, number of vacation days taken and ratings of the political stability in the countries of her suppliers. From her experience, as these numbers went, so went Illumina's market cap.

Her newly christened TM7 dashboard was a bit more complex for *what* it monitored and the myriad of data feeds required under its hood to generate the numbers. It tracked aggregates of global humanitarian figures on a monthly basis.

In one month's time since Biarritz, her figures reported this year's year-to-date totals and percentage/raw number changes from the last month:[66]

Number of reported rapes (65 countries reporting): 208,313 (+5%)

Number of reports of domestic violence: 1,954,724 (+7%)

Number of refugees: 12,415,786 (-3%)

Number of orphans: 127,650,000 (+2%)

Number of deaths from starvation: 5,912,678 (+4%)

Number of people who are hungry: 698,451,560 (+8%)

Number of children who aren't being educated (by gender): Girls: 26,941,423 (+3%); Boys:

---

[66] Please search for all appropriate terms as you'd like noting the appropriate caveats in the text

23,612,897 (+6%)

Number of people living on less than $2/day: 1,112,679,000 (+3%)

Number of tons of CO2 emitted into the atmosphere: 28,755,000,000 (+8%)

Number of significant armed conflicts: 14 (+1)

Number of active nuclear weapons: 17,215 (no change)

Number of countries with nuclear weapons: 9 (no change)

Number of female Heads of State: 22 (11% total) (no change)

Number of women in U.S. Congress: 104 (19% total) (no change)

The sad thing about some of these figures was that they constituted a very small fraction of what was actually happening. In the United Kingdom for example, where Heidi knew it was relatively acceptable to go to the police, the number of actual rapes committed in a year was over 65% higher than what was reported.[67] About only one-third of the world's nations actually tracked rape data, further underscoring the deceptive nature of her TM7 dashboard figures.

The sheer magnitude of the numbers, however, imparted a view of suffering on such an enormous scale that the human mind strained to understand—if not outright deny—its existence. Heidi was very aware of countries with large populations that viciously looked down on reporting rape or domestic violence. In these countries, individuals who courageously came forward could face personal, familial and social stigmatization, as well as other malevolent repercussions, including farcical legal processes or outright murder. Suicides in response to these pressures were not uncommon and the psychological trauma victims carried with them could be embedded for decades without trained support services which were usually unbudgeted and thus generally lacking.

She knew about "honor killings," when the slaying of a woman is "justified" because the killer's family has been shamed by a refusal for an arranged marriage. Extending this logic, a woman could be killed for wearing clothing deemed inappropriate or for homosexual behavior, and her murder would be endorsed and considered fully acceptable by local authorities.[68] Heidi was also aware of "bride burnings," when newlywed wives are doused with kerosene and lit on fire because their dowry is considered too small and husbands need more compensation. These

---

[67] Search "rape statistics" and "domestic violence statistics"

[68] Search "honor killings"

burnings were commonplace in particular parts of the world.[69]

Heidi understood that even if poverty estimates were 2% off, that 2% meant 16 *million* people with hopes, dreams and desires *just like the rest of us*, were facing questions of life or death every on a daily basis. She also knew that 13 current heads of state—all men—were worth an estimated 104 *billion* U.S. dollars combined.

Joseph Stalin observed, "One death is a tragedy, one million is a statistic." Heidi was out to make every death a tragedy.

The TM7 dashboard was prominently featured on every device she owned. In her home office, Heidi actually had a stock ticker set into a ceiling cavity that circled her desk, marching these numbers by her on a real-time basis. Given her personal experience, the "Number of reports of domestic violence" was of particular interest to her. She shuddered every time a Super Bowl or international soccer championship neared. Assault numbers perennially made significant jumps on those days.

Her father would call what Heidi was doing as "liberal guilt," which he seemed to correlate with liberal arts educations. "This is what an Ivy League education does to you? Shouldn't you be more worried about taxes, and how much the good-for-nothing government is taking from your business and personal accounts?" she would imagine him barking at her, drink in hand. Funny thing was, Heidi had no problem paying taxes. Yes, she was concerned about government spending, corruption, inefficiencies, ineptitude and shady backroom deals. From her perspective though, these issues were symptoms of a greater problem—patriarchy and testosterone run amok. She viewed the whole system as being built around men wanting and maintaining power. It was one massive "my balls are bigger than yours" contest with each successive government leader trying to retain control of his voters through whatever means possible, including making financially absurd promises for terms on end.

Heidi had had enough exposure to male politicians, regardless of culture, to posit this hypothesis as fact. She recalled one meeting with a government official in Asia. The official was trying to lure her to build a production facility in his province. He had the whole thing planned out, contractors already "selected" and briefed. "We can get all required permits filed and approved. And we can break ground in fifteen days!" he had eagerly assured her. But when Heidi started to ask him some of her typical due diligence questions, he stammered and then froze.

---

[69] According to Indian National Crime Record Bureau, there were 1,948 convictions and 3,876 acquittals in dowry death cases in 2008.

"What is the current birthrate in your province?"

"How long does it take a common woman to get to the closest hospital or clinic with OBGYN facilities and staff?"

"What percentage of your workforce is female and has a high school degree? A college degree?"

"What kind of community development efforts will the increased tax revenues support?"

"What are your plans to improve schools, medical care, housing and infrastructure?"

"What is your selection process for contractors, and what are your ties to them?"

Women, Heidi observed, were generally more transparent than men, and tended to focus on system-wide analysis of issues and policies. Analysis that not only included, but prioritized, human impact with bottom-line numbers. Women were also more inclined to develop better personal relationships, rapports that had a tremendous impact on getting things done in business. Heidi's involvement in a Silicon Valley-based women's group called Imprint had been pivotal to her ability to grow Illumina through the knowledge, introductions and counsel she had received.[70] In a similar vein, she was aware that recent impasses in the polarized U.S. Congress had been overcome by women on both sides of the aisle who came together and, without televised fanfare, chest-beating or the need to declare "victory" over the other side's political philosophy, pushed through pragmatic legislation that kept the economy and country moving.[71] These female politicians had apparently formed a group that met often to celebrate life events such as marriages and baby showers.[72]

Heidi felt that the positive effects of female leadership were not limited to politics either. A report by the consulting firm McKinsey & Company revealed companies whose top management had the highest percentages of women performed better, to the tune of 10% better in Return on Equity, 48% better in earnings and 1.7 times stock price growth over time than their industry averages.[73] Heidi, predictably, was leading this trend—the majority of her board members were women, not just because they gave good advice, but because they had earned the position through smart, hard work. It was no secret to anyone in

---

[70] Search "Watermark" and "Ellevate" for more information

[71] Search "Women getting things done, political parity"

[72] Ibid.

[73] Search "McKinsey Women Matter"

her circles that she longed for more candidates from which to choose. She knew women's natural management capabilities—listening, communicating, making teams work, tapping emotional engagement—were much better suited for the needs of 21st century organizations than men's.[74] She loved to share the turnaround of Xerox by her good friend Anne Mulcahey, who had inherited a company teetering on insolvency. With no flash and barely a public interview, Anne engineered one of the greatest corporate turnarounds in U.S. history.[75] "And, all financial and strategic decisions aside, she did it by focusing on what people, her customers and employees, needed," Heidi reflected.

Heidi also believed large corporations and higher-income individuals should pay, at minimum, equal taxes to what ordinary businesses and citizens pay. They, of all constituents, benefitted the most from government help, usually in an extremely disproportionate way. These businesses were able to tap an educated workforce. They benefitted from having roads and infrastructure available to power and move their people and goods. They profited from having a government regulate energy, education, food supply, climate and things that heal us. And they accessed public money through exchanges which, without government regulation, would most certainly lose investor confidence because of the testosterone-induced tendency to compete by cheating. It didn't matter if it was Enron or WorldCom accounting shenanigans, Bernie Madoff or Allen Stanford's multi-billion dollar Ponzi schemes, or hedge funds out of Stamford, CT. Men with extraordinary connections (managing directors and board members of premiere investment banks and consulting firms) profited constantly from non-public information. Man's primal need to compete for the kill at all costs was still alive and well; it just dressed in $2,000 suits these days.

There was so much to do, Heidi felt, and not enough time.

Oh yes, and over the course of one month, during the height of U.S. Congress' activity, a male-dominated faction of one party was able to thwart all progress on a multitude of important legislative issues, including immigration reform and rationally dealing with funding the government.

Yes, there was so much work to do.

And Heidi's time was coming...

---

[74] Ibid.

[75] Search "Anne Mulcahey Xerox turnaround"

# 14

## The Midterms

Heidi, and the rest of the civilized world, was in shock. The U.S. midterm election results had come in, and they could effectively set her agenda back decades. Senate and gubernatorial races revealed a voter bias for "conservative values," or so observed Reince Priebus, Chair of the Republican Party, in his smug frat boy manner. Heidi preferred to think of him as "Rancid Plebeian."

Well, she reflected sorrowfully, if conservative values meant maintaining a religiously-backed, corporate-focused, male status quo, then yes, the results did point in that precise direction.

With some exceptions, the Senate saw its balance of power shift from blue to red, with new seats occupied for the most part by aging white men.

This election was curious for a few reasons. The current President, who had been gifted with a nation on the verge of economic collapse by the prior administration, had done a remarkable job of bringing the country back, not only from the brink, but to a state that made many conservatives wealthier. There had been 65 straight months of economic growth. A record 56 months of private sector job growth. Unemployment had fallen from 10+% to sub 6%. The budget deficit also had been reduced by 60+%. No foreign terrorist attacks had occurred on American soil, and the Dow Jones Industrial Average had grown from roughly 6,700 to over 17,000, the strongest performance by this indicator...ever. In fact, the net worth of the Koch brother's, backers of all things conservative tripled from $32 billion in 2009 to over $100 billion in 2014.

So why the rise of conservative values? First, a fair percentage of the land of the free didn't much like having a man with black blood in the White House. Heidi had often wondered if it would have been a good campaign tactic for the President skin a knee while playing basketball, just to show the world that his blood was red, just like everyone else's.

Second, Heidi felt that voters were drawn to conservatives because even though the economy was growing, wages had not increased. The vast majority of jobs that created during the President's first months in office were low paying, often temporary gigs. To many it seemed like the great recession of 2008 had ended in the press but continued to cripple their bank balances. Virtually 100% of the gains that were created went to the top 10% of income earners, and 95% went to the top 1%. Which led Heidi to the third reason for voters' discontent.

The testosterone-dominated Supreme Court's decision in the Citizens United case essentially allowed any organization—for-profit, non-profit, labor unions and other associations—to contribute unlimited funds to back political candidates. Consequently, an estimated $4 billion was spent nationwide on these midterm elections, with the net expenditure in some state races reaching upwards of $100 million.[76]

*What that money could have been spent on: education, private investment, infrastructure, debt reduction, etc.,* Heidi imagined.

As it turned out, conservatives were able to take control of the Senate because of several crucial races where outside money surpassed what the candidates themselves were able to raise. And this outside spending appeared primarily in the form of television advertising, which was objectively the nastiest, most negative, demeaning and of the most questionable authenticity seen in years. Most of all, this publicity played

---

[76] Search "CNN 2014 elections spend"

to people's fears: immigration, random viruses from other continents, more terrorists.

Heidi was dragged into the morass kicking and screaming against the whole scheme. Not because of the cost. She could care less about what she was asked to donate. It was the principal of the matter. Money was blatantly buying elections. And for Heidi, that was not democracy. It was a façade of a system rigged against the common person. Unfortunately, many people saw it for what it was, but felt powerless to stop it. A full 79% of voters believed that the government was "run by a few big interests looking out for themselves" and only 19% believed government was being run for the benefit of all.[77]

For example, of the roughly 13 million citizens in Texas, approximately 2.8 million voted for the conservative gubernatorial candidate, 1.8 voted for the liberal, and a whopping 9.4 million just didn't vote.[78] From Heidi's perspective, a small, yet vocal, hardcore religious (and scared) portion of the population was being played by billionaire backers to vote the show. In fact, in the 2012 election, .00042% of the U.S. populace (162 citizens)[79] gave 60%, or approximately $500,000,0000, to "Super PACs," predominantly to support conservative efforts.[80] In these midterms, the Koch-backed network alone contributed an estimated $400,000,000 to political causes.[81]

Heidi liked to mentally compare these figures against those of Denmark for example, where 89% of the population voted in the last election and over 75% of the population belonged to a trade union. Health care and higher education were free in Denmark, and the minimum wage was almost double what it was in the States. Denmark was also coincidentally ranked in a 2013 U.N. report as the "Happiest Nation on Earth." All three party leaders of the coalition government were women.

Another one of Heidi's rotating quotes came from Bernie Sanders, an independent senator from Vermont. "When citizens become actively involved in the political process, government CAN represent ALL people—and not just the very rich."

---

[77] American National Election Studies; additional data provided by Alan Abramowitz, political scientist, Emory University

[78] Texas Secretary of State

[79] Lesterland, Lawrence Lessig. Search "Lessig Ted Talk"

[80] Center for Responsive Politics. Search "open secrets 2012 Super Pacs"

[81] CNN

It was also not long after the midterm elections had been decided (one day in fact for one overly eager candidate) that the sharks circling for the 2016 Presidential ballot started to stick their dorsal fins out of the water in preparation to battle.

And Dick Perry was ready…

# 15

## Right Under Their Noses

Qin's meetings with the Qatari royals were scheduled to start on Monday, December the 9th. When this news became known, flight and accommodation arrangements were immediately made for the rest of TM7 to arrive the afternoon of December 7th. What a coincidence, Heidi reflected.

"Yesterday, December 7, 1941—a date which will live in infamy—the United States of America was suddenly and deliberately attacked by naval and air forces of the Empire of Japan," Franklin Roosevelt had declared over sixty years ago. From her perspective, there was a high probability he both provoked the attack and knew it was coming. He needed a way to sway popular opinion, which at the time was very mixed on getting involved in another global conflict. A war would also extract America from the Great Depression. Japan, a country with few natural resources, had to marginalize U.S. naval power in the Pacific because the U.S. was threatening its vital oil supply coming out of Southeast Asia.

Japan needed to destroy the U.S. Pacific fleet, particularly its aircraft carriers, all four of which were conveniently exercising out of harbor when the attack came.

Never mind the 50+ million people who died in World War II. Never mind that the U.S. dropped two nuclear bombs on Japan—killing over 200,000 civilians—to rapidly accelerate the end of the Pacific war so Russia could not lay claim to lands it assisted in conquering à la Germany/ Berlin. Never mind it, because it's all just history and we can't go back and change it, no matter how necessary or unnecessary it was.

And we can't change it, Heidi mused. But we can re-write the future by not repeating the past, regardless of our judgment of it. December $7^{th}$ could again be a pivotal day, though hopefully this time with an ending that involved minimal loss of life and a marked improvement of it.

...

Stem cells are essentially generic cells that can be purposed to serve whatever capacity is needed in the body, from a muscle cell, to a white blood cell, to a brain cell. Wherever there is damage, stem cells can potentially help out—new kidneys can be grown from stem cells. Stem cells can help with the treatment of diabetes and hearing loss. An amazing feature of all stem cells, regardless of their source, is that they can self-replicate almost *ad infinitum*. Once you have a few, you can keep growing them as needed. All of this was very convenient for Heidi.

There are two basic types of stem cells, adult and embryonic.

Adult stem cells typically replicate the organ from which they are harvested. Heidi obviously could not use this kind of stem cell since E4 is synthesized in the fetal liver and is passed on to the mother via the placenta.

Embryonic stem cells usually come from the blood of an umbilical cord once the baby is delivered. They can only be used effectively on mammals with *that* specific DNA sequence. These were the stem cells on which Heidi's research had been focused. This method would also be difficult to use as Heidi was fairly certain the umbilical cords of world leaders were probably in very short supply. Additionally, both techniques, adult and embryonic, required a degree of tinkering within the cells, which slowed down the product's manufacturing, and added a considerable cost component to the equation.

But then something fortuitous happened. An anesthesiologist named

Dr. Charles Vacanti, out of Brigham and Women's Hospital in Boston, and in conjunction with the Riken Center for Developmental Biology out of Japan, came up with a novel hypothesis. When you scrape your knee, what causes the damaged cells to grow back into skin cells, versus kidney or bone cells? It turns out that adult cells, when almost killed, revert back to embryonic versions of themselves. They then become whatever area of the body needs them. Essentially, by having a person's blood, you can get the plasticity and effectiveness of embryonic stem cells— primed specifically for that person—without needing to fiddle with their insides.[82]

Supporting this breakthrough was an "anonymous investor" operating under the cloak of a little-known fund called Pucelle Capital Partners. The fund was guaranteed rights to various applications of the technology with its investment in the start-up, Genix, undertaking the research and development. Genix happily fulfilled their commitment to share in-depth updates with the investors' representative, a surprisingly young woman named Lexie who appeared for quarterly board meetings via video calls and the occasional cruise through the labs.

Leveraging this access, Heidi's team was able to develop a self-contained device about the size of a large boot box whose labyrinth of glass chambers, clamps and tubes resembled a miniaturized gerbil farm with hi-tech, motorized hamster wheels and other gizmos. It worked a lot like Henry Ford's production plant. You simply inserted a small vial of the target's blood in one end, plugged the device in, waited for about 24 hours, and out the other end came the required mixture of estradiol (E2) and estriol (E3) needed to synthesize with the target's liver to create E4. And because the E2 and E3 were made from the target's own DNA, acceptance and production by that body was guaranteed. Lexie named the mixture "the LoveTail," combining "love" and "cocktail," but also in wry jest knowing the target's biological desires for sex (she was aware a common male slang word for the female crotch was "tail"), and the love cycle initiated when they start to produce their own E4.

The innards of the process were slightly more complex. The subject's blood was first tested in a cyclotron, which measured testosterone levels and the state of the liver, both critical factors in determining the amount of E4 to produce. It was then acid-bathed to near annihilation to get it

---

[82] Search "STAP Brigham" however it should be noted that recent transpirations have cast questions on this particular pathway; http://www.newyorker.com/magazine/2016/02/29/the-stem-cell-scandal

to a pseudo-embryonic state, at which point very particular proteins were introduced to stimulate the production of the E2 and E3 ingredients. Through some novel feats of engineering, once one batch was finished the machine was good to go again, with the easy replacement of a few chambers and tubes.

The machine was built for field use and it incorporated some very well thought through *what ifs*? Before a run started, the machine automatically performed a contamination scan of the entire system, which could identify anything that might cause an errant end product. The device then either performed another wash cycle or flagged the item for replacement via blinking icons and celebrity voices (once assigned, all user information rained down from the Cloud). When in operation, the device needed to maintain a constant temperature of 65 degrees throughout the numerous steps, which involved both heating and cooling. Should the power go out, a lithium battery, with about 10 hours of run time, kicked in while a message alerting the owner of the loss of charge was communicated to all relevant devices. A spare battery also came conveniently attached to the underside of the base in a form-fitted pocket. Process updates, including the contamination protocol, that visually mirrored the labyrinth were transmitted real time to whatever device the owner desired. Any required modifications were readily served up, complete with the fix's probability of success based on past experience and associated calculations. This was a device built by the woman who started Illumina, after all.

When the process was through, the LoveTail was deposited into a brushed silver insulated metal container that resembled lipstick for nonchalant ease of handling. Based on Lexie's "love" theme, Heidi had named the device the "LoveBomb," to be transported in a stylish, sturdy, yet understated, shipping case (made from renewables) with wheels, whose innards had been custom designed and padded to carry all required components for multiple doses. To reduce the possibility of external contamination, the case was also fitted with an unobtrusive rubber lining which made it waterproof to 300 feet. And, to avoid raising any eyebrows in airport security, all sides of the containers had been lined with a thin sheet of silver, through which x-rays could not pass. The silver had been stamped with imprints of clothes, shoes, and other travel needs in such a way that to random security personnel who might be looking at a scanning machine, the case appeared to belong to a woman who was on a very well planned holiday. Heidi, for one, couldn't wait to start using her unlimited vacation plan.

...

The lab in Qatar was in Doha, the capital, as there wasn't really anywhere else it could be in the country. Though there were plenty of opportunities to get involved in the local biotechnology scene (via the impressive Qatar Science and Technology Park, or in partnership with U.S. universities like Texas A&M and the Weil Cornell Medical College), Heidi had decided to avoid the attention.

Instead, she chose to set up shop in a nondescript, walled-in compound right off a traffic circle near the park, adjacent to a supermarket and with a daycare facility called Giggles directly across the street. Heidi had actually checked out Giggles and, sure enough, the owner, staff and clientele did giggle. There was also a small mosque located adjacent to the property. Though she was at odds with the whole religious thing—organized religion of whatever strain, from her perspective, was a bastion and enforcer of male dominance—she also realized that most women weren't enlightened to the ways religion oppressed them. Yet.

Heidi wanted to make daily life as easy as possible for her colleagues. She liked the privacy of the walled-in research compound, and she required all colleagues to change from their lab outfits into street clothes for reasons of cleanliness before leaving the building. Outwardly, they looked like women employed in some kind of light manufacturing or call center business.

Qatar's social codes had been modernizing at a rapid pace in comparison to other countries in the vicinity. Women were allowed to drive with male permission (unlike in some neighboring states where women couldn't drive at all). Dress codes were relatively lax; head scarfs that covered mouths and noses were not required. A good portion of the female population was employed and could take on leadership positions across industries. The first female judge had been recently appointed and female athletes had competed in the most recent Summer Olympics.

All this noted, Heidi didn't want to take any chances. She knew that no matter how progressive a society was, certain individuals within it would react unfavorably to her efforts. No PR, no meetings with ministers. All recruiting was done by referral.

Who would guess, she would occasionally ponder, that someday Qatar's prevailing norms might someday be significantly evolved from this little facility situated off a random traffic circle? Who would guess the world might take some giant leaps for man—and woman—kind? Right under their noses...

...

The Gulf Stream planes (minus Qin, who had wisely chosen to make her own arrangements) queued up like the curled tail of a cat basking in afternoon sun in preparation to land at one of Qatar's crown jewels, Hamad International Airport. The ladies (again, without Qin) would be staying at the Le Cigale Hotel, in part because it served alcohol (alcohol consumption was generally not allowed in Qatar) and in part because of its location near the airport. Heidi's travels had made her aware of foreign driving habits; the less undue ground transportation the better.

After the planes landed and they passed through immigration and customs, the women broke into a mass of hugs in the hangar. Although they had been in touch over the last two months (the beta devices used to call each other had been very busy), they had all been looking forward to the reunion. It made Heidi glow. She had wondered if the women, being physically separated, might have doubts while on their own. But this did not seem to be the case...in the slightest.

Heidi whisked the group to the hotel in a van with darkened windows. During the ride, she underscored the need to minimize the risk of any information being leaked...anywhere. She had experiences with (male-run) media organizations and (male) financial analysts looking to get an illicit scoop on the next Illumina product...and *this* was a launch that would make history. She exhorted TM7 to view the world from a similar perspective. After all, "Loose lips sank ships" and "new ears bring fears." To outsiders, this trip was a review of the progress that International Verve Fund recipients were making toward their goals.

When TM7 checked-in to the hotel, Heidi suggested they unwind at the spa or lounge at the pool. Heidi and Lexie needed to discuss some corporate matters for an hour or so. The group planned to convene downstairs at 6:00 p.m. at the Di Capri restaurant for dinner. The meal would be followed by a high level discussion of everyone's progress with planning. Qin would arrive by then.

Dinner was served in a public space, and the women spoke judiciously. Qin showed punctually at 7:30, firmly hugging each of her colleagues. "Let's get this meeting going," she said with a smile the size of China, though Heidi could sense something was on Qin's mind. She made a mental note to have a one-on-one talk with her sometime during their stay.

TM7 retreated to a windowless, private function room in the interior of the hotel. As they settled into their seats, Heidi sensed a palpable bond of shared purpose so pure she almost started to tear up. TM7 was truly magnificent. Lexie did a quick pass of the room with her device looking for bugs. Satisfied, it was clean, she turned on the projector box.

The group had done an impressive job of self-organizing and had transcended individual boundaries to become a functioning team with roles based on respective assets. They were women after all, Heidi observed.

The team had created a presentation, with a purple and white theme Heidi obviously liked. They even designed brand elements that reflected both the group's purpose and psychographic profiles. First was a logo of what appeared to be leaves protruding from a twisted stem. On closer inspection however, the stem was actually the DNA double helix. "Kind of like Steel Magnolias," Qin commented with a prankster's smile— which was unusual for her. Heidi sensed that a good part of Qin's downtime outside of China was probably spent devouring American entertainment.

They had also chosen a font that combined a sense of style, substance and feminine mystique.

*TM7*

"If we are ever found out," Shalala giggled, "people will have a hard time believing what we're trying to do…our look and feel are more along the lines of a boutique flower shop than a super-secret organization with global game-changing technology!"

"Ladies, may I start the first official meeting of TM7?" Divine, who was chosen to facilitate the meeting, asked with her powerful voice resonating with the strength of camaraderie in the room.

"Yes!"

"Ok, here we go."

The agenda was to 1) discuss LoveBombs and 2) determine their targets and timing. First, Lexie gave a visual overview of the LoveBomb. How it worked. How it didn't work. And how to deal with a bevy of "what ifs." She directed them to icons on the LoveBomb, and on their MoPhones, for interactive video overviews of everything they would need to know. Tomorrow morning, they would go through practice runs using the contraption, changing parts, and tackling unexpected challenges. Heidi had done enough product demos with her sales colleagues to know that learning curves exist for everyone, regardless of technical skill. There was immense power in repeating product information four or five times to get the requisite mental and physical muscle memories imprinted.

"Oh darn, I should have asked you all if there's a man in your life who could use a good shot," Heidi jovially admitted.

Lexie obviously had spent a lot of time with the Bomb, and her ability to answer all sorts of questions exceeded Heidi's expectations. There were many good ones.

Elena: "Can it be damaged by the airlines or a fall?"

Lexie: "The external case has been stress-tested to 500 pounds in all directions and the LoveBomb itself has been engineered to withstand significant blows. The case could drop ten feet, tumble down a flight of stairs and end up at the bottom of a very deep pool and the LoveBomb would still operate beautifully." Lexie's response was spoken with a vague inference that an unplanned variation of this story may have actually happened.

Shalala: "If something still doesn't work, who should we contact?"

Lexie, with a smile: "Why, the LoveBomb AnswerFemme! If the audio-video instructions on either the LoveBomb or your MoPhone don't suffice, simply push this button," she said, motioning toward an orange, nickel-sized circle on her MoPhone that read 'WTF,' "and say 'Help me.' Then take a video of what isn't working, add your commentary, and the answer, my friends, will blow through the winds and project on your screen."

The ladies were duly impressed by this technological feat. Finally, a sensible way to fix things. Heidi sensed this and added, "This functionality will be available for all of Illumina's products in the next six months and for common fix-its next year."

Divine, being mindful of the time, politely suggested they move on to the second half of the agenda. There would be ample opportunity in the morning to fill in whatever blanks might still exist.

The topic turned to targets and timing. Divine started the presentation with a map of the world with red dots of different sizes. There were many. "These red dots represent current wars, and the size of the dot correlates with the amount of killing and refugee activity in each place," Divine shared in a somewhat stolid tone. She then pressed a button and yellow dots appeared on the map, in larger sizes and with more space in between them. "Yellow signifies hunger," she said. Purple meant human trafficking. Black stood for pollution. Pink, which covered most of the planet, showed female inequality and included rape and domestic violence. Grey marked nuclear weapons.

By the time Divine finished, it was difficult to tell there was a map underneath the panoply of paint ball splotches. TM7 sat very still throughout Divine's impassive delivery. They had all been part of putting this presentation together and, perhaps due to the enormity of the challenge and their personal experiences with a color (or two or three), they were deeply affected.

"So, we have a little work to do," Divine continued, with a hint of humble wit. She hoped to lighten the tone of the meeting a little despite the scale and scope of the problems they faced. "But as long as certain things fall into place, we can expect to be finished in a little over a year."

The most optimal forum for this "testosterone takedown" was the upcoming G20 meeting in Tokyo, Japan, which was scheduled on September 15th…roughly nine months away. It would give them adequate amounts of time to plan, prepare and practice.

Why the G20? All the key players, and their leaders, would be there: OPEC heavyweight (and Sunni leader) Saudi Arabia, the BRIC contingency (Brazil, Russia, India and China—and certainly Qin would be part of the Chinese contingency), the European cluster (U.K, France, Italy, and Germany), established Asian powers (South Korea, Japan and Australia), and, of course, the North American cascade (Canada, U.S. and Mexico). These 20 countries represented approximately two-thirds of the world's population, 85% of global economic output and 75% of global trade. Of particular fortune, Iran, a pivotal force, had been invited to attend this session as well.

The only big downside to targeting the G20 was that most of Africa, parts of which had rainbows of color layers, would would not be represented. But because the women felt they could make a profound impact by working with the G20 leaders, they agreed they should receive attention first. And if TM7 could pull off this feat, there was a good chance that particular organizations (WHO, Organization of African States, the U.N., etc.) would emerge from the shadows of men's narrow egos to truly serve their purposes, with more than adequate resources and combined political and economic strength. It was all about tipping gorillas.

Now whether each respective leader would show, given the current tenuous state of global affairs, was a pressing question Heidi posed to the group. "If someone big doesn't show, we'll need to make a house call," Elena responded with her usual matter-of-fact brio.

"Additionally, there should be an unusually large amount of chaos at this summit," Gilat noted (she was on quite a few mailing lists). "Groups protesting all sorts of issues, from Greenpeace and some other crazy environmental organizations," she said, her eyes merrily landing on Elena, "to the Occupy Movement and anarchists. All have pledged to show. Though security will be tight, there's a good chance that random events will foul up even the best laid plans…we can use this to our advantage."

The women shifted their attention to Heidi who, until this point, had said little. With a face that reflected the distant tone with which Divine began the meeting, Heidi leaned back in her chair, gently closed her eyes and clasped her hands in front of her as if she were getting ready for a quick meditation session. After a few long moments, she slowly stood up and, as she opened her eyes, it seemed she might be about to give some difficult feedback. Then she suddenly started clapping as if she had just learned that Illumina had been selected as Global Employer of Choice (for the ninth consecutive year). "Excellent work, my Magnificent Seven!" she cried. "Excellent!"

"So we have eight months. Plenty of time to get ready and prepare for this summit."

"Yes," Divine responded, "and for a few reasons, we'd like to do a practice run first. One, we want to make sure everything works in the field, as easily as we presume it will in the production facility. Two, we want to understand the impact of dosing two sides of a bitter conflict, just to see how things play out. And three, one of our members," she said, darting a mischievous glance around the table, "even before our first conference call, had developed a plan that was utter genius. It has some risks, no doubt, but we all believe it has a very good chance of success with minimal exposure for the member and the group. While G20 will involve all of us—and Heidi, we presume you can make a cameo—this initial test will be run just by one of us, so if she is discovered, TM7 will remain relatively intact."

Heidi digested this information as she took a slurp of her Cosmo. As soon as she finished swallowing she responded, "Another great idea. And yes, I will most certainly be in Tokyo during the summit." She continued, squinting her eyes around the table like a suspicious detective probing a lineup for the culprit, "And I'm very curious to know which one of you is behind this master test plan."

"Oh Heidi," Divine responded with a laugh of light-hearted sarcasm. "It really isn't all that difficult to figure out. Which one of us has a particular axe to grind?"

# 16

## Heads Up

The next thirty minutes was spent reviewing TM7's test plan. Though she had some reservations about this particular tack, Heidi sensed the winds were blowing very strong in this direction. To thwart her team would have deflated many sails that were presently trimmed and functioning well. The last thing she wanted to do was come in and take over. That would be way too penile…The women were on board and Heidi knew she could trust they understood the risks and were taking steps to mitigate them. And the plan, which had obviously been worked on for a while, was downright fantastic.

It was getting late and jet lag of various hues was starting to creep onto faces. Heidi called it a night and calibrated expectations with the team. All were invited to breakfast, though optional. She would be downstairs in a van at nine. The girls started to make their way toward the elevator bank.

Qin knew Heidi wanted to talk to her, and in fact she needed to speak with Heidi, which was why she had dropped the cue. She dawdled as the other women said good night to each other and left the room. Lexie lingered as well just to see if there was anything else Heidi might need or wanted to discuss. "Lex, I'll catch you in the morning...7:15 in the gym?" Lexie confirmed with a tired smile and a wave and quickly disappeared, leaving Qin and Heidi alone.

"I can't hide much from you, can I?" Qin observed with a smile that was probably a little more relaxed than usual due to the three quarters of a bottle of Malbec Heidi had passively watched her consume. Heidi hesitated for a moment, trying to decide if she wanted to broach what happened in the *Salon Edouard* or to get into what was happening now. She decided on the latter; when Qin was ready to discuss what happened in France, Heidi felt sure she would bring it up.

"Qin, I am not the best at reading people but, tonight, I definitely picked up a vibe," Heidi said. "What's going on?"

"Well, as you know, it's difficult for me to communicate freely from China sometimes," Qin started. Even though communications with the rest of the world had skyrocketed over the last fifteen years, there was still a huge governmental presence, a modern day Great Wall, controlling what the country's citizens could and could not know about the world outside of the central kingdom. No less than twelve governmental bodies, employing an absurdly large number of people, existed to control the flow and type of information the Chinese populace could consume. All so men could maintain control...and their wealth.

Illumina was initially at the forefront of efforts to liberate data from censorship, while keeping its customers' information confidential from governmental exploitation. Heidi pioneered a consortium of Silicon Valley powerhouses to develop an encryption standard not even the NSA could break. However, after several Chinese government crackdowns and multiple arrests of Shanghai-based colleagues (who weren't involved; the arrests were purely to provide leverage and PR for the Party), Heidi took a different approach. For Illumina to prevail, the company had to penetrate the Chinese market. The more widespread her technology became (especially in the hands of public sector mucky mucks), the less power the government would have to shut them down. And once TM7 started to kick in...who knew how much information might start to flow to the Chinese populace?

"Well," Qin said. "Some things that have happened since my trip to France that have me concerned that I may be under more surveillance than usual. Who knows? I may just be a little paranoid because nobody in China knows what I know…and knowing what would happen to me if they did know can be a bit wearing." She ended with a smile though this one betrayed her seriousness.

"Oh my," Heidi responded, her attention piqued. "What's been happening?"

"Little things primarily. Some emails and texts are taking a bit longer to arrive at their destinations, which could mean they are being monitored. This happens. When I arrived home one night, one of my mirrors was a bit off-kilter. If there is a video camera or microphone someplace—and they've become very good at hiding them—I certainly can't look for it or they'll know there's a reason I'm looking. I also have a sense that I'm being followed sometimes, possibly even on this trip."

"Now, I'm used to this kind of scrutiny. You have no idea how many attempts were made to discredit me by provincial autocratic postulants as I climbed the ladder. I've spent my entire life under magnifying glasses, so much so that at times I thought I would burst into flames. I'm used to being careful…so extremely careful about every aspect of my life. I haven't been wrong often, and I simply cannot take the chance of being wrong this time."

"I just wanted to give you the heads up so we can all be on guard. One slip and TM7 could come crashing down and that would be the absolute last thing I would want to happen." Qin continued, looking slightly more animated, "And I will do *whatever* I can to see *our* mission through to its conclusion." Though Qin's energy had returned, her last line was uttered with a degree of pained somberness that seemed to echo the fact that a wound, though perhaps cleaned and bandaged, had not healed.

Heidi leaned back in her chair and began to process everything Qin had just shared. With a matter-of-fact expression she said, "Well, I figured this would happen eventually, and I expected it would be either you or Gilat, or both of you, given your governmental ties. I just didn't think it would happen so soon." Her eyes became empathetic. "Qin, above all I want you to be safe. If anything were to happen to you, even though you know what you've gotten yourself into, I would feel horrible. Absolutely, utterly horrible. Truth be told, a part of me already feels badly that I've diverted TM7's life paths, perhaps irrevocably, to my cause. But, as we all agreed, it needs to be done…I have to let this go."

She paused for a moment to catch some breath. "Remember, and I cannot underscore this enough, if you ever want out just say the words.

And you know that—" she stopped.

Qin sat there, deep and complex emotions professionally hidden behind an emotionless face. She looked into Heidi's eyes as Heidi shared her concerns, and though her expression contained less life than the desert outside, her eyes conveyed utter respect and that she was inspired, almost worshipful, of Heidi. It was obvious that Heidi's words, while having meaning, would not mean a thing to Qin. She was on this ship until it sank. Heidi stopped speaking and the white of Qin's cheeks softly grew into knowing curves. She smiled.

"Yes, you know that," Heidi repeated to herself, seeing that she didn't have to remind Qin that she could get out whenever she wanted. "And I don't need to remind you to take every available precaution. If you need to go dark to stay inside, we'll completely understand. It's taken us lifetimes to get to where we are. There is no need to jeopardize that time by doing something too risky in the short term. In any case, I expect we will be developing backup plans, should members, for whatever reason, be unable to fulfill their roles when the time comes."

...

Although the trip from the hotel to the compound was just as unmemorable as most other routes in Doha, Heidi did her best to play tour guide. She let Divine drive (she knew the local terrain much better) and Lexie gladly took shotgun to scan for crazy male drivers. The confluence of wealth, bored young men with wealth, and not many opportunities for recreation, had created a culture of (very) fast driving and automotive acrobatics such as high speed slides and climbing out of windows while the car was tipped on two wheels.[83] Lots of fun if you were young and self-centered; not so much if you were hit and had mouths to feed. Heidi pointed out the local sights: the university, the Qatar Science and Technology Park and, of course, Giggles.

When they arrived, all they could see was a ten-foot high cinderblock wall, with a gate that slid open with surprising speed given the dusty environment. All were painted a light brown color whose blandness had been accentuated by a relentless sun and pockmarks from an occasional sandstorm.

Naijla, the facility's General Manager, greeted them at the front

---

[83] Search "Qatar crazy drivers"

door. Her relaxed manner was complemented by an equal degree of confidence and strength. The women could immediately tell she was just as passionate about the cause as they.

"Welcome everyone. Welcome to Doha!" Naijla exclaimed graciously. "You must be Elena."

The facility's interior reflected the stark difference between the parched environment outside the walls and the vibrancy of what was happening within them. Tasteful furnishings and a sleek, white tile floor complemented walls painted a familiar shade of purple. All appropriate rooms were filled with a multitude of plants and flowers and the floor plan included a well-stocked kitchen and a rather large "Rest Room" that was outfitted with couches, futons, a plethora of pillows, yoga mats and a variety of lighting and audio options for resting, meditation, etc.

After a quick view of the glass-enclosed lab where, among other projects, the proteins required to trigger the production of E4 were being synthesized, Naijla led the group upstairs to a sizable and similarly decorated "Production Room." Six shipping cases, presumably with LoveBombs snugly packed inside, had been neatly arranged in a semi-circle around a seventh for the morning's learn-by-doing session. And thankfully, against the far wall, a coffee, tea and a fruit presentation was waiting.

After making sure the group had everything they would need for the day, Naijla departed with a heartfelt salutation. "Gals, or The Magnificent Seven as I've heard you named yourselves," she said, "I wish you all the luck the universe can bestow. I hope what we have created does the trick."

Heidi then walked over to one of the cases, and sat down on it. She seemed to want to say something important, but she encouraged the group to get caffeinated first if needed. Soon enough, all were all seated on their own case.

"Before we start getting intimate with our machines," Heidi said, "something has come up that we need to be aware of." She shared Qin's concerns, and underscored that they could all get out whenever they wanted. Like Qin, they all just sat there on cases that housed potential weapons of mass construction, listening to everything she was saying with open ears and resolved hearts. When she was finished, there was silence for a moment, which Elena punctually broke, "Yeah, Heidi... We get it. We got it when we signed up for this. *No hay problema*, right sisters?"

"Yes!" they chorused.

"Now, can we get to this LoveBomb thing? I want to start making those motherfuckers into motherlovers…"

…

The rest of the morning went smoothly. The women found the LoveBombs to be even easier to deal with than they had imagined. The focus on user experience research and design for the software, machine, and how the two synergized (the hallmark of Illumina's success) paid off in spades. The devices were almost too easy to use and, after a quick review by Lexie as to what everything was, soon enough seven LoveBombs were whirring, clicking and mixing away. Heidi made sure that each member's actions and words were recorded on video since she knew from experience that if there was a problem and the AnswerFemme was needed, understanding how each member interacted with their machine could be useful in quickly diagnosing and solving the problem. If something went wrong in the field, the women would need answers, and fast.

There was one memorable question that was answered on the spot. During the cleaning process, some chemicals (marked with "Cleaner" on the bottle that had its own shape in the shipping case's foam innards) needed to be poured into a funnel-shaped indentation (coincidentally marked "Cleaner") on the top of the Bomb. As the audio-visual step-by-step instructions continued, there came a point where the polished voice suggested that if any cleaner splashed onto the device, the user should simply use a napkin or cloth to soak it up.

Upon hearing these instructions, Shalala momentarily froze, eyes and mouth opening in a mix of registered shock and curiosity. "I am sorry Lexie," she delicately inquired, "did the voice just say we should use a napkin to soak up the cleaner?"

"Yes, Shalala. Is there an issue with this?" Lexie deferentially replied.

"But what if you aren't on your cycle?" Shalala asked dubiously.

TM7, who had overheard the entire interchange, immediately broke into hysterics. When Lexie regained enough lung capacity to speak, she informed Shalala that "napkin" in U.S. English was something used at meals to wipe one's mouth which, she now recalled, differed from the U.K. definition that Shalala was accustomed to, which meant "sanitary pad." Lexie immediately sent an email to the internal production group to flag "napkin" in all future Illumina audio releases.

...

At 12:15, the group broke for lunch, which was delivered to the Production Room ("with plenty of napkins in case we get messy," Shalala deftly observed). Heidi was stoked. The members of TM7 were very quick learners. The only real issue, as far as she could see, was making sure particular pieces and tubes of glass didn't get too slippery to handle during the clean-up process. Though replacement parts were included, she didn't want users to deal with broken glass, potentially cutting themselves, which could also pose a contamination risk. She made a note to investigate using glass with etched sides for better gripping.

"Ladies, excellent work today. You're all naturals at making things work for the better. I hope you found the education session easy to understand and informative. You each will be taking your LoveBomb with you, everyone except Qin. Although you could buy a "suitcase" like this in Qatar, given Qin's concerns about being followed, it doesn't make sense to take that chance." Qin nodded her agreement. Heidi continued, "But don't worry, Qin. If and when you need your device, it will be there."

Then, quite unexpectedly, Heidi felt a flush of panic. While speaking, she had seen six women happily sitting on top of their LoveBombs, attentively listening to her every word. But in an instant she found herself assailed by thoughts of potential discovery and danger. Perhaps it was Qin's confession that she might be a "person of interest" that had shaken Heidi. Perhaps it was because the plan had now become real, and their lives would become increasingly at risk.

A hideous image of the folly of her actions formed in her mind. She imagined the women "yee-hawing" and flogging their LoveBombs with cowboy hats as they fell from the sky, just like the neocon Major Kong, played by Slim Pickens, in Dr. Strangeglove. He also believed he was in the right, in his own twisted and deluded way. And while Heidi had no questions as to the moral nature of this real-life plot, the irony of the lengths belief could take you, in both good and bad ways, was not lost on her.

Her vision quickly returned from mid-60s black and white to next millennium color with Lexie's hesitant probing "Heidi, is everything alright?"

"Oh, yes. I'm fine. Sorry everyone. Just a little flashback…Where were we? Oh yes. We have another four hours before we must go, and we can't have Qin disappearing for too long any more. She needs to be visible and doing her thing. So, how do you want to spend our time?"

Divine snagged a green whiteboard marker and walked gracefully over to a wall that had been finished with whiteboard paint. "Ladies, what do we want to cover? We are diverging here, so no idea is too out there." The group immediately came up with some practical questions, including:

Which countries do we want to prioritize as "must dose" versus "nice to dose"?

How are we going to get blood from 10 to 15 men (only three of the G20's leaders were women)?

Who would be responsible for what?

How would the doses be administered?

Where is the best handbag shopping in Tokyo?

The last question was immediately answered by Lexie who started raving about a little bag shop in Shibuya. The group, which was quick to pick up technology, asked her to repeat the name on camera. A button press later and a map appeared with a picture of the shop, its address and walking route keying off landmarks from the closest subway.

"I believe we should start with the first question," Gilat said. "Start with the biggest questions as they often frame smaller questions…"

TM7 agreed and a priority matrix was constructed using the Mo-Phone's interactive spreadsheet function and projected on the wall. Coming up with criteria proved a bit difficult. However, Heidi knew from experience that if the criteria were not appropriate and agreed upon, the results wouldn't reflect the group's prime desires. One part of the group wanted to use the color labels from Divine's world map to rank the most important issues and apply them to the respective countries.

Others, while seeing value in this approach, posited that some countries might not *appear* influential on the world stage because of the limited nature of their geo-political, economic and religious influences, but they could be very important for the TM7 cause. Saudi Arabia was a great example of immense potential to affect change because its wealth, oil supply, alleged funding of terrorist groups such as Al Qaeda ("15 of the 19 suicide bombers behind 9/11 came from Saudi Arabia," Shalala demurely reminded the group), and geographic location in the thick of Middle East and North African conflicts.

Predictably, the women came up with a compromise. Based on Divine's world map, they would review potential impact for each country by checking the size of the country and the number of lives that could be affected. They would then create a list of issues and apply these to the G20 countries with a filter they decided to name "Impact." Each woman would go through the exercise herself and then all the scores would be tallied up.

The women got busy and seven MoPhones started humming. The resulting ranks, with notes, and a special column Elena added to denote particular emissions per capita "offenders" appeared on the wall. Brazil, Argentina and Germany all showed up with a pink background that signaled their leader was a woman. However, this color code did not necessarily remove them from scrutiny; combinations of conditioning, religion, genetic dysfunctions, and lack of courage can trump biology.

| Country | Rank | Notes (in no order of importance) | Elena's Motherfuckers |
|---------|------|-----------------------------------|------------------------|
| Russia | 34 | Run by a sociopath, military power, energy supplier, climate change, women's/human rights, nuclear weapons, human trafficking | X |
| China | 31 | Military power, human/women's rights, climate change, immense economic power, nuclear weapons, human trafficking | X |
| India | 30 | Women's/human rights, climate change, poverty, lack of education, nuclear weapons, human trafficking | X |
| Saudi Arabia | 28 | Religious influencer/theocracy, economic power, oil supply, women's/human rights, climate change | X |
| Brazil | 28 | Poverty, lack of education, climate change, human trafficking, women's/human rights | |
| Iran | 28 | Religious influencer/theocratic, women's/human rights, economic power, oil supply, nuclear weapons (?), climate change | X |

| | | | |
|---|---|---|---|
| United States | 24 | Climate change, military power, women's rights, poverty/income inequality, religious elements, oil supply, nuclear weapons, economic power | X |
| Mexico | 20 | Climate change, women's/human rights, poverty, lack of education, oil supply, human trafficking | |
| Argentina | 19 | Sociopathic leader, human trafficking, climate change, poverty, oil supplier, women's/human rights | |
| France | 18 | Xenophobic elements, climate change, women's/human rights | X |
| United Kingdom | 17 | Climate change, women's rights, military power, nuclear weapons, economic power | X |
| Indonesia | 16 | Poverty, lack of education, women's/human rights, large population, climate change | |
| Turkey | 16 | Climate change, women's /human rights, regional force | |
| Japan | 15 | Climate change, economic power, women's/human rights | X |
| Germany | 12 | Climate change, women's rights, economic leader of Europe | X |
| South Korea | 12 | Climate change, women's/human rights, economic power | X |
| Italy | 10 | Climate change, economic power, women's rights | X |
| South Africa | 5 | Climate change, women's/human rights | |
| Australia | 5 | Climate change, women's rights | |
| Canada | 3 | Climate change, women's rights | X |

TM7 sat back a bit on their LoveBombs to soak it all up. After a while, Heidi broke the silence. "Anything unexpected here? Any surprises my Magnificents?"

"Not really," Gilat responded, "though there certainly are other countries not on this list that would probably rank very highly using this process, *and* Elena's criteria," she said, shooting Elena a humored look, which Elena proudly returned.

"Yeah, there are many other motherfuckers out there with very high emissions per capita, mostly countries that produce oil or natural gas," Elena added. "It will be interesting to see what might happen to their economies, and political systems, when the gorillas tip…"

She continued in a matter-of-fact tone of voice. "What is also kinda' cool, is that two countries from my continent on this list both voted the way of the V recently," she said, making the peace sign with her left hand. "Vagina!" She smiled gleefully to a chorus of giggles from all present.

"Yes" Heidi echoed. "I've been following those elections closely. I'm very, very pleased that in the midst of all that machismo, women have taken the reins. I hope one day, sooner than later, many more of these countries will be in pink."

Shalala shared next. "What I find interesting is that there are a few countries with strong and influential economies that don't score as high on the list as I thought they would. Countries like Japan, Germany and South Korea."

"Good observation, Shalala," Heidi responded. "Anyone venture a guess as to why?" The group reflected a bit and then Shalala, an apparent history aficionado, observed, "Well, all three countries were involved in relatively recent and bloody wars, and Japan had two atomic bombs dropped on it. The Japanese constitution forbids spending more than 1% of their GDP on military expenditures, and that can only be spent on "defensive" weapons. With the United States' protection, both Japan and South Korea have avoided "arming up" again, and instead focus on building their economies, with great success. Germany, which was obliterated during World War II, is also a leading proponent of peace in Europe and focuses on its economy instead of war. It's unfortunate that so many millions of people had to die to cause this change, though they are great examples of what is possible."

"I agree completely," Heidi replied. "I have a theory that the odds for peace, at least when men are involved, are much higher directly after the brutality and suffering of war have penetrated a populace's, or the world's, consciousness. The Geneva Protocols, signed in 1925, banned the use of chemical weapons because of the million plus men killed or injured by chemical warfare in World War I.[84] The Geneva Convention, signed in 1949, finally defined the rights of wounded and captured soldiers, after thousands of years of killing. Hell, even Republicans were swayed back then. There's a great quote I have…" she said, fumbling with her MoPhone and asking the amicable actor/activist for help, which he was more than willing to provide.

"George, please find my Ike quote."

"Comin' right up. Anything for you, honey."

From the top of her device, a hologram of a black and white picture of president and five-star World War II general, Dwight D. Eisenhower, appeared with a quote. Ike's expression reflected the geo-political uncertainty at the time, as the Soviet Union's military-industrial complex, fed by the recent Korean War experience, was kicking into serious gear and he was very hesitant to join that zero-sum race. The quote came from a speech dubbed "A Chance for Peace" and it was delivered directly after the death of Stalin, in an apparent effort to derail a very high-stakes Mutually Assured Destruction[85] scenario:

> "Every gun that is made, every warship launched, every rocket fired signifies, in the final sense, a theft from those who hunger and are not fed, those who are cold and are not clothed. This world in arms is not spending money alone. It is spending the sweat of its laborers, the genius of its scientists, the hopes of its children.
>
> The cost of one modern heavy bomber is this: a modern brick school in more than 30 cities. It is two electric power plants, each serving a town of 60,000 people. It is two fine, fully equipped hospitals. It is some fifty miles of concrete pavement. We pay for a single fighter with a half-million bushels of wheat. We pay for a single destroyer with new homes that could have housed more than 8,000 people. . .This is not a way of life at all, in any true sense. Under the cloud of threatening war, it is humanity hanging from a cross of iron."[86]

---

[84]  http://en.wikipedia.org/wiki/Chemical_weapons_in_World_War_I

[85]  MAD also stands for Mutually Assured Destruction. See http://en.wikipedia.org/wiki/Mutual_assured_destruction

[86]  http://en.wikipedia.org/wiki/Chance_for_Peace_speech

TM7 sat there, soaking up Ike's prescient words. "Unfortunately, I'm not sure there was any other way we, we being the United States, could have played this one out. While I believe we women support defending ourselves, dealing with a hegemonic power whose economy depended on military expansion would have eventually led to conflict…as it did in Vietnam."

She continued. "But things have changed. Though Russia seems to want—or need, unfortunately—to get into another Cold War, its global military power has diminished dramatically and international trade has become another critical driver of its foreign policy." She paused. "There is also this little country called China," she said, warmly glancing at Qin, "which has emerged as a power that must be contended with."

"This new power paradigm means that we need to make sure we dose our targets at roughly the same time…We don't want an Ike needing to deal with a Stalin…or a Putin. We like Ikes all around." She completed her monologue with her usual cheery smile.

Predictably, Qin one-upped her. "Oh you mean, the 'I like Ike' button from the Indiana Jones movie?" she logically inquired with a grin. "I really liked the role Cate Blanchett plays…"

Heidi laughed. "Yes…Qin, I can't sneak anything past you, can I? I can imagine why you like her role. She's intelligent and a bit imperious in dealing with her thuggy Russian comrades…"

Even if they hadn't seen this particular installment, the reference brought smiles all around, and relieved TM7 of a little tension the whole group had been accumulating due to the rather heavy topics being discussed.

Perhaps emboldened by Heidi's affirmation, Shalala spoke up again in her slight yet refined British-Pakistani cadence, "Heidi, I agree with your observations. In this context, I believe we should re-examine our list of targets. Although the U.K. and France are numbers 9 and 10, it would seem Indonesia and Turkey, both of whom are only one rank behind them, should replace them. My thinking goes like this: in the case of Indonesia, there is a population of roughly 250 million people. Although the country has long been considered a model for tolerance and religious freedom, social and religious conservatism seems to be growing. Some local governments have introduced Sharia law, controlling how women can act, dress and behave. Since Indonesia is the largest Islamic country on earth, I personally don't want to see movements like the Taliban infecting the populace."

"As for Turkey, it borders and buffers Europe from many hot spots: Syria, Iraq and Iran, and parts of the country have remained relatively secular. However, its future is uncertain. While Erdogan, the Prime Minister, seems to have distanced his Islamic beliefs from the more conservative strains, the fight for women's rights, which blossomed in the 80s and 90s, was recently dealt a huge blow when he informed women's organizations he does not believe in gender equality. The Kurdish issue is also a major regional concern."[87]

"And the UK and France?" Heidi logically inquired.

"While they both have issues…and nuclear weapons," she started, "neither is particularly capable of doing anything too damaging, and their human rights records are stronger. The only potential downside of not dosing them, at least in the short-term, is they could regress and start Channel feuding again. But I don't believe this is a high probability."

"Yes," Heidi echoed. "The French are stilled bummed Napoleon lost." The statement drew a subtle chuckle from Divine. "Great analysis, Shalala," Heidi exclaimed, as Shalala leaned back on her LoveBomb to give Heidi the floor. "I'm on board with this switch. Any detractors?"

She was met with silence. "Sheesh, Shalala, you could've been my history mentor in university," Divine laughed humbly. Shalala blushed a bit, though her notoriety and public appearances had prepped her for this kind of spotlight.

"Anything else?" Heidi inquired.

"Yes, one last thing," Lexie piped up. "Although I understand that, given how the scores were calculated, it would seem the U.S. President could use a sizable dose, I believe he is doing a very good job given everything he's had to contend with internationally and domestically, literally from the first day he stepped into the White House."

"I also believe that because his parents divorced when he was young and he was raised primarily by his mom, he wasn't exposed to the typical 'male roles' to which most men are socialized. You can see these elements in his overall platform. His focus on health care, equality from pay to human rights, education, getting us out of wars and 'changing the mindset that got us in them,'[88] make him, in my mind, the least 'male' president the U.S. has had, with very good results. Does that make sense?"

---

[87] https://en.wikipedia.org/wiki/Recep_Tayyip_Erdoğan

[88] http://www.ontheissues.org/2008_Dems_Super_Tuesday.htm

Heads nodded in agreement.

"So, I propose that although the U.S. seems like it should appear on the top 10 list, we should give the president a pass for the moment. We don't necessarily want him to lose his edge, particularly given the recent, disastrous mid-term elections."

They all agreed and Divine put back on her facilitation hat. "So, it looks like our top seven, must-dose targets are the leaders from Russia, China, India, Saudi Arabia, Iran, Mexico, Indonesia and Turkey. Ladies, we will be focusing the predominance of our time on these characters going forward."

"This looks really great and geographically smart," Heidi observed. "There'll be vital pockets of estrogen in key locations in Europe, Asia and North and South America…and from a timing perspective, given historical animosities and geographic proximities, it doesn't seem anyone will be invading anyone else. It's a real shame we're not going after anyone in Africa on this pass but, again, the domino effect of reeling in the big fish may help tremendously in bringing these countries out of their testosterone traps. Should things go our way, it's not a question of *if*, but *when*."

Divine glanced at her watch. "OK girls, let's move on to the next important issue on the list: *how do we collect the blood?*

Heidi jumped in, "Ladies, what I'm about to share with you could be considered a TM7 'state secret.'"

"If you were a head of state and you were traveling abroad, maybe off the beaten path a bit, what would you want to make sure you had with you, just in case? Think life or death."

There was a momentary silence. Then Elena exclaimed, "A converter for my hair dryer." She pushed back her long dark hair and smiled satirically.

"A pound of dark chocolate," Divine said, shivering with the guilt of pleasure.

"Movies on a hard drive if I can't access Netflix," Qin said, cracking a smile.

"A PETA-reviewed shopping guide," Lexie said with a deadpan tone of voice, echoing Elena's irony.

"A liter of chilled Cosmopolitans," Shalala blurted, and then covered her mouth, bluntly aghast as to what had just jumped from her lips.

"A vibrator," said Gilat, with a face so straight, a few present imagined her carving out a custom-fitted pocket in her case's interior for her special friend.

Heidi had tried to take control after Lexie's response, but upon hearing Shalala's startling 'must have,' she lost it. And Gilat's statement almost sent her, and the rest of TM7, laughing all the way to the ER for abdominal spasms.

...

The answer, of course, was blood. It was common practice for international V.I.P.s to travel with a few units of their own stuff in the rare but real case that something unforeseen—an automobile accident, an assassin's bullet—happened to meet them. TM7 would need to get a hold of the correct blood bag, peel back a corner of the label that identified whose blood the bag carried, stick a needle in the bag where the label was, extract the needed amount (plus a little extra to be sure; who knew, after all, if there might be another use for it?), and press down the label again to seal the bag. 30 seconds max. No muss, no fuss. The trick was simply figuring out where the blood was stored, which was actually easy as it needed to be kept refrigerated.

Heidi was already working on a plan she was confident would work. She had tried it out on Roger with brilliant success. The real issue, from her perspective, was how they were going to get the therapy into the target.

And then hold on as the changes kicked in…

# 17

## KISS

Lexie peered over the top of her laptop as she sprawled on an over-stuffed couch on board Heidi's jet. While her MoPhone could do everything the laptop could, and a whole lot more, there was something to be said for the size and privacy of the screen, and the physical fulfillment of touching keys. These would require non-trivial behavior changes if the MoPhone, with its light-sensitive keyboard and holographic projection capabilities, was to gain significant customer acceptance. Besides, she didn't necessarily want Heidi to be able to see what was happening in her friends' love lives, or the latest internet flash sales.

"Heidi, do I really need to do Putin? He's really creepy...I mean like, REALLY creepy." Lexie was scrolling through images of the Russian dictator from a web search and had stopped on one of him looking decidedly smug, decked out in camouflage pants and what looked like Russian Timberland boots. He was topless with his chest shaved (or waxed?), and strolling on the edge of a river with a fishing pole over his shoulder. What was most unsettling was the look in his eyes. Lexie quickly reviewed his eyes in other shots, primarily portraits. The look was there in all of them, whether smiling, stone-faced or thoughtfully posed. It was a look that lacked any vestige of life; there was nothing but emptiness behind the blue.

"Lex, we've been through this twice. You know why you were chosen to dose him," Heidi sounded more like a mother who knew when her kids were pushing well-worn buttons. "You fit his profile."

"Yeah, but I mean, do I really have to show interest in him? That's going to be very difficult with Mr. Macho. I mean, if we're strong and smart women, why resort to this kind of child's play?" She paused and recalled a takeaway from prior conversations. "Oh yeah, to *us* it's child's play. I forgot."

"You have nothing to be worried about, Lex. You'll be fine. If you have any serious concerns, keep thinking of other ways you could LoveTail him. I'm sure you can figure out something else."

The day in Doha had ended on a very solid note. Heidi had briefly shared her plan for "specimen collection," which purposefully sounded more like TM7 was embarking on a biological rainforest expedition looking for undiscovered species than infiltrating and procuring blood from some of the most heavily guarded men on the planet. The fact that they would be going after blood sacks (versus "sacks of blood and a few other miscellaneous body parts") made the task a whole lot easier. This was a guiding principle of Illumina's success—KISS: Keep It Simple Stupid—and she urged the women to apply this acronym as they developed plans to administer the therapy. "This isn't an *Ocean's 11* or *12* screenplay," she said. "No need for tunnel-making using Chunnel machines or wiggling around dancing light beams. We just need to get the serum in them somehow."

Like many things in life, her plan was born out of her own experience, for she too travelled with a few pints of her own blood, stored in a small, paneled refrigerator in her jet, away from the galley. "I don't want my staff to get too grossed out or accidentally nick one of my blood bags with something sharp," she had commented. She presumed their targets would travel in similar fashion. And there were only a few custom-interior design outfits for top-end, private jets in the world. Heidi had intentionally become a customer of all of them.

Getting through computer firewalls via 'customer sign in' links, Heidi easily found floor plans for each country's fleet. This was just the start however. Particular countries, like Saudi Arabia, had so many planes it was difficult to figure out which one the King would be using. After accessing flight manifests from prior trips, she was able to triangulate on the top three potential selections. That meant there were only three sets of plans to dissect. In any case, they could get a visual of the plane once it arrived to determine which plans fit.

She was also able to deal with Lexie's final objection to her target, which she burbled in an annoyed, twenty-something dialect, "Heidi, like, you know he has 58 planes. Fifty-eight! Have you been able to procure plans for like, all 58? And how will anyone be able to remember 58 schematics?" Heidi pointed out that for trips like this one, where Putin needed to show off, he would likely use a larger plane, probably the one with the gold-finished bathroom that alone cost him $85,000."[89] This information actually made Lexie curious and caused her to reframe the mission in her head. "Wow, 85 G's on a bathroom. I'd like to take a pee in there!"

The only other preparation TM7 needed was to train as aircraft cabin cleaners. This would be their cover to collect the blood "donations" while the planes waited for their passengers to return (hopefully 2ml heavier). Training wouldn't take long, and Heidi had already assembled the proper uniforms, badges, and cleaning kits per what she had experienced on prior trips. Before they scattered, she proudly showed TM7 pictures of the local, smiling cleaning crews, their security badges easily discernible. She then pulled out of her case a brilliant, pressed replica, down to a little wear and tear on both the uniform and the card. Heidi would be there as well of course. Since the private jets had their own special playground, they could easily walk from one plane to the next.

The women also decided who would head up the team for each target: a position they called the "Lead Tailer." The Lead Tailer's job was to get to know that particular target's every predictable pattern and peculiarity, medications and meditations, tastes and troubles. Their job was to find anything that might provide a means to dose the targets safely and invisibly. Drawing on this intelligence, the Lead Tailer's were to map out a Plan A and a Plan B, and then work with other TM7 members to get feedback on their plans, test them and eventually execute them, with each other's support if need be.

These selections were made based on pragmatic overlaps such as

---

[89] http://heavy.com/news/2014/07/vladimir-putin-wealth-forbes-net-worth/

appearance, language, skin-color and origin. Each of the three most protected men would be assigned a Lead Tailer, while the other five world leaders would be divided among the remaining three women. In the case of Putin, his public preferences for a certain type of woman, per a publicized affair with a Russian gymnast who happened to vaguely resemble Lexie, bestowed Lexie with that odious honor (though she had found allegations that he was latently gay and the affair was contrived for PR purposes).

They fell out in the following manner:

| Country | Leader | Lead Tailer |
|---------|--------|-------------|
| Russia | Vladimir Putin | Lexie |
| China | Xi Jinping | Qin |
| India | Narendra Modi | Shalala |
| Saudi Arabia | Abdullah bin Abdulaziz | Divine |
| Iran | Hassan Rouhani | Gilat |
| Mexico | Enrique Peña Nieto | Elena |
| Indonesia | Joko Widodo | Shalala |
| Turkey | Recep Tayyip Erdogan | Divine |

Heidi would be The Grand Dame, the behind-the-scenes organizer, technology wizard, purchaser of whatever might be needed, and arranger of anything else.

As always, the devil was in details. Shalala had such international renown that she would be hard to hide even with her veil, which it was agreed would stand out a bit in Tokyo. If she was discovered, the team worried how Shalala would explain being incognito. She'd need to leverage her popularity, not hide it.

"No problem," Shalala responded, her "public figure" side magically appearing from nowhere. "My foundation will arrange an appearance and a press conference at the summit. It fits perfectly with our mission. If countries want to grow and reduce poverty, women must be educated. With the right prodding and positioning, I'm quite confident the proper meetings can be arranged." With a wry grin that conveyed an understanding of her influence, she continued. "It's in their political best interests to get photo ops with me."

Gilat taking on Iran was another concern. On the plus side, she was relatively familiar with Iran and, given her husband's profession, had an understanding of their security protocols. On the negative side, Gilat might be too personally invested in this particular target at both a state and personal level. Iran-Israeli relations hadn't been the most cordial recently. The former Iranian president had repeatedly called for the elimination of the Zionist state,[90] while Israel publicly threatened to destroy Iran's nuclear efforts. The real elephant in the mix was the fact that, for decades, Iran had sponsored groups such as Hezbollah, the Islamic Jihad, and Hamas. "Gilat," Divine diplomatically inquired, "given the reason you are here, I'd imagine a part of you would rather do away with him than dose him?"

Gilat, who had already thought through this issue, replied with uncharacteristic softness, her protective armor relaxed, "Divine, if this were ten years ago, I'd have killed him without thinking. But things have changed. The world has changed and it must keep changing...and we have the power to change it. Believe me, not a day passes when I don't reflect on what has happened to me, and how tragedy has altered the course of my life. Perhaps it's just being a woman," she said, giving Heidi and then the entire group a look of respect, "but I don't want any other mother to lose her child over something as archaic as religion. In grieving for my sons, I'm grieving for all mothers—past, present and future— who have lost children for this reason. And I will grieve until *we* have no reason to grieve any longer."

Gilat stopped speaking and Divine led the hug parade.

The final issue was Divine going after the Saudi King. Although Saudi Arabia officially banned slavery in 1962, at which time there were an estimated 300,000 indentured servants, Saudi Arabia had been able to remain essentially an apartheid state. "Blacks" (whose local name meant "slave") constituted 10% of the population, but did not have equal rights, could not hold many governmental positions and were still viewed as objects, not humans. A grandson of the King was recently sentenced to life in prison in England for brutally killing his black "servant" in a posh, five-star London hotel.[91] In Saudi Arabia the hierarchy went local men first, local women a distant second (they had to wear veils, weren't allowed to work certain jobs or drive) and local blacks and guest workers, a very distant last.

The heart of the issue, like most cases of disenfranchisement, was the

---

[90] http://en.wikipedia.org/wiki/Mahmoud_Ahmadinejad_and_Israel

[91] http://www.theguardian.com/uk/2010/oct/19/saudi-prince-servant-murder-guilty

need to control, to retain the male status quo, supported by an obscenely (in this case) patriarchal and misogynistic version of a religious creed. While the Qu'ran has some noble (for the time it was written) clauses that mitigate (while allowing) slavery, Sharia Law (the extremist Islamic legal and moral code) and more recent *fatwahs* (orders delivered by authoritative clerics) clearly support the notion that women are, at best, second-class citizens. Sharia law states that slavery is a part of Islam, and that sexual slavery and rape of women of particular religious/ethnic backgrounds is both permissible and should be practiced.[92]

"So Divine…any issues with knocking off the Saudi Grand Poobah if you had the chance? He could rape you and think he was doing God's will," Shalala clinically asked. As with Divine's inquiry to Gilat, these were questions that needed to be broached.

Divine laughed with an echo of confidence. "Like Gilat, I have fortunately been able to move past my past, and now I look at the experience as setting me free for I know now, having been to the edge and back again, that whatever happens to me, no one can control my soul. I do not believe killing is the answer. Death will only lead to more death and hate, more hate. There is no positive end game in this scenario. My target could have global implications for the future of the world, and Islam's part in it. This is huge. I will do whatever I must to try and make our plan work."

"Even the Bible and the Torah condone slavery, multiple wives, sexual slavery[93] and incest.[94] I was raised Catholic yet, like Gilat, I've since broken free of those bonds. Religions can be used for good. But because they were created by men, at their fundamental core they all treat women as property to be bought, sold, and physically, mentally and spiritually desecrated."

. . .

The van ride back to the hotel was quiet. They were all internalizing the immense progress that had been made in the last 24 hours and thinking about what lay ahead, in the near term (the prelude), the short term (their next meeting) and the medium term (the summit). As for what happened

---

[92] http://en.wikipedia.org/wiki/Islamic_views_on_slavery#Sexual_intercourse

[93] http://en.wikipedia.org/wiki/The_Bible_and_slavery#Sexual_and_conjugal_slavery

[94] http://en.wikipedia.org/wiki/Incest_in_the_Bible

long term, well that was anyone's guess, and though they realized their work probably wouldn't end in Tokyo, that was their prime focus for now. They would jump off at the next dock when the time came.

At roughly 8:05 p.m., five planes queued up for takeoff. One was bound for Tel Aviv, bringing with it a very special piece of cargo.

Qin, who had informed her Chinese colleagues she wasn't feeling well and had needed to rest in her hotel for the day, showed up for dinner with her group, still tired but with a minutely perceptible degree of levity.

# 18

## Heidi's World

Heidi loved to fly. She relished the freedom, the existential escape from earth-bound commitments and other man-made concepts like time. As soon as the wheels left the ground she felt liberated, a weight of meetings, communications and schedules being lifted from her shoulders. This was especially true on longer flights, since she could control the information flow as to "where she was" and "how much longer she had to go." Her pilots had been kindly instructed to refrain from the standard "we are crossing into the [blank] time zone so please adjust your watches accordingly" announcements.

Heidi had a prop license, and when she was younger, she would rent a random, one-seater Cessna merely to play hide and seek with her shadow in the clouds. She particularly liked the Stratocumulus Cumulogenitus "species" with their thick, freshly whipped cream shapes that resembled the foamy aftermath of breaking waves. The rental agency quickly learned she'd need a radio call to remind her that her session was 45 minutes over time and she might want to check her fuel levels.

She particularly enjoyed the long flights, the flights from the West Coast to Europe or Asia because, in her mind, she was breaking space/time symmetry, even for a brief moment. From her perspective, it was the displacement in this symmetry—which was being investigated, and possibly even proved, at the Large Hadron Collider in Europe—that caused the universe to come into being. Perhaps unconsciously, she reflected, she looked at landings as a re-birth of sorts, a return from the (relative) lack of rules of the skies to the maddening masculine paradigms of the ground. She always touched down re-charged, with ample energy to change these paradigms. It was in the sky, looking down, that Heidi could imagine her world.

It was a world that, from 30,000 feet, probably didn't look too different than our current one, with a few exceptions. First, the air would be clean enough to actually see the ground clearly from that height. The once glaringly visible logging swathes, deforestation wounds and coal incisions would be healed. The polar ice sheets she had regularly flown over for both work and pleasure wouldn't be markedly crumbling into the oceans.

In the States, football stadiums would be repurposed or dismantled, though she might not need to attack that issue since the "sport" (she perceived it more like a modern-day gladiator event with high-paid slaves) seemed to be going through a reckoning. Through their own testosterone-induced focus on profits and power versus human health and well-being, the National Football League had recently conceded to paying unlimited damages to its former players for essentially denying and hiding the fact that repeated head trauma could lead to tragic consequences such as Chronic Traumatic Encephalitis, Amyotrophic Lateral Sclerosis, dementia and other related life-shortening conditions.[95] The supply of players was thankfully dropping; learning of the risks, parents, especially mothers, were wisely directing their sons to other pursuits.[96]

It was around 5,000 feet where more detailed transformations would be observed.

Slums and shantytowns would be transformed to environs with basic human dignities—access to clean water, sanitation facilities, power,

---

[95] Search "NFL concussion lawsuit"

[96] http://www.bloomberg.com/politics/articles/2014-12-10/bloomberg-politics-poll-half-of-americans-dont-want-their-sons-playing-football

and refuse collection.[97] The countryside would be dotted with schools, universities, hospitals and clinics, connected with paved infrastructure and sidewalks. Children would be fed, clothed and shoed, a pre-requisite to going to school. Trees necessary for viable ecosystems would be plentiful, coal emissions would either be stringently treated or halted, wind farms would proliferate and reflections of solar-panels of varying sizes—from farms to individual devices—would provide electricity and light, two critical elements to survival and growth.[98] Though she instinctively didn't like nuclear power, Heidi was behind it, at least until a safer form of electricity production became scalable enough to replace coal for baseline production. Advancements in the design, materials and fuel sources of next-generation reactors had satiated her concerns and there were some novel advancements in fission generation that could also prove to be cost-effective and scalable.[99] And she was most intrigued by efforts to harness the power of the ocean (while not disrupting the local habitat).

Mothers, particularly in the United States, would be outside pushing baby carriages instead of sitting childless inside offices due to paternalistic and nonsensical maternity policies (Illumina gave every colleague a minimum of six paid months of parental leave and encouraged job-sharing as long as parents desired until their kids were of school age). There would be no prostitution for, as Sweden had successfully done, this act would be reframed for what it was—violence against women and children—and the police and prosecutors would be enlightened to this fact.[100]

Coral reefs, critical to ocean ecosystems (and commercial fish stocks), would stop losing their color and longevity due to warming seas absorbing a 30% increase in $CO^2$ emissions since the Industrial Revolution. The estimated 270,000 tons of plastic floating in the ocean,[101] hallmarked by the coincidentally Texas-sized dead zone in the Pacific, wouldn't exist.

---

[97] Roughly 2.6 billion humans lack access to clean cooking facilities and sanitation. 783 million lack access to water. Search for "Number of people without electricity IEA" and "number of people without water"

[98] 1.3 billion humans lack access to electricity. Ibid.

[99] Search "TerraPower" and "Lockheed fission"

[100] Note that Sweden's government, like most of Northern Europe, is run by women. http://esnoticia.co/noticia-8790-swedens-prostitution-solution-why-hasnt-anyone-tried-this-before

[101] http://www.huffingtonpost.com/2014/12/10/tons-of-plastic-in-ocean-study_n_6305216.html

Fish, dolphin, whales, rays and sharks would be visibly abundant.[102]

Perhaps the most important, yet least obvious change to the untrained eye would be the dismemberment of the (male) military–(male) industrial–(male) government complex. In 2012, the world spent approximately $1.7 trillion on military expenditures, an amount equal to that spent at the end of the Cold War, the costliest "war" in world history.[103] What was ironic, Heidi mused, was that there was excellent research, generated from the same university some particular U.S. presidents attended, that showed military expenditures in times of war inevitably caused all the great empires of the last 600 years to collapse for *economic* reasons, rather than being conquered militarily.[104] One of her favorite quotes in her screensaver queue was from James Madison, political theorist and the fourth president of the U.S.:

> "Of all the enemies to public liberty war is, perhaps, the most to be dreaded because it comprises and develops the germ of every other. War is the parent of armies; from these proceed debts and taxes... known instruments for bringing the many under the domination of the few...No nation could preserve its freedom in the midst of continual warfare."

$1.7 trillion was a large number, even to Heidi, whose company market cap was roughly in the $620 billion range. She was intimately familiar with the corporate budgeting process, had researched similarities in the public sphere and knew the implications of a reduction, a.k.a. re-allocation, to fund her world. And she understood that spending, particularly on stopping terrorism, was needed. But the amount spent on impractical efforts (a trillion dollars to create one new fighter plane[105]—really?) were, in her humble opinion, ludicrous and self-serving. Governments had a responsibility to protect their citizens, no matter the scale of expenditures, but the impact of constant war on domestic economies, debt loads and consequent interest rates was causing global suffering, especially when the opportunity costs of those allocations were included.

What if the global amount spent on education could be buttressed by

---

[102] Search "cod stocks", "bluefin tuna stocks", and "shark definning"

[103] http://www.globalissues.org/article/75/world-military-spending

[104] See "The Rise and Fall of the Great Empires," by Paul Kennedy

[105] http://www.businessinsider.com/the-f-35-is-a-disaster-2014-7

just 20%—$370 billion annually—of these "defense" funds? If it only cost $16 billion per year to send all children in low-income countries to school[106] (.009% of the total military expenditure), what was the big deal? Again, the more educated the male populace was across countries, the less likely they were to go to war. And the more educated the female populace, the higher probability their country would experience economic growth and consequent social stability.

Similarly, what if health care, infrastructure, water supply, climate change and energy production were to receive an additional 20% in annual funding? How many jobs would be created? Lives saved? Species saved (including our own)? Conflicts reduced or avoided altogether?

Heidi readily understood these changes would not happen overnight and would require some very serious work. Global workforces (primarily men) would need significant retraining to take on new functions, which was not a trivial exercise. However, she had first-hand experience with this dynamic; as long as you performed at Illumina, support to grow your abilities to meet new demands received top priority. She never lost colleagues because they had "inadequate skill sets."

What she found fascinating about these very possible transformations was that if given the chance, most people, regardless of gender and personality, would much rather dedicate the time of their lives to something that helped humanity rather than potentially hurt it.

She really wanted to give them this opportunity.

Certain companies (and countries) that relied on military expenditures as a significant part of their income/GDP would take some hits. And the pushback from testosterone-fueled dissenters would be fierce in congresses around the world, particularly in the U.S., which supplied 40% of global arms sales.[107] Though not a conspiracy-minded person, Heidi did occasionally wonder if an underlying driver of America's significant involvement in arms sales was to provoke the threat of foreign conflicts to ensure recurring revenue from all involved. It was difficult to get into wars if you didn't have "enough of something deadly the other guy didn't have." The fact that millions of people might have to die to support the lavish contracts and perks that riddled the "defense" industry was something she surmised certain leaders overlooked in the name of "national security." After all, being male was all about the double-edged

---

[106] UNESCO

[107] Search "US global arms sales"

sword of fight or flight, aggression and fear.

More than a few (male) dictatorships would also go extinct with this shift in spending. The cost might be bloodshed. Heidi knew the charge she was leading could unfortunately cause loss of life, as evidenced by the recent Arab Spring and other pro-democracy movements. The footage of those incredibly courageous protestors taking on the tanks in Tiananmen Square would forever be burned into her memory. Sadly, there was no way around this. Revolution, when appropriate, was in the best interests of her species, and all species. It simply had to be done.

At the root of this dynamic was religion of whatever mainstream flavor. She readily understood most people needed something in which to believe, something to explain the inexplicable, a way to justify and soothe the anxieties surrounding our inescapable end. Why though, should women (or anyone for that matter) believe books written by men, about men, and for men that, at best, treated women like side characters and, at worst, blamed them for the "Sin and Evil" that existed on earth? Religious texts were not very positive starting points for narratives on how to live…or love.

What if the prevailing "religious" texts had been written by women, free of men's influences? How would they read? What would *their* ethical standards look like? Would there even be a God, Gods or Goddesses? If so, how might their temperaments differ from our current incarnations? Would Satan and the notion of "evil" exist, or even need to exist? Would there be a Heaven and Hell and would there be different means of payment to avoid the latter? Would we be born guilty of sins not committed? How different would our world be without the wanton fear, pomposity, self-righteousness and doom-laden finales that oozed from men's testicles to the pages of these fictitious propaganda pieces that formed the basis of a major portion of the world's social mores, penal codes and governing systems?

And perhaps most importantly, how would these texts be *used?* As guidance to build open, just, equal and free societies, with an emphasis on education and caring for all? Or as tools to control, to maintain the power of a few (by enslaving many), and to inject the poison of superiority over others as a rationale for subjugating and killing…millions? Beyond the rhetorical aspects of these questions lay a domain whose vastness would require some non-superfluous mental adjustments to adequately imagine. Breaking away from what was instilled in childhood via parental role models can be extremely difficult.

To be fair, Heidi would acknowledge in conversations with certain peers, the Qu'ran, for example, was written in a time of dark and barbaric bedlam and it was very effective in uniting warring tribes. However, over the nearly 1,500 years since its roll out, the number of deaths and oppressed women attributable to this faith was mind boggling. Why did this anarchy, the war and destruction of the Dark Ages exist in the first place? She would also note that the Qu'ran did call for a more "socialistic" focus on income distribution and support for all people than did Christianity. Al Qaeda was birthed from income inequality—the Saudi Royal Family was viewed as corrupting the word of Islam, with its tens of billions of dollars set against the peninsula's high unemployment (12~20%).[108]

What if places of worship were turned into museums or art galleries, community centers, local incubators for education, invention and innovation, housing for homeless or simply places to meditate? What if tithed funds were redirected to these efforts? Heidi doubted the sea change would be visible from the air, but it would be undeniable on the ground.

Another issue that piqued Heidi's imagination when she traveled aerially was the notion of borders. She was fascinated by the immense amount of money, personnel and politics surrounding them. She had flown over many boundaries around the world, and the elaborate and ridiculously expensive one with Mexico was in her backyard. She'd had to deal with the immigration issue head on and had not backed away. Many people of Mexican descent worked at Illumina, from engineers and HR heads to executives and custodians, and Heidi had fought diligently to protect their working status in the United States. She felt that hard-working, tax-paying people should be respected and protected in the workplace regardless of their immigration status. From her perspective, they were human, just like her. Their place of birth and upbringing shouldn't be a barrier to improving themselves. Besides, for Social Security to survive, roughly 35 million more people would need to pay taxes to the U.S. treasury by 2050. Given the declining birthrate in the States, tax-paying workers would need to come from foreign lands.

Heidi's border observations represented a larger vision. Why so many fences at all? She understood the useful purposes—to keep animals and random kids off roads, for personal privacy, etc. What if theft of property was a rarity; no fences needed. Taking something that was not yours was, in Heidi's opinion, an overriding male characteristic. In her world, there would be minimal need for police, incarceration and prisons. If testosterone could be tamed, crimes would decline precipitously: from murder, rape, domestic violence, thievery, and drug infractions, to white-collar transgressions and the National Rifle Association's perspective on the state of the Second Amendment.

Heidi would habitually peer down from her window at the random towns, cities and farmlands beneath her and wonder what was happening at street level. What sort of violence was permitted and perpetrated by men in uniform, in white hoods, in work clothes, in suits? How many lives, including the lives of kids who witnessed these acts (and were more apt to commit them as adults), were being forever scarred by these male power trips?

With incidents of this nature occurring once every nine seconds in the United States (and possibly more often around the world), Heidi knew that 1 in 4 women in the States, and 35% of women globally (approximately 1,250,000,000) would at some point in their lives be victimized by someone they knew, usually by a partner.[109]

This fact underscored Heidi's personal experience with abuse. The memory of seeing her mother's body slumped over the side of her easy chair, bullet hole in the back of her head peeking through wisps of blonde hair scorched by the explosion from the pistol's barrel, had a permanent place in her mental screensaver. Violence wasn't just a statistic to Heidi. It couldn't be. Every time she traveled, every time she watched the world below from her airplane seat, she thought of how many violent acts against women were occurring at that exact moment in time. For no apparent reason, these moments would suddenly rush to her from within, surfacing in her consciousness with the speed and intensity of an erupting volcano, protrusions from her psyche that obviously had not been, and never could be, fully dealt with. In sub-30 seconds, she would go from high-flying, uber-wealthy technology CEO to a sobbing wreck. No amount of money or therapy could heal her completely. When she had these moments, she would readily consume her ever-present bottle of chilled Chardonnay.

Above all, she wanted women to feel safe, to be able to walk wherever and whenever they pleased, without fear. She wanted them to be equal

---

[109] Search "Global domestic violence statistics" and "US domestic violence statistics"

beings with equal rights and equal protections, humans who were subject to equal enforcement of the law and equal and transparent prosecution of crimes against them. She wanted them to be able to get into a cab and not need to worry about being raped or murdered.[110] To feel safe knowing that if they were pulled over by a male police officer, they wouldn't be sexually assaulted.[111] To know that just because a man didn't orgasm did not mean a woman hadn't been violated.[112] To know they could go out and have a few drinks without becoming an assault target. The world she wanted was one in which women wouldn't be targets at all.

Heidi realized her *what if women ran the show* thesis was a gargantuan piece of pie in the sky to unprepared minds. Maybe even space, probably deep space. Fortunately, examples of matriarchal societies—landscapes of a completely different earth—had existed throughout time and still exist today. Heidi relished pulling these examples out of her purse and had the knack for knowing precisely the right time to casually interject her contrarian viewpoint with maximum impact. She fondly recalled an interchange along these lines that subsequently became an Illumina legend. She was negotiating an acquisition and was settling on terms with the chairman of the board of the acquired firm, who she observed was "a bit of a narcissistic pig." After seemingly endless circular discussions, they settled on a reasonable price and payment terms. The only sticking point was the Chairman was dead set on keeping the CEO, a man of similar character, in his position. Heidi had a stellar female executive she'd been grooming for a few years ready to go.

The Chairman really went ballistic. His melodrama surprised even Heidi, who knew maintaining her calm would only piss him off more. She simply sat there with a placid and relaxed grin, as he frantically paced her boardroom, hands gesticulating, a semi-delusional stare fixed on nothing but the air in front of him. Wiping the froth from the sides of his mouth multiple times with both coat sleeves, he finished his diatribe with the comment, "Throughout history, men have been the leading force of civilizations…you need a warrior to lead this company, to captain it through its future battles, and to deliver its ultimate victory." That was all Heidi needed.

"Bob, allow me to share some history. The Iroquois Indian Nation,

---

[110] http://www.cnn.com/2013/12/04/world/asia/nirbhaya-india-rape/

[111] http://www.huffingtonpost.com/2014/08/30/daniel-holtzclaw-cop-rape_n_5740714.html

[112] Ibid.

whose origins trace back to between 1142 and 1400 AD, wisely believed warriors should not have a vote in the strategic decisions of the nation. They were simply too impulsive and couldn't envision the impact their choices would have on the collective whole. From family names to mediating disputes to setting tribal direction, women were in charge. They were the Creator's stewards of the land. They appointed leaders and were held in the highest regard as they raised the children. In fact, their system of government somewhat influenced our Constitution.[113] Having women in charge worked extremely well for 450 years, longer than all Continental dynasties."

She continued, "While your claim supports short-lived stereotypes, given Illumina's performance, we would seem to be a better model. The world will always need warriors of different stripes...but more importantly it needs women to guide them."

Heidi delivered her response with her natural grace and matter-of-fact manner. The Chairman couldn't argue with a word she said and just stood there, his ballooned cheeks, eyes and ego, astutely and diplomatically deflated. He didn't say a word, but simply made a hand motion like he was asking for the check at dinner. Heidi could have taken offense at this "motioning-to-the-waitress" proxy, but she graciously handed him the documents and a purple pen.

This hand motion had become a fixture in the company, and was used by both sexes as visual shorthand in situations where men's delusions were trumped by female rationality. As for the outcome of the meeting, the female executive took her position the next Monday...and, with support and guidance from Heidi, proceeded to surpass all expectations.

There were two other examples of present day societies where women were in charge, and Heidi had visited them both.

One, the Mosuo "tribe" in China near the Tibetan border, only numbered 50,000 people but was large enough to provide a glimpse into a matriarchal culture with longevity and scale.

Among the Mosou, women managed the money and social mores. Men's role was essentially to do the more muscular work during the day, rest and then service the women, at their behest, at night. There was one key rule: the men had to leave the women's beds by the time the sun rose. No one was to see a man come or go, and the floor plans of Mosou houses were laid out so as to make this *daytime friend, nighttime lover*

---

[113] http://www.nytimes.com/1987/06/28/us/iroquois-constitution-a-forerunner-to-colonists-democratic-principles.html

dynamic easy to navigate. These "walking marriages," as they were called, flipped the patriarchal order on its head; many children didn't know who their father was, and yet there was no cultural bad karma about this in Mosouland. Children were raised by the community of men and women (a very estrogeny concept, Heidi noted) and carried the woman's family name.

It was a true win-win, from Heidi's point of view. Women could select who they wanted to sleep with and to father their children on their terms, while men, so long as they were nice to the women, could enjoy themselves to no end with a variety of partners. And all without the inevitable squabbles that plagued most relationships over time. A video clip with a Mosou man conveyed the arrangement nicely when, in response to the interviewer's question of "Do you like this kind of social system?" he replied with the Cheshire cat grin of a college sophomore who has just realized how easy it is to get laid, "Yes, we get to sleep around a lot."

There was one part of the Mosou experience that was still male-based: men ran the local government. This was more appeasement than anything else as, from Heidi's perspective, those who control the testosterone make the rules. The difference from Western models was that here the social norms were contrived and controlled by women.

Estrogen's influence, the need to care for all, was deep and profound. For example, profits from each village were distributed to all inhabitants thereby eradicating homelessness. Some could argue this system was more than a bit "socialist." It certainly had a few of the hallmarks, but Heidi preferred to call it "humanist." She was a firm believer in the power of free-market capitalism, particularly its reliance on innovation. However, she also was quite aware of its shortcomings. In Mosou society, the elderly were dutifully taken care of by both sexes. And like her vision from 5,000 feet, there were no prisons, no crime and no police. In fact, there was no word for "jealous" in Mosou vernacular. While Heidi was concerned by the inevitable Western influences, her visit had revealed that their culture was incredibly resilient to the intrusion of outside influences; the people she met mostly chuckled at modern syndicated TV content.

The other, much larger example, was also an Asian society, the Minangkabau. Probably not coincidentally, it shared characteristics with both the Iroquois and Mosou norms, namely that women owned and passed down property and assets, while men ran the politics. The Minangkabau people, also known as the Minang, hail from Western

Sumatra and currently number three million on that island, with an estimated additional four million who have spread out through South East Asia.

What made the Minang so fascinating was that a very "female" topic—education—was at the root of their culture. This focus on learning (versus fighting) had profound effects on the region. From political leadership—Minang men founded the modern day states of Malaysia, Singapore and co-founded Indonesia—to leading and growing industrial sectors including textiles and media. The focus of the society on education had enabled economic growth in locales where the opportunity for civil unrest due to the "young unemployed men" syndrome would be relatively ripe.

What was also notable, and on the surface probably a bit paradoxical, was that this matrilineal system had flourished in a country where Islam was by far the most prevalent religion. Apparently, Muslims educated in a sensible interpretation of the Qu'ran could create notable to extraordinary economic growth and social order. And though the recent rise of radical Islamist elements was a definite concern, Heidi predicted the fringe would have a very difficult time upending this successful structure.

Back up at 30,000 feet, Heidi observed something else. A strong reason why these societies flourished, going back to the Goldman Sachs 10,000 Women initiative, could be because of who controlled the household spending decisions. Men in developing countries (and developed countries as well) liked to spend on arms and alcohol. Women preferred education, consumer durables, insurance and savings—the necessary components for financial stability, banking and lending, and economic growth.

Heidi understood that, while she would love to be able to wiggle her nose and with a flourish of an Illumina device convert the world to some facsimile or combined permutation of these cultures, the global status quo, with its millennia of masculine religious oversight, would be difficult to budge. This noted, the mere fact that these social mores existed and had real numbers behind them was all Heidi needed to provide her with the hope and promise that with education, re-socialization and possibly some très groovy stem cells in appropriate bodies, women could one day share an equal seat at whatever table they invited men to share with them.

This was Heidi's world.

# 19

## Dick Perry

From Wikipedia, the free encyclopedia

George Richard "Dick" Perry (born July 6, 1952) is an American politician and businessman who served as the 47th governor of Texas from 1996 to 2002, Texas Senator to Congress from 2002 to 2005, and Secretary of State under George H. Bush, from 2005 to 2008. He is currently a leading contender for the Republican Presidential ticket in 2016.

Dick is the only son of Dorothy and James Perry, both immigrants, and was born at Presbyterian Hospital in Dallas, Texas. His father served the U.S. in World War II in the European theater, rising to the rank of Captain. Post-war, he founded and grew Perry Enterprises, which provided construction services to the burgeoning global oil industry.

**Early Life and Education**
Dick was raised in privileged circles, bouncing around the Dallas private school circuit (reasons not stated), and often accompanied his father on business trips around the world in his corporate jet. Though his grades were only marginally better than average, with a substantial and discreet donation, Dick was admitted to Yale University, where he

studied European History. He graduated on the "five year plan" in 1974, as he needed to take some time off to deal with purported cocaine and alcohol excesses[114] and their impacts on his studies. After a briefly working for his father, he attended and graduated from Harvard Business School in 1979.

**Career**
Though lacking investment banking experience, in 1980 he was hired by a boutique investment bank in Washington, DC, Influere & Co., as a "strategic advisor to corporate and institutional client's needs as they intersected with government policy."

In 1990, after making an unsuccessful bid for a Texas House of Representatives seat, he joined Jeff Skilling, a "good amigo" from business school, in the then nascent Enron Capital & Trade Resources Corporation and played a role in liaising the "mark-to-market" accounting rule with the respective governmental overseers that eventually contributed to Enron's demise. [115]

In 1993, with substantial contributions from power generators who wanted to deregulate the markets, Dick entered politics one more time and won.

**Family**
Dick has been married three times and divorced twice due to affairs and, according to court filings, "substance and domestic abuse." He has two children, Thomas and Amy, from his first marriage, and twins, Abigail and Elizabeth, from his second. He also has a step-child, Martin, from his third marriage. His family life has been an ongoing source of frustration as it has not mirrored conservative values: Thomas died in 2009 of an apparent drug overdose, Abigail came out as homosexual[116] in 2011 and Elizabeth had a child out of wedlock with a Mexican landscaper of questionable citizenry when she was 17.[117]

It is reported that after his second divorce, with the weekly support of evangelical minister Ted Haggard and some "extensive therapy," Dick became a clean and sober born-again Christian. Mr. Haggard led the National Association of Evangelicals, representing 30 million followers, from 2003 to 2006, when a male escort alleged that Mr. Haggard paid him for sex and methamphetamines over a three-year period. "Pastor Ted" as his parishioners called him, later confessed to "sexual immorality" but not to using drugs. Fortunately, with the counseling assistance of four other Evangelical ministers, Pastor Ted was later deemed to be "completely heterosexual.".[118]

**Political Philosophy**

---

[114] Search "George W Bush cocaine"

[115] Search "Jeff Skilling Enron"

[116] Search "Mary Cheney", daughter of Dick Cheney, Vice President

[117] Search "Bristol Palin", daughter of Sarah Palin, Vice Presidential Candidate

[118] Search "Ted Haggard" and "George W Bush Ted Haggard"

Dick's political positions are a unique combination of conservative Texan tradition, free market capitalism, a devotion to Ayn Rand (a devout atheist) and his strident religious morals. "Of course I support the separation of church and state," he has said. "I absolutely do not condone bringing weapons with more than 50 round drum magazines into church."

On social issues, he has positioned himself as "the last vestige of American family values" and has vigorously backed pro-life causes, the war on drugs, anti-immigration laws and anti-LGBT equality efforts. He staunchly believes climate change is a "complete hoax fabricated by scientists who don't understand science." He is a proponent of the dissolution of the Department of Education, the Environmental Protection Agency and the Internal Revenue Service. He has called for "significant literacy" in English as a pre-requisite to "earning" public education. He successfully had the words "evolution" and "big" and "bang" deleted from all secondary textbooks and lesson plans in Texas. He has supported efforts to drop all limits on domestic hunting and fishing. He has characterized monitoring any and all parts of the food supply, from soil to seed to meat, as "spurious wastes of time and money."

Economically, he is a fervent apostle of "trickle down" economics. He has publicly derided any efforts to regulate financial institutions, voted against governmental bailouts of companies deemed "too big to fail" and views Social Security and Medicare as "non-essential" services. He has railed against the Affordable Care Act, publicly stating, "If you can't afford health insurance here, go someplace else," and has tried to set the Texas minimum wage at 50% of the national rate "because we can work longer in Texas."

In foreign-policy contexts, Dick is an outspoken advocate for the "democratization of the world." However, his views on exporting democracy include inferences of "Western democracy and its requisite Christian underpinnings." Some pundits have speculated this was a driving factor in his support of the Iraqi invasion and why the number of Jewish GOP members in Congress has fallen precipitously. This observation is supported by Dick's overall performance as Secretary of State, described by an Asian Prime Minister who chose to remain unnamed as having "a palpable disregard for any country that does share his religious ideology." Known as "Mr. Isolation" in diplomatic circles, Dick's perspective that "the American way is the only way" has generated many negative responses from polite disagreement to public resentment across most of the world's governments, including those he considers to be allies.

### Campaign Tactics

Dick's rise to power was enabled by voters from four main GOP demographics: white evangelicals of both sexes, older and mostly wealthier white Republicans of both sexes (the majority men), the white and relatively uneducated Southern block of both sexes, and a younger, more idealistic, primarily male voting bloc.

A common theme (that has worked for decades; see McCarthyism) in bringing these four demographics together is the fear of losing the social status quo. During his run for Congress in 2002, Dick leveraged the terror alert color system, pushed by FOX News after the 9/11 attacks, by extrapolating that all illegal immigrants, especially those involved in the drug trade, were probably Taliban terrorists. He aired footage of similarities between selected Middle Eastern and Mexican terrains, with a grave voiceover, "Evil can come from anywhere." The Texas "risk of attack" was purportedly driven by the number of undocumented immigrants and drug-runners that had been caught that day.

Doomsday propaganda is an historically effective tool to tap voters' fear of loss of control: loss of Christian values, loss of income, loss of white power and loss of American hegemony abroad. Dick understands that scared constituents will donate vast amounts of money to their choice savior. In this context, his relationships with the Texas and DC elite, business school "amigos" and other members of the "1%" (the Koch brothers of particular note), have generated huge war chests of "super PAC" funds to support his and his party's campaign efforts. As a result of the predominantly male and conservative Supreme Court's "Citizen's United" ruling, Dick's Congressional bid elicited over $200 million from mostly unspecified donors.

Domestic and foreign correspondents have referred to Mr. Perry's presidential campaign, projected to raise over $2 billion, as the "Triple Dick" campaign—drawing on the Koch brothers' contributions.

. . .

"All you'd need," Heidi bemusedly observed, "is to add in one or two Bushes to the mix and you'd have a verifiable cluster fuck."

# 20

## In a Dramatic Turn of Events

Heidi cupped a just-poured mug of morning coffee in one hand, as she leaned against the stand-up desk in her home office, which was backlit by the morning light. She was dressed in a light pink one-piece pajama with non-skid feet and an open white terry cloth robe, though her relaxed attire did not match the state of the body within it. Her form was stiff, eyes transfixed, senses consumed by a much more powerful wake-up jolt than her usual strong dose of caffeine.

She was stunned. Absolutely floored. And she was beside herself with joy.

Israel and Palestine were making peace happen.

And she knew why…

From her speakers, a newscaster with a British accent excitedly conveyed the news.

"In a dramatic turn of events, Israel, The Palestinian Authority and

Hamas have signed a Letter of Cooperation and Goodwill that will pave the way for a lasting, peaceful co-existence between Israel and Palestine. Elements of the deal include:

- a mutual recognition of statehood and lands between the two countries
- apologies and acceptance of responsibility by all sides for past mistakes, losses of life, destruction of property and hardships caused by the conflict
- the cessation of new settlement construction in the West Bank and opening of all settlements to habitation by people of all religious backgrounds
- the immediate dismantling of Hamas
- the recognition of the human elements that bind us all: our hopes and dreams for better lives for our children"

"The Letter was signed by all parties late yesterday afternoon after an apparent breakthrough in negotiations that morning. The timeframe with which the Letter was signed after the breakthrough occurred is truly astounding and the entire global foreign policy apparatus is reeling in amazement at the pace, scope and nature of the deal."

The newscaster continued, "Leaders of all three organizations stood side-by-side, an unthinkable act in and of itself, and delivered the news in their respective languages. They underscored the need to compromise, the need to put their children and grandchildren's lives, liberty and happiness first, and the need to coexist if, in their terms, 'our species is to survive itself.' They also underscored that aggression or martyrdom by any group wanting to disrupt this peace would be retaliated against using the combined forces and intelligence of Israel, Palestine and, by default, Hamas."

"Reactions from many conservative Islamic militant groups have been blunt and divisive. Numerous *fatwahs* coming from mullahs throughout the Middle East and North Africa are branding all Palestinians and Hamas members as infidels, with typical jihads being launched. Similar pronouncements have been made by conservative Jewish factions."

"The triumvirate, which was obviously prepared for this sort of reaction, finished the press conference in bold defiance of these orders by not only shaking hands, but hugging each other with an emotional bond unseen in these lands for decades."

"John Bonner, the Republican Senator from Virginia and Chairman of the U.S. Foreign Relations Committee, echoed 'This is absolutely unheard of…nothing like this in the history of the civilized world has occurred with such scale and speed. I know I speak on behalf of the entire global community when I praise the efforts of all involved in making this utterly historic event happen.'"

"Yes, Mr. Bonner," Heidi reflected as she turned down the volume, a novel concoction of irony and smugness momentarily flooding her pores. "Nothing in your 'civilized' world has happened because your definition of 'civilization' is fundamentally flawed and self-destructive… and we are going to change it! You are very welcome," she laughed.

Heidi was well aware of Mr. Bonner (or "Boner" as she would amusedly refer to him). Charismatic, handsome, connected "up the ass," exuberantly powerful and with an ever-present Florida Keys tan, he was the granddaddy icon of conservatism. She also saw through his "broadcast rhetoric," as she liked to refer to statements like this one. It was no secret his state's economy was heavily subsidized by the U.S. military, through personnel and hardware/software services. In 2011, almost 14% of the state's economic output, $56.9 billion,[119] came from military contracts and facilities. Though there were many other conflicts requiring arms sales, the loss of this specific antagonism, and its potential ripple effects throughout the Middle East, would undoubtedly concern many generals, politicians at varying levels, and corporate chieftains. For Mr. Bonner, it would mean a drop in his state tax revenues. "Sucks to be them," Heidi commented to no one. "They'll have to spend more time with their families…"

TM7's choice of Gilat as the first test of their capabilities and overall strategy was risky on multiple levels. Israel/Palestine was a pivotal conflict (not that all the targets weren't pivotal in their own right, but this WAS a biggee). If Gilat was found out, the effect on TM7 could be profound in a few ways. It could be a morale downer, though given what each woman had endured, Heidi knew a little adversity would not deter them. Awareness of TM7 could also increase security needs on a global basis and make subsequent dosing significantly more difficult. And no

---

[119] Bloomberg Government, Defense Spending Impact on States, 2011.

matter how hard it would be to track Gilat back to Heidi and the others, given her knowledge of all things digital, Heidi knew the odds were good a connection could be made.

The gravity of the situation in the Middle East, combined with Gilat's brilliant plan, won TM7 over, however. Tensions in the region had reached another boiling point. The Palestinian Authority, which Heidi respected, had become a shell of a negotiating force as Hamas, primarily through violence, had become the de facto spokesperson for the anti-Israeli coalition. No matter the good intentions of Palestinian leaders, with Hamas in the driver's seat, those efforts would fail, usually with deadly consequences as Israel seemed to be looking for any opportunity to go after Hamas militants or supporters. And though the Israelis would politely inform Palestinians when attacks would be coming, innocent civilians would inevitably be killed and wounded, which only furthered the hatred and polarization of the populace, the majority of whom wanted peace. And this happened on both sides of the fence, with random Hamas rocket attacks on Israel having the same effects.

Like most conflicts involving men, this was as an excellent example of people overlooking their common humanity and resorting to religious and ethnic stereotyping—and in the process perceiving others as non-humans—as a basis for actions that only served to justify their self-deception.[120] In Heidi's view, women were much more likely, even after being socialized by misogynist societies, to view situations from a human versus abject object perspective. There was a TEDx quote by an enlightened gentleman named Jim Ferrell that had stuck in her brain. He was speaking with a Middle Eastern leader who confided in him, "You have to understand. We and our enemies are perfect for each other. Each of us gives the other reason to never have to change."[121] Heidi defined "change" in this context as "lose my power and control," two fundamental manifestations of testosterone.

. . .

---

[120] The Arbinger Group, *Leadership and Self-Deception* and *The Anatomy of Peace* (Berrett-Koehler Publishers, 2009)

[121] Search for 'TEDx, New Hampshire, Jim Ferrell'

Gilat knew the characters involved well. The Israeli Prime Minister, Benjamin Nutandyahoo was a good friend of her husband and she was very close to his wife. Though Gilat liked him, she knew the PM was a significant part of the problem. His brother had been killed during a ground assault operation in the 80s and Nutandyahoo's actions, though seeming to have peaceful intentions, would always default to pulling the trigger when things got hot.

By far though, the pillar that had to be felled was Khaled Mashal, the leader of Hamas. While Gilat understood why Mashal was dead set on securing a Palestinian state, she felt his means fell way outside the realm of what was appropriate. Calling ongoing military action against the State of Israel justifiable and moral, while purportedly squirreling away billions of dollars in relief funds meant for ordinary citizens was simply wrong.[122]

Gilat had attracted women to her blog from some very useful quarters particularly, as it turned out, Mashal's personal nurse. It took an extraordinary amount of time and digging to identify her. Communicating via Gilat's blog required significant stealth as both women were aware of the many forces, from all directions, incessantly scouring the online world for intelligence. One slip up by either of them and they both could have landed in serious, even deadly, trouble. These concerns noted, they realized that two women fighting for peace could overcome the machinations of men agitating constantly for war. Biology can trump dogma.

Eventually, the two met in Barcelona on "vacation." Both were able to lose their tails, and they hooked up in the Gaudí Gardens, in the quiet and reclusive section of the park that looked like a wave breaking overhead. During this meeting, Gilat learned this nurse's son had also been killed by the conflict. The nurse, who shared that her name was Adeelah, said she would do whatever she could to stop the senseless deaths. She, like the son of the founder of Hamas, could not morally live with the brutality extolled by her male leaders.[123]

"I have tended to so many young men, Israelis and Palestinians, who have so much promise to add to the world. I've gotten to know them,

---

[122] http://en.wikipedia.org/wiki/Khaled_Mashal
[123] Search "The Green Prince movie"

as I try to heal them, in hospital gowns without flags stitched over their hearts. I realized that there is no difference between them at their core. They all have the very same hopes and dreams for the future—fall in love, raise a family, die after living a long life. And yet they get swept up by this stupid "national and religious duty" to give their lives? For what again? Honor?" Adeelah confided that she'd thought about killing Mashal, but recognized he would only be replaced by another rabid idiot, probably at the cost of her own life. Without giving details, Gilat revealed "I may have a way to make this happen without killing him, and it involves pigeons," It was then that she enigmatically asked for a favor.

...

Mashal's annual checkup had gone well. His vitals were looking good, save his blood pressure, which was predictably high. Knowing you're at the top of the *most wanted* list of one of the planet's most militarily advanced countries that happens to be within mortar distance, apparently can cause a bit of hypertension. An extra blood sample was needed to make sure there was nothing else going on…

...

The light grey-breasted pigeon with speckled wings and a vial attached to its left leg arrived at Gilat's apartment at 2:00 a.m. and left again within 26 hours without incident. The LoveBomb worked beautifully.

...

In a single bedroom, whose decorations were less plentiful than the amount of natural light eking through four opaque glass bricks facing an internal courtyard, Mashal eyed his daily pill and vitamin regimen, served to him on a cold, metal plate. He was tired and worn; he wondered why he was taking so many supplements if he could be killed by his enemies long before his health failed him. Nonetheless, with a slow saunter and a gulp of lukewarm water from a small, thick-sided glass, Monday's meds went down his throat. Only on very close inspection would three capsules have stood out. The inquisitor would need to crack open the shells to realize the contents were not what was advertised.

...

Timing was a critical element of Gilat's plan. She would need to administer LoveTails to the two leaders at roughly the same time; if one became sane too far before the other, the insane one would have a window of opportunity to be, well, insane.

Gilat had shared in Qatar that she'd been mentally working on her plan since the lunch at the Hippodrome on the first day in Biarritz, even before the target conflict zones had been selected. From the get-go, she knew why she'd been selected by Heidi and had started laying the groundwork for her "intervention," as she wryly termed it.

Trying to get blood from one of the most well protected men on the planet was no small feat. Fortunately, Gilat had backdoor access: Nutandyahoo's wife, Sara, who she'd come to know extremely well during the rise of their spouses' careers. Gilat recalled many a wine-infused afternoon with other wives of moral fortitude whose husbands in the Israeli political-military establishment were "dramatically lacking" in that realm. The wives shared similar desires for Israel. They wanted *peace* and *safety* and *prosperity* for their nation and their children, and while they may differ on *how* to secure the first objective, the consensus was very strong. Gilat had observed a positive correlation between the women's willingness to compromise and the length of time since a loved one, especially a son, had been killed. The farther along the grief cycle, the more open they were to talking first and shooting, rocketing, bombing or shelling later.

As it turned out, Sara loved sex, another favorite topic that would usually perk up about three glasses into their lunches. The women enjoyed sex, though for the most part it wasn't the kind of sex their husbands had been trained (by society and porn) to think women wanted. Rather than the much-hyped "boom boom" version, they preferred slow, tender intercourse. They liked the lure of fondled foreplay, the utter sensuality of touch, the impalpable yet perceptible knowledge that they were receiving their bedmate's entire focus for those ephemeral moments.

They loved being pleased, and pleasing even more. They liked feeling the details of their husband's (and for a few, their lover's) anatomies incrementally making their way in and out of them. And at their age and in their physical condition, the women would laughingly say, if their husbands could just make this happen, it was a good start.

This was Gilat's point of entry, in a matter of speaking. Though they were very dear friends, she realized using the same tactic she had used with Mashal's nurse was too risky. Sara's alliances to the State of Israel and her husband were far too strong; she would undoubtedly ask more questions of the request. Gilat had dropped off the social map for a few months, and she knew she could use this, and the fact that things with her husband were not peachy, to provide cover for her plan. She began by making a phone call on a random Tuesday morning.

"Hi Sara, it's me, Gilat…How have you been?"

"Oh my word, Gilat, what have you been up to? How is life out in Haifa?"

"Life out here is pretty good for the most part. The air is clean, the sea is beautiful, and I am healthy."

"Oh, good for you! It's been too long since we've spoken…"

"Yes, I'm so sorry for not being more in touch. I have needed to work through a few big things."

"I completely understand, Gilat. How goes it? You know you're always welcome back here."

"Thank you so much Sara. It goes well. Some days are better than others, but I'm making good progress all around. Being away from Moshe has been helpful."

"Yes, I can understand that. When you're in the thick of things, you can lose sight of what's really important. Given everything going on right now, and with the men so focused on their work, I need to send an electronic invite just to get a 20-minute breakfast with Benji."

"I remember those days. Not very enjoyable. You feel distant and unimportant, and the men are so wrapped up in their stuff they don't even know how unhappy and cold they've become."

"Ha-ha. Yes, unhappy and cold to everyone, even their kids. Gilat, you sound strong," Sara said with a slightly tired laugh. "Are there any apartments to rent in your building?"

"Well actually, that was the reason for my call. I'd love to have you over for a night, just to connect, and find out how you're all doing in Tel-Aviv."

"Oh Gilat, that sounds like a wonderful idea. I'd love to. Let me check my calendar."

A few weeks later, after the usual sweeps of the surrounding area and the appropriate security preparations had been made, Sara arrived punctually at 11 a.m., in a glorious azure floral, knee-length summer dress and matching blue walking flats, a distinct break from the more conservative outfits she was obliged to wear to official gatherings and photo ops. Gilat wore relatively short beige shorts, a mauve camisole that doubled as a bra, with a light yellow button down blouse and broken in running shoes. They exchanged an elegant hug and cheek kiss, and immediately Gilat took Sara on one her favorite walks through the adjacent forest to the water. The walk wasn't planned, which triggered slight panic mixed with obedient frustration among Sara's body guards— Mossad agents—who scrambled to make sure all was clear. They were used to this sort of behavior, particularly with Gilat, who became known as a "shmuck" in Mossad circles for the perceived bad treatment of her husband and her overall "erratic" behavior. Gilat knew this and, while not overdoing it, she had fun keeping them on their toes.

The rest of the afternoon was spent in the local town, window-shopping, café bopping, gallery-hopping, the whole time spent catching up on what was happening in the highest echelons of Israeli power circles. Predictably, things weren't pretty. The intractable and bloody Hamas conflict, Iranian nuclear progress, the aftermath of the Arab spring, Al Qaeda and the rise of groups like the Islamic State (and Saudi Arabia's purported funding of the latter) and managing the internal divisions/agendas within Israel, not to mention their Western allies, was taking its toll on everyone. Hushed stories were circulating about relationship tensions manifesting themselves in all sorts of destructive ways.

Gilat was happy to let her friend do most of the talking. Sara shared it seemed that Moshe had easily boxed Gilat out of his daily life, due in part to the inordinate stresses he was dealing with and in part to his nature. It was generally understood that one should not to mention her in his presence, and he certainly wasn't sharing anything about Gilat with anyone Sara knew, which made sense as there was really nothing to share.

It was later that evening, after a delectable meal of fresh grilled fish, and tomato and garlic salad at a nearby local restaurant, that Gilat made the ask. The two women had retreated to Gilat's apartment, kicked off their shoes and cracked open a buoyant bottle of Italian red which Gilat served in voluminous wine glasses. Gilat made sure they were out of earshot of the Mossad agents before speaking.

"So Sara, are you able to schedule any time alone with your husband?" Gilat asked with a look and smile that conveyed both prior intimate conversations and a bit of empathetic womanly concern.

"Are you?" Sara replied with a slightly inebriated laugh, "I mean with *your* husband, not mine."

Gilat returned the laugh, even though things were not going well in this realm. Sara took a deep slug of her drink, and any appearance of being the wife of the Israeli Prime Minister seemed to fall away.

"Tell me, Gilat," Sara continued with a blend of innocent curiosity, comic relief and a slight ring of quiet frustration, "what are you doing to keep yourself happy? I mean, petting your kitty is fun and all but it only goes so far." Gilat knew whatever she shared with Sara would stay between them; they had shared enough dirt between them to keep the Israeli media machine churning for months. She also knew Sara wasn't necessarily fishing for anything. Nor would she pass judgment. The conversation was simply two women fulfilling their evolutionary imperative of helping each other.

"Well, you know those Mossad boys are in prime physical condition… and most of them are single," Gilat responded with a flirtatious smile. They both laughed, knowing an intimate relationship with a married woman would ruin an agent's future, and neither of them would ever wish that fate on anyone.

Gilat continued, "Actually, with all my time, I've recently developed an interest in biochemistry. It's absolutely amazing what is happening scientifically out there…particularly as it pertains to intimacy."

"Really? Like what?" Sara responded with piqued interest and another healthy sip.

"So," Gilat started slowly, with a hint of a teasing in her voice, "what if there was a way to make Benji want to reprioritize his time…not all or even most of it, he is the leader of our country after all," her tone became empathetic, "but just a little quality, focused time on you. On your family, on nurturing, on loving you like he used to before he became so important that he started to think of you as just another meeting invite?"

Gilat knew she was nearing some slightly painful ground here; the notion of "just another meeting invite" had come up in many an afternoon drink fest and while humorous on the surface, she knew "in jest there is truth."[124] She also knew Sara wouldn't be offended by the remark and, given her living situation, Gilat had also faced the same difficulties.

"Yes. I remember those days…vividly actually," Sara said, matching Gilat's nostalgic tone. "In the kibbutz, when we had nothing but each other and everything didn't matter. When we were in love…Now, he is just so wrapped up in his compartmentalized world. And there is no compartment for me. I just want to be loved. I want to be important to him."

"What if you could bring back those feelings in him? What if you could feel that raw rush, the power of love again?" Gilat asked, eyes lighting up, cheeks flushing with the passion of purpose. She'd been preparing for this moment for a while, and she knew she was in control of the situation. It was hers to lose. But if she succeeded, potentially tens of thousands, even millions of lives, regardless of religious or ethnic dogma, could win.

"There is a way to make this happen," Gilat said.

…

The pigeon fluttered in eight days later. When it arrived, Gilat smiled with the smug confidence of an evangelist who knew her time in the spotlight was coming, but without looking for recognition. Wrapped around the large vial was a small hand-written note that read, "He wanted his genome sequenced."

The LoveBomb functioned as advertised again. There were no issues at all, though it did make a little more whirring noise than she recalled

---

[124] William Shakespeare, *King Lear*

from her tutorial in Qatar. Perhaps it was because the room she used was smaller and lacked the sound-deadening drop ceiling. The digital timer on the bomb counted down to zero, then a gentle female voice announced, "Tah dah…Ready to go," and the small brushed-silver tube rolled down its little ramp and stopped at the bottom, its progress thwarted by a pink rubber bumper. It lay there, waiting patiently for its journey to begin.

Like the prior run for Mashal, Gilat gingerly picked up the tube and inspected it, for what, she had no idea. But she *did* know why. Within this unobtrusive, thumb-sized cylinder resided the potential salvation of the world. She kissed it and fit it into the leather straps that would be affixed to the pigeon's legs. In about an hour, as soon as it was dark, it would be on its way. Per their plan, Gilat texted Sara a rather bland message about how great it was to see her. Sara would be on the lookout for the pigeon and tomorrow morning, Benji's orange juice would contain something extra-special in addition to "moderate pulp."

...

At 6:32 p.m. Greenwich Standard Time, six devices around the world subtly alerted their owners that a message was waiting for them. A brief, yet prescient message greeted them—a string of characters that would be meaningless, in the remote event the device was hacked, or fell into dangerous hands. To the girls of TM7 though, it was a pivotal message…a message of hope, of progress, of confirmation that their vision and purpose could be, and was being achieved.

The doves have flown.

...

The Chief Medical Officer at Knome Genomics in Cambridge, MA got an early call from the CEO. A very special person needed a very special favor. This person recently started offering Knome's services to her global workforce as a benefit. The CMO made sure to give her a quick turnaround. A full human genome review, all disease types was needed. Blood was on its way. The CMO was to set up an interpretation meeting through Sara Nutandyahoo.

Yes, it was that Nutandyahoo.

# 21

## Purposeful Pastimes

Heidi loved patterns. Everything from patterns on clothing, furnishings and walls, to patterns in data and populations. She loved trying to catch patterns that could lead to breakthrough products or new business models as they teetered on the brink of adoption. She liked to track patterns that came from responses of young people whose egos hadn't been bruised by failures yet, and who didn't limit their thinking to what they were sure they knew. They could come through with some game changing stuff. And working with them kept Heidi young, or at least thinking younger.

She also loved looking for patterns of patterns. Meta-level information—*the why* behind *the what* that was happening—was the most fascinating and sometimes disturbing information to study.

Take consuming the news however you'd like: TV, the printed word or online channels. She would challenge anyone to randomly scan headlines with some novel filters:

- What are the overall themes of the headlines?
- To what extent is testosterone behind what is being reported?
- How many women are mentioned in the headlines?
- What is the nature of the mention?

Predominantly, she would casually point out, themes revolved around men needing to retain (and in the process misuse) power and control—politically, financially, socially, religiously, and militarily—from legal and policy decisions to terrorism to climate change. Men being aggressive, men conspiring, and men being criminals, from local thieving, rape and murder to actions resulting in multi-billion dollar fines, to starving their own populations. "And this is just ordinary, day-to-day reporting," Heidi would muse. "Wait until an election cycle hits."

The degree to which testosterone, in all its glories, was behind what was being reported was unshakably obvious. The need to win, often at all costs and without moral compunction, was the core of most issues that were fit enough to print. Heidi understood that, to sell content, it had to be interesting and useful to the consumers' demographics (a frightening thought in some contexts). But she was very enthused by the growing opportunities technology provided to convey different perspectives. Her company was named Illumina after all.

In most mainstream channels, there usually was at least one highlight of a woman someplace in the news line up. More often than not, Heidi noted, the nature of the story was essentially based on estrogen. Women who, against all odds and at risk to their careers, well-being, and sometimes lives, were working for justice, equality, safety, and peace.

Like a recent obituary for Dollree Mapp, whose objections led to a 1961 Supreme Court ruling that extended limits on police power and evidence.[125] It was Cleveland, Ohio, 1957. Ms. Mapp was being investigated for purportedly housing a man the police suspected of being involved in a bombing. Officers showed at her door demanding entry. Ms. Mapp asked for a search warrant, which they didn't have. More officers showed a few hours later, forced their way in and searched her entire house, including her daughter's room. Again, Ms. Mapp asked for a search warrant and an officer held up a piece of paper, which she immediately plucked from his hand and put into her blouse. The officer retrieved it, handcuffed her, and called her "belligerent."

The suspect was not there, however in the process of the search,

[125] http://www.nytimes.com/2014/12/10/us/dollree-mapp-who-defied-police-search-in-land-mark-case-is-dead.html?_r=0

police found sexually explicit books and drawings, which Ms. Mapp explained belonged to a prior tenant. They arrested her and convicted her on charges of obscenity. Her case made its way to the Supreme Court on grounds of obscenity and the First Amendment.

The judges threw out her conviction because the police did not have a warrant to search her premises. This has become a pivotal touchstone of legal precedent in the States. For this, Dollree has been called "The Rosa Parks of the Fourth Amendment."

Ms. Mapp's interactions with the male establishment were not over. Two years after relocating to Queens, NY, she was arrested on suspicion of possessing narcotics. The narcotics were found in the apartment of one of her renters, two miles from her domicile. The arresting officer was later discharged for taking money from a narcotics dealer. Nonetheless, her conviction was upheld and she was incarcerated until 1980 when the governor commuted the sentence, setting her free.

For all her idiosyncrasies and parts of her life story that some might find questionable ("We all have 'em," Heidi would reflect with a grin), Dollree was a great example of a woman who saw an injustice and simply would not stand for it.

Like Alayne Fleischmann, the attorney who worked on a team repackaging home loans as securities, whose persistent insistence that something was really foul at JP Morgan Chase led to a $13 billion fine levied against the financial services giant.[126] Were others on her team aware they were misleading investors? Absolutely. But she had the hormonally-induced moral fortitude to weather all the criticisms, name calling, insipid pressures and banishment from that industry to see justice delivered.

Like Bayan Mahmoud al-Zahran, who set up the first all-female law firm in the Kingdom of Saudi Arabia to represent women and bring their issues to the courts. She fought for the right of women to drive vehicles, which was illegal in the country.[127]

Like women in Afghanistan who defied death threats by the Taliban and cast their ballots.[128]

Like women in Brazil who, in a rejoinder to a survey revealing 65% of male respondents agreed that "if dressed provocatively, a women deserve to be attacked and raped," started a viral campaign with powerful

---

[126] http://rt.com/news/205327-fleischmann-keiser-fraud-jpmorgan/

[127] http://www.buzzfeed.com/rossalynwarren/badass-women-alert?bffb

[128] Ibid.

photos.[129]

Like the Moms Demanding Action on Gun Sense in the U.S. who took on a well-funded and politically powerful opponent, the testosterone-juiced N.R.A.

Like the American nuns who broke away from their dogma and voiced their support for contraception.[130]

Like Professor Maryam Mirzakhani, an Iranian-born mathematician working in the U.S., who was the first woman ("long overdue," Heidi thought) to receive the Fields Medal for her work on complex geometry.[131]

Like Benal Yazgan, chair of the first Women's Party of Turkey, that sought equal political representation for half of its populace (nearly 38 million citizens). She observed, "Once again, hegemony is being passed from man to man. The patriarchy is the same; they always leave women out and pass the roles amongst themselves."[132]

Like all the other women throughout history whose daily acts of courage to uphold what they believe is intrinsically fair and moral, no matter how "newsworthy" their story might be.

Heidi fully realized that men, perhaps whose testosterone had waned due to age, or who were raised in liberal households, or whose life experiences brought them outside the U.S. for spells of time, could also "do the right thing." There were gentleman like Edward Snowden, who caused her industry to rethink its priorities in a fundamental fashion, and John Kiriakou, the C.I.A. whistleblower who raised the first flag on waterboarding terrorist suspects.[133]

And then there was President Jimmy Carter who, in 2009, severed ties with his church of 60 years because, like most religious institutions, he felt it trampled women's rights.[134]

> This view that women are somehow inferior to men is not restricted to one religion or belief. Women are prevented from playing a full and equal role in many faiths. Nor, tragically, does its influence stop at the walls of the church, mosque, synagogue or temple.

---

[129] Ibid.

[130] http://action.groundswell-mvmt.org/petitions/stand-with-the-nuns-for-birth-control

[131] http://www.bbc.com/news/science-environment-28739373

[132] http://www.buzzfeed.com/rossalynwarren/badass-women-alert?bffb

[133] http://en.wikipedia.org/wiki/John_Kiriakou

[134] http://abcnews.go.com/US/story?id=95311&page=1

This discrimination, unjustifiably attributed to a Higher Authority, has provided a reason or excuse for the deprivation of women's equal rights across the world for centuries.

At its most repugnant, the belief that women must be subjugated to the wishes of men excuses slavery, violence, forced prostitution, genital mutilation and national laws that omit rape as a crime. But it also costs many millions of girls and women control over their own bodies and lives, and continues to deny them fair access to education, health, employment and influence within their own communities.

The impact of these religious beliefs touches every aspect of our lives. They help explain why in many countries boys are educated before girls; why girls are told when and whom they must marry; and why many face enormous and unacceptable risks in pregnancy and childbirth because their basic health needs are not met."[135]

"WOW", Heidi exclaimed every time she read this passage, which was a fixture in her revolving screen savers. "HE GETS IT!"

---

[135] http://www.smh.com.au/federal-politics/losing-my-religion-for-equality-20090714-dk0v.html

# 22

## Practice Makes Perfect

Heidi peered out of her window at the skyscrapers along the bay as her plane made its final curve into Hong Kong, descending over water to an airport literally built on water. Hong Kong had changed dramatically over the years. As the mainland Chinese economy had mushroomed, so had the accounts of companies providing financing to support the growth. In addition, gobs of money had come back from these investments through China's nouveau riche class of ministers, politicians and businessmen who all wanted a domicile away from the miserably polluted, people-laden and sometimes frosty sprawls of Beijing and Shanghai.

It had been decided in Doha that to avoid risking Qin's exposure even slightly, the next meeting of The Magnificent Seven would be on her turf. This said, a troupe of women of non-Chinese descent (even with the requisite breathing masks due to the filthy air[136]) traipsing around the 21

---

[136]  http://aqicn.org/city/beijing/us-embassy/

million other inhabitants of the capital could attract attention, and maybe even surveillance, given Heidi's presence. Possessing an Illumina product had become an enormously popular marker of economic success in the country. Heidi wasn't paranoid. She could discern between rational and irrational fears quite easily, but she trusted that the hotels, restaurants and phone systems were less buggy in Hong Kong than Beijing.

Qin had known for weeks about a series of meetings she would need to attend in Hong Kong. Once she received the message that the doves were in flight, she confirmed the dates. She was giddy with excitement and had a more difficult time than usual retaining her composed exterior. She planned to fly down on Saturday for a day of shopping, or so she stated in her government-issued phone that she had faith was being monitored. Her meetings started Monday, promptly at nine.

Heidi and the other samurai also arrived on Saturday. Heidi, who was coming from Boston, picked up Lexie in San Francisco. Elena surprised Gilat, greeting her with an ebullient "Mazel Tov!" and a Capybara hug in Tel Aviv, the two slightly demur personalities developing a predictably special rapport. Divine, who had been back in Doha, showed up with Shalala, who may have had one too many Cosmopolitans on the flight as she gaily pranced down the jet's air-stair as it was still being unfolded, tripping a little over her kurta on the last step and landing, with giggles, into the arms of the waiting immigration authority. It wasn't until they had arrived at their hotel that Divine noticed Shalala was without a headscarf. "Oh, the air in Hong Kong is too humid for a veil," Shalala glibly replied.

As a rule, Heidi preferred smaller, more homey/funky boutique hotels to the gargantuan chains. "For some reason," she said, "they seem to have more estrogen in their design, and probably management." It was during a two-block detour going into downtown Hong Kong, en route to the J Plus Hotel, that they saw the notes. Post-It notes to be precise. Thousands, perhaps tens of thousands of them, pastel colored, adorning walls, outdoor stairwells, windows and street lamps. Some had drawings of umbrellas, the official meme of the democratic demonstration. Others had notes of support, of dreams, of visions of a world where every citizen simply had one vote.

TM7 had been tracking the televised movement of over 100,000 protesters who filled the streets of downtown Hong Kong and parts of Kowloon, facing beatings, tear gas, jail and potentially death, just to secure a right that less than half of Americans typically exercise. Heidi recalled a televised picture of a banner, probably 30 square feet, hoisted by the crowd that read in English, "You can't kill us all."[137]

Upon seeing the Post-Its, and a giant man made from wooden blocks, arm extended, hand daintily holding an open yellow umbrella, conversation stopped as the women internalized what had happened. It was just a feeling, but Heidi sensed Shalala and Divine, both coming from nations where voting was either not allowed, "not suggested," or not available, quivered the most. Heidi thought of Qin, as she and her 1.357 *billion* fellow Chinese citizens never had the ability to choose the people who led their lives. The rest of the ride transpired in contemplative silence.

. . .

Qin felt conspicuous as she dawdled through the complex of streets called Fashion Walk. She didn't particularly like to shop, nor did she possess the financial resources of her male counterparts. Nonetheless, this was her cover. So she explored a good number of stores and made a few inexpensive purchases of sizable items, as larger bags would underscore that she was, in fact, shopping. Physically fatigued, but more mentally drained, Qin was uncertain how much longer she could continue this slightly painful practice while projecting a carefree smile. She did one final scan of Cleveland Street for sales and started back to her hotel.

She was staying at the Mandarin Oriental, whose reputation as a best-in-class destination was not contrived. It was a very nice perk of her position that China's officials, being men, controlled most of the money in the country and could spend it quite lavishly on themselves. She could recall many occasions where, after a night of rich dining and entertainment, her male colleagues found themselves accompanied by much younger women. A party of five could easily go through US$5,000 a night, including hotel costs, which was roughly equal to the average worker's yearly salary,[138] and 13 times more than approximately 100 million of their fellow citizens had to scrape by over a 12-month period.[139]

She did like the Mandarin, appreciating its spacious, beckoning lobby, and stylish, modern furnishings. These aspects were surpassed by its

---

[137] Search "Hong Kong protest 2014" web and images

[138] http://qz.com/170363/the-average-chinese-private-sector-worker-earns-about-the-same-as-a-cleaner-in-thailand/

[139] http://www.worldbank.org/en/country/china/overview

exemplary service. She cruised to the hotel elevators and proceeded up to her room on the eighth floor, overlooking the harbor, whereupon she immediately ordered room service.

Now to the untrained eye, and even the professional peering at her through a telescopic device, her movements in the room would not have seemed unusual. In fact, they weren't. Qin relaxed on her bed, got up occasionally, went to the bathroom, turned on the bedside light, fiddled with the TV remote and then got back in bed, her senses apparently fixed on whatever she was watching. And, after room service came and went, and darkness started to envelop the tower, she closed the inner drapes that showed only a silhouette of movements within. What the eyes watching her would not have known was that a nifty little black box (courtesy of Heidi as an outgrowth of an Illumina artistic education effort) located next to the bedside reading lamp had been recording all of Qin's movements. She would take this footage, edit and loop it at her leisure. She could even change the movements, or skip to a different segment remotely using her MoPhone. Once the drapes were closed, with a flick of a finger, the device started to softly project her movements against the folds of the curtains, using the same wattage of the lamp's bulb. Any probing eyeballs would only discern a woman who was in love with Western media. And who wasn't?

Qin programmed the device to start precisely at 6:44 p.m., just as she was putting her room service tray in the hallway. The door closed, a figure came back to bed and resumed watching the dancing light emanating from the 48" plasma screen. Qin had practiced this routine more than a few times and, though confident the ruse had worked, kept her MoPhone on just in case something went awry. Taking the stairs to avoid the cameras in the lifts, she exited the Mandarin on the city side and discreetly slunk into a cab. Fifteen minutes later she was in the J Plus, glass of Malbec in hand, in the glorious company of TM7, sequestered in the shmancy penthouse conference room.

After the usual quick catch-ups and sharing of pictures—it had been five months since Qatar—Heidi started things off with a toast. "My Magnificents," she said, "I'm sure your excitement was piqued when you got the message about the doves…but did you expect what happened next? For the first time in history, it looks like peace has come to a pivotal part of the Middle East…It is absolutely amazing what happens when estrogen starts calling, or at least influencing, the shots. Congratulations Gilat, on a masterful effort!"

"Congratulations!" chorused the women, the confidence and resolve of their purpose at an all-time high. "Woot woot!" Elena echoed with a fist pump.

"And while that deal must still survive the many tests of time and testosterone," Heidi continued effervescently, "so far, implementation is going well and there have been no deadly reprisals. I'd say those LoveTails really did the trick. What's more, the leaders of the three groups have been making appearances together as a show of collaboration and support for their mutual decision. They want this thing to work, and they're putting their lives on the line to make it happen."

"To Heidi's point," Gilat added, "there are predictably elements out there, predominantly male within and outside Israel and Palestine, that want to see the peace fail. Their identity is inextricably wrapped up with blame and history to justify their enmity. Perceiving the other side as non-human makes it so much easier to demean, desecrate and destroy."

Gilat continued, "This said, people's love of their families, especially their kids, seems to be working. They want to give future generations a better life than they've experienced. Even in my little community, there has been an upsurge in cross-cultural events that celebrate life and lineage."

Gilat stopped and let her words sink in. It was really happening. TM7's dreams of a safe and peaceful world were materializing. And the woman sitting in front of them had made this shared rêve into reality.

Heidi, who sensed the group was quickly going from processing Gilat's words to deifying her, quickly redirected with a humorous close. "And, per his genome's results, Nutandyahoo now has an explanation for his bad breath and a proclivity to digest certain nuts with a gaseous output."

...

The girls had come prepared to have Divine run the agenda again. First topic: Feedback from Gilat regarding how the LoveBomb worked.

"No issues. The only surprise was the whirring noise when I ran the Bomb in a quiet, small space," Gilat shared. With a playful jab, she continued, "But when Elena is in the room, the noise tends to drown out the machine."

Second topic: Rehearsing their cover as cleaning staff to the leaders' jets without raising suspicions from the crew that something unusual was happening, while in fact something unusual was.

Heidi took this one on. "Tomorrow morning, everyone except Qin will scoot back to the airport, leaving the hotel at 5:00 a.m. sharp. Your uniforms, badges and cleaning kits are on my plane, ready to go. I'd like to start dry runs at 6:00 on our planes, which I've asked airport staff not to touch. We should be able to run through three or four times before the airport starts to get too busy. I don't want to attract too much attention," she said with a grin, "having Narita uniforms in Hong Kong worn by non-locals. I believe Lexie sent you all the translated instructional videos used to train Tokyo cleaning crews. If you've reviewed them, you'll know how serious and precise the Japanese take service of any sort. I've found getting the bow right can take a lot of practice…"

The women had obviously devoured the videos, which had a special segment on the bow. "We can work on that over time, however getting the bow right can make a huge difference, especially if you really need to pass yourself off as a legitimate airport employee."

Third and last topic: profiling our targets and reviewing suggested plans to dose.

"Who wants to start?" Divine inquired, mild excitement running through her voice. "And by the way, I presume you all got the message about the new application we just perfected in Doha?"

"Yes," Shalala replied. "It's an aerosol spray, yes? Very ingenious! This will be very useful. I believe you were to bring the equipment we'd need to convert the liquid into a spray?"

"Yes," Divine responded with humble pride. "I have it with me. It's supremely easy to do. I'll show you all in a bit. So, who's first?"

"Well, as I'm the loudest one here," Elena started, jovially volleying Gilat's earlier reference to her, "I might as well start so as to not drown out anyone else."

The group had developed a template for data relating to the target's accessibility, with a picture in the upper right hand corner. Elena's jumped on the screen.

"Enrique Peña Nieto," she started. "Pretty boy…and motherfucker."

Relevant data: He's fathered two kids out of wedlock. Likes brunettes with short hair. Likes tequila but prefers single malt scotch. Doesn't like Japanese food. Likes action movies. Lives on coffee. Very concerned about his looks.

"While I'd like to personally give him his dose through a suppository, I think our best bet would be to spray him. I'm quite certain I can get close enough to him," Elena said, hinting that would harness the power her gender could have on the male species, from bodyguards to presidents.

"Heidi, I'll need a wait staff uniform."

"Done!"

"OK, I shall go next," abruptly proclaimed Shalala who was working on her second Cosmo.

"Narendra Modi, India and Joko Widodo, Indonesia." The screen expanded to show both reports side by side.

"The verdict on these two gentlemen is that they both must *appear* to care about educating women and focusing on poverty. I'd like to dose them with the spray application during my foundation's press conference at the Summit. I've already confirmed meetings with both of them."

Gilat went next, "Let's have a look at a real target." She shot Elena a competitive smile to which the Latina replied, "Whoah... getting a little testy there aren't we amiga?"

Hassan Rouhani's information filled the wall.

"Unlike his predecessor, Rouhani is relatively sane and I believe he's what the Persian world needs," she started, with a surprising tenor of respect in her voice. "He's actually pretty much on our side already. No vices or stupid interpretations of the Qu'ran. The only weakness I could glean is a love of afternoon tea, specifically Earl Gray, possibly due to his studies in Scotland. I believe that will be my point of entry. Heidi, I'll need access to the conference kitchens."

"No problem."

"OK, you want a REAL target?" Lexie interjected, joining the competitive fray with the impudence of youth.

Vladimir Putin's soulless blue stare materialized. "Decades of psychotherapy won't help this guy. I hope our stuff can work on sociopaths like our research suggests," Lexie said with a hint of annoyance, but more exasperation in her voice. "Gals, I am having a really hard time figuring out a way into this guy. He's kind of a paranoid control freak. He has his own chefs cook for him, and his rooms are swept for bugs after every cleaning. He even brings his own rocket-proof car on a separate transport plane...And I still think he could be gay, so that play," she said, glancing at Elena to emphasize the double entendre "may not work."

Qin, predictably, delivered the surprise of the night. "Lexie, there is a movie called *Colors* that was made before you were born, so you may not be aware of it."

Heidi's ears would have bulged as big as her eyes if they could when she heard Qin refer to a movie about gang warfare in Los Angeles in the early 80s…

"There's a scene where two policemen are discussing how to get information from gang members. The rookie wants to go after them, while the experienced officer shares the wisdom, 'Let them come to you.' Although this is fiction, I believe it's very useful advice. Instead of going after your adversary, ask yourself, how can he want or need to come to me?" To Heidi, Qin's voice was much like Robert Duvall's, the movie's sage: methodical and fatigued from hard-knock experience.

"Wow Qin, that's awesome," Lexie observed. "Thank you! I'll think in those terms…and if anyone has a good idea given his background," she said motioning to the projection on the wall, "please let me know."

Heidi couldn't contain herself. "Qin, how do you know about this movie?"

"Heidi, as you may know at the time, Sean Penn, who played the younger officer, was married to Madonna…and I'm a huge fan of hers," Qin responded with a subtle mix of raw idealism and the reserve that came from being unable to express it for decades. Heidi pictured Qin, daughter of the Cultural Revolution, dressed up in some skimpy Madonna get-up, doing a vogue routine and singing "Material Girl."

Qin knew Xi Jinping intimately since she had access to his inner circles and worked with him on occasion. Like Gilat with Rouhani, she had some respect for him as, unlike Putin, he didn't seem all that interested in exploiting the power of his position. She shared, with her usual subdued confidence, that she had a plan in place and, aside from wanting to understand how the spray technology worked, didn't need anything more from Heidi at this time.

As she finished her section, her MoPhone chirped a reminder. Apparently, the movie was ending and Jodi Foster's erudite voice inquired if Qin wanted to watch another. "Yes please, Jodi," she spoke to her phone on whose screen outlines of a hand directing a remote at the TV (which was Intelliphone/box enabled) appeared. After scrolling through a few selections with a smile, she settled on the original *La Femme Nikita* and the shadow hand once again rested on the bed. "I LOVE this movie," she said.

"I am very glad that motion capture device is working for you," Heidi said. "It is amazing. A concept that was originally designed for kid's play can have so many different applications. We may be rolling it out for athletes soon, to help them work on their form."

"Yes, it is working beautifully," Qin responded, giving Heidi a warm look. "No complaints."

The other members of TM7 were intensely curious about this technology. Qin gave a brief overview of how it worked and Heidi, spurred by the interest but more importantly realizing what might happen once their efforts started having material impacts, decided to provide one to each member of TM7. "I had given Qin this prototype as I thought it would be useful if she was being followed. However, I believe we all should have one going forward, just in case."

"It can take a little while to master," Qin said, "but the learning is very fun. I will share with you all whatever information I have been able to gather." The women responded thankfully.

Divine, perhaps because she was the facilitator, spoke last.

"Abdullah bin Abdulaziz and Recep Tayyip Erdogan," she mused as their dossiers flashed. "Erdogan should not be a problem…as he's another prolific tea drinker. Gilat, lets connect on our tactics here. All I'll need for him will be hotel access."

"Now Abdullah, he is another matter completely. From my research, he is on the verge of dying from lung cancer and I don't know if he'll be able to make it to the conference. He's in really bad shape. Predictably, there is a power struggle happening in the house of Saud and presently nobody knows who will emerge on top. I'm afraid we may need to wing this one, or at least wait and see who is selected to attend on his behalf. The website still lists him as the official delegate."

"No problem Divine," Heidi replied. "I've been following this very closely as well. There is a chance, depending on who takes his place, that things could get very ugly. Saudi Arabia has a long-standing religious and military relationship with Pakistan, and there are those on the peninsula who want nuclear weapons that the Pakistanis would be happy to provide. Abdullah has been reticent to go down this path, however it seems his reign will be ending soon."

She continued, "We still have a little more than three months before the summit, however it would be great if those without obvious reasons to be there," she nodded at Qin and Shalala, "could plan on arriving a week prior to get used to the time zone and get to know the layouts of buildings key to their targets and the airport. As the summit gets closer, it would be best for you to fade into the background of the hotel. Security will be very tight, and the hotel will become increasingly difficult to access. Everyone will undergo an additional layer of scrutiny.

I don't want to raise any eyebrows." She paused for breath. Realizing her demeanor had become mission-serious, she closed the pre-week agenda with a lighter tone. "And, of course, everyone will have to consume mass quantities of some very yummy ramen." Heidi knew what she was talking about—she could recite instructions from the film *Tampopo* on how to properly down the noodles and broth, while paying homage to the pork slices, by heart.[140]

The girls all laughed, perhaps to release a little tension. The plan had been getting more real by the minute, and Heidi's instructions regarding what would be happening in around 90 solar revolutions had instantaneously fast-forwarded the group's mental frame to those future moments. They could picture the airport, the hotel, the conference rooms, the elevators, the security cameras and personnel, and of course hot, steaming bowls of exhilarating ramen. Their time was approaching, and it could not be stopped.

Their laughter was interrupted by a loud buzz coming from Qin's pocket. She immediately withdrew her MoPhone, looked at the screen, and held her other hand up quickly yet politely for silence. In the background, the women could hear a gentle but firm knock on the door. Qin froze a bit, her pupils dilating with a tremor of tension, though there were no other muscular movements neck up.

She pushed a button, practiced a smile in order to get her intonation to sound positive, and in a slightly fatigued and loud voice to compensate for the distances, said in English, "Who is it?"

A male voice said something sing-songy in Chinese.

Though her face didn't change all that much, a minute drop in the corners of her smile and a perceptible narrowing of her eyes, transmitted a film of fear that immediately suffused the entire room. The women all focused on Qin and her MoPhone. Elena, who was sitting across from Qin, abruptly edged forward to get a better look at the screen, and apparently forgot about her glass. Her elbow knocked it with just enough force to send it sliding across the tabletop on the edge of its base, like a crystal ballerina on point glittering across a stage. Elena froze, realizing the glass would either topple on the table or fracture on the floor. Both scenarios would produce an unmistakable crash that would be difficult to explain coming from inside of the carpeted hotel room.

Meanwhile Qin had responded with two languid bursts of Chinese,

---

[140] https://www.youtube.com/watch?v=L9m6FoSw4jE

separated by a thoughtful pause, and then waited with visual trepidation for her visitor's reaction.

Elena started to lunge at the glass, trying desperately to reach it before it obeyed gravity.

By this time, everyone else in the room realized what was about to happen and jumped to divert disaster. The mass movement was enough to redirect Qin's concentration from her device to the potential giveaway scenario that was unfolding in front of her. Her face went from a state of subdued panic to veritable panic, and the MoPhone quivered in her hand. She was already dealing with the unexpected visitor 15 minutes away, but she valiantly tried to multi-task.

In a flash, three options emerged, each with its own set of risks. Being in the glass' direct path, she could join the fray, though she might not be able to get to it in time and could potentially bump someone with better odds out of contention. She would also risk dropping her MoPhone, which could be problematic if she needed to finish the conversation with the visitor and couldn't. Worse, what if something got stuck when the MoPhone hit the floor and Barry White started melodically grunting about being dropped. Multiplying risks = high probability of failure.

She could ask her MoPhone to mute itself, though she hadn't done that before and she didn't know if Barry might make a similar appearance and ask her, "Baby, why do you want to shut me up?" This would go over extremely well coming through the device, even if the visitor didn't speak English. Medium probability of failure.

She could also try to press the mute button on her MoPhone, and she knew where it was. The issue was getting to it in time. All things considered, she surmised this option had the lowest probability of failure. She made the decision in the half-blink of an Asian eye.

Elena got to the glass first, as it teetered on the edge of the table, though her fingers couldn't quite get a grip, slipping on condensation that had formed on its exterior. With a look of abject horror, she watched it twist like diver in into the abyss. All was lost.

Qin's visitor, after a brief pause, was apparently satisfied with her story, and started leaving with a polite and apologetically sounding statement.

Qin, her eyes following Elena's failed attempt, mistakenly pressed "Speakerphone," which was vexingly right next to 'Mute.' The visitor's voice started resonating from her speaker. All was really lost.

Elena's touch though, had delayed the glass' downward arc just enough for Divine's graceful fingers to gingerly snatch its stem, abruptly halting its kamikaze descent about six inches from its target. The only sound generated was some liquid taciturnly gracing the floor.

Qin mumbled a perfunctory "Thank you" to the man's supplications, located the silence button on her MoPhone and collapsed back in her chair as the visitor's voice faded.

Divine, in the same flowingly circular movement, handed the insolent vessel back to an immensely relieved Elena with a placid smile, saying, "I believe this is yours."

"Rabble rouser," Gilat growled satirically. This time, Elena had no response but just reclined, hugely relieved, hugging her glass.

Heidi glanced at Lexie, who noted that the "mute" and "speaker" buttons needed to be on opposite sides of the MoPhone screen.

"What happened there, Qin?" Heidi asked with peaked curiosity, once the members of TM7's had calmed down and the anxiety-induced laughter had subsided. "Why did you look so concerned?"

Qin sat there for a moment, her synapses still trying to interpret what could have happened, both at the Mandarin and at the table.

"Well," she started pensively, "two things confused me. First, the man spoke in Mandarin Chinese, the mainland tongue, not Cantonese, which is confined pretty much to Hong Kong. This is unusual and could have been a tip off that he was working for my government." She continued, "Second was the fact he asked me if I had finished my meal, which I had and informed him the tray should be outside the door." She paused, almost meditatively.

"On reflection however, I believe this was not someone checking up on me. Service at the Mandarin is extraordinary, and I'll bet the staff knows I am from Beijing so they should speak to me in Mandarin. Second, another hotel staff member may have already picked up my tray and this gentleman was merely following up to do his job. Again, their service is legendary…"

"This said, I should probably return immediately. I have a very good sense that I'm being followed on this trip and the longer I'm away, the greater the possibility my absence will be noticed." She stood. "I look forward to seeing you all in Tokyo!"

After receiving a hug from each Magnificent, and a particularly firm one from Heidi, she left the women with a sense of both profound hope and earnest apprehension. The game was on and the opportunities for failure were as well.

...

After unobtrusively catching a cab back to the Mandarin, Qin slipped in a side door and climbed the stairs. It was after 11 p.m. and she knew from experience the hall lights would be dimmed, which would help ensure that her final act of duping any watchful eyes would work. Outside her room, she extracted her MoPhone from her purse and located the clip that would show her shadow getting out of bed and going to the bathroom, whose door was adjacent to the hallway. The trick here was to enter her room just as the projected bathroom light turned on, as the momentary blaze would block whatever luminescence might sneak in from a quickly opening and closing door. To make the ruse work, she would need to time this delay, and coordinate it with the two-second window when the door would be unlocked after inserting her key card, which she had pragmatically put in a different pocket than her MoPhone so as not to inadvertently take its magnetic identification away.

She had practiced this move many times, though given what had just happened at the J Plus, she was operating in a state of heightened awareness. She tried unlocking the door once, just to make sure the card was facing the right direction and that she was applying the correct pressure so the reader would work. She also wanted to make sure her insert/withdraw cadence aligned with her expectations. All this to open a silly door. "What ever happened to keys?" she thought. The green light on the lock came on and she could hear the door release. She pulled it open just enough so that when the door lock timer had expired, the mechanism couldn't re-lock.

She took two deep breaths and pushed a button. On her screen, she could see her shadow get up out of bed and slowly make its way to the bathroom. She began to count. One one thousand…and now. She hurriedly opened the door just as the bathroom light flickered on in the recording and slipped inside, making sure the hall door shut behind her. It was heavy, with a rather strong auto-close mechanism on it, so she wasn't too concerned it would stop, but again, she couldn't afford to leave anything to chance. The door shut, Qin took another big breath, turned on the bathroom light, and turned off the projector, which by that time, was showing nothing. She donned her nightgown, brushed her teeth, and calmly "returned" to bed, where she was gleefully able to get lost in an episode of *The Walking Dead*.

...

The eye in the telescope instinctively blinked once to help its pupil adjust to the increase in light coming from the bathroom. Its owner jotted down something in Chinese in a notebook, which had been divided into rows of 15 minute increments from top to bottom. Nothing out of the ordinary had occurred. The eye closed for a night of sleep as soon as the TV turned off.

...

Though working through jet lag and drinks, the women were up and ready the next morning promptly at 5:00 for transport to the airport where their planes were waiting in a partially-closed hangar. Aided by their pre-work, they quickly picked up the ins-and-outs of private jet service. Aside from the standard that everything be fastidiously clean, it was imperative to understand the specific needs of the passengers. Knowing what kind of newspapers they liked to read, the kind of drinks and snacks they preferred and, in her case she said with a grin, remembering "the kind of flowers I like to have in onboard...orchids of course." Adding these personal touches could make a huge difference, Heidi explained. Additionally, providing exemplary service would be vital to their mission because in Japan it was a source of national pride and identity.

It was decided that Gilat, Elena and Lexie should be the primary cleaners, with Shalala and Divine acting as backup in case something went wrong. Shalala's notoriety and meetings with two of the attendees could easily give her away, while Divine's height and skin color "just might stand out a bit." It wasn't the guests Heidi was concerned about fooling, for it was common to bring on contractors to service large events. It was the actual Narita staff that worried her, in case their paths happened to intersect and TM7 couldn't pass muster.

Heidi had tapped into Narita's customer relationship databases and had a good idea of what each target liked, down to his particular brand of alcohol (the Saudi King and Iranian president included even though spirits were religiously forbidden in their countries). She would take care of inventorying these items.

After getting comfortable with all the tools in their cleaning kits, learning when to use them, how the vacuum cleaners worked and how to carry everything correctly, only one thing remained—the women needed to practice their bows. Heidi lined them up and, following the video's instructions, they bent over until their lower backs were sore and they felt like they would keel over from the blood ebbing and flowing to and from their foreheads.

"Motherfuckers," Elena snapped. "Why do women need to bow lower than men? I can't wait to show them respect."

"You don't know?" Gilat responded, her voice faltering a bit as her breath was forced from her lungs at the nadir of a bow, "it's because they believe their penises are smaller than other races and the women, knowing this is true, don't want to upset them. It's all about self-preservation," she said with a knowing tone. "I learned this from my blog." Elena, Divine and Lexie, who were in the midst of a downward motion, lost it laughing and finished on the ground.

Heidi suggested they stop and urged everyone to practice two minutes a day, in a mirror, until they met again. They agreed with a tone of forced (and humored) compliance—"It's all about size!" Gilat interjected after Heidi made the request. Despite the teasing, Heidi knew the women would follow through. A noble pursuit can require many sacrifices, including a bit of physical discomfort.

The women changed out of their uniforms and placed them in their sleek black denim bags for packing. Heidi took Shalala's, as Shalala would be at the Summit on official business. All vacuum cleaners and cleaning kits were collected for Heidi's transport as well.

By this time, the hot Hong Kong sun was starting to burn through the morning haze. It was going to be another scorcher. Heidi asked the girls to let her know at their soonest convenience where they would like to be picked up to make the summit trip. She also promised, referring to a checklist of "To Dos" on a tablet, to provide plane plans for all targets, to have hotel uniforms, IDs and shoes produced, and to make inventories of each target's specific plane requirements. Finally, she made sure to underscore her and Lexie's availability if anything else was needed for preparation. "Divine and Gilat are to share tea strategies. And Divine, you're going to keep us posted on Abdullah's status and how you plan on dosing him if he shows. Did I miss anything?"

No, Heidi rarely missed a thing.

"Well, I think that's about it," Heidi concluded with a smile. "Before we leave, does anyone have any questions or FUDs: fears, uncertainties or doubts?"

Most of the women shook their heads. Then Gilat spoke. "Naturally, I've been tracking things in Israel and our experiment there seems to be working extraordinarily well, though we aren't out of the desert yet," she said cheekily. "There are still many, many opportunities for our plan to be severely impacted, and quite possibly collapse. 99% of them are beyond our control. All it takes is one fanatic..." She paused to let the words sink in as well as to prepare for her final comment.

"I believe the same risks exist, and get even larger—much larger— once we add more countries to our plan. Specifically, those we are targeting in Tokyo. The complexities of international relations are vast and deep, and my fear is that we may be opening a Pandora's box of uncertain outcomes with our actions. This isn't to say I don't believe in what we are doing. I *absolutely* do. It's the fact that we are breaking decades, even centuries, of paradigms, foreign policy structures and animosities. I just don't know how the world, and the multitude of actors, will behave in this completely new—and probably never imagined—landscape."

"As crazy as it sounds, my fear is what we unleash—peace—will trigger both domestic and international backlashes. When men are threatened or don't like something, they tend to push back. Look at racial relations in the States under the current president. The incidence of white officers killing unarmed black men, oftentimes for no justifiable reason, has increased during his time in office, at least given the available data."[141]

"So much vitriol and dehumanization has been used to justify hatred of others...I just don't know how we'll be able to change people's mentalities, at all levels, quickly enough to sustain the change at the top."

She stopped as her words, penetrating the group's consciousness, filtered down to their cores. Heidi, for once, didn't respond but seemed to agree with Gilat's statements. The silence started to become uncomfortable when Shalala, in her stridence-masked-by-meekness voice, declared, "Gilat, everything you say is true...and I have had similar concerns. For example, in my case, how will the Taliban react to peace? Might they take out their vengeance on more innocent people? How might the military in my country react if tensions in the region subside? How will men across the world continue to justify their actions if those actions are no longer needed?"

She continued, "These are all very good questions. Excellent questions,

---

[141] http://www.cjcj.org/news/8113

and I have no answers. All I know is that the current path of our planet as a whole must change. And even if we fail, or our plan goes haywire, who knows who else might be able to learn from our experiences, pick up the pieces and then keep carrying on. Inaction will only perpetuate the status quo. And I am here to fight."

Shalala's sparrow voice rose in pitch, but not volume, causing a slight echo in the hangar. And though the high timbre of her voice made her sound overwhelmed, the adamancy of her words affirmed her strength.

Heidi smiled and simply said, "Thank you both."

The women, who had been seated in a circle on folding plastic chairs, instinctually grasped hands and let the combined power of the beating hearts and minds course through the loop. It was a power of exponential order and it shone through in the eyes of all present.

Gilat was right. And Shalala was right. Who knew—who could know—how the world might look in six months or a year from now? Only time would tell...And time would stop for no woman. All eyes lit up with the flame of purpose.

In unison, the group spoke as one voice. "Tokyo here we come!"

# 23

## Putin: Round 2

"Good evening. This is Christiane Amanpour, CNN's Chief International Correspondent and I am reporting from Tehran on this day, August 26, 2014, on the recent buildup of Russian armed forces on its border with Azerbaijan. An estimated 1.6 million military personnel, complete with tank battalions, and supported by air and naval power have amassed in Derbent, a city on the Caspian Sea, roughly 50 miles north of the border."

Images of maps displaying the geography and satellite pictures of massive temporary military camps appeared on the screen.

"The buildup started in early August and has accelerated quickly. Per Russian Prime Minister Vladimir Putin, the forces are there solely for military maneuvers. However, it is very difficult for any nation to believe what he says given his unprovoked seizure of the Crimean Peninsula last year while Russia hosted the Winter Olympics, and his ongoing support of the Russian-sponsored rebels in Ukraine."

B-roll of Russian troops entering Crimea took over the screen.

"The primary question on the minds of global leaders is 'what is his end game?' The U.S. and E.U. sanctions on Russia's financial and trade activities, in response to Putin's invasion of the Ukraine, are causing significant domestic issues within Russia. Rising consumer prices, combined with a plummeting ruble as Russians continue to pull money out of the country and the resulting inflation, have triggered a recent increase in the prime interest rate to 17% by the Russian Central Bank, a full point higher than analysts expected. The lending rate has risen 12 points in the last year and it is forecasted that the Russian economy will go into a recession next year."

B-roll of empty supermarket shelves and digital foreign exchange boards.

"An even larger issue threatening the Russian economy and Putin's hold on power is the falling price of oil, which has dropped roughly 35%—over $40 a barrel—in the last year. Fracking efforts have enabled the U.S. to become the largest oil producer in the world, generating approximately 14% of global output, overtaking Russia and Saudi Arabia, who are now second and third, with 12% and 11% respectively. Iran is fourth, with 5%."

B-roll of U.S. fracking operations.

"Now, if Russia was able to acquire Iran's oil supply, it would gain significant influence on the global price of oil, by some estimates $10 to $15 per barrel. This is the prevailing fear in Tehran that, as crazy as it may sound, Russia is intending to blow through Azerbaijan, which coincidentally has significant natural gas deposits and would add another 1.2% to Russia's global oil control. The eventual target would be Iran's oil fields, which are clustered in the southwest corner of the country in a province called Khuzestan, which sits on the Persian Gulf. Experts agree that a full country takeover would not even be necessary, merely a north-south corridor from Azerbaijan to the gulf, avoiding Tehran. This move would also be another geopolitical win for Russia, as having access to these ports would enable much cheaper transportation to regional buyers and provide a military presence that would upset the balance of power in an already perilous region"

B-roll of the map showing potential military movements.

"NATO and the United States, and the Azerbaijani and Iranian governments, are pointedly asking Russia for clarification on what kind of "maneuvers" Russia is planning on carrying out. The American aircraft carrier, George H.W. Bush, has been deployed to the Gulf."

B-roll of a U.S. carrier majestically slicing through seas.

Iranian forces are amassing in Tabriz," she said. The map behind her flickered. "And reservists are being called up, though their total available force is less than half of Russia's. NATO countries are discussing a similar cooperative strategy as was used to defeat Libya, and additional 'mercurial' sanctions are being developed. The feeling here in Tehran is very tense."

B-roll of Iranian citizens holding protest placards.

"Needless to say, if Putin, whose Rambo-like image appeals to many old-guard Russians," she said as pictures of Putin bare-chested, looking manly while holding an assault rifle appeared on screen, "sticks to his persona, this could erupt into a regional and potentially larger conflict. What is difficult, and critical, for many Western viewers to understand is the current Putin-induced climate that has engulfed Russia. He is trying to resurrect the fiery environment of the Cold War. He has consolidated financial, industrial and natural resource power amongst a small circle of friends, is re-writing history in classrooms and is blaming the West for the hardships the Russian population has been forced to endure.[142] He may stop at nothing to retain control of his empire, including going to war."

B-roll of Russian citizens at a pro-Putin rally thumping their chests.

"The real question," she said, "should Russia choose to take this short-sighted path, is what role China might play in the fracas. Russian-Sino relations have warmed significantly recently, as evidenced by a recent 30-year, $400 billion natural gas deal,[143] and the fact both countries vetoed the UN Security Council resolution that would have referred the atrocities in the Syrian conflict to the International Criminal Court.[144] China is also concerned with its ally's domestic economic issues. To ensure that its vital gas supply stays stable, China could find itself drawn into this mess to ensure the Putin government stays in power."

"All this is happening with the annual G20 meeting of the world's major economies scheduled in Tokyo in October. There have been several international protests to Russia's participation. True to form,

---

[142] http://en.wikipedia.org/wiki/Putinism

[143] http://www.bloomberg.com/news/articles/2014-11-10/russia-china-add-to-400-billion-gas-deal-with-accord

[144] http://www.theguardian.com/world/2014/may/22/russia-china-veto-un-draft-resolution-refer-syria-international-criminal-court

Russia has responded by conducting air and naval exercises in the Sea of Japan. In an unusual move, the U.S. has dispatched a full fleet, including two super carriers, the USS Ronald Reagan and USS John C. Stennis, to the west coast of Japan.

A map of the Sea of Japan showing Vladivostok's position vis-à-vis Japan and the U.S. fleet's trajectory appeared on the screen.

"Tensions are also running very high in Tokyo. We will be following this story very closely. Thank you and good night."

# 24

## First Blood

The queue of jets lining up to land at Narita International Airport, according to the dots on Heidi's radar screen, wound their way for miles. An image of an anaconda she had seen in Brazil came to mind. Anacondas can grow to longer than 15 feet, and their mouths can accommodate animals as large as wild boar. "Whatever is going on inside my head, she reflected with a wry smile, "it's certainly appropriate… female anacondas are generally larger than males."

Heidi was used to the borderline chaos that surrounded the planning, parking and servicing of private jets at these types of events. Even the Japanese, with their excruciatingly delightful attention to detail and planning, had a hard time making everything work just right. It could be something as simple as someone arriving later than expected. Because of whatever ego-driven, undies-in-a-wad reason, that person might claim that his jet could not be parked in the same hangar as another fellow human. Because of this, the system could buckle and occasionally break.

What were these masters of the universe afraid of, cooties? It occurred to her that she might actually want to cause some of this confusion this time—the more the better for the blood collection part of TM7s plan to work. But she decided she probably wouldn't need to. Men are men.

She and her three planes were ensconced right in the center of the action, per her request. There were benefits to arriving early. She'd been able to glean from the airport staff where their target's planes *should* be parked, and was delighted to note that most were within a quick walk of her location. Only Russia, due to Putin's obstinate behavior, would require a golf cart to access. As always, Putin had to make a big deal of his arrival, and it wasn't until he actually left Moscow that his Japanese hosts knew which airplane he would be using, causing the hosts to scramble for hangar space.

Putin ended up in a fancy hangar, as Heidi had predicted. The fact that he insisted his jet be accompanied into Japanese air space by two of his fighter planes, Sukhoi Su-34s, for "safe passage into hostile territory" further incensed the Japanese and the rest of the G20 nations. Eventually, he relented.

The Fearsome Fivesome of TM7 were enjoying the Tokyo experience. The Summit was to happen at the Imperial Hotel, the granddaddy of international corporate and diplomatic stays, located smack dab in the center of the city, nestled next to Hibiya Park, which caressed the moat surrounding the Imperial Palace. As it turned out, all of the dignitaries would be staying at the hotel. Given the predicted protests from the usually law-abiding Japanese, getting through the picket lines increased the risk of physical harm. Many heads of state would be behind bulletproof windows in transport from the airport. Once they had arrived, it was usually better to just stay put.

Heidi was able to secure three adjoining suites on the second floor of the Imperial Hotel, with no real views of anything but buildings. As the day crept closer, she realized it would be rather impossible to get in or out of the hotel without scrutiny. Shalala was also able to get a room, based on her notoriety and the fact that a press conference with two foreign leaders had been scheduled on the premises. Qin would also be staying in the hotel, and TM7 knew not to look like they recognized her. Shalala, in contrast, was definitely more approachable in public due to her fame.

Arriving in the morning and having a bit of time to kill while the rooms were made up, Heidi gave her *bushi* ("warriors" in Japanese, a word with a distinctly male connotation) a tour of the premises. Even five days prior, security was tightening up. However, no one noticed the camera in Heidi's broach that took video of every step and turn so that the women would know the exact layout of the hotel and, more specifically, the conference area and routes to and from the massive kitchens. The Imperial had 900 rooms and 26 conference facilities. Lexie, using a wireless device developed by Illumina's "Perfumed Parts" labs (Heidi's version of "skunk works") was able to tap into the hotel's surveillance system wirelessly so the women would have an understanding of what the security folks would be seeing. Timing was going to be critical in making their moves.

The five LoveBombs, cradled in their outer containers, and swaddled by foam, had been immaculately positioned in the rooms at the end of each bed. They decided to run the blood in the hotel, primarily due to the time required to convert the blood, the distance to and from the airport and the need to get through the groups of protestors. The women would do two more dry runs prior to the main event. Heidi had installed a biometric lock on each Bomb, just in case a snoopy cleaning person (or somebody else) was curious to have a look inside.

Heidi broke out the staff uniforms and wigs, which the group readily tried on, breaking into overly dramatic nice and naughty poses to a Madonna mix that Divine had created in honor of Qin.

Heidi had asked Lexie to record the processes of porting trays to rooms as the Japanese had it down to an artful science. Every movement, including walking down hallways (even with no one around), getting onto elevators, knocking on doors (and taking two steps back and turning the face so as not be threatening), to the actual service had been perfected by decades of experience and *masu masu* ("little by little") improvements. While Heidi knew there was little chance the women could adopt the precise actions so quickly, all she needed was to fool the security monitors long enough to deliver the goods. Lexie ordered room service with different dishes—a meal, a drink and, of course, a tea service—and recorded those interactions with her broach. She had wisely packed serving trays and the women practiced the cadenced interplay of body and voice protocols of service for hours, watching video projected from their MoPhones.

*"Douzo yoroshiku onegai itashimasu."* (Pleased to meet you)

*"Douzo yoroshiku onegai itashimasu."*

*"Douzo yoroshiku motherfuckerimasu."*

Each practice session ended with a bow off, which Elena ironically won. With two days to go before the start of the conference, and one day before they would return to the airport, Heidi felt comfortable they would clear whatever hurdles lay in their path. Elena's ever-present swearing notwithstanding.

...

When the training sessions finished for the day, Heidi pushed the women to get out and explore Tokyo for cultural indoctrination, to help get them time-adjusted, and to appear like they were on vacation to government security forces that had permeated the area. Everything brought into the building was open for inspection and, as they left one evening, one man, ignorant to the ways of security, had unintentionally left his roll-on suitcase unattended in the lobby. He was immediately engulfed by plain-clothed agents.

One excursion was the mandatory visit to Akihabara or "electric town," a quick cab ride from the hotel, where the latest technological appliances were introduced for public consumption and feedback. If a product proved particularly popular, it was "marketed like a dog in heat," Heidi explained jokingly. Visiting Akihabara was an excellent way to stay abreast of what was happening out there in the digital domain; her Tokyo sales office, which she also visited one afternoon, had one colleague dedicated to roaming the district to see how her patents were being used. Heidi realized that oftentimes, particularly in the case of developing and bringing hardware and software to market, sharing her patents with the world could actually create markets the technology was built to serve. Would she like 100% of a $50 million market with low margins, or 60% of a $1 billion market with the profits that come with scale? Not to mention the absurd expenditures on the legal side of enforcement. Those monies could be much better spent investing in her colleagues' growth, or on innovation and engagement, which were the real keys to building products people wanted to buy. To her knowledge, hiring the most prestigious law firm to represent claims had no impact on any of those key drivers.

Heidi had been entertained more than a few times in Tokyo, and she understood some of the local rituals. One, called *hashigozake* ('climbing the ladder') involved going from bar to bar, where respective hosts had their own bottles of whisky or sake in specially marked nooks. With each stop on the circuit, the liquor became more expensive and lower-level managers were shed, until the V.I.P. (Heidi, in this case) reached the leaders' hangout where the real business was conducted.

Heidi had developed her own version of the ritual. It started with a delectable meal at a variety of spots (a personal favorite, depending on the season, was *Nakame no Teppen* due its close proximity to the cherry blossom trees), followed by (not hard to guess) karaoke at some random spot, perhaps in Shinjuku or Ebisu. After exhausting her voice (and hopefully keeping her clothes on), she would make her way to dance "with the kids" in Roppongi at some underground clubs. "Japanese dancers are some of the finest in the world," she would croon, with a bit of gushing in her voice, recollections of excitement perking up her blue eyes. The whole evening could not end without a trip to *Kaotan Ramen Ya*, a venerable hole in the wall conveniently situated in Roppongi. It was usually packed until the wee hours of the morning. The group was amazed by Heidi's endurance and her knowledge of the Tokyo scene which, much like New York, took on a completely different visage after midnight. No one moved until after noon the next day.

...

"Mexico just touched down," Lexie reported in a matter-of-fact voice, looking at her laptop and then furtively peering out the window of Heidi's parked plane with a set of binoculars. "Looks like an Embraer 600. Gilat, are those the plans you have?"

"Yes," Gilat replied, with a slight sigh of relief that she wouldn't need to memorize another plane's interior.

"Good," said Heidi, "five down and three to go, yes?"

"Yeah," Lexie replied, her eyes glued to something on her laptop. Heidi couldn't tell if it was another target plane's landing schedule or a great Rue La La deal that had entranced Lexie. Probably the latter given her probing gaze.

"Where do we sit with the Saudis again?" Heidi asked Divine. "I've been checking the list of attendees on the website and it hasn't been updated."

"We still aren't sure who is coming," Divine answered, "though I'm fairly certain it is not Abdullah. He hasn't budged from his hospital in New York City and he seems to be on his last legs. We also have no idea which plane from their fleet they're using, unless Lexie can access the flight manifests."

"Cannot," Lexie replied somewhat curtly, her eyes still glued to something on her screen. Her fingers typed furiously and finally clicked the "buy now" button. "Though they should be arriving in the next two hours," she reported, breaking away from her screen and again peering outside. "Hopefully we can get a visual ID on him if there's enough light."

"And if there isn't?" Heidi said to the group that was decked out in their cleaning uniforms, wigs on, faces made up, badges clipped, walkie talkies on hips with cords snaking up to headsets and print outs of plane schematics on the tables in front of them. Two large cardboard boxes near the door housed the inventory of "special items" tagged for each leader.

"Then we'll have to meet him," Gilat replied, with a glint in her eye.

"Quite right, Gilat," Heidi underscored. "When does Putin get in again?"

"He should make his grand entrance in about four hours," Lexie said. "Can't wait…"

. . .

Two hours, a few games of backgammon and bridge and a few more purchases later, the Saudi plane descended with the setting of the sun. It was a Dassault Falcon 7X, probably chosen because of its ability to fly non-stop from Riyadh to Tokyo. Heidi quickly searched her databases and narrowed the potential owners to four. To her glee, Prince Muhammad bin Nayef was one of them. She'd known Prince Muhammad for a while as he had risen through the Saudi governmental ranks to the role of Minister of the Interior (the Saudi version of Homeland Security). He was an ally of the United States, was younger (54-55) than most members of the family, had studied in the States and, from her point of view, was a great candidate as successor of the throne. He'd also overseen the purchase of a small fortune of Illumina products.

Though a bit risky, Heidi decided to confirm for herself. After bringing TM7 up to speed on her relationship with Prince Muhammad, she got up, quickly donned a suit jacket and hurriedly left the plane. Four sets of unblinking eyes followed her.

The women watched as a host of men in *shumaghs* started coming down the stairs. Upon seeing Heidi walking towards them, one of them immediately raised a hand in a welcoming gesture. They met at the bottom of the stairs, shook hands and seemed to engage in a "what's up" conversation while luggage was being transferred from the belly of the plane to the waiting transport vehicles, which had lined up in front of the limousines. Four minutes later, they shook hands again and Heidi returned to her plane.

"Yup, it's Prince Muhammad," she reported. "It seems he's the prime candidate for the next King. However, as Abdullah's end nears, there are predictable plots at play, some just talk, others with movement behind them. As you know, the King of Saudi Arabia can have a massive impact on the world. He was almost killed a few years ago by an Al Quada suicide bomber who actually had the device surgically implanted in himself.[145] Gals, I just had a great idea about how to dose him." Speaking to her MoPhone, Heidi said, "George, please remind me tomorrow morning at eight to set up a meeting this week with the Prince to discuss Illumina's biosensor endeavors."

"Why sure thing Heidi. But who is this Prince character? Should I be jealous?"

...

After another two hours, Putin's Airbus ACJ319 touched down and was met by an obviously impenetrable vehicle, which quickly scuttled him away. His fatigued-looking coterie, which did not seem as plentiful as would befit a man of his importance, trudged to the main gate, with roller boards in tow and computer cases slung over their shoulders, where they were met by two cabs. "Economic troubles, Mr. Putin?" Heidi mused with the steeliness of a Kremlin guard.

"Ok ladies," Heidi started. "We all know the drill. Everyone turn on your headset and say something." The walkies, though charged to show their lights were active, were merely ploys. The headsets were connected to MoPhones wirelessly and Heidi initiated a group call.

"Here," Gilat said.

"Yeah," Lexie said.

"Yo," Elena echoed.

"Oui," Divine said, though she was merely back up.

Heidi smiled, "All right…Let's get some blood!"

---

[145] http://en.wikipedia.org/wiki/Muhammad_bin_Nayef

Given the high traffic of private jets and the non-immediate need for turnaround since the conference was four days long, no one really expected the cleaning crews to do their thing immediately upon arrival. From experience, Heidi had observed that the crews usually started at one end of the hangar and worked right to left (possibly because that was how Japanese writing was read?) though again, this was an unusual set of circumstances with a high chaos factor. By the time the women would be hitting the planes, the only people in the area would be random maintenance crews if something needed fixing, airport security and possibly a guard from the respective country.

It had been decided that the women responsible for dosing their targets should not also go after their targets' blood in the event they bump into the same security forces. Not likely, but possible. They had also decided to go all at once, so if one of them was discovered, the others might be able to collect their specimens before security really cracked down. Heidi followed all three women via GPS on her screen. Lexie had shown her how to use the surveillance software, which wasn't of immense help, particularly at night, though it afforded Heidi some visibility and it would warn her if her *bushi* encountered anyone.

The women picked up their cleaning equipment, shouldered their vacuums and rummaged through the cardboard boxes for their target's personal stash. They then quietly made their way down the stairs and fanned out.

The President of Turkey's plane was right next door to Heidi's jet, and Elena had chosen it. It was an Airbus ACJ318. There was a small refrigerator near the floor in the galley. Heidi could see Elena on one of the camera feeds as she made her way toward the plane. No one was outside, apparently. Elena made her way up the stairs, knocked, peeked her head in and then disappeared inside.

"So far so good," she reported to Heidi. She quickly located the fridge, opened it, and found two pouches of crimson liquid with Erdogan's name on a label, just like Heidi had described.

"Ok…Found the stuff. Just like Heidi said," she continued, aware that all five women could hear what she was saying. "Peeling back the label… getting my needle out…inserting it…withdrawing the specimen… replacing the label…fridge is closed…and…one motherfucker done!" The women could hear Elena plunking down a bottle of Sambuca, Erdogan's favorite, on the table. "Next!"

Lexie's first target, Indonesia, also went swimmingly. It was a smaller plane, a Bombardier Learjet built for middle distance trips, with a small fridge in an overhead container. There were no complications en route and no guard on board. Simple as pie. "Done!" Lexie cried! A bottle of Pimms hit wood, which was followed by a rustle of pages and an "Oh my god! Gross!!"

"What?" three voices exclaimed, with Heidi's unique laugh starting to kick in. "He...he...likes pictures of nude, very fat women." Lexie stammered. "Like size 50...With snakes!"

"I was wondering when you were going to notice that, Lex," Heidi wryly admitted. "Heidiiii!" Lexie retorted, her initial reality-rocking surprise quickly being replaced by the humor of the situation.

Gilat had made a beeline for Putin's plane. There were two countries whose leaders TM7 absolutely had to dose: Russia and China. Heidi decided to put Gilat on both of them, as she knew challenges might arise that would require the confidence and pressure-tested mettle of maturity. Heidi watched Gilat as she commandeered a nearby electric cart and slowly started wheeling toward Putin's Taj Mahal in the sky. Heidi's heartbeat increased a bit when she saw an airport security man unexpectedly emerge from the shadows of a hangar and start to motion at Gilat. Gilat, who apparently had seen him, gave a meek, fatigued wave and kept going. The security guard stopped and, sympathetic for the overworked cleaning lady, retreated back into the darkness.

"No problem," Gilat said assuredly, reading Heidi's mind as she approached his location, "though there is a guard outside his plane... and it looks like someone else is inside." She could see a silhouette in the interior. "This is going to be fun."

Putin also had an Airbus, an ACJ319, which he had marketed as an interior designer's dream. Putin was very proud of his $89 million aircraft and had nicely provided the design firm (and Heidi) his schematics as a benchmark for others to try to emulate. There was a small refrigerator in a hidden panel behind his desk, which was located at the end of the plane, adjacent to the slightly gaudy bathroom.

The guard was leaning back in a plastic folding chair, away from the plane, smoking a cigarette. Gilat let the cart slowly stop about ten feet from the stairs, got out, and went about her business collecting her box of cleaning supplies, strapping the vacuum cleaner to her back and gathering up Putin's personal gifts, all the while under the inspecting gaze of what was undoubtedly a former member of the KGB. She was just about to start climbing the stairs when he barked a command at her that only could have been interpreted as "Stop."

She did so, gave him a slightly embarrassed and wearied look, and said in slightly stuttered English that conveyed it wasn't her native tongue, "I need to clean plane." She held up a bottle of Russian vodka and the latest U.S. edition of *Field and Stream magazine*. After a few moments, the guard, obviously just wanting to exert his power as he didn't even get up, simply jerked his head toward the plane, eyes emitting a misogynistic glare at her. Then he took another drag of his cigarette. Gilat carefully mounted the stairs and entered the plane.

Once inside, she immediately started preparing for the cleaning routine so as to not attract the attention of the other man inside who, hearing his comrade's shout, had spotted Gilat out the window but was two rooms toward the back of the plane. Gilat wasn't sure of how to deal with him, but she was sure she could figure something out. Maybe she could snag the blood and then take it in the bathroom to collect.

Sure enough, the other man came sauntering up to her and Gilat, following the local customs concerning respect, hurriedly looked down at the floor and repeated, "I need to clean plane." There was an uncomfortable silence during which her intuition softly screamed that she was being checked out, considerably more than usual. And it did not seem like this man had the most noble of intentions. She peeked up. He was brawny, bald and, though a little older than what Gilat would have expected, looked stronger than usual for his age. "Vell, hello," he introduced himself in a slightly unsettling, quasi-predatory tone. Gilat's defensive mindset immediately kicked in. This guy could be a problem. She shuffled a bit and then inquired, "Start at back?" She felt his eyes disrobe her. Then he smiled and slowly nodded.

Gilat gingerly brushed past his body, which took up most of the doorway and did not move. She was careful not to let the vacuum cleaner smack him *too* hard in the side. "Oh, I am sorry!" she quickly followed with a ring of heartfelt sarcasm in her voice. It was going to be difficult to play the subservient Japanese female role much longer, at least in dealing with this lump head. He might have been KGB, but she had been trained by Mossad...and she had the advantage of surprise.

He obviously didn't pick up on her tone, but kept smiling while voraciously watching her scurry toward Putin's office. "Men are so oblivious," she reflected, trying as hard as she could to mentally distance between herself from his probing gaze. "Well, if this is the way he wants to play it, I'm ready," she thought. He didn't seem to notice that she had not deposited her bottle of vodka in the galley as she cruised through.

Heidi, extrapolating solely from the conversation, also became concerned. She chimed in, "Gilat, is everything ok?"

"Yes. May need to take care of something," Gilat murmured.

"Ok, I'm here if you need me."

Gilat reached the end of the plane and, per the cleaning protocol, immediately started wiping down Putin's bathroom, her back to the doorway. She mused that the bathroom was rather small, which surprised her since the jet was outrageously expensive.

Through the headset, Heidi heard the security thug lumber up behind Gilat. "Hey, yoo vant some wrodka?"

Gilat, who realized she needed to take on the subservient role to aid with her escape, played along famously and put her right hand up to her mouth, fingers extended, to suppress a feminine giggle that on the surface conveyed discomfort, but also seemed to appreciate the attention. She coyly looked up in the mirror and saw that the man was just within striking distance. He was carrying a bottle by its neck in one hand, and two small glasses in the palm of the other. Probably not his first glass for the evening, Gilat surmised.

"Who? Me?" she replied, turning slowly clockwise, her hand still on her mouth so as to distract attention from the bottle centrifugally swinging upwards in her left hand, catching his chin—and brain—completely by surprise. She felt and heard his teeth gnash and chin break. In fact, everyone listening in heard his teeth gnash and his chin break, followed by the "thunk" of an overweight body falling unimpeded onto thick shag carpet. He might, Gilat mused, remember hearing the crash of glass on his jaw, and he will most certainly feel it when he wakes up. "No motherfucker," Gilat demurely purred, adopting the Elena meme, "let me serve you." She placed her bottle squarely in the center of Putin's desk.

"Hey Gilat, don't waste any vodka there," Elena piped in, surmising what had happened.

"Gilat, are you OK?" Heidi repeated cautiously, uncertain as to what had just transpired.

"Yeah, I'm fine. Just had to take care of something," Gilat responded, as if she had just swatted a fly. She hopped over the slumped figure, whose hands still loosely held the bottle and glasses, and made her way toward the hidden fridge.

Three minutes later, two full syringes had been collected, one from each unit so as not to raise any suspicions regarding uneven quantities. She hid the samples in the bottom of the cleaning box underneath some rags. "Got em," Gilat reported, and glancing outside to locate the whereabouts of Thug No. 2 (he appeared to be chain-smoking), quickly made her way toward the exit, where she paused.

She knew that in order to effectively signal Thug No. 1's malevolent intentions, she could dishevel herself and run screaming or crying from the plane. But that may attract too much attention, which was something she did not want. Instead, she decided to simply scamper to the cart, giving Thug No. 2 a healthy and prolonged glare of contempt as she disappeared into the night. No. 2, upon seeing her and realizing it was way too soon for her to be finished, immediately stood up and started walking quickly toward the stairs, a look of concerned yet familiar disbelief on his face. "I'll bet their balls this wasn't the first time this happened," Gilat observed into her headset. "And I'm quite certain there won't be any investigation."

Unknown to all, an act of testosterone-driven defiance was just being reported off the local coast, which would dramatically ramp up security around this particular plane for the rest of the Summit. TM7's timing had been randomly perfect.

Though Heidi knew Gilat could probably still handle the Chinese collection, she understood, as all women have to, the emotional and mental toll of being in that kind of body and soul threatening scenario. She redirected Gilat to India and, since Elena was closest, Heidi asked her to take on China. Elena was in the middle of chatting up the Iranian pilot, a man of British descent who lived in Switzerland. Elena, as it turned out, was a very good storyteller, and she explained to the pilot (and the other members of TM7) that the airport's staff wasn't adequate for the size of this event. She had been flown in from the Philippines for the job. He laughed, gave her his number and suggested she look him up in Tokyo over the next few days. "There's a sucker born every minute," Elena chortled.

The remainder of the specimen collection missions went relatively smoothly. Lexie nailed Saudi Arabia and Mexico with very little fanfare. Everything went according to plan and, emulating Elena's precedent, she proudly thumped down a bottle of tequila in the Saudi plane (wondering how they kept the alcohol a secret once in Saudi airspace). She then perched a bottle of scotch on the Mexican plane's mahogany bar. She was actually very happy to use her Spanish on the Mexican plane. Growing up, she had a nanny from Guatemala, who spurred her interest in the study of languages.

Gilat deftly handled India with Heidi's guidance, though the fridge in the galley area was right next to the sound system controls, which Gilat accidentally turned on and couldn't figure out how to silence. The entire time she was in the plane, all the women could hear was the blare of Indian Pop, whose lively synthesized violins never seemed to stop undulating across the same frequencies regardless of the song. Elena kindly suggested that Gilat hit the console with a bottle. Gilat retorted with a reference to Elena being propositioned by Iran's pilot "if she got into Tokyo over the next few days."

China was the last and final collection target, and it provided a few challenges. First, the Chinese guard was a bit skeptical as to why Elena was servicing the plane. The language barrier was difficult to overcome, but Elena's fun-loving attitude and animated hand gestures eventually got her past him. He gave her 20 minutes to do her job. "Jerk head," quipped Elena, once inside. "It would take a *skilled* worker 20 minutes to complete the job without needing to locate and punch a bag with a needle." Further, Elena wasn't familiar with the layout of the Airbus ACJ319, the same model as Putin's but with a vastly different interior configuration. Heidi's plans seemed to be a bit out of date, as the cold storage locations weren't where they were supposed to be. Elena found two refrigerators in the galley area, but both had only normal consumables in them. Momentary panic set in until Divine, being very familiar with temperature-controlled spaces per her laboratory pursuits, pushed an application to Elena's MoPhone that could detect heat loss, depicted as rainbow-colored waves radiating from black shapes on the screen as the MoPhone was tilted in particular directions. Elena simply had look for what was generating heat and she would quickly pin down the fridges. "Muchas gracias, Divinita!" she thanked her.

After about six minutes of frantically pseudo-vacuuming through the plane, she located the fridge hidden in an overhead compartment. "Halle-fucking-lujah," she breathed heavily as she peered into its interior. Then she realized there were what looked like a good two-dozen bags of plasma with "those fucking Chinese hieroglyphics" on the labels. Momentary panic proliferated again, particularly as Qin was unavailable, until Heidi pointed out all she had to do was to search the Web for "Xi" and match up the characters. "Yeah, but there are three fucking characters that all mean 'Xi'!" Elena replied after doing the search, frantically comparing and contrasting. "Well, if they are fucking, I hope a fourth isn't created on the spot…That would really slow things down," Gilat lazily observed.

By this time, Elena had roughly ten minutes left. A quick glance outside revealed that the guard, who had apparently noticed her super-charged cleaning efforts, was focused more on what was happening in the plane than around it. He could not have imagined what looked like dusting was actually a frenzied pawing through bags of blood.

After what seemed to be an eternity, she located the match, peeled back the labels, and plunged the needle in so hard she thought she might have punctured both sides of the bag. "Motherfucker!" she gasped as she turned the bag over. No leaking.

"What's up Lenikins, you flip your wig?" Gilat chimed in.

"Gilat, when I get back, be ready to work a bottle," Elena responded only partially focusing on what she was saying. She actually liked the humor as it softened her anxiety about getting everything right, and she knew Gilat knew this. She smiled at her psychic support. "Got 'em," she reported to all, whose audible collective sigh of relief calmed her down as well. "Time to clean up."

The guard had already made his way up the stairs and had peeked into the main cabin, when Elena, with an apparent final flourish of a cleaning rag, popped her head out from behind one of the bathroom doors in the middle of the plane and gleefully said, "Finished!"

The guard, surprised by her sudden appearance, just stood there dumbfounded as Elena, whose wig and makeup were all equally tousled by her manic efforts, cruised by him, solidly plunking down two bottles of liquor on the main table en route to the door. He was even more perplexed when, at the bottom of the stairs, she turned to meet his distressed stare, grinned and confused one of the only Japanese words she knew, "Sayonara" with "Toyota." While Heidi and Lexie froze fearfully upon hearing this faux pas, Divine and Gilat's projectile laughter must have been audible to the guard through her headset, 20 feet away.

Elena could tell from his expression that he was seriously regretting his decision to have let her on the plane. She thought, however, that it was more than likely he would not report sighting an "unusual" character in the vicinity (much less on the plane) for fear of incurring undue exposure. He would rationalize to his superiors that whatever cleaning discrepancies were found were simply another example of Japan's waning global economic influence. After all, as a man, it was always better to guard your personal interests, than be transparent and apologetic for the group.

"*Qué tipo!*" (What a man!) Elena laughed out loud to the guard as she sped back to Heidi's hangar. "Gotta' love you."

...

A soft purring sound could be heard coming from rooms 287 and 289, if one was walking slowly down the hallway, which very few people were at 2 a.m.. The maids had been politely asked not to show for the turn down service. As it was early Monday morning and Shalala's press conference wasn't scheduled until Thursday, her two doses and Qin's, would be processed after the other five, in order to give the other Magnificents ample opportunities to deliver their doses. Heidi was confident that Qin could dose Xi, even if it had to be on the return flight with him to China.

The women had decided not to show their faces any more than necessary beyond the doors of their rooms starting on Friday, when security became really tight. Going outside was being discouraged for everyone by the hotel and summit organizers unless absolutely necessary given the growing numbers of protestors outside the hotel doors. The women spent their time playing games, napping, watching TV and movies, eating room service (making sure Heidi answered the door), monitoring the Summit's proceedings, rehearsing their moves and speech and, in the case of Lexie, keeping tabs on eBay watch lists and her Instagram friends (with location tracking turned off for security). Heidi occasionally made a cameo downstairs or in the spa so as not to seem like she was in the middle of running a revolution.

As the days passed, Heidi noticed an underlying current of anxiety building in her crew. This was understandable. She likened their current situation to being on a troop carrier as it neared the beaches of Normandy, or Iwo Jima or Okinawa. They had volunteered, had been training for this mission for months and were finally about to meet their enemy. Their success at the airport was like making the landing unscathed. But now, with a foothold in the soil, the real battle was about to begin. The big difference in this endeavor was that the only blood spilled so far had been extracted from bags. And while Heidi understood the parallel wasn't a fair comparison—her girls wouldn't be facing cannon, mortar, machine gun or rifle fire from bunkers—she also knew that stress was relative to one's personal set of experiences. Though their lives weren't on the line, their anxiety was real, particularly when the women began to speak about the global stakes of the mission. And they spoke often about their fears. Heidi made sure there was ample alcohol in the room and suggested (really commanded) each woman to take a nice hot bath once a day to relax. In addition, Heidi led a morning yoga session and reserved her suite room, using Illumina scheduling software, as a late afternoon meditation studio. She also made sure to check in one-on-one with each woman to see how she was doing. And Heidi made sure she, and the entire team, laughed…a lot.

A little past midnight, five vials rolled down their ramps. Gilat, the only one (aside from Heidi and Lexie) that had experienced this process before, had excitedly notified her colleagues that the time was coming, though their MoPhones had already given them a heads up. The clinks of the metal canisters hitting the stoppers at the end of the ramps signaled more than just the finality of this part of the process. They were a call to arms. TM7's weaponry, the means to intractably reverse a few millennia of testosterone-driven atrocities, policies and decisions that now threatened to destroy the human species, was innocently sitting in five small berths waiting patiently to be deployed. Like Gilat after her first run through, the women just sat there for a while, tentatively eyeing their version of nuclear missiles, contemplating their potential impact on the entirety of the world: people, animals, oceans, climate and, most of all, children. Even Heidi and Lexie, who had been through this moment of reflection a few times, were transfixed by the power housed inside these innocuous-looking ampules.

Eventually, Heidi moved to the closest device and gently scooped up its product, holding the LoveTail between her thumb and index finger for all to see.

"Riddly, riddly, I dee dee, I see something you all can see," she started with the guiltless freedom of an adolescent game usually reserved for long and boring car trips. "I see peace."

While none of the women save Lexie had any exposure to this game, Heidi's cadence and spirit conveyed its playful essence, adding a layer of levity, while succinctly encapsulating the reason they were all there.

"To peace," Divine reiterated in a voice resonating with the power of confidence. "To peace," the group refrained, gathering around Heidi in a group hug.

...

In their rooms on the fifth and eighth floors, Qin and Shalala's Mo-Phones vibrated with the notice of an incoming video text. Separated by only eight seconds, their responses came back.

"TO PEACE!"

# 25

## What Happens at the Imperial

The genesis of the G20 had been the U.S. financial crisis of 2007, which exposed the fact that the global economy was not only interconnected but regulated by a relatively small number of financial service businesses (mostly U.S.-based) that had become too big to fail. In the past, if America got a cough, Europe could catch cold. Now, the need for metaphorical defibrillators in every country to deal with the local shocks of spiking American heart attacks became glaringly obvious, and the coordination of treatments to proactively reduce the drastic costs of a visit to the financial ER was a necessity. It was all about prevention.

The G20 host country had a surprising amount of influence on the agenda for these powwows, and Japan had chosen to focus attention on further buttressing the global financial system, with a special track for developing economies and climate change efforts. Unlike the last summit, where organizers didn't want to "clutter" economic discussions,[146] this

---

146  http://en.wikipedia.org/wiki/2014_G-20_Brisbane_summit

one wisely saw the critical overlaps of these efforts; building economies requires energy and lots of it.

A wide variety of protesters had been planning peaceful displays for months. Even if their cause wasn't directly linked to the stated topics, it was an excellent forum to raise awareness, do press releases, flood online social channels, and perhaps do a stunt to get some media coverage. The more of a splash they made, the greater the donations. A few leaders—all men—actually seemed to relish the fracas to which they were linked.

Greenpeace was present, its members sending inflatable bloodied sea mammals to surf through the crowds. Occupy Wall Street/*Kabutocho* was there with the support of a horde of protestors with Guy Fawkes masks and a large digital sign showing the global deposits of the largest 20 money firms. Free Hong Kong was represented, with a large swathe of yellow umbrellas. And the Jehovah's Witness proselytizers were seemingly on every available street corner, their unmistakable polished faces and cheap suits on a mission to convert.

By far though, the largest target was Russia. On Sunday evening, just as Putin's plane landed, the Japanese Navy reported an unidentified "large underwater vessel" (a.k.a. submarine) lurking a mere 20 km northeast of Tokyo harbor. It could have belonged to some other nation. The report could have been fabricated. It didn't matter. Once the media got a hold of it, the Japanese public was catapulted into an accelerating vortex of hysteria. Building on historical enmity with Russia stretching back a century, Putin's present-day naval and air maneuvers in the Sea of Japan, the buildup on the Azerbaijan border and his crumbling economy, the Japanese (and the world) were bracing on the glazed edge of a *katana* (samurai sword) for what this high-stakes dictator was going to do next.

By 8:00 a.m. Monday morning, a crowd of roughly 200,000 people had gathered in Hibiya Park and the streets around it, and had spilled over the bridge onto the public space in front of the Imperial Palace. The park had been chain linked at Hibiya Road, the divided thoroughfare separating the park from the west end of the hotel. The Tokyo Metro's Chiyoda subway stop in the park had been shut down to prevent quick arrivals and exits, and the entire area within three blocks of the hotel had been blocked off to anything motorized. The area was secured further by heavily armored police, who also stood lined up next to the hotel-side of the fences on Hibiya Road. All cars entering, for whatever reason, were hand inspected with munitions-detecting swabs and mirrors to review the vehicle's underbelly. A strict no-fly zone was also in place, with Japanese military helicopters making cameos, accompanied by the occasional fly-by of a camouflaged jet.

Placards of Putin in likenesses of Hitler, replete with the copyrighted mustache, seemed to spring from the crowd like *Shimeji* mushrooms on long white stems. The action in the outdoor auditorium in the park was in full swing, with various voices taking turns cranking up the crowd with their rhetoric which, from Heidi's point of view, was pretty much spot on (save the Jehovah's preachers, who thankfully didn't get a turn at the microphone). It's a shame, she reflected, that people need to point out the obvious with so much force.

The women of TM7, whose windows had an angular line of sight and could hear the throngs bunched up against the ten-foot metal fences were dazed by the human storm that woke them. They had sensed something was brewing when they had returned from the airport around midnight. As they neared the hotel, they saw multiple checkpoints and noticed a palpable tension in the lobby. But none of them were prepared for a display of this magnitude. Shalala, whose room was on the other side of the hotel and had a view of the palace, sent the group a picture from her vantage point with the brief descriptive, "Oh my!"

The outside hubbub raised the anxiety that continually tried to overpower the multiple incense sticks Divine had brought with her and was chain-lighting. It didn't need to be said that the root cause for the demonstrations was precisely what TM7 was trying to change. No additional pressure to perform, Divine thought wryly, just 200,000 people incessantly chanting "Save the dolphins," "Too big to fail," "You can't kill us all" and "Putin go home." Not to mention the 120 deluded converts merrily asking people if they were happy with their lives.

But Heidi knew the women were up to the challenge, no matter how stressful the situation became. From her first exposure to their stories years ago, to the profiling for funds, to Biarritz, Doha, Hong Kong and their successful escapades at Narita, there was no one else she would rather trust to execute this plan.

The LoveBombs had been cleaned, and the three final doses started humming. They would be ready with plenty of time. For the respective *bushi*'s desires, Divine atomized doses into cute, white spray bottles, adding a hint of fresh lavender and mint so that the spritzes could pass as either breath freshener or a facial pick up. "A squirt on the tongue is better, though a deep inhalation should work fine as well. So long as it gets into their blood stream somehow, we are golden, ladies," Heidi instructed.

TM7 tracked their targets as they arrived via the surveillance cameras. Not all targets would necessarily attend each session, and many had arranged side meetings. It was these smaller and impromptu convergences that Heidi and TM7 felt would be the easiest to infiltrate. Trying to break into respective governmental scheduling systems was just too risky as hack prevention was on full alert. While it would have been ideal to plan a time and place for the dosing to occur, the women, aside from Shalala, realized they'd need to go with the flow, which meant they'd all have to be properly attired and ready to go at a moment's notice.

Mr. Clooney's resonant morning voice casually reminded Heidi in a pillow-talky way to set up a meeting with bin Nayef. Heidi reached out to him later that morning and secured an afternoon spot on Wednesday at four in his suite. "Oh yes, may I bring along a colleague who is very familiar with our latest advances?" she said. "OK. Super. I will see you at four."

...

The first opportunity to strike came Tuesday afternoon at around three courtesy of Lexie, who had been able to tap into the hotel's room service order system. Prime Minister Erdogan, after some seemingly successful discussions, had contentedly retreated to his room whereupon he ordered some tea. Lexie peered up from her laptop long enough to alert Divine that her target was available. "Yup, he's hot," she reported, "but not *that* way."

For a brief moment, Divine hesitated, uncertainty forming on the smooth contours of her elegant, long face. The moment troubled Heidi. Was Divine uncertain because she wasn't sure if this was the best time? Or was Divine unsure as to whether she could pull off the mission? All eyes focused on Divine and, for a second, Heidi's presumption that TM7 could weather all storms wavered.

Divine predictably dashed those fears, her expression returning to calm and effortless deportment. "Well, as Heidi is taking on bin Nayef in about thirty minutes, it looks like I will be off for the rest of the week," she said, her beautiful white teeth glimmering through her grin. Heidi and the rest of the girls shared her smile, tension dissipating more quickly than Lexie could "Like" a friend's Facebook post.

The girls had figured out the details well. Once the decision was made to engage, Lexie would cancel the room service order in the system and immediately place the same order to TM7's room, which Divine would then deliver to Prime Minister Erdogan with a little something extra. And, given their rooms were on the second floor, the delivery time would not be markedly compromised. The Imperial, like most Japanese hotels, prided itself on punctual service, even with a full house and elevators working overtime.

Hotel management tried to be as cosmopolitan as possible with their staff, and non-Japanese contractors were common for this kind of brouhaha. Besides, TM7's name tags were in both English and *Katakana* (the Japanese alphabet reserved for Western words). And while their personalities were distinctly *gaikokujin* (foreigners), they *looked* pretty freakin' official.

The only real issue would be making their way as unobtrusively as possible as hotel staff from their suites to the staff elevators down the hall (curiously, there were no cameras in them). There was also the possibility of bumping into other staff during delivery. But given the resource-exhausting demand and the intrinsic chaos of the event, this didn't raise too many concerns.

While Divine did a final makeup and hair check, bobby pinning her staff hat so it wouldn't inadvertently slip off and knock anything off the tray, Heidi retrieved Erdogan's LoveTail from her fridge. Divine would need to add the LoveTail to the appropriate vessel once in his room. Research had shown that LoveTails had a shelf life that dropped exponentially as the ambient temperature became warmer. The highest probability of a successful dosage would occur with the cells spending the least amount of time in hot water. After learning this, Divine said with a gleeful smile, "The water will be even hotter once they are in it."

A knock at the door sent the women scurrying to the other suite. Heidi opened the door, let the tea service wheel in, signed the bill and graciously slipped a 1,000 yen note to the staff member who, after more than a few bows and a litany of humble thank-yous, left. The women filtered back in, circling and eyeing the service with a similar feeling as when they first viewed the shaken and stirred LoveTails. This was it. Game on. The delivery mechanism was before them, steam wafting out of a polished metal spout, a pink carnation in a thin glass vase on the side. It sure beat a missile for efficiency and collateral damage, Heidi reflected.

"Well gals," Divine announced, confidence lodged in every word, "here we go!" The women gave her quick hugs. She was almost out the door when Heidi, who was deeply entrenched in the moment, remembered…"Divine, I believe you'll need this," she said, handing her the petite metal canister from her pocket. "*Ah oui, merci.*" Divine replied with a laugh, her graceful fingers grasping the vial and putting it in her pants pocket. And she was gone.

Like at the airport, her MoPhone was live so the group could listen and learn. Divine had also commandeered Heidi's broach for a visual feed. The women were perched on the edge of whatever was available—chairs, couches and bed—transfixed on the projection spouting from the top of Heidi's MoPhone, which was placed on the central coffee table. Lexie shifted from her laptop to a tablet to keep an eye on what was happening on the security cameras.

Erdogan's room was on the seventh floor, and Divine encountered no resistance accessing the staff elevator, which made its ascent unabated. When its doors opened however, she looked down, mentally preparing and practicing her lines one more time. The cart was two front wheels well across the gap before she looked up and realized a startled service sister, who was maybe a nudge over 4'11," was frantically trying to avoid being run over while not losing a tray of empty martini, red wine and cocktail glasses tenuously swiveling on one hand in the process. The onlookers, Divine included, held their breath.

Fortunately, with a practiced finesse, she deftly regained control, took a step back to make sure her footing was secure and directed a smile of camaraderie at Divine. Divine, obviously impressed by the woman's balancing prowess, bowed, a very low bow, to convey her deep apologies for her lack of attention. Heidi likened the scene to a giraffe trying to mollify a gazelle. The staffer laughed, bowed back and gingerly stepped out of the way to let Divine pass. "*Mata ne*? (see you later)," she cheerfully chirped. Once past her, Divine stopped, turned to face her and deeply bowed again. The staffer bounced into the elevator and with a quintessentially cute wave, and was gone.

Divine couldn't hear it, but the suite had erupted with fits of relieved laughter. Heidi, seeing no one else around, took her phone off mute and quietly (above the background din) said, "You go girl!" which was all Divine needed to hear. After that run-in and its happy ending, she was unstoppable.

With the sexy swank of a fashion model, hips swaying, palm tree legs gliding, back poised, eyes fixed straight ahead, Divine sashayed down the hallway. The Turkish guards saw her coming and froze. It wasn't every day in Tokyo that a tea cart was pushed by a gorgeous black Amazon.

"*Du thé pour le premier ministre?*" (Tea for the prime minister?) she politely asked in her native tongue, betting that at least one of them spoke French.

"*Oui, un moment,*" (Yes, one moment) one replied. He knocked on the door, said something in Turkish, which received a prompt reply, a pause and a final confirmation. "*Oui, entrez, s'il vous plaît,*" (Yes, please enter) he continued, opening the door.

Divine graciously smiled and completed her runway walk. Erdogan was sitting in the living room of his suite, at the end of an elegant sofa. "*Bon après midi, Monsieur Premier Ministre,*" Divine greeted the prime minister. "Entrez, entrez," (Enter, enter) he eagerly replied, eyes trying to soak up Divine at full scale. "*Merci, Tolga, fermez la porte s'il vous plaît.*" (Thank you Tolga, please close the door) Once it was closed he said, "*Mon dieu, il ne plaisantait pas. Comment vous êtes belle!*" (My god, no joke, you are beautiful)

"*Merci, Monsieur Premier Ministre,*" Divine demurely replied, positioning the cart next to him and, standing behind it, gracefully presented five miniature vessels, located in front of the pot, each with various colors and textures of loose-leaf tea. "*Quel genre de thé souhaitez-vous aujourd'hui?*" (What kind of tea would you like today?)

"*Nous sommes en Japon, alors, le thé du Japon,*" (When in Japan, drink Japanese tea) he responded cheerfully, still distracted by her enviable proportions.

"*D'accord,*" (OK) she continued in a professional voice, eyes shifting downwards to focus on methodically meting out the appropriate amount of leaves from the first vessel into the little wire basket to steep in the pot. "*Comment prenez-vous votre thé?*" (How do you take your tea?)

"*Généralement je préfère un peu de citron,*" (Generally, I like it with lemon) he said, not so covertly hiding his desire to make conversation. "*Mais, c'est Japon. Je prends comme un Japonais.*" (However, this being Japan, I will take it Japanese-style) It was clear to Divine that Erdogan was trying to appear worldly to impress her.

"*D'accord,*" Divine said, following Japanese tea-making protocols, pouring the hot water into the pot and gently setting the lid on top. "*Nous devions attrendre pendant trois minutes.*" (We must wait three minutes) Giving her watch a quick glance she said, "*Comment appréciez-vous Tokyo?*" (How do you like Tokyo?)

The next three minutes seemed to last an abbreviated eternity, as Divine's politely feigned interest in the Prime Minister's trip soon transitioned to where she liked to hang out when she wasn't working. "It's a shame I didn't know of any gay bars," she would later share with the girls. "Imagine his surprise, and the stories that would circulate in the press."

All the while, Divine busily took care of all last minute preparations, including emptying a particular liquid into the oversized drinking cup. Erdogan, entranced by her features and form, didn't notice her ancillary hand movements.

"*Ah bon. Trois minutes. Vous êtes pret?*" (Well, three minutes are up. Are you ready?) she docilely inquired, carefully pouring the slightly green liquid into the cup, which she immediately handed to the Prime Minister. "*Profitez-en!*" (Enjoy!) she said, with a divine grin.

And he did. He drank the whole cup in three quick gulps that must have burned his throat a bit going down. "*Encore!*" (More!), he delightedly requested.

"*Sans doute,*" (Absolutely) Divine replied, happily pouring him a second cup, as she imagined the stem cells coursing toward his kidneys. "*Et voila!*" (Here you go)

She waited until he was midway through his second cup to start her departure. "*Puis-je être d'une aide supplémentaire?*" (May I do anything else for you?) she meekly asked, though her body language read differently.

The prime minister sputtered a bit, the timing of her question not matching the cadence of his swallows. "*Comment vous-appelez-vous, Mademoiselle?*" (What is your name?) he asked, trying to make out her name tag.

"*Oh, cela ne fait rien,*" (It isn't important) she replied, dodging his question and quickly retreating to the door. "*A la prochaine fois...*"

And with that, Divine departed with a low bow, but not as low as the one she had given her staff sister. Her stride back down the hallway to the service elevators had the same visual impact, though something had changed. While still naturally fluid, her paces were less about sex appeal and more about the power of confidence and conviction. Like a soldier returning to base camp after enduring a full frontal attack on the line, Divine knew she had done her part in trying to make the world a better place. The last ten minutes might have been the most impactful of her life. Merely knowing she had been part of it was all the recognition she needed. "She has met the enemy and he is hers," Heidi remarked with an unusual tinge of solemn gaiety as she watched Divine approach the elevator.

"One down, ladies!" Divine murmured into her MoPhone, her mind still processing the fact she had just met her mission with flying colors as she pressed the down button. "That was easy!"

…

Emboldened by Divine's success, Iran fell next. An order for two gin and tonics and a Manhattan (with bourbon) came from the room of Hassan Rouhani at 6:03 p.m. Pre-dinner cocktails, Gilat presumed. "I'm glad these are all non-alcoholic or I would have to tell Muhammad on them," she sarcastically quipped. The delivery was a bit complicated as Gilat didn't know who would be imbibing each drink. However, according to Lexie, only three men had entered the room so chances were good that Rouhani would be getting at least one of them. Fortunately, the Imperial's in-room drink service called for in-room mixing and pouring of whatever libation was ordered. It fit TM7's needs nicely.

Gilat sprang into action, swiftly transforming her slightly tanned and freckled face to a quasi-kabuki visage of cake face and overstated red lipstick. "How do I look?" she facetiously queried Elena, who was researching how to make a Manhattan on her MoPhone. Elena gave her a quick look and flatly responded, "If I had a bottle I'm not sure if I'd drink it or use it on you." Gilat, who almost started tearing up with laughter, was advised by Lexie to try to stop lest her makeup drip on the drinks. Another application of powder had just been completed when the order showed.

"Don't forget your hat," Divine chided as Gilat headed for the door.

"Oh crap," Gilat said with a predominantly positive smile with a hint of "you'll be on stage in five" anxiety. "The effing hat…Anyone have a bobby pin?" Divine plucked one out of her hair and affixed the hat, albeit at a slightly cocky angle. "There you go, you are Madonna Kabuki," she observed with pride. Heidi handed her the dose and Gilat was out the door.

It wasn't until Gilat was in the elevator that Heidi realized she forgot her broach and MoPhone. "She'll have to go in dark," Lexie said gravely.

As it turned out, Gilat had wisely and purposefully left her MoPhone and the broach in the room, as she expected to be searched. And searched she was, by a hand-held flat wand that most certainly would have detected the unbranded device. She had also buried her LoveTail in the ice bucket while in the elevator to avoid detection if the cart and service was searched, which they were. Gilat's foresight to deal with the particular security measures of the Middle East was dead on brilliant.

Other than forgetting to add the cherry to the Manhattan, everything went smoothly. "Rouhani had a G&T, with a stiff dose of gin," she reported upon her return. "They were all discussing something in Persian and essentially ignored me. A quick twist of lime, a quick twist of the tonic cap, and a quick twist of this," she said, bringing the empty vial out of her pocket, "and two down! Lenikins, would you please hand me a bottle…"

...

Later that evening, three more metal tubes, whose contents could dramatically improve the lives of more than 2.5 billion people, rolled docilely out of LoveBomb's innards. Heidi, who had scurried over to watch, hoped that the revolutions these tubes might spawn would be as harmless as the revolutions they had just made coming down the ramp. She simply didn't know, and couldn't know, what would happen next. There were too many factors to contemplate. "First things first…Let's hope all these doses are delivered," she ruminated. There was strength in numbers and the more numbers on their side, the stronger the hope for non-violent change.

...

Early Wednesday morning, at around 4:00 a.m., a hotel staff member was making her rounds, slipping bills in envelopes under doors. If a surveillance officer had been watching very closely (in fact he would needed to be actively looking for the discrepancies with a very trained eye), he would have noticed that the envelope being delivered to one particular room occupied by an international celebrity was a little thicker than usual; it required some angling to get under the door. He might have noted that this particular staffer delivered envelopes to this room only, and, if his suspicions had been aroused, he may have wanted to checked to see if this particular guest was supposed to receive their invoice on Wednesday morning. But no surveillance officer would know to take an interest in what was happening.

Still, if he had wanted to look into the envelope, he would have been confronted with a surprise—not itemized accounts of nightly charges, taxes and orders for Cosmopolitans—but a note written in classic cursive that read 'Turkey Iran doneski,' and what appeared to be small, white plain spray bottles that, on first blush, were probably either a knock-off perfume or breath freshener.

. . .

Of all the TM7 members, Heidi was most concerned about how Lexie would do under pressure. It wasn't a question of trust or capability. Lexie had been there for her in so many contexts, from overseeing the formation of TM7, running the creation of LoveBombs and Tails, to frankly saving her from public shame on the occasions she had gotten smashed. Heidi just didn't know how Lexie would perform when she needed to dose one of the scariest men on the planet. Perhaps it was a function of Lexie's age combined with the fact that her life story, while powerful in its own right, wasn't nearly as intense as the other TM7 member's. She had resolve and grit, but did she have the mettle? To help answer this question, Heidi discreetly decided Lexie should accompany her on her visit to bin Nayef.

On the surface, it made complete sense. Lexie was very familiar with Illumina's explosive sensing efforts, as they drew on fields that Lexie had a liking for: bio- and nano-technologies combined with big data. But Lexie knew Heidi better than to just think she was there as a data source, a role she had comfortably played in countless prior meetings. This was a test, and while Lexie knew she wouldn't fail Heidi, she felt a bit slighted by Heidi's perceived lack of faith in her, especially given the relative ease of the first two forays. And given Lexie's relatively young age, her disappointment in Heidi bubbled up.

"So Heidi, about our meeting with bin Nayef tomorrow," she said at dinner after Gilat had made her triumphant return, "what kind of scoring system will be used to judge my performance?" Though the question was posed in a casual, almost off-handed manner, Heidi knew what was up, especially because it was presented in a group setting.

Heidi responded with true leadership style—transparently, honestly and human to human—looking Lexie directly in the eyes. "Oh Lexie, I am so sorry. I've been fretting about your assignment ever since it was decided, and I haven't shared my concerns with you. This is completely my bad. My concerns are around what could happen if Putin should find you out. Of all our targets, he is by far the most heartless, and best protected." Lexie just sat there. Her big, green-brown eyes, initially piercing, softened considerably as the full gravity of the situation sunk in. "And truth be told, a part of me isn't sure you're ready to take him on, which is why I thought about seeing how you might do tomorrow with bin Nayef. It's not a question of your capabilities; it is more about wondering how you will do in a very high-stakes setting. Putin is on the verge of starting a regional conflict with global reverberations."

The other women didn't need a reality TV host to fill in the blanks. They understood what was transpiring and could empathize with both Lexie and Heidi's positions; above all their respect for both was impregnable. Divine re-crossed her legs while Elena discreetly smacked her fingers of soy sauce drippings after a rather large bite of vegetable tempura.

Lexie, who had apparently finished processing, spoke. "Heidi, you're right. Taking on Putin is something I've been fretting about ever since I was chosen…and I've been in denial about what a big deal he is. I'm sorry for my outburst. I'm frankly still not sure what would be the best way to dose him, or what location to choose. I've been monitoring his entourage, and he's more closely guarded than Amazon Web Services' server farms."

"No worries at all Lexie," Heidi replied. "Again, I should have trusted my initial instincts…Well, I'm glad you brought it up. Ladies, we need some help here. Any thoughts regarding how we can get to Mr. Putin given he is presently The No. 1 Contender for The World's Most Wanted?"

...

Putin's participation at this G20 Summit had been rough from the get-go and had only gotten worse. Russia, it seemed, was on the verge of becoming a pariah nation. Even its largest trading partners (the E.U. and China), and political ally (China) were deeply and publically concerned by its recent expansion into Ukraine and the massive force amassed on the Azerbaijan border. Putin received a chilling reception on the opening day, with many heads of state politely refusing to shake his hand. The ritual group shot, which made the front page of most of the world's leading publications, said it all. Putin was in the front row, left of center, with a discernible physical void around him, his emotionless face staring into the flashes. Flanking him was Angela Merkel of Germany and Shinzo Abe of Japan, both looking markedly uncomfortable. Behind him, to his right, stood Rouhani, who looked like he was preparing to put Putin in a choke hold once the cameras stopped snapping.

After Putin was escorted away from the site of the shot, Wolf Blitzer of CNN reported in a more charged voice than usual, "Vladimir Putin, a man only Russians can love. But it would seem those numbers are dropping quickly as the common Russian is increasingly unable to afford the basic necessities due to rampant inflation brought on by sanctions, and job losses of the recession. His government's debt has exceeded junk bond ratings and, with oil in the sub $50 range per barrel, his ability to fund his government is increasingly questionable. He is in a world of hurt, brought on primarily by himself."

Numerous effigies had been ceremoniously burned in the park, and the multitudes, regardless of persuasion, joined the choruses of anti-Putin chants that regularly rocked the skies above the Chiyoda district. Whatever the ill, it applied to Russia. Even the Jehovahs temporarily ceased their efforts and joined in the refrains.

To compound matters, Putin seemed oblivious to the pressures his government and people were facing. He was his usual obstinate, Russia-first self when topics of global and regional economic growth, energy production, climate change and human rights were raised. By the end of Day Two, Xi Jinping, his only tangential friend at the table, politely suggested he reserve his remarks for later sessions. This comment infuriated Putin, whose bald head turned red as his flag, though he remained composed, sat back in his chair, and started playing with his cell phone. This scene went viral and when it hit the giant screens that had been erected at various locations around the park and palace grounds, the crowd went so wild, the roar could be heard in the meeting room. While there was speculation that Putin might leave the conference early, it was obvious he needed to make some back room deals happen while he was there, or even his prized military machine would stop dead in its tracks.

And with whom would these deals be made?

Heidi messaged Qin. They had to meet…

...

Qin was working non-stop behind the scenes to make this conference a diplomatic success for China. There were many pressing issues to be discussed, and each required its own analysis of impacts. There were discussions amongst internal stakeholders, studies of international appetites for particular initiatives, and finally outreach, either publicly or informally, to key players (typically governments, oftentimes corporations and more recently NGOs) to formalize decisions through policies, conventions and agreements. And she was outstanding at her job; Qin had been the background warrior in the landmark U.S.-Chinese emissions agreement which, though not nearly what she had wanted, had stunned the world.

Her sleeping hours had been few, and whatever shut eye she enjoyed was mere dozing, as her mind just couldn't let go enough to get into a deep, re-invigorating state of dormancy. Day Two had just ended and things were looking good for the most part. Everything, including TM7's agenda, had gone according to plan.

She was elated when Xi made his statement. A planning session was scheduled later that evening in preparation for a closed door meeting Putin had requested with Xi the next evening.

Qin had just entered her room, and was eying the bed for a quick 45-minute nap before the evening cocktail hour and dinner cycle started, when a familiar vibration peaked her fatigued senses. Rummaging through her suitcase, she extracted a small black device from a hidden pocket and tapped a button to bring the device back from the mode she had been missing for the last few weeks. Whatever it was, it must have been extremely important, as it had been agreed that the women should take no phone calls due to scanners, and should engage in only minimal messaging to avoid random detection. Qin kicked off her shoes, slid into bed, ducked under her comforter, and pressed another button. It was a message from Heidi that read, "Need to meet ASAP. Whenever, wherever. You rock."

Qin, knowing full well the reason why, reflected for a moment and then replied, "Spa. 10:30 p.m. Steam room."

Two seconds later her MoPhone blinked again. "Can't wait!"

...

"Oh Qin, my dear," Heidi softly exclaimed upon seeing her exhaustedly open the steam room door, "come here. I've been watching out for you on the Summit telecasts. You look like you haven't slept in a week and I can't imagine everything you are doing. You need a hug." She extended her hands.

The embrace seemed to immediately break through the separation of time and culture that had rusted Qin's fatigued joints. It was a hug of warmth, of camaraderie, of amity, of love.

"Are we alone?" Heidi lightheartedly asked.

"Ha!" Qin replied, whatever weariness had enmeshed itself in her bones was instantly banished by Heidi's energy. "You know, I don't believe I was followed this trip and even if I was," she said, looking around the empty steam room, "I simply told my boss I had to relax. He understood…"

Heidi briefly recounted the highlights of both expeditions, including Gilat's Madonna Kabuki appearance and Divine's Top Model exploits to Qin's fatigued fits of laughter. "So, we really have dosed Erdogan and Rouhani? That is amazing!" Qin remarked upon hearing that news.

"We wish you had been with us, however your position may be of even more tantamount importance," Heidi started to segue.

"Let me guess…That thorn called Putin?" Qin replied. "His leadership style isn't geared for this millennium. I just got out of a three-hour meeting preparing for negotiations with him tomorrow."

"That was my prediction," Heidi observed. "He needs friends, friends with money, lots of money and credit and influence, and China is all he has available to him. But of all the leaders at this summit, he needs to be dosed the most…and we, just like all the folks outside, are having a very difficult time figuring out a way to get to him. Pariahs are usually paranoid."

"Ha ha, you are quite correct," Qin reflected, her mind momentarily rushing back to the days of Mao. "I know where you're going with this and I'd be happy to try. Do you have the LoveTail with you?"

"Yes, it's in the locker outside," Heidi affirmed. "Given the difficulties getting to him, I had two doses created, one in liquid, and one in spray with scent. More flexibility. I'll sneak them to you when we change. And Qin…"

"Yes Heidi?"

"Please don't take ANY unnecessary risks. If you can't make it work, we'll try another way. You're way too important to TM7…and to me, to lose you."

Their eyes locked as if each was willing to let the other into the inner sanctums of their souls, recesses where they alone had only ventured and never were able to fully explore. But the time wasn't right for this. Not now. "Thank you, Heidi," Qin delicately replied. "I don't want to lose you either."

They hugged again, deeply and, once outside the foggy glass door, were just two women who happened to have shared the pleasure and random conversations of a good steam session.

# 26

## X Is for Exogenous

Nieto was next. Knowing that most Mexicans started their days with a rousing cup of coffee, Elena made sure she was up, showered and dressed by 6:15 a.m. She cheerfully woke a slightly pissy Lexie, who threatened to tie Elena up and sculpt a Japanese wig style out of her hair with kid's scissors if her premature stirring was in vain. Sure enough, the call came in at 6:45. Gilat, who'd gotten a little drunk the night prior celebrating her successful mission, woke up briefly to wish Elena luck with "Señor Suave," and retired once more to sleep. Divine, who'd celebrated with Gilat, didn't even stir. Heidi, who surprisingly hadn't imbibed too much, perhaps because of the soothing steamer, was up and monitoring.

By now, the process was slightly old hat. Elena, following Divine's lead, traipsed down the hallway in a tango-like step, much to the delight of the security guard stationed outside the room. Her moves were so pronounced one could see her rhythm through the broach video feed.

"*Buenos dias!*" Elena exclaimed in a leading, sultry voice. "Are you armed and loaded?" she followed in Spanish, knowing full well firearms were forbidden in Japan. She was obviously implying something else.

Lexie started to freak out while Heidi just giggled.

"Why, yes I am," the guard perked up, with a knowing smile.

"Well, I need to deliver some coffee first," Elena responded, matter-of-factly. "Want to search me?"

"Why yes," came his enthused reply. "I should do that."

The video quivered a bit as the man's hands made their way along Elena's limbs and up her chest.

"Find anything...dangerous?" Elena inquired.

"Not yet." His hands fondled something very close to the broach.

"Ahem, the coffee is getting cold," Elena said, with a *first things first* tone in her voice.

"*Si, senorita, un momento por favor*" (Yes, miss, one moment please). He hurriedly knocked on the door and reported, in an overly happy voice for someone who'd been sitting outside a door all night, "Mr. President, your coffee is here." Upon hearing a short response, he opened the door, ushered Elena and cart inside, and closed the door behind her.

Elena, on a roll, readily engaged Nieto. He blinked a few times upon seeing her. "How do you take your coffee, Mr. President?" she asked with a voice that could be described as a Latin version of Marilyn Monroe asking JFK what he wanted for his birthday.

By this point, Lexie was going apoplectic and Heidi started to tear up.

"With cream, and a little sugar," he stammered. Perhaps a bit like Erdogan, he wasn't expecting his Tokyo hotel room service would be delivered by a bombshell who spoke his language.

"OK," Elena responded, her back to him, letting him imagine her nude ass in a variety of positions, while she deftly emptied the contents of a small metal casing into his filled coffee cup.

"Here you go, Mr. President," she said, turning to present him with his cup on saucer, bending over in such a way that if the hotel shirt wasn't buttoned up to her neck, her voluminous cleavage would have been in his face.

"*Muchas gracias,*" he replied, and then asked a question with a slight squint of his eyes that scared the crap out of Elena, and of the women watching from afar. "Do I know you from someplace? You look vaguely familiar."

Elena, not expecting this question, froze for an interminable moment, wondering if her likeness had ever come across his TV screen or desk. It was a possibility that would require some seriously fleet-footed explaining. How did a South American eco-warrior end up serving coffee in Tokyo?

This same logic chain also flowed through Lexie and Heidi's synapses, petrifying Lexie and instantaneously putting Heidi into support-at-all-costs leader role. Her blue eyes fixated on every detail in the room, her mind racing as to potential means of extraction.

"Why, I don't believe so. I certainly would have remembered you," Elena replied, regaining her role with a smile. Her voice, at least to those accustomed to it, conveyed less confidence.

"Lexie, what is his room number?" Heidi asked unflappably, picking up the hotel phone. Though risky, as the call could be traced if desired, her first thought was to get Elena out of there before things got too hairy…But there was no response from Lexie. Heidi glanced away from the dial pad to see an immobile statue, turned to stone by the Nieto medusa.

"Could it have been in Hong Kong or Singapore?" he asked discreetly. "Have you worked either of those locations?"

"No, not yet," Elena replied, uncertain if he'd actually seen someone like her in one of those locations or he was just using the standard cosmo-jet-setting-President-impress ploy. Regardless, her cover seemed intact. "Is the coffee to your liking?" she followed, wanting to make sure her mission was completed.

Naturally, he took another big sip and commented, "It is delicious."

"Fantastic, the beans are Costa Rican. We wanted to make you feel at home," she said with another smile. "Well, if that is all, I must be on my way." Elena turned and started toward the door. "Please ring if you need anything else."

Her hand had just reached the handle when Nieto, perhaps triggered by her Costa Rican reference remarked rhetorically, "Oh…I know, you remind me of a woman from Brazil, I think she does…environmental work…"

Heidi, who'd replaced the phone in its cradle after the false alarm, reached for it again, while Lexie started looking for a nearby leftover glass of anything to drink.

Elena, still riding her wave of stress hormones, was much better prepared this time, and in perfect form replied, "Haha. I wish I could do something like that. I'm just looking forward to saving enough money to finish school. *Adiós* Mr. President."

Feigning she had just received an urgent call on her headset, she elusively made her way past the guard, blew him a kiss and said, ironically echoing the Terminator, "Hasta la vista baby." She was quite certain the hotel would be receiving high customer service marks from Room 535.

Later that day, she would admit she found the guard cute.

. . .

Nieto almost catching Elena was a foreseeable event—particularly because Elena had a prominent profile. Not inevitable was Lexie's reaction to the event: paralysis. It confirmed Heidi's fears. To avoid embarrassing Lexie, who was a little sensitive to this "area of growth" (though Heidi knew the other women wouldn't think any less of her), Heidi did a quick feedback session with her before Elena returned with the buzz of a bullfighter who'd just tamed the biggest steer in the country…with some eyelashes and coffee beans. "No worries at all, Lex. It's one of those things that comes from experience," Heidi observed with a smile. "We'll get you there."

Lexie's annoyance with herself quickly transitioned to appreciation for Heidi's discretion. "Heidi, you're right. When something out of the blue comes into the picture, I just freeze. While more planning might help, there are just some things I realize I can't plan for. I must be more mentally nimble…and truth be told, being cooped up in here, with everything happening outside, has made me feel a little claustrophobic and even more nervous."

"I understand. Me too. Why don't you go have a workout and a steam? It'll do you good," Heidi suggested, thinking, briefly, of Qin. "When you get back, we can meditate on this, and then discuss what will happen this afternoon. I've been thinking about our meeting with bin Nayef, and there'll be some interesting details we should consider. The Saudis always occupy the Imperial Suite, and there will probably be a few more people present, which will make dosing more complex. We need to think through who is doing what and when…and come up with some back up plans," she finished with a kind smile.

"Thanks, Heidi," Lexie said appreciatively, just as Elena gently burst into the room, waking everyone up, even those in the adjoining room. She started impersonating some rap star's swagger about "taking down the man."

"Awesome job, Elena!" Heidi remarked effusively, as they rained down congratulations on their flamboyant mercenary. "Three down!"

...

News of the Chinese Prime Minister's smackdown of Putin and Putin's lack of response, in addition to roiling protestors outside the Imperial, was having global reverberations. Hotel rooms occupied by foreign correspondents were ablaze that night, as commentators speculated on the evolving dynamic between Russia and China. Sound bites, with the usual provocative extrapolations, burst from all news channels.

BBC: "Has Putin created a corner he cannot escape without serious Chinese help?"

Sky News: "What options does Putin, Russia's Bad Boy, have available to him? His lack of response could be very troubling. No one knows what is going through his mind right now."

Fox News: "We are hearing talk of a major closed-door session scheduled tomorrow night between the two superpowers. What comes out of this meeting could determine Putin, and Russia's, fate."

The financial markets predictably reacted with much the same degree of speculation. Oil and natural gas futures, already frothy given Putin's military buildup on the border, zigzagged precipitously as traders placed bets on a spectrum of potential scenarios ranging from full-scale invasion to Putin stepping down. The price of natural resources coming from Russia tumbled, and the ruble, already flimsy, fell precipitously. Russian bond values continued to plummet as investors knew that their beta values, their riskiness of repayment, would go nowhere until a resolution was reached. Logic dictated that Putin should strike some major deals with China or face economic collapse, but these deals might only delay the inevitable. The trouble was that Putin was not a logical man. The higher the pressure and the stakes, the more irrational his responses seemed to become.

Later that night, satellites detected four Russian armored divisions and three battalions of infantry starting to make their way south toward the Azerbaijani border. More troubling was increased activity picked up at the Tatishchevo silos, the closest such installation to the Middle East, which housed an estimated ninety SS-19, ten SS-24 and twenty SS-27 class intercontinental ballistic missiles,[147] each capable of carrying

---

[147] http://www.nrdc.org/nuclear/planphoto/planphoto1.asp

nuclear and non-nuclear payloads.

In a brief press conference Wednesday morning, Putin downplayed the activity as merely normal military training, and refused to comment on anything else, including the purported meeting with the Chinese that evening. This blow-off communications tactic, which he had used countless times before, sometimes (but not always) masked his true intentions. It also further agitated local and international sentiments, and trading on the Russian bourse was halted outright for fear of a mass sell-off. Putin responded to this crisis in his best way possible, by instructing regulators to slash the price of local vodka so people could still afford it given its crippling inflation.[148]

Al Jazeera: "Interestingly, neither the U.S. nor China has tactically reacted to Putin's threat of force, instead issuing a joint statement that denounces Russia's ongoing aggression and making it known that any military actions will be met with a coordinated response. Additionally, Iran, which is at this G20 Summit, aside from reporting more exercises on its side of the border, seems unaffected by Putin's saber-rattling."

CNN: "Back in the States, Congressional hawks are squawking about the lack of U.S. action. Dick Perry, governor of Texas and a strong contender for the GOP presidential candidacy was quoted as saying, "I cannot believe our President is not taking this bull by its horns. We have the firepower, let's use it." His remarks were countered by Senator Elizabeth Warren of Massachusetts who stated, "We see no reason to further inflame an already delicate situation. I am quite certain President Putin realizes military action of the sort he seems to be messaging would not sit well with anyone.""

TM7 had to crank up the TV volume to deal with the din of protestors outside, whose ranks had doubled to an estimated 400,000 concerned citizens. Tokyo had now officially shut down while the summit was in progress, and the riot police had been joined by armed members of the Japanese military.

...

"Well, these certainly are interesting times," bin Nayef said as he greeted Heidi at the door of the Imperial Suite. "Come in and apologies, we will only have about 15 minutes to talk. Should Putin do the unthinkable,

---

[148] http://money.cnn.com/2014/12/31/news/economy/russia-vodka-putin/

Saudi Arabia will most certainly be involved in a response. And who is this?" he smiled, shaking Lexie's hand.

Heidi responded, "This is Lexie Seekay, my right-hand woman, and she is extremely knowledgeable about our biosensor programs."

"Very nice to meet you, Lexie," bin Nayef graciously said. "Come in, come in." He motioned them toward a semi-private sitting area. "May I offer you anything to drink? Tea? Coffee? White wine?" He winked at Heidi. They had obviously entertained each other a few times.

"Yes, coffee would be great," Lexie responded, giving the room a quick scan. There were two security guards inside the door who, after gracing her with a quick once over, more for her form than looking for weapons she surmised, would return to a heated game of backgammon after serving her desired beverage per bin Nayef's glance. She could tell the guards didn't necessarily like having to serve her as she was a woman, however they weren't in Saudi Arabia and the boss had commanded it. Without a word, coffee, cream and sugar were placed in front of her, though a spoon was forgotten or overlooked. No matter, Lexie thought, I won't be having too much of it anyway.

There were four other men working on laptops and on phones at the dining room table, obviously engrossed in planning economic and military responses to Putin's potential belligerence.

"And I will have some white wine," Heidi replied with a smile.

"Chardonnay, yes?" bin Nayef confirmed, his mustache rising at each end with a grin as he reached for an open bottle in an ice bucket stand that looked like it had been recently delivered particularly for Heidi's consumption. "You know Heidi, this stuff is going to be your downfall someday."

"Yes, Muhammad, you're probably right. I'm just happy to know you'll be there next to me," she retorted demurely. "What is your latest scotch infatuation? I understand there are some excellent selections coming out of Japan these days…"

"You're quite right Heidi. I simply cannot get enough of the Yamazaki Single Malt Sherry Cask…and in fact, in your honor, I will have some right now." A bottle and glass materialized, seemingly from his robes.

"So, Lexie," he said in a suddenly subdued voice, "as Heidi may have briefed you, there will be a changing of the guard soon in my House. This is a very big deal as the Kingdom's evolution is at a major point of inflection. There are internal forces, very powerful forces, who want to continue the old ways…and others, predominantly younger, that realize things need to change. I am concerned for my family, and my personal well-being." He paused to inhale, clearly thinking of his own mortality. "Heidi mentioned you have some interesting technologies that might be useful in protecting us, and perhaps the future of my country…and the world."

Lexie had been briefed extensively, and what bin Nayef was saying was very true. Saudi Arabia, in what seemed to be a gesture to its ancestral Wahhabi fighter's beliefs, had funded hundreds of madrassas throughout the Middle East, in Afghanistan and Pakistan in particular. These madrassas taught a very conservative form of Islam. So conservative, in fact, that women caught driving in Saudi Arabia were being brought up on terrorist charges.[149] The desire to educate had given way to a religious pedagogy that had returned to haunt the Saudi Royal Family, as this particular interpretation called for the distribution of wealth and support of the poor, which were being blatantly ignored by the privileged few. Both Osama bin Laden and ISIS publicly decried the House of Saud as heretics. Dealing with the mess would require leadership of a sort that hadn't been seen in Middle Eastern circles…ever. It would require, as Heidi would off-handedly say, "Leadership without veils."

"Yes, your excellency," Lexie started, leaning forward to match his low tone, and to be within easy reach of his drink. "I believe I have an understanding of the nature, the tenuous nature, of the situation you face and we would really like to support you. We have three technologies you may find interesting. First—"

Heidi delivered right on cue, her tilted glass passing its test of gravity, soaking her lap and splashing on the floor.

"Oh my," she exclaimed with an embarrassed grin, "what a klutz I am." She started to get up slowly to draw the attention of all present away from her colleague who, had she been spotted, would seem to be fumbling with a small metal canister.

Bin Nayef, ever the gentle host, immediately stood up and motioned to the guards. Dropping dice, they snapped to, hurriedly procuring two napkins from a room service delivery tray that, surprisingly, had not yet been retrieved.

Out of the corner of her eye, Heidi saw Lexie was still scrabbling. Crap. Heidi started walking toward the bathroom drawing all eyes to her, gladly thanking the guards as she passed them.

---

[149] http://www.ibtimes.co.uk/two-women-face-terrorism-charges-driving-saudi-arabia-1481331

"I'll be back in an instant she said at the last possible moment before closing the door, hoping Lexie had fixed her fumbling.

After a light pat down with cold water, and a quick check of her hair and makeup, Heidi returned to the sitting area with the humorous observation, "You know Muhammad," she said, looking down at the wet spot on her lap, "people are going to wonder what we were up to in here."

The meeting went five minutes over its allotted time and bin Nayef was very impressed with Illumina's prowess, particularly with an application that could detect trace amounts of explosives, even those embedded in bodies, with the swipe of a diminutive handheld device two feet away from pretty much anything. Heidi promised to send him ten beta versions for his testing and feedback ASAP. They toasted and downed the rest of their drinks.

"Heidi and Lexie, thank you both so much for your time," he said, getting up and politely ushering them toward the doors being opened by the guards. "You are a godsend."

"As are you," Heidi echoed with a smile that only Lexie, knowing his potential role in future world events, could interpret.

And out they went.

Heidi could tell by Lexie's post-meeting demeanor that her fingers had eventually triumphed, and the dose had been successfully delivered. Though it was also clear that she still had issues, and her confidence wasn't fully where it might need to be for anything more complex.

Oblivious to the subtext, the other TM7 women, who'd been following every word and movement, prepared to give Lexie huge hugs upon her return to the rooms. In their eyes, she had performed. Lexie, whose mind was still dismembering and analyzing every single solitary error, perceived error and even errors that could have happened and didn't, was very surprised by the outpouring of affirmation and support. Four down.

It was Cosmo time…

...

The vanity play made a ton of sense, especially for someone like Putin whose self-worth was so tightly bound to his public image. Qin fingered the two canisters in her suit pocket. She had wisely made a little etch on the bottom of the perfumed spray to distinguish it by touch. Visually reviewing three canisters in a clutch moment could kind of give things away.

The negotiations with Putin were to be all business, though the terms of the deal clearly displayed Beijing's weariness with the state of its political half-sibling's dealings. Some Party-line Chinese pundits claimed that the reason Russia was in its current state was because it allowed a Western-style democracy to exist within its borders. There were also those who understood that such simple rationalizations rarely apply under the scrutiny of fact. Yes, transitions to any new system of government, particularly those from dictator to democracy, were always bumpy and could take decades to firmly establish themselves. Economic and financial systems key to showing progress were typically so backward and non-productive that establishing centers of manufacturing with the requisite scale to compete in international markets, while keeping the public fed, housed and warm, was incredibly difficult. When was the last time a Russian car was sold anywhere outside of Russia? For countries with vast natural resources like Russia, these resources were their linchpin of growth, their ticket to a better economy, and life. However, given the Russian people's history of allowing tyrants to run things, all you needed was another greedy, aggressive and power-hungry (not to be redundant) "male" leader to take over and you had all the ingredients for a global crisis.

The meeting, which was leaked to the press, was to start promptly at 7 p.m. True to form, Xi, Qin and crew were all seated and waiting at 6:55. And true to form, Putin, who had called the meeting, wasn't there. At 7:08, Putin and aides shuffled in, with a slightly pugnacious allusion to being held up that could have been construed as an apology if it weren't for its pathetically transparent lack of sincerity. Xi, always polite in these settings, simply sat there, hands calmly folded in his lap, a serene look on his face, waiting for Putin's self-importance to wane enough to start discussing the terms of his bail out. This was, after all, a tremendous opportunity for China to secure many valuable assets—more natural resources, shipping routes through the Arctic, further protections against the falling ruble, etc.—on very favorable terms.

After the usual five-minute diatribe on the harmonious and historical cooperation between the two superpowers, Putin made a vague insinuation to some "current, short-term, and Western-conceived issues" (a.k.a. the low price of oil) threatening to destabilize their present relationship. He, of course, was not so subtly referring to the recently signed $400 billion natural gas deal, which required Russian investment of monies he did not have and could not borrow. The Chinese were prepared for Putin to play this card. If Putin had expected shock or exasperation from his largest trading partner, which he would take as a signal of weakness and could leverage in the ensuing negotiations, all that registered was an impenetrable Great Wall of stolid faces.

Xi, letting the silence descend upon the room like a soaked, cold blanket, eventually spoke in a measured voice. "Mr. Putin, we are well aware of your issues and we see no reason why they should interfere with our relationship. To assist in your time of need, we have prepared a list of agreements we believe can benefit both of us." China clearly had the leverage and no matter how big a hissy fit Putin might throw, whatever was coming from China was going to be on their terms. Xi motioned and Qin's boss stood up and approached the Russian delegation with copies of documents that were numerous enough to require large-sized binder clips. The Chinese had been waiting for this and they were ready. "I understand there is a lot to review here, however I believe we can reach some high-level agreements this evening and work out the details over the next few days," Xi coolly observed.

Putin, not eliciting the desired response from his minor threat and upon seeing the thickness of the negotiating points, started to crack, his puffed up bravado losing its hot air, revealing a sullen, skull-framed countenance that knew it had lost. "How did he think he would prevail going into this meeting?" Qin reflected. Delusion or denial or both?

The next two hours were spent reviewing the main topics. Secured oil supply at current world prices plus 10% for twenty years. Secured wheat production at current world prices plus 10% for twenty years. Secured mining rights for copper, gold, and diamonds for 30 years. All with upfront payments to help Putin weather his perfect financial storm. Putin had little choice but to agree, at least in principle. As he verified each point with an indolent shrug—he apparently was having difficulties expressing defeat—Qin wondered how his close circle of friends, most of whom controlled Russia's natural resources and whose net worth would be dramatically dinged, would react to his decisions. There would be some rather serrated conversations, with him and about him in London and Spain, where many of Russia's billionaires had relocated. This wasn't her concern yet, though these agreements could cause any regime, this one in particular, to fall.

With the last point broached and agreed on, Putin, fatigued and battered by his pasting, blearily motioned for the ceremonial shot of alcohol to consummate the deal, with a look on his face that conveyed more of those were to come later that evening.

Qin sensed this was the time. Putin had just shaken hands with Xi, had sat back down and was gathering up his notes when in the corner of his eye he saw a Chinese woman appear to spray her face with a small white bottle. Eyes closed, deep smile, relaxed breaths, she obviously was thoroughly enjoying the brief existential respite from the rather warm room where he'd just agreed to denigrate his nation from declining superpower to economic colony. Not to mention the ego bash pursuant to his demotion in the *Forbes* 100 wealthiest people list.

He watched as she placidly re-entered the tumult of reality, slowly standing and walking toward his table. Apparently she was on their negotiating team, probably a support staff given her gender. "Maybe I can get something, anything, for me out of this session," his eyes conveyed.

"Miss," he started in surprisingly good English, distracting Qin as she approached his main deputy. Qin pointed at herself as if surprised the President of Russia had a reason to speak to her.

"Yes," he said with a slightly lording smile that conveyed, all arrogance aside, he does his homework on those with whom he negotiates. "Forgive me, I don't speak Chinese and I know you speak English. I couldn't help but notice how much you enjoyed your face spray. Could you tell me about it?"

Qin was ready. "Oh President Putin, was I so obvious?" she started, "I'm so sorry. That meeting was just so long and…wearing." Qin was very good at playing ignorant of the fact her country had just essentially disemboweled him.

"Yes it was," he said grimly, though she could tell his mental calculus was already honing in on her weakness. "So, about your spray."

"Well, it's from France. It is nothing really. Just some nice fresh water with mint and lavender mixed in. I find it takes me away, ever so briefly…" Qin stopped, looked Putin in the eye and with a polite tone said, "Would you like to try some?"

Of course he did.

"Why, yes, I'd love to," he replied, eagerly looking forward to escaping his present hell, even for just a fleeting moment.

Qin, feeling the etch, extracted the correct bottle, removed its cap and suggested she administer it. He nodded, smile forming, closed his eyes, and just as she was about to spray, she gave him the instruction "Breath deep."

It must have looked a bit odd, a Chinese delegate applying what looked like a facial mist to the Russian President in the aftermath of a brutal negotiation session. Well, people are human. Somehow, a picture was snapped of this interchange whose caption, when syndicated in a variety of foreign papers, ranged from "Putin gets vaporized by China" (*The Economist*) and "China comforts its Russian ally" (*Beijing Daily*), to "Russia allows help from China" (*The Moscow Times*). And though Qin was a little upset that a picture of her, even just her backside with no readily recognizable features, had made its way into the global media sphere, she would be very pleased to receive a group hug video text the next morning attached to the picture, which had been forwarded to her MoPhone.

Qin excitedly watched as Putin's modified blood was inhaled into his system. She was elated. Her feelings of triumph penetrated the practiced neutral expression on her face; she smiled without meaning to. She couldn't tell if the mist had the effect Putin was looking for, however he seemed to thoroughly enjoy it. His eyes and smile remained motionless for a few seconds, mind possibly wandering to a late spring day in the lavender fields that dotted Provence. After a few additional inhalations, he opened his eyes and simply said, "Thank you."

"You're welcome," Qin replied. "Did you like it?" she said, playing the classic supporting role perfectly.

"Yes, very much. It does take you away."

Qin then, in a typical female act of giving, pre-empted Putin's predictable ask by saying, "Would you like the bottle? I have many at home."

"Why yes. If it isn't too much to ask," Putin replied, sincerity in his voice. He was obviously touched by Qin's generosity. It would be the only thing he could claim, at least to himself, he had gained from that meeting.

"Certainly," Qin affirmed and, with a submissive smile, handed the capped spray to him. In parting she added, "Oh yes, it also makes a great mouth freshener."

Qin's parting image of Putin was of him spraying the cells of his transformation onto his tongue.

. . .

Shalala was exhausted from the lack of sleep from the pandemonium outside that just seemed to be getting larger and louder with each passing hour. She'd tried to stay abreast of what had been going down at the summit, particularly with her targets, but she was distracted by the sheer force of humanity sending tremors through the concrete and steel of streets and buildings to her room. And while she was there with her absolutely extraordinary father, who had provided her with moral guidance from as far back as she could remember, she missed her sister companions, and wished there was a way to physically share her feelings, a hug and a drink or two with them.

"Shalala, my flower," her father said, picking up signals of her duress, "you seem not yourself. What can I do for you?"

"Oh thank you, father. There's a lot going on right now and I'm just trying to make sense of it all." She returned her gaze to the window on her computer screen that showed closed-circuit summit meetings, and glanced up from time to time at the window of the hotel, where protestors could be seen below.

Although the major focus of the summit was overshadowed by The Putin Problem, the overall agenda was well-maintained. Shalala sat in on a few topical sessions—Governments' Roles in Expanding Microfinance Options, An Update on Developmental Economics and Technology's Role in Global Education—knowing her mere presence would have an impact on what the participants would take away. In sight, in mind.

On Thursday afternoon at 1 o'clock, Shalala and the prime ministers of India and Indonesia would discuss her proposal for girls' education in a conference room on the third floor. The press conference announcing their agreement was scheduled for 3 p.m. later that afternoon, in the media chamber upstairs on the eighth floor. Her plan was to get on the elevator with her targets once the final terms had been agreed to where she would casually refer to a fantastic facial spray that made you look so much more youthful and vibrant on camera. Coming from a woman with her ever-present glow, she was confident they would want to try some. She had five floors to make this happen.

At the nexus of Shalala's well-researched proposal was the requirement that all girls be provided an education that met high school-level proficiencies. She had come up with a novel curriculum geared to help girls escape the classic trap of marital malaise and to be able to flourish independently. This could easily be afforded by a slight shift in spending—"from military defense to economic offense." And this did not include the economic benefit of a dramatic reduction in corruption that would accompany, over time, an educated female workforce, and thus administration.

While Shalala's intuition was that neither of the leaders would follow her proscriptions to the paragraph, much less the letter (they were meeting her more for the PR windfall), if TM7's plan worked, her points would be amazing guidelines that almost any woman would happily push for.

Everything was falling into place when, at 12:50 PM, showing at her purported meeting room, she found there had been a mix-up and the room was actually being used by another group (which she walked in on) until three. Things didn't start getting frantic until it was discovered that there were no available rooms until 2:30, and she couldn't reschedule a press conference with the heads of two countries whose combined populations exceeded 1.5 billion people just because there wasn't a meeting room. Prime Minister Modi immediately offered the use of his suite, located on the seventh floor, which Shalala and President Widodo both graciously accepted. She contemplated, as she got on the elevator, whether she should try to help them look better then, but the timing just wasn't right. The deal needed to be sealed first. Inwardly frantic, she and her father, who perceptively noticed something was amiss, entered Modi's suite and the discussions commenced. What was a five floor trip became one.

The usual, "last minute" modifications to the proposal focused on timelines and checkpoints for implementation, rather than the actual points. This was typical, from Shalala's experience. The men were more concerned with having backdoors to leave the agreement "should adequate funding not be available" or "presuming proper facilities are available." It was all a question of will and priority. How important was educating their countries' most value-adding and productive assets?

Shalala was able to push back, playing a bit of rehearsed good cop to her father's bad cop, securing the livelihood of most of her points and potentially millions upon millions of fellow humans in the process.

At 2:45, everyone was in alignment and Shalala suggested they go upstairs to prepare for the actual signing of the agreement and the subsequent Q&A with reporters in front of cameras. This was going to be big news as no one outside of very close circles was familiar with the precise points of the agreement.

She led the entourage, including a few ministers from both governments and her father, to the elevators. While waiting, she started to pull out her white-capped bottle to initiate her mission. Just then however, Modi's mobile phone started ringing. Shalala realized she would lose the attention she needed to pull off her ruse. Her hand went back in her pocket.

The doors opened, people started piling inside and she started to sweat. She knew that once they reached the floor above them, their announcement would take center stage, and it would be near impossible to command the requisite attention of her targets. Shalala's opportunity was fading faster than the doors were closing, and no matter how laterally her brain could think, no other options were making themselves available.

It was then, when she closed her eyes out of sheer abandonment of hope, that the lights went out and the elevator, between floors, stopped moving. She could tell from the change in Modi's tone and facial expression in his phone's light that the topic of his call had shifted to what was happening to the elevator, though no details were apparently immediately available.

As it turns out, Putin had just publically backed out of the deals he made with the Chinese the night before and the protesters, upon hearing this news, successfully hacked into the hotel's mechanicals and had shut everything down as a metaphor to what would happen to Russia. It took about nine minutes for the hack to be located and the respective systems rebooted, and that was more than enough time for Shalala to work her facial magic.

After escaping the cramped confines of the stuffy metal box, who wouldn't want to appear in front of glaring bulbs and polished, professional lenses looking refreshed and relaxed, especially at the recommendation of an international celebrity who'd been on the cover of *Time* magazine?

The only thing Shalala forgot in the heat of the moment was which spray was which. "There was just so much confusion starting with the meeting room fiasco," she would later share, "I simply couldn't remember which pocket was for Modi and which was for Widodo. I actually thought about trying to get them to share their bottles somehow to cover all bases, but I couldn't figure out how to pull that off. We'll just have to wait and see what happens. There is nothing else we can do."

. . .

Qin originally thought of slipping Xi's dose into a random drink at some point, however the circle that surrounded him day and night due to Putin's pissy party was too difficult to penetrate without severe risk of being discovered. There were a couple cracks in his coterie that might have afforded an opportunity, but she took Heidi's cautionary dictum to heart. If she were found out, there was little chance of Qin ever seeing the TM7's faces in person again. Not to mention she knew the interrogation process would either kill her or make her choke out indicting information, or probably both. Nonetheless, she kept both containers with her at all times, just in case a confluence of exogenous events assembled themselves in a pattern with an opening.

It was then, in a random stroke of luck, that that Xi came to her. The picture of her giving Putin a facial with her spray caused quite a stir in China. Everyone, from newscasters to ministers, was paying attention. Differing accounts of what had started the interchange by those "who were there" were bouncing around with the velocity of the light particles carrying encoded messages over global fiber optics networks. No one had yet asked Qin what had happened. The next afternoon, Xi motioned her over to a sitting area in his 5,000 square foot suite.

Qin was ready. She explained apologetically how she had selfishly wanted to "take a mental break" from the proceedings and how President Putin happened to see her. He too obviously needed a break, and reached out to Qin. Xi chuckled, saying that everyone needed a break from Putin and commented on how the picture, from an internal Chinese PR perspective, was a brilliant hit. Qin lowered her head, thanking the president for his gracious thoughts. She was about to leave when Xi abruptly asked her in a slightly lowered voice if he could try the mist, mentioning how it seemed to have had a marked, albeit brief, effect on the death-warmed-over features of Putin. "I could use a break every now and then too," he said with a little wink.

This unforeseen request almost broke Qin's patent-pending poise, however her "tempered by fire" spirit didn't miss a beat. After the customary "It isn't good enough for you" interchange, where Xi affirmed his request, Qin somewhat abashedly produced a white bottle, removed its cap, and, picking up the president's signals, offered to apply it.

"Breathe deeply!"

Xi had a similar reaction to his processed plasma as Putin did. He opened his eyes and smiled. Qin, noting his pleasure, insisted he take the bottle which, after the customary interchange, he accepted. As with Putin, Qin added that it made a great breath freshener. She gave him another parting glance and another squirt of cells to improve the odds of absorption. She calculated that the absorption rate could reach as high as 100% for Xi with this level of exposure.

Six devices merrily hummed with a text message later that evening confirming Xi's dose.

In a rare event, Heidi responded before Lexie with a simple "WOOHOO!!" She added a note about looking forward to their next group meeting, implying she had an idea as to when and where it possibly could happen. "And even if the odds aren't in our favor, 6 out of 8 confirmed is extraordinary! Congrats to everyone. SUPER job!"

...

Indeed, the women had done a super job, given everything that could have gone wrong and the many things that didn't go as planned. Much like life, Heidi ruminated. The key was to focus on what you could control, accept the vast scope of what you couldn't, and have the wisdom to know the difference. And to understand that what you can't control doesn't always hurt you...and sometimes could be quite helpful. She made a note to discuss this with Lexie on the way back as it might help her with her anxiousness. Then again, Lexie was still young...

...

The organizers claimed the summit a success, which it was for the most part. Advancements were made on many fronts, though Putin's backpedaling, then stalling and then silence, aside from stunning financial markets that pulverized anything Russian, threw the local protesters into frenzies. Everyone, except for seven women who shrank into the bamboo backdrop behind the insanity surrounding the mad leader's mayhem.

Transporting the Russian delegation via automotive means to the airport, regardless of the type or number of vehicles, could be hazardous to both dignitaries' and demonstrators' well-being. In a picture reminiscent of the American embassy being evacuated from Hanoi, Putin was photographed climbing aboard a military helicopter, with stoic disconnection to the teeming hordes of connected citizens behind him. He smugly waved, seemingly to show that he was in control, and that he had great affinity for the proletariat beneath him. While the image made for great PR in the motherland, the majority of the world wrote it off as his final hurrah. Heidi wondered how different the global picture would be if his mother had loved him as a child.

As soon as Putin's plane entered his airspace, Russian armored and ground forces started moving south toward the border of Azerbaijan and the Russian Finance Ministry kicked off a prolific domestic ad campaign for war bonds to fund Russia's "Renaissance."

# 27

## *Tsugi wa…*

### ("Next…")

TM7 made it out of Tokyo with no real issues. A few hours after Putin's departure, the crowd dispersed enough to allow transportation to resume fairly normal schedules. Heidi needed to get back to San Francisco for meetings with her staff and board to determine their next steps should Putin do something really "boner-headed" (especially if the stem cells didn't kick in). Divine departed with Gilat. Divine was given explicit authority from Heidi to protect and potentially relocate the Doha staff and their families, given their proximity to all that was happening in the region. They couldn't be too safe, Heidi felt. While Elena wanted to hang with Gilat, it was decided there was simply too much risk in this plan. There was the danger Israeli surveillance posed, and then there was the danger if the two were let loose unsupervised in civilized quarters.

So, Lexie and Elena, while in the general vicinity, took a plane to

Indonesia to work on protecting the last national park in Sumatra from deforestation. They hoped to publicize its impacts on both climate change and species extinction. Unlike Brazil, where the main beneficiaries of deforestation were cattle ranchers, this violence against nature supported the production of palm oil, which permeates the global food supply.[150] Shalala returned to London to milk the PR from her agreements. Qin travelled on to Moscow with a cadre of other comrades to attend special "last ditch" negotiation meetings "in an environment more conducive to rational thought" the *Moscow Times* announced. These meetings apparently halted the Russian forces who had advanced to within five kilometer of the Azerbaijani border, where they were reportedly subsisting on vodka shots.

To appease the hawkish forces in their respective administrations and militaries, the U.S., E.U., China and Iran all countered Putin's saber-rattling by expanding sanctions, shutting down all forms of capital in- and outflows and unveiling government-sponsored deals to supply Europe and China with oil and natural gas from the States, Iran and Saudi Arabia. U.S. and NATO forces were being deployed to the area, a no-fly zone had been erected above Azerbaijan and Iran had started amassing its military south of Tabriz, the closest main city south of the border.

Meanwhile, Azerbaijan's robust military of approximately 50,000 troops of various backgrounds and experience started digging in a bit west of Khachmaz near the border with Russia to defend the North-South highway. They also spread out along the coast of the Caspian Sea and around Baku, the capital to deter an amphibious assault (which could isolate the border forces). Their air force, which could be easily housed on two U.S. aircraft carriers, was scrambling all over the place with some degree of logic. Their naval forces, primarily patrol and torpedo boats, had formed a revolving blockade at the invisible line in the water. Their four submarines were all out of sight and were detecting similar, larger fish in the general area.

Putin, reacting to these reactions, immediately declared a state of martial law in Moscow, shut down all natural gas pipelines leading out of the country "It will be a very cold winter in Europe and China," he matter-of-factly growled when making the announcement. And he scheduled the classic, retro-60s military parade in Red Square where

---

[150] http://www.saynotopalmoil.com/Whats_the_issue.php

tanks, foot soldiers and missiles all marched by his unwavering gaze. He also forbade any further emigration to other countries (Russians with money were leaving in droves by buying residencies in compliant nations), and held numerous press conferences denouncing Western capitalism and greed. He intimated that his enemies wished to destroy the Russian economy—and spirit—and that, as a virtuous leader, he needed systematic aggression to liberate particular oil fields from their sordid situations. In an apparent attempt to leverage a popular image of American hegemony, he replaced Uncle Sam with a similarly stern, pointing-directly-at-you picture, fur-bound Russian trooper chapeau in lieu of Sam's top hat with the words "I want YOU to buy Renaissance Bonds." The irony—the U.S. version supported democracy, the Russian version, tyranny—was lost on no one outside of Russian borders, and more than a few internally.

Given Putin's crackdown, Heidi was particularly concerned about Qin and her physical safety. She would put nothing past Putin, including a hostage-for-cash deal. She had sent Qin a message and was starting to fret when she hadn't received a response in over 48 hours, though she also understood getting a message out of Russia, given the assured pandemonium, would be difficult. Finally, after three days, Qin was able to send Heidi a quick note. "Am OK," she wrote. "Bad situation all around."

Days felt interminable as sleepless negotiations and global nerves stretched out like the sinews a yogi doing a camel pose (which is more particularly painful to men than women). Things were crazy. From the neurotic Russian government and corporate bond holders, to oil and natural gas futures markets twitching like the traders were on crystal meth. From the Azerbaijani border where 500,000 Russian troops were camping out and practicing making S'mores, to Tehran, which hinted it might have a nuclear weapon after all, to the floor of the U.S. Congress, where the military-testosterone complex, with the N.R.A.'s explicit backing, was screaming to proactively "Show the world who's boss." The degree of tension and anxiety could have been compared to the build-up to the final episode of *The Bachelor*.

It was then, when all hope and emotional logic seemed lost, something completely unexpected happened.

...

Carl Donnerstag's aged linebacker frame reclined in his sleek black leather desk chair. He stared dazedly out the large, Plexiglas window of his expansive, recognition-paneled office into the autumnal forest that surrounded C.I.A. headquarters in Langley, Virginia. His sturdy fingers were spread like a five-legged spider, occasionally drumming against his desk, starting from his little finger and moving sequentially to his thumb.

He could not believe what was going on. The global order, the decades-old backbone of commonly understood foreign policy, seemed to be changing, fundamentally, right in front of his eyes. It was his job as Director of the C.I.A. to not only foresee these changes, but to proactively make sure they happened in the United States' political, economic and military favor. His entire career, after graduating from West Point and serving in the Army, had been at the C.I.A. Through it all, even with unexpected surprises like the events of 9/11, he believed he, and the U.S., maintained control of what happened abroad to varying degrees. Though he oversaw 21,000 people and had a yearly budget in excess of $15 billion, a limbic-inspired feeling told him, based on what had unfolded in the past two weeks, that America's knowledge was intrinsically flawed and its power was slipping fast.

Echoing the Israeli-Palestinian deal earlier that year, which had "blown his jock strap off," India proactively reached out to Pakistan to schedule "mutual understanding, reconciliation, and co-investment" meetings aimed at dealing with past atrocities on both sides and moving on. This included dramatic reductions in military spending, decommissioning all nuclear weapons and exploring ways to bolster trade between the two nations. In the same breath, Prime Minister Modi underscored his commitment to Shalala's education contract, redirecting defense budgets to these ends, including all "necessary" expenditures for infrastructure including access to clean water, sanitation and health services. He made a strident commitment to reduce air pollution in India's cities. He also recanted his government's position on marital rape[151] and declared, "The only way India can reach both its economic and, more importantly, quality of life potential, is by treating women with the same dignity, respect, and legal transparency that men have received for thousands of years."

Indonesia followed suit by redirecting significant military expenditures to infrastructure and education, per Shalala's contract. The country also abruptly stopped all deforestation efforts for whatever purpose. "We

---

[151] http://blogs.wsj.com/indiarealtime/2015/04/30/modi-governments-reasons-why-marital-rape-is-not-a-crime/

will not continue to jeopardize the future of our planet and the future of Indonesia's plant, reptiles, birds and animals for short-term money," Widodo stated emphatically with a curious emphasis on "reptiles."

Mexico similarly piped up, with dramatic decreases in its military spending. "Who might we need to attack?" Nieto asked his Congress. "Who might we need to defend against? Guatemala? Belize? Cuba? Really?" He concomitantly increased expenditures for education, workforce development and infrastructure. He broached the drug trade problem head on, stating, "The drug business is a supply and demand problem. We need to supply our citizens with resources and paying prospects that demand their attention, commitment and focus. While this will take time, I am confident we can replace this plague that has killed far too many of our people with truly value-adding industries."

Erdogan of Turkey also grabbed copious numbers of pixels by acknowledging Turkey's leading role in the Armenian genocide. Prior to this moment, mere mention of the genocide was punishable by jail time.[152] He called for meetings with all neighboring states, including a delegation of Syrian rebels. "I will not deal with oppressive dictators," he said, "We will establish a regional economic bloc that will bring together Asia and Europe, starting with forgiveness." He delivered this statement in a surprise visit to Yerevan, the capital of Armenia, with its slightly bewildered President and Prime Minister, who had just been briefed an hour prior, clapping with both hope and hesitancy in the background.

The news from Turkey, while groundbreaking, was dramatically out-shined by the decrees coming out of the Kingdom of Saudi Arabia, which could only be described as revolutionary. In a carefully worded and rather lengthy statement, the Royal Family decided it was in neither its citizenry's, nor the world's best interests to continue supporting the Wahhabi interpretation of Islamic conventions. The state would no longer allow these teachings in its schools or the madrasas it had funded throughout Central Asia, Western Europe and North America.[153]

"Too much hatred and blood has been spilled between Muslims and throughout the world because of these doctrines that, if allowed to continue, will create an impenetrable divide between generations and cultures."

"Holy Jesus!" Carl Donnerstag exclaimed upon hearing the statement.

---

[152] 1.5 million deaths, http://en.wikipedia.org/wiki/Armenian_Genocide

[153] For more on this fascinating topic: http://www.pbs.org/wgbh/pages/frontline/shows/saudi/analyses/madrassas.html

He said it with the same degree of excitement as if he'd been invited to Hooters by co-workers to down some suds and watch football. "They're flippin' coming around."

"Further, we acknowledge and apologize for the blatant hypocrisy we have shown, as very few members of the Royal Family abide by Wahhabi law outside of Saudi Arabian borders."

"Sweet mother of God! What's gotten into them?" Carl continued.

But the real bombshell was yet to come.

"Finally, building on our movement away from our Salafi roots, it is our belief that the roles that existed for the sexes should have evolved since the 7th century. We see no reason why women cannot fulfill duties with the same capabilities as men in business, government and religion. In fact, we see no reason why women cannot be religious leaders."

This part was so unbelievable Carl simply didn't react. He couldn't react. Not only would women be able to drive and not be brought up on terrorist charges, they could go out in public dressed however they'd like (though this might take time). *And* have a previously unimaginable influence on the direction of their religion, their politics and their social order.

The 300-year agreement between the House of Saud and the Al ash-Sheikh, the ruling religious family behind the Wahhabi sect of Sunni Islam, and second only to the House of Saud in public image, had been broken. The power of the *ulema*, the caste of religious figureheads and jurists that provided the moral authority critical to the Saudi family's control, had been on the wane in recent decades. The contradiction of extravagant wealth in the hands of the few while publically preaching religious codes stridently antithetical to these pursuits had triggered conflict between these families. This proclamation could very easily trigger a full-fledged civil war.[154]

While there was a government-sponsored personal army (Saudi Arabian National Guard) dedicated to the King, Carl wasn't sure how the internal religious politics of these factions, and the rank and file soldiers, would line up.[155] "Man, whoever made this decision has balls the size of a fucking dromedary on steroids…" Carl observed with a perceptible degree of respect, a rarity for someone who occasionally believed he controlled the world.

---

[154] http://en.wikipedia.org/wiki/Saudi_Arabia
[155] Ibid.

Iran, in an equally surprising declaration, echoed the Saudi assertion that women should be able to function in the highest levels of religion, business and politics. But Iran also took the opportunity to reiterate it would use "all means possible" to defend itself from foreign forces (which many foreign correspondents deciphered as involving a certain grade of uranium).

"After thirteen hundred years, the Sunnis and Shiites may finally be coming together under a female flag," Carl quipped, his initial humor quickly giving way to worry about the potentially serious ramifications of what could happen if Islam, all one billion plus adherents, were able to self-organize, possibly under a single entity. From his point of view, this lack of an Islamic 'Vatican' was a massive part of its problem.

In many Muslim states, there were avowals for more women in governmental positions, of general gender equivalence and, coincidentally, a strident focus on eliminating corruption. This was mind-blowing, coming from Muslim leaders such as Erdogan who formerly held the Islamist view of the role of women as commodities for reproduction.[156] Carl envisioned global demonstrations by Muslim women on the BBC carrying placards reading "Get your ulema out of my uterus."

Responses from the more advanced economies were quick and extremely encouraging. U.K. Prime Minister David Cameron remarked how the world "had just taken some giant leaps toward self-preservation." Japanese Prime Minister Shinzo Abe, drawing on the Japanese experience at the end of WWII, observed "how important acknowledging your nation's faults is to moving forward." German Chancellor Angela Merkel elatedly lauded the changes "I sincerely applaud the recent events that have been sweeping the world. They renew our hope for peace, equality and prosperity for all."

Carl's boss was ecstatic, jumping up and down in the Oval Office with each new announcement. He made a special televised address to the American public and the world announcing America's unequivocal and steadfast support for the courageous leader's "radically necessary" actions, as they were "critical to the world, and its children's futures."

Shalala's schedule was booking up fast.

None of this would have been possible, in Carl's view, if it weren't for the "out of left dimension" turnaround in Moscow. Negotiations with the Chinese had gone nowhere as Putin seemed to be completely locked

---

[156] http://www.theguardian.com/world/2014/nov/24/turkeys-president-recep-tayyip-erdogan-women-not-equal-men

up internally. He had public bouts with his ministers, ignored calls with friends who controlled the natural resources he was selling and, most pointedly, seemed to be at odds with himself. There were times during the negotiation sessions when his already confused countenance took on an extra layer of discord that seemed to emanate not from the details of the discussion, but from a fierce philosophical battle within his own mind. During these mental mêlées, he would abruptly stop speaking, close his eyes and just sit there, appearing almost dumbfounded, as if he'd realized for the first time the severity of Russia's problems and their impacts on its citizenry, not just his ego and monetary worth.

These breaks became more frequent over the course of the week, and Putin took longer to recover from them. After such incidents, it was noted by a deft Chinese female delegate that his positions became even more muddled. What he'd previously (and audaciously) laid down as table-stakes became humble starting points. He displayed flexibility and a willingness to compromise for the first time in his career, shocking both his team and himself. It was as if his mouth was being run by a different master.

Even with these changes, the two sides were still too far apart for the Chinese to believe a deal could be struck, particularly as Putin's negotiating strategy became more and more bizarre as the week had progressed. At 11 a.m. on Friday, in fact, his behavior was in such a state of flux that he somewhat timidly requested a two-hour break "to be able to return with something clear and defined." The two hours stretched to four, and anxiety over whether any deal would be reached at all began to infect the negotiators and international observers alike. One fatigued and jittery international correspondent appropriately described the scene as, "450 degrees Fahrenheit. One more degree of indecision and the agreements will combust."

Actually, a lot more than the agreements would blow up, Carl reflected. At stake was the balance of power in Central Asia, the state of Russia and many, many human lives.

The weight of the world weighed on Putin as he quietly, without his usual hullabaloo, re-entered the negotiating chamber and sat down facing his Chinese partners. What came out of his mouth next, many PhD theses would later assert, incontrovertibly proved he was not only a sociopath, but had a severe multiple personality disorder that expressed itself in periods of extreme stress.

"Thank you so much, my fellow comrades, for your time this past week. After some deep and revealing thought, I have decided on a new course of action that may or may not require your assistance. First, Crimea will be immediately returned to its rightful owner, Ukraine. I will be extending my sincere apologies for my actions to the Crimean and Ukrainian citizens who have been impacted by this intrusion."

"Second, all Russian support for the revolutionaries in the Ukraine will cease, with similar apologies for these senseless acts of belligerence."

"Third, Russia apologizes for shooting down the Malaysian Airlines plane earlier this year. It was an act I sincerely regret. We will be making financial restitution to the families of all those who died in this very unfortunate event."

"Fourth, all Russian military forces will be withdrawn as quickly as possible from the Azerbaijan border and missile activity in the region will stop."

"Fifth, Russia, with its Chinese comrades and U.S. allies, will immediately embark on dramatic drawdowns of nuclear forces."

"Sixth, our military spending will be radically reduced and redirected to improving the state of our education, infrastructure, investments in science and technology, and health care, with special emphasis on treating alcoholism, smoking and AIDS,[157] which are having a more pronounced effect on our population's longevity than whatever kind of war we could find ourselves in. And besides, *why* would anyone attack us?"

"Finally, over the course of the next week, all political prisoners will be released, all Russian media channels that have been shut down may resume operations, the ban on foreign emigration will be lifted and everyone can once again acquire a driver's license."[158]

"WHAT THE FUCK!" Carl blurted, his thick-rimmed black glasses seeming to ski down his nose by the force of his eyes popping out of his head. "What's next? Pussy Riot is going to play at his birthday party? What is going on?"

Putin continued in what normally would be considered a humble tone of voice if it weren't for the fact that no one had ever heard such nuance coming from him before. "We genuinely hope these actions, which are but the first of more announcements I will be making over the next few weeks, will provide satisfactory proof to world governments and the investment community that Russia does not want to be regarded as

---

[157] http://en.wikipedia.org/wiki/Healthcare_in_Russia

[158] http://www.huffingtonpost.com/2015/01/08/russia-drivers-license-transgender_n_6439000.html

an outcast, but as a nation with flaws that we will try our hardest to fix so that it may contribute to the overall growth and peace of all of its peoples and the world. It is my intent that these directives will have a positive impact on our economy by lifting sanctions and allowing foreign capital flows. If these measures do not have the requisite effects, we will gladly continue our current discussions with you. I thank you on behalf of the people of Russia for your focused and prolonged efforts this week."

The interpreter for China who, like the entire team, had started sputtering with astonishment at point two, finished translating to a Chinese delegation that was frozen in utter disbelief. Even Qin was shocked. TM7's plan was unfolding right in front of her eyes in a way the historical system of power-hungry hegemonies had never imagined: *the way of the female.* As the scope of Putin's transformation started to sink in, Russian team members, especially those who'd been involved in its first modern break from totalitarianism, started to clap. Out of the bluest and hottest part of a flame, the phoenix of perestroika and glasnost had returned. The clapping rapidly hit a crescendo and then the room just as quickly fell silent as everyone waited for the Chinese response.

It was at this moment that the final bud started to bloom. The lead Chinese negotiator, finishing a hushed conversation that had started sometime during Putin's seven-point plan, slowly stood and, while trying to speak with the classic Oriental unemotional composure, erratically read a statement. Perhaps he couldn't read it smoothly because his hands were shaking so much.

"My fellow Comrades, I bring you a statement from our President. After much reflection and given the current global situation, we have decided that entering into the proposed financial transactions is not in Russia's or potentially even China's long-term best interests. In order to achieve regional and international harmony, Russia must be able to support itself. Entering into the kind of agreements we have been discussing would not only weaken its economic prospects but even worse, weaken the will of its people."

"Not to mention that they might provoke a revolution in a country with the most nuclear weapons on the planet," Carl reflected.

At this point the delegate stopped reading, looked up and continued, this time with a smile. "President Xi is extremely encouraged by your change in direction and he informs me that, should your new course not yield the scale of financial response you require, we will make short-term support available. Lastly, President Xi is contemplating other related initiatives he would like to discuss with you in the very near future."

At this news, the Russian delegation stood and uproariously put their hands together. Not only had an island of refuge magically appeared in the midst of an unbeatable storm, but they would keep their boat and have access to a safe harbor. Some shed tears and hugged each other. Qin worried they might do something like jump over the tables separating them and embrace their fellow humans. But she knew both sides were far too manly for that to happen.

Subsequent announcements from the two countries solidified Carl's suspicions that *something* behind the scenes was afoot.

China and Russia pledged to dramatically reduce carbon emissions in a special Sino-Russian deal that exceeded targets agreed upon by China and the U.S. They committed to wiping out "the senseless destruction of animals," by imposing mandatory life sentences on anyone caught smuggling parts of endangered species, and agreed to push PR campaigns conveying facts such as consuming a tiger's penis did not make men better in bed.[159]

Upon reviewing video clips of Putin and Xi's speeches, and extending the analysis to the other countries who'd made similar "radically progressive" statements, Carl noticed a previously unseen commonality of their presentation styles: a heartfelt passion being expressed for their newfound positions. While most leaders knew how to get a crowd riled up, this was different. These leaders seemed to be connecting with their audiences at a deeper, more empathic level. Human to human versus rehearsed puppet to audience. Carl sensed there was a real and inexplicable shift at play, at least on the surface. Given his nature, he was determined to find out what was happening under the skins of these former dictators.

What was even more troubling to Carl was that significant portions of these regimes' populaces, women included, were either not ready for these changes or were dead set against them. Deadly set in some cases, especially in the case of Iran and Saudi Arabia and their new stances on Islam. By his reckoning, internal conflicts could easily invite intrusions by players who might have a flag but lack a currency. All it would take is a few fundamentalist fuckheads to come in, do their thing, and ruin the whole ride.

---

[159] http://en.wikipedia.org/wiki/Tiger_penis_soup

He also noted how the timing of these repositions was both risky and pure genius; if everybody dropped the tug-of-war rope, or in this case decided not to play Army any more, at the same time (and meant it and could survive the internal dissent), the only thing you'd be defending your country from, other than the occasional terrorist (whose *raison d'être* may also be impacted), are migrating birds. The concurrent reduction in militarism could seriously dent global military spending, led by the U.S., whose budget was larger than the next eight countries (China, Russia, Saudi Arabia, Germany, Japan, India, France and the U.K.) combined.[160] As Putin and Nieto so aptly put it, "Who would attack us?"

What was happening? There had to be a pattern here. One was that each leader in question was at the recent G20 Summit in Tokyo. Carl quickly transcribed the list of attendees on a large whiteboard adjacent to his desk. He noted, after reviewing the list a half dozen times, that none of the women on the list had come forth with major announcements. Instinctively he knew there had to be a whole lot more at play than what was merely meeting his eyes. He just had no idea what it could be. And not knowing was a big cause, perhaps the greatest cause, for fear.

"Lucy, I'd like to review all the video we can get of each prime minister and president who was at the G20. I gotta' sense something fucking big is happening and we'd damn well better understand what the hell is going on. We could be next."

---

[160] http://pgpf.org/Chart-Archive/0053_defense-comparison

# 28

## Hurricane Thelma

### Winter Storm Louise

From the Weather.com Website

**NEWS FLASH: BRACE YOURSELVES FOR THE STORM OF THE MILLENNIUM!**

November 18, 2015 3:34 p.m.

In a bizarre confluence of events, the nation is facing what climatologists have termed as "Snowpocalypse." While the main push behind this "storm to end all storms" are the contrasting warm and cold fronts typical of Nor'easters (the greater the difference in temperatures, the more violent the storm becomes), this particular weather anomaly has previously unseen qualities.

First, we have a massive Winter Storm Louise coming off the Pacific, much like the "Snowmaggedon" storm of 2010, which was a Category 3 (major) event. That storm dumped as much as 2 feet of snow over most of the country and was accompanied by very high winds. Deaths were reported from Baja California to Maine.[161] Louise is already tearing up parts of the West Coast, and giving them much needed rainfall, as it makes its way directly east at a very rapid clip. No slowing this one down.

Second, the nation is facing an unprecedented and unseasonably expansive cold snap. All states (save Hawaii) will experience sub-freezing temperatures over the course of the next week due to an Arctic thrust of freezing air blasting down from Canada. This intrusion, known as a "polar vortex," is a recurring theme in North American, European and Asian weather patterns and, until recently, has not been a large concern. Over the past few winters however, these dips of Arctic temperatures have become more pronounced with greater geographical spread. This is the first time the polar vortex has reached so far south, touching every continental state. Record low temperatures are being set across the board with some locales registering levels 40 degrees below normal, before wind-chill. Many deaths are expected due to this extreme cold.

The last component of Snowpocalypse is Hurricane Thelma, which started off the west coast of Africa as a mere tropical storm. However, much like Hurricane Katrina, once it hit the unusually warm waters of the Gulf of Mexico, it picked up immense speed and power and has adjusted from a Class 2 to Class 5 hurricane in just 8 hours. This is the greatest accelerating hurricane on record, with winds exceeding 180 mph. It will probably be amongst the top five most intensive Atlantic hurricanes ever, of which three of those—Katrina, Wilma and Rita—all occurred in 2005.[162] Satellites tracking the storm predict it will hit land at approximately 10:30 this evening, somewhere between Galveston and Port Arthur, Texas.

What we really don't understand is what will happen when Louise and Thelma collide. Both are arriving with very warm tropical air behind them which will boost the intensity of the storm once it hits the extremely cold air of the polar vortex. Our computer models just don't know what to make of this trifecta in terms of overall effects and directions once they have met. Some predictions are calling for as much as 4 feet of snow in Texas, Oklahoma, Louisiana and Arkansas. There is a possibility that Thelma, whose power should decrease slightly once she hits land, could join or "bounce" off Louise and head east, potentially magnifying the power.

The majority of the country is on full alert and states of emergency have been declared in almost every state within projected paths. The President is expected to declare a national state of emergency in the next few hours. Some

---

[161] Search "Snowmaggedon, 2010"

[162] http://en.wikipedia.org/wiki/Hurricane_Katrina

states are considering curfews. There are reported runs on food, batteries, boats, warm clothing, ammunition, and water along the Texas/Louisiana coast as memories of Hurricane Katrina are still vividly in people's minds. The National Guard is on alert and the Army Corps of Engineers has been called to Houston in case of bridge, canal and levee failures.

Steven Binn, chief meteorologist of NOAA, has stated "The polar vortex was a major cause for concern by itself. Many people, particularly in the South, aren't used to dealing with that kind of cold. But when you throw in Storm Louise and Hurricane Thelma, this could be a formula for disaster on a massive scale. I do find it ironic that the two disturbances are named Thelma and Louise, like the movie duo. I suppose, picking up on the feminist theme, Mother Nature is going to kick us where it hurts."

## Snowpocalypse Subsides, Leaving Death and Destruction in its Wake

CNN.com: November 21, 2014  11:02 a.m.

At last, the main brunt of Snowpocalypse is over, though "obscenely" frigid temperatures will persist for most parts of the country throughout the weekend. In its wake, an estimated 16,000 people have died, mainly due to exposure and lack of heat as power was lost in approximately 50% of the country, stretching from Texas and the Great Plains states to the Mid-Atlantic and down to Florida. The southern states were particularly hard hit since they've had no reason to prepare for this kind of scenario in the past. Many of these geographies are still without power and predictions as to when rural populations in particular will get electricity back are presently unknown.

To recap, Winter Storm Louise didn't let up at all, her winds staying constant at around 100 to 125 mph as she marched inland from the Pacific Coast in an eastward direction, dumping massive quantities of rain and mostly snow along the way. She then hooked up with Hurricane Louise, who had trotted across the Gulf, turned north at the Texan coast and then, due to the high pressure polar vortex and Louise's staying power, turned east and boomeranged back toward the Atlantic. Essentially, the two storms became one massive front, Louise on top, Thelma on the bottom, pulverizing everything in their path.

Jackson, Mississippi; Montgomery, Alabama; Atlanta, Georgia and Charleston, South Carolina all recorded over three feet of snow. All major highways and rail lines in those geographies are impassable. Many will remain closed until temperatures rise due to a pronounced dearth of snowplows. Damage estimates, which are still very preliminary, are placing the cost of this natural disaster at upwards of $61 billion.

The President has been working tirelessly with FEMA, the Pentagon and Governors to triage the issues as quickly as possible. He has issued an executive order releasing $5 billion of federal aid to assist those families in dire need of help. "This is a tragedy of immense proportions," he said, fighting back tears. "We just aren't prepared for an event of this magnitude."

Blame for what caused Snowpocalypse has begun, with conservative senators, including the Senator from Oklahoma who is Chairman of the Environment and Public Works Committee, issuing a statement "global warming, if it exists, is of actual benefit to mankind and, per the Bible (Genesis 8:22), 'as long as the earth remains there will be seed time and harvest, cold and heat, winter and summer, day and night.' God's still up there. The arrogance to think that we, human beings, would be able to change his creation is outrageous."[163] He also observed that Snowpocalypse was a cold event, which would refute the "global warming" thesis.

These themes were also magnified by personalities such as Rush Limbaugh, who observed how Snowpocalypse neatly avoided all the blue states, and was somehow contrived by liberal politicians and scientists to "promote the absurd hypocrisy of climate change while trying to literally kill red-blooded tax paying citizens who vote their conscience."

Refrains from Katrina have also appeared, with Pat Robertson leading the charge claiming the event was God's will because He is angry that Supreme Court Justice Roberts upheld the Affordable Care Act.[164] Dick Perry, a prime presidential hopeful and former Governor of Texas echoed these sentiments, "Once again, natural forces have come together to support the scientifically disproven theory of climate change for if God had intended for there to be snow in Texas, he would have made cowshit white."

Coincidentally, the most comprehensive and analytical study ever undertaken was recently released by a team of Korean and American scientists linking arctic melting due to climate disruption to the weakening polar vortex. Using sophisticated computer modeling and statistical analysis, the team has assembled a thorough explanation for the pronounced cold snaps which have been occurring with increasing frequency around the world.[165]

---

[163] Senator Inhofe: http://www.newrepublic.com/article/120134/climate-change-denier-james-inhofe-lead-environment-committee

[164] http://mediamatters.org/research/2005/09/13/religious-conservatives-claim-katrina-was-gods/133804

[165] http://www.slate.com/blogs/future_tense/2014/09/03/new_study_links_polar_vortex_to_climate_change.html

# 29

## Introducing Sarah Bachman,[166] Your Next Vice President

Politico.com, Politico Magazine, December, 2015

**Does the North Dakota House Rep have what it takes to compete with the big boys?**

For those of us who've followed Sarah Bachman's meteoric rise, from mayor of Casselton, a small township (population 2,491) roughly 25 miles west of Fargo, to her current position representing North Dakota's State At-Large Congressional District in the U.S. House of Representatives and a potential Vice Presidential candidate next year, one theme runs through most of her media's coverage: she is conservative and built to stay that way.

Born in Fargo to an auto and snowmobile mechanic, she attended North Dakota State University, also in Fargo, where she studied Communications and Journalism. Raised with evangelical Christian morals, she realized she

---

[166] http://en.wikipedia.org/wiki/Michele_Bachmann; http://en.wikipedia.org/wiki/Sarah_Palin

was a Republican when "I was made aware of the fact our Founding Fathers had secretly wanted to establish a Christian theocracy, a fact which the liberal media has completely distorted."

She eloped with her high-school sweetheart, Todd Bachman. They "took the major leap" and moved to Casselton where they opened and managed a Christian counseling service, which specialized in homosexual conversion therapy "with a 100% success rate," per their website. *(Editor's note: while their business received over $200,000 in federal and state support from 2008 to 2012, according to an interview with Bachman these funds were used for education purposes; she still eschews "any and all government spending that is not defense-related.")*

After becoming Mayor of Casselton in 2010, she "quickly observed the vast corruption and profligate waste in government." To combat this, she replaced the City Council, reduced budgets and closed all governmental services she deemed non-essential including the library, local museum and community center. She fired the police chief because he had issues with her managerial style. Bachman subsequently ordered all city employees to speak with her first before making any public comments "to make sure we are on the same page." She also pressured all city employees with amity for her predecessor to resign.

To reduce property taxes, she pushed through local sales tax and bond issuances for street and water improvements and a $15 million sports complex. Casselton's long-term debt grew from $1 million to $25 million, which was justified by a City Council member as due to the 25%population growth (600 people) during Bachman's tenure. Bachman was also able to earmark federal funds for sewer repairs and a transportation hub.

It was during these bond issuances that Bachman became aware of the North Dakota Oil and Gas Conservation Commission, whose charter was overseeing the safety and efficiency of this sector, which was starting to expand dramatically due to fracking. She was appointed a member, and it was through this organization that Bachman was introduced to donors with "super PAC" funds. When the former House Rep announced his retirement in 2014, Bachman, with her newfound backing, made a successful run for the House in 2014, outspending her opponent 15 to 1.

Bachman's policy positions run the conservative party line. She is a staunch proponent of trickle-down economics "so long as the money trickles up first." She has proposed legislation banning same-sex marriage, has voted against the College Cost Reduction and Access Act, and is fervently anti-abortion in all cases. In addition, she has referred to climate disruption as "voodoo science," observing that $CO_2$ is a naturally occurring substance and thus cannot be harmful. Finally, she's said she would have voted *against* any government bailouts during the financial and automotive crises.

Bachman has called for media exposés of the President and members of Congress to "let the American people know who is for America and who is against it," has refused to answer census questions because they "aren't Constitutional" (*Ed. note: they are*), is diametrically opposed to healthcare reforms, has called for the elimination of a federal minimum wage, has called for the phasing out of social security and Medicare, has characterized federal policies as "overseeing a centralized and state-controlled economy" and famously threatened to "disembowel" the Environmental Protection Agency while touring a Monsanto Round Up production plant.[167]

Foreign policy is an admitted weakness for Bachman. While not owning a passport prior to her election to the House ("we'd just sneak across the border to Canada to get some of those Molson Bradors...I'll show you some spots"), Sarah has made some interesting observations about international affairs, including the fact that you can see a foreign country from her state, India and Indiana are not related and, should France disagree with American decisions, Americans do not need to ban French Fries, necessarily. She also expressed virulent opposition to the U.S. becoming part of the international global economy..."I don't want," she said, "to see our children's futures tied to financial decisions being made in Kenya or Tanzania. I will have no part of it."

Some analysts have noted an uncanny similarity between the positions of Dick Perry of Texas, a strong presidential contender and Bachman, to the point that they have been dubbed the "Carbon Couple." The designation is one they both downplay, though on matters of immigration Bachman has proudly quipped, "So long as Perry is defending the Southern border, I've got the North covered."

---

[167] http://articles.mercola.com/sites/articles/archive/2013/06/09/monsanto-roundup-herbi-cide.aspx; http://web.mit.edu/demoscience/Monsanto/index.html

# 30

## Dancing Suns

Fortune smiled on Qin. Perhaps things were going her way because she'd performed superlatively at the G20 Summit and Moscow negotiations. Or perhaps it was simply luck. Regardless, she found herself being selected to visit the Sundance Film Festival in Park City, Utah as the official representative of the Chinese government. She was chosen because of her "deep knowledge of American cinema history and trends," per the official letter she received and had shared with TM7. "For once, being scrutinized pays off!" she happily reported. The Chinese market was huge and growing, and China wanted to establish itself as an equal, if not superior force in the global movie market. India's dramatic success with Bollywood, and the fact the U.S. was blatantly ripping off Korean productions, only fueled this fire. "Fantastic!" Heidi responded to Qin's group text informing TM7 of her availability. "Finally, in honor of our name, we can all wear cowboy hats and fit in."

Heidi was a veteran Sundance attendee and had actually funded several productions that had been selected for judging. Aside from being able to sometimes hang out with "handsome at any age" Robert Redford, Heidi felt a very strong connection with the vision of the institute that ran the festival—it was all about impacting empathy, understanding and social change through pushing boundaries and delighting audiences with powerful stories.[168] Aside from the written word, Heidi knew of no better way than film to enable scaled shifts in mindset, and thus, culture. Upon hearing Qin's news, Heidi immediately rented an on-slope chalet in Deer Valley, the ritzy sister resort to Park City, and made travel arrangements for Lexie and Divine. It had been decided, now that the "cells were out of the tube," that to avoid any undue suspicion, the more well-known members of the group should travel independent of Heidi's jets.

It was an easy thing to explain to the world. Shalala, whose global popularity and recognition kept surging in the wake of the education platform she had signed with Modi and Widodo, known simply as "Her Contract," pushed out her planned attendance through her channels. Requests for meetings with executives to discuss projects came pouring back. Elena used a similar strategy, though she only had two requests for meetings with people who ranked low on a Google search. "If only I had been shot in the head doing my thing," she noted satirically in a group message. Sundance was also a natural fit for Gilat who was very interested to see a particular screening called "The Only Way" that recounted the real story of a former member of Al Qaeda transitioning to atheism and peaceful existence.

Lexie and Divine quickly RSVP'd, Divine noting how much she'd like to try skiing. Lexie offered to show her some ropes, proudly noting her only ski accident had happened coincidentally at Park City when she was a child and a tree moved in front of her, knocking her out. "The worst part of the whole experience was being strapped up in a toboggan and having to breath in the exhaust from the snowmobile on the way down," she cheekily reported. Divine, predictably undeterred, replied, "Well, so long as we both have helmets on and we don't go too fast, I'd love to play dodge-tree with you."

Sundance was scheduled from January 22 to February 1. The women couldn't wait to regroup, particularly with Qin and Shalala, though Qin warned she would likely be tailed. "No worries," Heidi said. "I have an idea. We have a lot to discuss."

---

[168] http://www.sundance.org/about/us

. . .

The world had not only returned from a brink, it seemed to be heading in some very promising directions. Russia carried through on its promises. Its sanctions ended, the ruble rebounded, inflation subsided, its interest rates returned to pre-crisis levels and its natural resources were still owned by Russians. More global progress on climate disruption ensued, discussions on reducing global nuclear stockpiles began and the topic of the power of female leadership was taking center stage in the global media. NPO, NGO and academic budgets started to focus on Northern European countries where women had some of the highest percentages of top jobs in the world, and coincidentally some of the highest, and happiest, standards of living. The U.N. actually started functioning as originally intended.

The Pope, who'd been creating some remarkable evolutions in his own right, leveraged the Saudi's announcement and declared that he saw no reason why God, though created in Man's image, would bar women from taking on equal positions in the church and society at large. "Their roles in society notwithstanding, women are what bring, raise, nurture and defend life. Why shouldn't they be involved in contributing to and running the governmental and religious systems that have been constructed purportedly with the same purposes?" He had apparently wanted to make this change since the commencement of his Papacy, and had been building up to it.

The United States reassured the world it unequivocally supported these polemic-shaking events as they were completely in line with the President's agenda on virtually all counts. Specifically, they afforded a great opportunity to further reduce military expenditures, including mothballing as many nuclear weapons as possible, one of his largest desired legacies.

Predictably, especially given the scale of the changes, the residue of the past was still clinging quite closely to the present. "Like tighty-whiteys on testicles," Heidi merrily said. And in some quarters men were both overtly and covertly fighting back. Global reports of political-military infighting, oftentimes with blatantly religious tenors, started making the rounds.

Pakistan was of considerable concern in this context, being blind-sided by both India's overtures for peace and by the Saudi's decree, which would have major social and economic implications particularly in the fragile, somewhat lawless, countryside. The divide widened between the conservative religious lobby, which had a degree of military and political support and were anti-everything, and the more moderate progressive groups. 24/7 protection of the latter was initiated to prevent another assassination of a Prime Minister.[169]

Things in Saudi Arabia were much, much worse, as the schism between the ruling family, the factions inside it and their once-religious backers devolved into full-scale conflict. Wahhabi clerics embarked on Congressional filibuster-length rants, imploring their adherents to denounce the Royal Family and to pick up arms against them. Outbursts of violence were reported in all major cities, demonstrations erupted around the world and the Royal Family went into a state of secured hiding around the globe. A few attempted suicide killings, via bombs sewn into flesh, were thwarted by an amazing technology that had just come to market. Fortunately, the military stood strong behind the Royals, in large part because its command structure had been inextricably bound, by bloodlines, to the King.

Heidi had foreseen these divisions, though her experience of feminine consensus building gave her a degree of confidence. She knew whatever coups might be building would be quickly quelled—hopefully without bloodshed. Though this dynamic would probably not hold up in places where people regularly killed themselves for a belief and an unproven promise they could not realize in this life.[170] What she had not expected, which eventually turned the tide in many such locales, was the outpouring of emotion, support and steadfastness of the women within the Saudi's geographical diktat. Mosques that had been male-only for 1,500 years were surrounded by throngs of women of all ages chanting two cries that quickly went viral, "Kill us, no kids" and "Would you kill your mother?"

Not surprisingly, *fatwas* started flying around the Muslim world faster than women started removed their veils and learning to drive. Their sheer numbers were too much for anyone to keep track of. While Catholics had the Pope for global guidance, Mormons had a President-Prophet, Jehovah's Witnesses were led by their Governing Body, and Born Again Christians looked up to Ted Haggard, there was no central authority for

---

[169]  http://en.wikipedia.org/wiki/Assassination_of_Benazir_Bhutto

[170]  http://www.islamhelpline.net/node/6495

interpretation and direction of the Muslim religion.

Membership spiked in fundamentalist groups of all sorts around the world—from right-wing radicals, Evangelicals, and white supremacist groups in Europe (including Russia) and America, to Salafi-inspired groups worldwide, with a particular reference to ISIS, whose ranks swelled by an estimated 40,000 in a matter of weeks. It was terribly sad, Heidi mused, how people's fears of the unknown could express themselves in such blind and hateful ways. Religion was more than an opiate of the masses; it was a convenient, flimsy and fear-driven excuse to avoid reality.

Within the U.S., the same split emerged between moderate progressives and conservatives that had formed abroad. Those who were more open to change were exuberant over the quantum leap in policy that seemingly appeared from a different dimension right in the nick of time. Those stuck in past ruts were terrified, as their read of events pin-balled between conspiracies of cunning collusion ("Russia and China have obviously joined forces and have embarked on this *lie* to lower the West's defenses so they can finally destroy their ideological enemies") to seditions of faith ("We are undeniably approaching the final pages of Revelations. Only tithing and voting as Lord Jesus commands will forestall this inevitability.").

Much more disturbing than this rhetoric, however, were murmurs Heidi gleaned from her funding network. The oil men, whose net worths had been decimated by the drop in barrel prices, would spend anything to make sure the next U.S. President was as conservative as possible. "Someone who sees the world from our eyes," was how they put it. These men had no qualms about leveraging the current global uncertainty to "control" the territories needed to buttress America's influence of the supply, and hence price, of oil. Dick Perry was a commonly suggested candidate. "He has the pedigree and is clueless enough to be played and not even know it," one oil man said.

. . .

"Greetings Ladies! Welcome to Utah!" Heidi hollered, trying to one-up the streams of exuberant chatter bouncing off the rustic pine planks in her mountainside chalet. One by one the women had trickled in. Qin and Heidi had switched outfits, boots included, in the women's room of the Deer Valley main lodge to throw off whatever tails might have their eyes on Qin. Under helmet, goggles and face warmer, it was impossible to tell who was who.

"It is *so* great to have you ALL back, and safe, in one place again. We did it!" she said, raising a glass to all present. Her infectious optimism, already rock solid given her professional successes, had taken on a new manifestation; its fire had burned through whatever layers of doubt or fears might have constrained her plan. Behind her on a huge plasma TV, were rotating headlines exalting the "unbelievable" events sweeping the world. Sweeping, Heidi would often reflect with a grin when she saw this term used in the media, was, coincidentally, typically the woman's job.

"And Shalala, it would seem you made the right decision," Heidi said, motioning to some reverberations in India and Indonesia on the screen. Shalala's visage beamed brighter than the sun's dancing reflections off the snow outside the chalet.

"I'm sure you've all been keeping up with current events," Heidi continued, with a slightly facetious tone as if a spouse (or father) might demand they do for social purposes. Laughter followed. "Your efforts are having some pretty amazing impacts, I'd say." She made a motion and the screen changed to the home page of *The Bulletin of the Atomic Scientists*, a group started 70 years ago with the development of the nuclear bomb and had expanded to include climate disruption in its predictive calculations, using a timepiece as its tracker and midnight as the witching hour.[171] "The Doomsday clock has been set back 3 minutes!"[172] There was cheering and hugs all around.

"This said," Heidi continued with an air of seriousness, "we aren't out of the woods yet. Saudi's position on bringing Islamic fundamentalism into this century, I mean millennium, was a complete surprise. I didn't see that coming. Nobody," she said with another wave and relevant articles filling the screen, "can predict where the door that has been opened with this announcement will lead. There's a good possibility it could provoke a full-on civil war in Saudi Arabia, which would undoubtedly draw the U.S. and perhaps China into the fray. There's just too much oil and global investment hanging in the balance, not to mention the peninsula's geopolitical position." She hesitated ever so slightly, and then, to underscore the seriousness of the situation, shared, "Yesterday, Divine made the decision to temporarily shut down Doha operations."

---

[171] http://thebulletin.org/

[172] http://thebulletin.org/three-minutes-and-counting7938

Qin reiterated. "Heidi, what you say is spot on. There've been meetings in Beijing recently with our stance toward Saudi Arabia being the top priority. There's a lot of talk of potential coups, and perhaps even a small-scale nuclear strike on the Royal Family by a rogue force." Qin shared this intelligence with her usual voice of objective resolve, though a slight change in tenor implied there was something else she wasn't comfortable revealing. "There are also the links to Pakistan which are worrisome in this context."

"Yes, my country is in a state of chaos," Shalala reinforced, her face reverting back to serious without emotion. "Without Saudi support, who knows what might happen? There will be many, many men with fundamental beliefs without income, which is always an unsettling proposition. Combine this with allowing women into the religious ranks, an uneasy alliance between the military and government, and Pakistan's nuclear weapons, and we have a religious powder keg."

"Agreed," Heidi echoed. "Pakistan is a top concern. I wish they'd been at the G20, though having Iran there was a big help. We may need to deal with that situation, and quickly…We can discuss more Middle East in a bit though I'd like to make you all aware of what could be the most important and tenuous key to helping us realize our purpose: the upcoming U.S. election."

Heads nodded.

"As I'm sure you've noticed, our actions have sent reverberations of various sorts—religious, political, economic, military and possibly even moral—around the world. Many individuals want to see arms put back in place, and they'll fight hard to try and maintain their state of control. We've noticed this around the world, even in countries where women have contributed to the betterment of the society," she said, giving Gilat a knowing glance. The rise of the Haredim in Israel had not slipped by Heidi's radar.[173]

Heidi continued, "There is no other more forceful pendulum in the world, given its economic, financial and armed might, than the U.S. The internal pushback here is reaching a fevered pitch. The Republican majority in Congress is trying their best to derail the current President's foreign policy and domestic efforts, the recent attempt to cause the Iranian nuclear arms deal to collapse being a great example."[174]

---

[173] http://www.newyorker.com/news/news-desk/jerusalem-haredim-women-equality

[174] http://www.huffingtonpost.com/james-zogby/boehnernetanyahu-so-smart-theyre-stupid_b_6536964.html

She continued with the strident confidence of the power of a few concerned citizens, "In fact, right now, two states over in Palm Springs, California, a group of very powerful and rich conservatives are meeting to decide who they want to back as the Republican candidate for president. Operating under the auspices of the non-profit Freedom Partners Chamber of Commerce headed up by the Koch brothers, these "kingmakers" donated almost $300 million in the last mid-term elections.[175] And, my sources tell me, they're ready to direct over $1 billion to this presidential election.[176] All it takes is a 5% lean by the voting public, and come the end of this year, the U.S. could either support, drive and build on the remarkable changes happening around the world with our favored candidate," she said with a wink, "or we could find ourselves in isolationist, 'we-have-the-weapons-so-yield-to-us' mode again. And not to the mention the tremendous impact the next President will have on the U.S. Supreme Court."

"The paradigm we've built only works if ALL the big guns decide to put them away at the same time. My gut tells me, given the degree of the spurious babble spin on FOX news, there's enough fear and ignorance out there in America that the religious right has a verifiable chance of being able to charade their ignorance. We cannot let this happen. We are *so* close to tipping the gorillas!"

"What can we do?" Elena asked, standing suddenly, with a glint in her eye that she would give life and limb for the cause.

"We could dose their candidate," Gilat suggested, as if it was something she liked to do between blog postings.

"Yes, that is a possibility, though I have perhaps an even better idea than that," Heidi responded.

"What if—"

...

The woman trailing Qin was frantic. She had lost Qin amid the swarm of stylish parkas and ski pants in the Deer Valley Resort Center. She knew where Qin was staying. However, a listening device planted above Qin's door had picked up nothing but the maid service the entire afternoon. She thought she had sighted her mark, but it turned out to be an older

Caucasian woman in a very similar outfit. She took a picture of the woman anyway. Why, she wasn't completely sure. All she could do now was wait. She uploaded the picture file to her laptop.

# 31

## Lies, Lies, Statistics and Lies

*This is Dick Perry's Presidential Republican Candidate Acceptance Speech, which he delivered at the Republican National Convention in Indianapolis, Indiana on July 16, 2016.*

"My Fellow Patriots,
First, I'd like to thank our hosts, the great people of Indiana, for their Christian hospitality in welcoming the Republican National Convention to their capital city. I sure feel at home being able to see 'In God We Trust' on license plates!

<pause for applause>

Tonight will be remembered as a turning point of change for America's future, and the future of the world. Domestically, we face problems of unspeakable gravity. Immigrants, I mean rapists, thieves, drug-dealers and terrorists, are streaming across our border. The Affordable Care Act is a joke. Unemployment is at all-time highs. Reductions in military spending are putting our country in the most serious risk **ever** of attack and invasion. Federal education standards are calling for absurd notions such as evolution and climate change to be taught in our schools, to **your** children. I ask you, would God really allow this concept of global warming to happen to us?

<pause for applause>

Marriage outside of what the Bible sanctions—between men and women—is happening across our land and these people's rights are prevailing over those bestowed by our Creator. There are concerted efforts to raise the minimum wage and to give women the right to make the decision to murder their unborn children. Extraordinary efforts are being made to prevent our police officers from doing their jobs and to limit campaign financing by corporations. And finally, I believe we all share a profound derision to see our Second Amendment rights taken away!

<pause for applause>

Each of these topics is at a critical point of no return, a point that will require tenacity, proven leadership and someone who knows how to get things done, to roll back the last eight years of a Muslim's attempt to force Socialist ideology onto every facet, from education to spending, of our great nation.

<pause for applause>

Eradicating these intrusions that have consistently failed the American people will be difficult and could possibly be like rolling a big, I mean large (can't forget what's in my state's textbooks now can, I? —chuckle) ball of stone up a mountain only to see it roll down again. But we must try.

<pause for applause>

Internationally, we face similar dilemmas. Russia and China are growling on our doorstep via their partner-in-ideology, Cuba, whose influence must be contained at all costs. The axis of badness—North Korea, Iran and Syria—is still with us, and grows radically more powerful and deadly by the day. And the fall of the global price of oil, while nice at the pump, will spell long-term demise for our economy, our society and your family's standard of living.

Fixing these problems will also be a superhuman task. But we must try and, with your support, I know we will prevail.

<pause for applause>

Which is why I, Dick Perry, do hereby solemnly accept the honor, responsibilities and God-given rights of the Republican candidate for the position of President of these United States of America. I pledge to all those listening, from Ed the Electrician in Wisconsin, to the law-abiding police force of Ferguson, Missouri, to my Christian brothers and sisters around the globe, to the thousand points of light, to the Prime Ministers of China, India and Russia, to the leaders of every terrorist organization on the planet, the age of America isn't passing, it is just beginning. You hear me? The age of America isn't passing... it is just beginning!

<pause for applause>

Now, I understand what I'm going to do now may be a bit unorthodox, but the term 'unorthodox' describes, to a T, the person I'd like to introduce to you all right now. Throughout her entire life, this woman has bucked convention, taken on the established powers that be, and frankly kicked the hell out of them them until they relented. Since coming into power, her state has recorded the highest percent job growth of any state in the union... even beating out Texas. It is for these reasons I want to nominate, right here and now, Ms. Sarah Bachman as my official Vice Presidential candidate. Sarah, come on out and say "Hi" to the American people. Folks, the next Vice President of the United States of America...

<pause for applause, shake hands and hug Sarah, let her say Hi, but DON'T let her push you away from the podium—she will probably try to—and DON'T let her speak!!>

Ok. Thank you Sarah.

My fellow Americans, in closing, when this November 8 arrives, I ask you all, to ask yourself, "Do I want to see four more years of wasteful and inefficient government spending of my hard-earned tax dollars allocated to useless programs like the Environmental Protection Agency, the Internal Revenue Service, the Food and Drug Administration, and the Department of Energy? Do I want my Christian values, on which our great nation was founded, to be even further corroded by the insidious blasphemy of the liberal machine? Do I want America to fulfill its biblical destiny, ensuring a safe and prosperous future for my children? The choice is yours to make.

<pause for applause>

We look forward to the campaign and we look forward to November 8th! WHITE HOUSE HERE WE COME! YEEHAW! God bless my fellow patriots and God bless the United States of America. Good "night."

# 32

## Catch Us If You Can

Carl hadn't been able to get more than a few hours of sleep per night for weeks, and his face showed it. The eye bags, filled by decades of late nights in different time zones, were getting notably droopier, and his stubble had increased significantly. He managed only a weekly shave, if he could muster it, on Sunday.

The world was figuratively exploding around him in ways he'd never foreseen. The very premises on which the U.S., and thus the world's foreign policy, had operated for the last 60 years had been dismembered in a relative blink of an eye. The new world order was of utmost concern and distress to him. This was uncharted terrain, a landscape now seemingly based on trust, cooperation, domestic priorities and improving the planet, versus power, geopolitical positioning, and profits. He was having a very difficult time wrapping his head around these transformations, as they simply made no sense, at least from his perspective and hardened, historical experience. How could anyone have enough trust to assume that another country wouldn't attack? How could these countries slash their defense spending by 80%?

His staff at Langley and his network of foreign "correspondents" had been working similarly long hours. Their main directive was to monitor the inner-workings of their respective region's political, military and oppositional structures to avert potential blowback not advantageous to U.S. interests. The Middle East bureau had been particularly stressed, as it seemed every potential terrorist group was surfacing in response to the Saudis' cathartic proclamation. He'd been able to inform bin Nayef of one such attack (Carl was keen to know who manufactured the bomb detection units that foiled two other attempts). Of course, the swelling of the ISIS ranks, having settled their ideological issues with Al Qaeda and leveraged their networks, was of critical import as they were the most obvious threat to U.S. objectives in that area. Every byte of information going in/out/or through that region was scrutinized for intel.

He wasn't alone. Across the world intelligence units were on full alert, from MI-6 to Mossad to the FSS. No one seemed to know how to deal with this new world order. To Carl, the global level of uncertainty had swollen dramatically. And uncertainty meant vulnerability on a dramatic scale. He was briefing the Oval Office and Joint Chiefs on a daily basis.

Yet for all his caution and "what ifs?" nothing *actually* seemed to be falling apart. The system was holding together. Leaders with newfound resolve were valiantly attempting to subsume the theory that nations are solitary actors duking things out. Suddenly, powerful nations were working as a model of collectives, bound together with common purposes for peaceful versus pugilistic intentions.

What caused this change? Why now? Was there a conspiracy of some sort, of which he, and other intelligence chiefs were unaware? He had pressed his networks to unearth anything that might be of use. He'd also tasked some of his best people with piecing together what, on the surface, seemed to be random yet coincidentally timed earthquakes in the plates of international relations.

He and his aides and lieutenants had spent countless hours reviewing the tapes from the G20 meeting, looking for any patterns in leaders' faces or body postures that might reveal a shadow connection, a backroom agreement that had evaded scrutiny by domestic congresses and global media. Aside from picking up a potential sexual attraction by Putin for Nieto ("figure he likes the Latin swagger," a deputy quipped), they found nothing. This was a dead end.

It was a happenstance glance at a picture one of his female staffers had printed out and tacked to her cubical wall that set his inquiry in motion. It was of a Chinese negotiator spraying the calmed Russian President's face with something looking like a breath freshener after the first negotiation session in Tokyo. The caption read, "China mists Russia." Maybe it was because Carl knew how utterly destroyed Russia *should* have been at that moment. But here was its leader looking like he'd just come out of an Ayurvedic spa (whatever the hell that was). Or maybe because it was the last thing in the world he would have expected a modern-day, command-and-control dictator to do. Or maybe it was because a woman was administering whatever it was to him. Carl would never know for sure. Looking back however, he would thank himself for listening to his intuition and making the right call.

"Lucy, would you please let me know more about this woman? Nothing special, just her file and recent intel."

"Sure thing, Carl," Lucy replied, her late twenty-something, pre-marriage and no kids vivacity perking up. "It may take a bit of time to get a positive ID on her as we can't see her face, but I'm sure we can figure it out."

"Thanks."

...

Qin Liu was the woman's name and there was very little information about her life prior to graduating from Beijing Law School. This could mean a few things: nobody was particularly interested in her before this accomplishment; there was no reasons to have an interest in her; or her parents were killed in the Cultural Revolution when many files were destroyed in a vain attempt to wipe out the past. "Whatever is swept under the rug, will only cause bumps down that rug," Carl would say when holes of historical denial, from nations to individuals, were found. "And inevitably someone is going to trip on those bumps."

For the first ten years after her graduation, there wasn't a lot either, most likely because she was outnumbered 100 to 1 by gender in a man's world. And why would anyone surveil a woman? In the mid-90s however, as China started emerging from its shell, details started to propagate. Qin had risen in the judiciary, and then made the ambitious jump into policy and trade. She could speak English fluently and understood business and international finance. She, by all accounts, was an excellent, yet quiet negotiator, often taking the back seat when the accolades were bestowed. Carl initially didn't understand why she hadn't been pegged for a particular seat or ministerial position, until Lucy patiently referenced the life of Ruth Bader Ginsberg and the trails she had to blaze to secure a modicum of equality for all; best to use examples that are close to home and let his mind eventually extrapolate. In Qin's file, her endgame was unknown.

"Hmm…so she's more than a pretty face," Carl observed. Lucy, who was sitting facing his desk and had just explained the reason why Qin did not fit the (male) profile, demurely rolled her eyes as if to say, "Yes, and she could have your job in a second if she were a U.S. citizen."

"Looking where she's gone in her career, I'll bet she's pretty good at reading emotions, faces and situations," he continued slowly, as if he was making a profound statement. Lucy's eyes stopped rolling, and fixated on Carl's wrinkled forehead, as if she was trying to penetrate his skull with fMRI capabilities to see just how much cranial matter was *not* operating. "Yes, you're probably right," she echoed in as objective a tone as her vocal chords would allow. "She is probably pretty good at reading people."

"You know something, Lucy," he began.

*Yes, I do. In fact I know MANY things,* she thought. *Why else would you have hired me?*

"While this picture looks completely innocuous," he continued.

*Aside from the fact it caused a major PR scandal worldwide.*

"There could be something else going on here."

*Yeah, what you can't see are the hot massage stones in Putin's undies.*

"I mean, what if—"

*Here we go again, another Carl theory.*

"The Chinese put something in that spray…something that could alter or mess with Putin's thought processes. It could explain a lot."

*Are you sure they didn't try it out on you first?* Lucy let out a frustrated breath.

"Or maybe even," he paused to convey the frank seriousness of his hypothesis, "MIND CONTROL."

*OMG, he HAS lost it!* Lucy smiled ironically. "Carl, I'm not sure about that last possibility, though there could be something there. This Qin woman intrigues me. How did she come to spraying Putin at that moment? I'll do some digging."

...

Lucy liked digging, extracting the molecule from the organism that simply shouldn't, and probably couldn't, be there without some covertly planned intervention. She wanted to know Qin, to understand the spirit behind the reports. To understand what drove her, what her end game(s) might be. Reflecting on her own career path in the C.I.A., and what she'd needed to do to survive and thrive in that slightly gender-biased environment, Lucy couldn't imagine what this woman had to endure to rise in the male-ruled Chinese kleptocracy. She uncovered Qin's involvement in a non-profit out of London, her love of American movies and the apparent void of partners. The hole in Qin's early history probably held more secrets, and possibly terrors, than what her striking yet purposefully subdued face might show. The more she dug, the more Lucy's fascination grew.

...

As it turns out, though there were spray misters in China, none came in that particular sized bottle sans labels or branding. In fact, there were no retail misters in the world for sale, at least through what Lucy could discover online, that were in plain white bottles. This presented a few options: the distributor was a small, local producer who didn't sell online (a possibility), or whatever was in the bottle was either made by Qin (a low probability) or had been custom-made for her (which would fit a finger of the two gloves supporting Carl's conjecture). As a next step, Lucy sent in two requests: one to identify who made those white bottles in the first place and get a list of purchasers; and two, to see where Qin had visited in the last year. Given her position, Qin was probably on the road frequently and she could have picked up the mister someplace. Using data from both searches could help Lucy begin lifting the veil behind which this enigmatic woman existed.

...

There were nine manufacturers of mist bottles of that approximate size and shape scattered throughout the world and they shipped all over the place, particularly to developing economies since the means to produce whatever they held—both mists and breath fresheners—required neither skilled labor nor regulation. The challenge was that these factories shipped the finished goods everywhere, and to a variety of resellers of incredibly different scales—from international perfume purveyors to "onsie-twosie" specialty shops. Potential strike out, Lucy thought.

In the past year, Qin had visited Qatar (probably for gas talks), Sudan (a principal Chinese trade partner and recipient of more than $500 million in direct investments), Hong Kong (nothing of note; possibly to help with the local election problem), Tokyo (for the G20) and then Moscow (for the showdown). On cursory review, there was no overlap between the destinations of bottle shipments, at least that Lucy could find, and where Qin had been, except for Hong Kong. Research is all about dealing with a dearth of "Yeses" and "Nos" floundering in puddles of "Maybes." She should have expected this. After a week of focused searching, all Lucy had been able to uncover about the bottle's origins was that it (obviously) existed and it could have been purchased in Hong Kong. Woo fucking hoo. She decided to intensify her search.

...

"Carl, I want you to see something," she began. It was two weeks after the bottle road kill, and Lucy had appropriately burst into Carl's office, tablet in hand.

"Yes, Lucy. What have you found me," Carl responded, glancing up from yet another interminable report.

"Look," she exhorted, excitedly jabbing at her screen. "See?"

"All I see is a security cam of what appears to be a hotel hallway with an unidentifiable employee shoving what appears to be a bill under a door," he replied with a whiff of exasperation.

"Exactly," Lucy said, springing up and down as if Carl's wood-paneled office had suddenly become a children's inflatable bouncy house that she happily had all to herself. "Oh yes," I forgot to tell you…She wasn't checking out that morning. Shalala, that is," Lucy continued with the understanding that she didn't need to fill in the rest. Carl might be a bit dense, like a black hole, but he wasn't stupid. "I'd been looking at this film for a week and then it finally dawned on me to ask the obvious question. Why was a bill being diplomatically issued at four in the morning? Or could it have been something else?"

"So, if it wasn't a bill what was it?" Carl said slowly.

*Didn't I just say that?*

"And if it wasn't due that morning, who was delivering it?" he continued lethargically.

*You might report to me someday.*

"Could it have been delivered by mistake?"

*Always the downer.*

"Carl, this is the Imperial Hotel, not some random Hilton property. They don't make mistakes, at least ones like this," she rightfully observed.

"So, who is this person?" he said.

*Good Carl. Very good Carl...*

"That is the question," Lucy admitted with a tone that was 90% *Thank goodness you came to that conclusion because I would never have on my own,* and 10% justifiable sarcasm.

"Well?" he continued.

"Well, we are currently trying to match up all hotel employees who were working then with this description. Though I don't believe we'll find anything there. I believe it was either someone outside the hotel who snuck in somehow...or someone who was already at the hotel."

"Couldn't you find this 'mystery employee' on any of the other cameras?" Carl asked.

"That's the funny thing," Lucy replied. "This person simply disappeared into thin air. We looked high and low for them, and even supposed they changed costumes. Nothing we've seen meets the time stamp on the cameras—which leads us to believe something is up. There are too many coincidences at play here for this to be a random event."

"So what are next steps?" Carl inquired with a slight smile, his ego buoying as he was beginning to feel he'd found something.

"In addition to tracking down every employee who was supposed to be in the building that night, we've procured the list of all guests who were registered at the hotel at that time and we're looking into their backgrounds," Lucy reported, in a matter-of-protocol-factly manner.

"Good," Carl said in an overtly practiced, command-and-control voice that dropped two octaves; Lucy sometimes deemed it offensive and, more often, laughable. "Keep me appraised of any further intel."

Lucy started to leave his office knowing full well he meant to say "Good job" but he simply didn't know how to. This ability to translate man-speak was a behavior Lucy had learned to keep herself sane and engaged, especially at the C.I.A., though she imagined the skill was necessary everywhere, at least if you were a woman.

"Oh yes, Carl. One more thing," she said, half turning her body, but fully rotating her face.

"Yes, what is it?" he replied with the classic note of impatience in his voice. He'd apparently been distracted from his briefings for long enough.

"I've been thinking about Putin, and frankly some of the other heads of state who have made some rather mind-blowing statements recently."

"And?" Carl replied, his attention obviously pulled in the direction of the *rational* analyses that lay on his desk, drafted by men, for men.

"Well," Lucy started, without offense. She had been through this cycle a few times. "I started thinking to myself, you know, I'll bet a woman is behind this whole thing."

"A woman?" Carl resounded, as if it was the first time he'd heard the word. "Why a woman?" he said with a hint of incredulity.

"Well, men are pretty up front," (aka simple and predictable) she began. "If they don't like someone, they usually just try to kill them. Done deal." She knew that even if Carl could think of anything different, he'd have little data to refute her claim; begrudgingly, he might need to agree with her.

"Women," she said with a mischievous and sparkly grin whose subtext would keep Carl awake more than the state of the world for the next few weeks, "are much more cunning. We can destroy people emotionally before breakfast," she said with a quick, unconscious yet effective glance at Carl's bare ring finger. It was common knowledge that his divorce had taken a tremendous psychological toll on him. "No, I think this is a female job, and a very smart one at that."

Lucy left him sitting there with a look of vapid blankness, as if someone had just enlightened him to an obvious fact he'd overlooked since high school that explained more than a few imperative failures over time.

...

It wasn't difficult to track down the women who had registered at the Imperial that night. There were the usual reservations made on behalf of a prime minister or president or other such leader, the 15% of the G20 invitees who were women, some support staff (Qin was one of these) and the occasional wife, who, for no apparent reason other than to visit Tokyo for fall fashion forays, had made the reservation. Other than this, there were foreign media correspondents, their supporting crews and

Heidi Delisle, who apparently was there with some staff as she had two suites. Not a lot to go on and there could be many female guests who were staying there under a man's reservation. Though it seemed like a probable 'out of inventory' situation, Lucy decided to very gently start probing warehouses out back.

...

It wasn't until three weeks later, after a few misses, and a rethinking of the scenario, that Lucy got a hit. One female correspondent from Iran was seen on a security camera with a white, spray-looking bottle in her hand. Given Iran's advanced scientific community and significant diaspora, as well as the Russian threat, it made sense to Lucy that the spray bottle could have come from this Iranian reporter. However, after some in-depth background checks and seemingly endless reviews of feeds of half-lit corridors, she concluded the correspondent wasn't involved in an international biotech plot. The whole line was a reach anyway: just because she had a look-alike device didn't mean she was in cahoots with Ms. Liu (even though Iran and China's interests, at least when it came to Putin's most excellent border adventures, were in relative alignment). Sheer coincidence, versus cause, was the most probable explanation.

One by one, all the available women were being crossed off Lucy's list, which she admitted to herself and Carl, might not have been complete. There could have been other women who simply weren't registered, and though Lucy did an excellent job of cross-referencing everyone who had checked in for the summit (thank goodness for the camera behind the reception desk), she couldn't be 100% certain that everyone who was staying at the hotel had been present at check-in. In fact, if someone was trying to avoid being identified, they probably knew not to be there at check-in.

It was at this point, during a meditation session, that Lucy had a reflective breakthrough. Obviously, Russia wasn't the only country acting in ways that were diametrically opposed to historical precedent; many other powerful nations present at the summit had "gone crazy sane" in her terms. This was an obvious fact. The question she hadn't pieced together was why, or potentially more revealing, *how*. What if there were other spray bottles that simply hadn't been caught in the act of being used? What if there were other delivery mechanisms? What if one person—or group—was behind all of this "absurd nonsense" with which the C.I.A., and other similar agencies, needed to deal?

She could tell she was onto something when she came during sex with her boyfriend, Max, later that night, the first time since the nonsense began. She'd been feeling extremely stressed by the uncertainty of simply not knowing was going on. But at the same time, she knew she was onto something…and in that moment with Max, she relaxed. Max, who had noted this causal relationship between relaxing and breakthroughs, slumped on top of her afterwards and, in a deep, post-orgasmic voice whimsically whispered, "Work is good for you too?"

It couldn't be just one renegade woman behind all these transformations. More people had to be involved for this change to reach all the countries now choosing to trust, rather than taunt or terrorize, their neighbors. Lucy expanded her reviews of security gigabytes to include other countries exhibiting these about-faces. After many arduous days and nights of fast-forwarding until people appeared (and then needing to rewind a bit to play from the beginning of the action), it was a replay of a room service delivery to the room where the Turkish delegation was staying, supported by similar service to the Mexican delegation's room, that really started to make her juices flow. While it was not uncommon for places such as the Imperial to hire foreign staff, there was just something about the way two hotel employees walked, particularly the lighter-skinned one, that made her pause. It just didn't fit in with the whole Japanese ethos. When she found out the Imperial had no such employees on staff, Lucy was sure she'd found something real. "Whoever you two are," she smiled with a look of "you can run but you can't hide," in her eyes, "I am going to figure you out."

Further video exploration of guest and employee entrances revealed these two suspects probably didn't enter, or leave, the hotel on that day, or the day prior, which really narrowed down the possibilities. Either they were professionally sneaky, though their flagrant hip action should negate this possibility, or they were amateurs and part of a hotel reservation Lucy had somehow missed. She was determined to figure out how and when they had come in and out of the hotel. She started looking forward in time, and came across a clip of Heidi Delisle and an associate (later identified as Lexie Seekay, one of her right-hand women) going to visit the Saudi delegation. The fact that Heidi was traveling with support staff explained why she had rented the two suites. Lucy passed the meeting off as mere business, though she astutely made the connection that, given its advances in the crossover of bio- and nano-technologies, the next generation of bomb detecting technology could have come from Illumina. She flagged Carl, who, after saying the predictable "Good," immediately set up a video call with Heidi.

...

At the appropriate time, Heidi's face appeared in HD harmony on the plasma screen at the end of Carl's office facing his desk. She seemed to be in a home office, judging by the profusion of plants in the background and a cat tail that moved back and forth across the screen until it eventually slunk down, most likely on Heidi's lap.

Carl and Lucy were both present, she sitting in one of the chairs that now faced away from his desk, he not having the apparent ability (or respect) to move from behind his desk to the adjacent chair. He spoke somewhat gruffly and louder than necessary, his camera insert in the screen revealing a discernible Lucy and a thickly-bespectacled Dilbert look-alike.

"Hello, Ms. Delisle. This is Carl Donnerstag, Director of the Central Intelligence Agency."

"Why yes, Carl, what can I do for you?" Heidi graciously affirmed, his male demeanor instantly dismembered by her effusive openness.

Carl continued in full-on interrogation style, apparently oblivious to (or purposely ignoring) her open posture. "Ms. Delisle, we here at the C.I.A. have information that leads us to believe your company is producing some next generation bomb detection devices and, as part of the Patriot Act, I need to remind you that you are compelled by law to disclose any technical information that could be used against the U.S. or our allies. Further, if you don't disclose such information—"

"Oh Carl," Heidi politely interrupted, without wrinkling a brow. "I am fully aware of the Patriot Act and its terms. You must be referring to my recent meeting with our Saudi friends about some devices that are still in beta-stage testing. I was made aware of potential internal strife while in Tokyo, and had these devices delivered directly from our labs. The team had to pull an all-nighter just to come up with the skeleton of an owner's manual, and I don't think the devices even have our brand on them. This said, I understand they have been quite useful, and I hope I haven't stepped out of diplomatic line here."

Lucy absolutely loved Heidi's response to her boss's unwarranted flexing of his (now sagging) pectorals: Heidi was being up-front, transparent and at ease with revealing she'd directly helped one of Washington's main frenemies stay alive/in power. It should have put Carl in his place, but it probably wouldn't.

Carl, who appeared not to have heard a word Heidi said, continued, eyes on the prize, "Heidi, you know you could face some very stiff penalties and could even prison if you don't make us aware of these technologies, per Section 4, Number 3A…"

*Oh Christ, here he goes again. Doesn't he get it? She just saved your wrinkling ass in a MAJOR way.*

Heidi was well used to this protocol, and didn't flinch. "Carl, I'd be very happy to share our intellectual property with your folks and, in fact, I intend on making it open source so that if anyone else can improve on it, they can, quickly and easily. I see these kinds of applications, the kind that save lives, as being in the world's best interest, not just Illumina's."

Lucy and Carl momentarily became fixtures in Carl's dark-paneled office, stunned by what Heidi had just shared.

"I'm sorry, Ms. Delisle," Carl deliberately repeated, her words now evidently registering in his head. "Did you just say you were going to share your technology with organizations outside the U.S.?"

*You are quick today, Carl. Wow. Blisteringly quick. I'd better go put my crash helmet on for safety. Who knows how fast your next comment might be?*

"That is correct," Heidi cheerfully responded. "I believe my free intellectual property will increase innovation and accelerate better developments, which will save lives. And the increased competition will keep price points from spiraling out of control, which will save everyone money. I can't imagine you'd have any issues with this Carl, do you?"

*OMG, I'm in love with her. She is brilliant and sane. Brilliant and sane… Hmm…*

Carl leaned back in his chair, put his hand on his chin in apparent deep-fathomed thought, vainly looking for an angle to respond with, if for no other reason than to shelter his ego. The silence was becoming a bit uncomfortable when Lucy posed what on the surface would appear to be a standard, information-gathering inquiry.

"Heidi, I'm just curious, what were you doing in Tokyo for almost two weeks around the G20 event?"

If it weren't for the monstrously large screen that was occupied by Heidi's larger-then-life visage, Lucy probably wouldn't have noticed an almost imperceptible hardening in Heidi's eyes, which Lucy interpreted as her guard going up. But that was precisely what Lucy was looking for when she asked the question. And she saw it.

"Lucy, is it?" Heidi started inquisitively.

*Wow, she's good. She knows who I am, probably through some facial recognition application that is cross-referencing the C.I.A. website. And that picture was three years old and my hair was an utter mess and four inches shorter. She's sizing me up.*

"Yes," Lucy responded professionally.

"Well, I absolutely love Japan in the fall. I needed to stop in for meetings with our Tokyo office, of course check out Akibahara and then I had meetings with customers, including bin Nayef."

Heidi seemed to be offhandedly sharing her agenda with the patina of practice that came from recounting her adventures to friends or work colleagues…or because she foresaw the question and had already responded a few times in her head or to a mirror.

*She knows I'm on to something.* "Oh. Ok. Just a standard question," Lucy innocently replied, writing something down on a pad of paper resting on her lap.

"No worries at all, Lucy," Heidi said, her eyes fleetingly drawn to what Lucy was writing, though there was no way she could read it. "Anything else I can do for you?"

Lucy glanced at Carl, whose mind was still struggling to fully comprehend the new paradigm Heidi had just introduced to him, and the world, oblivious to the link between Heidi's work and the changes that had gripped the global order in the last few months, at least from Lucy's perspective.

"Carl, I'll send over all technical specs on our detectors within the hour," Heidi continued. "And Lucy, it was great meeting you. Let me know if I can ever do anything for you."

"Great Heidi. Thank you."

The screen went dark for a brief moment, and was then was engulfed by the C.I.A. logo.

"Lucy," Carl asked, his senses still a bit dazed. "What was that last question about? It would seem kind of obvious why the CEO of a global computer company would be in Japan."

*Look out land speed record. Here we come!*

"Oh, I was just following the playbook," Lucy answered nonchalantly, with a degree of forced feminine naïveté. *And I may have just made your career.*

"Well, watch yourself…We don't want to look sloppy," he advised.

*I don't know if I should laugh or cry.*

"Let me know where things sit with your investigation at 0900 hours on Thursday."

"OK. Will do. See you then Carl."

. . .

60 seconds later, six devices in six time zones softly vibrated as a message, beamed from satellites, towers and Wi-Fi routers appeared in faint blue light. It read, "Beware. Woman at C.I.A. is snooping. More as I learn."

. . .

It took less than an hour to find the dark and lighter-skinned women seen in the hallway videos. They were with Lexie, Heidi and another woman stumbling in at four a.m., five days prior to Putin's arrival. Even though the image was as blurry as most people's eyes at that time of night, the similarity was incontestable. Lucy donned her metaphorical miner's brain bucket, complete with halogen headlamp and carbon monoxide detector, just in case the darkness she was entering could use a shot of lucency, and the air from many unexpected mouths got too thick to breath. She sensed she was on the edge of a catacomb of potentially profound depth, and she knew from experience you just couldn't know how far or deep it could go. For some, this was terrifying. For her, it was her calling.

# 33

## State of a Fearful Nation

Heidi wasn't sure which of the rules applied to the situation. In fact, they appeared to be piggybacking each other, or perhaps more appropriately colliding. First there was the classic, Murphy's Law: if anything can go wrong it will. Then there was the Law of Unintended Consequences that observed outcomes not intended by purposeful action occurred often. In her anarchist days, Heidi would have combined them to form *The Law of Unintended Laws* to define that a law itself was patently bad or unnecessary. Laws were needed because people couldn't be trusted to do the right things…and why the lack of trust again? Why did humans need criminal laws to begin with? Mostly to thwart the vices oozing from a particular male pouch.

She had predicted many of the current socio-political scenarios with a degree of precision. Putin was behaving himself. China was diverting funds from military buildups to grow its domestic economy, critical to paying promised benefits to the massive wave of retirees on the horizon.

Optimism had returned to the E.U., in large part because the bear to the East was hibernating indefinitely. India and Pakistan were making amazing strides forward with minimal friction. Iran had signed a nuclear deal with the U.S. and the U.N. The Israeli conundrum continued to de-escalate, and Mexico was making major amends for some very bad prior deeds.

Most joyfully to her, however, were changes in the numbers on her stock ticker board. Military spending had been curtailed in most advanced countries and budgets were being redirected. Renewed focus, enforcement and new legislation on issues to which prior global administrations had merely paid lip service—things like rape, prostitution, human trafficking, domestic violence, gender equality, gender preference equality, lack of education, malnutrition/hunger, child care, $CO_2$ and methane emissions, abortion rights and contraception—were having a marked impact in a very short period of time. They were only six months post-dose, and notable drops were flowing through her aggregated numbers. She couldn't wait to see where things might sit in six years.

All this said, there were some major snafus that would have made Robert Merton, the first observer of the Law of Unintended Consequences, very proud. First there was the fallout from the completely unforeseen rejection of conservative Islam by the Saudi ruling family, a few of whose 5,000 members were assassinated as a result. The reaction amongst the more militant tranches of the Muslim faith was predictably raw, the net sum being a massive influx of fighters from around the world into ISIS, whose ranks had now swollen to roughly 400,000 in a matter of months. Aside from expanding their hold on parts of Iraq and Syria and brutally beheading any non-believing citizen they could get their hands on, its leaders decided to go after the biggest gusher in the world with its greatly enlarged army, and their former patrons: Saudi Arabia. They had circumvented Baghdad and were pushing south through the Anbar province of Iraq.

This news did not bode well for the oil futures markets, which went into an absolute tizzy when it was apparent that ISIS was gunning for Riyadh and the oil supplies around it. The price of a barrel of crude skyrocketed, translating to a seemingly overnight doubling of pump prices in the States. This effect was immediately pounced on by the GOP spin doctors who started an extremely aggressive campaign (funded primarily by American oil producers) portraying the current, and potentially future, Democratic administrations as inept at predicting world events, soft on terrorism, oblivious to the needs of the common man and, in private fund-raising meetings, "lacking the balls to put those sand niggers in their place." The last taunt, which was secretly recorded and summarily went viral, was a special jab at the Democratic candidate, who was a woman. Bumper stickers started appearing on Made-in-U.S.A. pick-up trucks that read "Where's the balls?"

Heidi was troubled that a good portion of the American voting populace could, and would, be swayed by these "arguments" whose simplicity was only exceeded by their idiocy. But then again, people usually don't vote with logic, they vote with their hopes and fears and, at times, a fear of hope. They'd rather vote for a philandering nut job extolling hypocritical family values than a grounded and intelligent leader who might acknowledge he or she couldn't control the future but was certainly going to go after it with an open and impassioned mind.

This was Heidi's biggest worry: even though the rest of the world was on a positive trajectory, the U.S. could foul things up. Very badly and easily. For the female foreign policy platform to work, the other parties must act in good conscience. Given the duplicitous natures of recent Republican administrations (i.e., Nixon, Reagan, and both Bushes), she wasn't convinced it would happen. Yes, it took two to tango, and those presidencies certainly contended with their share of backstabbing, testosterone-riddled adversaries. But they also happened to set the global political agenda.

There was something else that really bothered her about the GOP— something at a psychological level, and possibly genetically driven. Heidi believed in the theory that all humans are made up of selfish genes, however she also believed they could overcome them.[177] It could have been the GOP's support for religious groups that claimed to love the word of God until a non-white or non-heterosexual, or in some cases a non-man, wanting basic rights (over their bodies for example) entered the discussion. It could have been the GOP's misguided economic policies: trickling down benefits only those who controlled the initial flow,[178] while the dramatic schism in the wealth divide worsened. It could have been Republicans' obsession with defense spending which, given

---

[177] "We can even discuss ways of cultivating and nurturing pure, disinterested altruism, something that has no place in nature, something that has never existed before in the whole history of the world…We have the power to turn against our creators. We, alone on earth, can rebel against the tyranny of the selfish replicators," Richard Dawkins: *The Selfish Gene*, (Oxford University Press, 2006), p. 201

[178] http://talkingpointsmemo.com/dc/warren-buffett-trickle-down-theory-hasn-t-worked-video

the number of lives lost on American soil due to war, somehow justified a $1.5 trillion dollar plane with questionable utility.[179] It could have been conservatives' dangerous denial of scientific facts, from the age of the earth to climate disruption.

Fundamentally though, it was the lack of humanity—of care, of concern for others—regardless of their social, ethnic, gender, religious or economic standing. This, the lack of humanity, was what Heidi identified as the root of her dislike. She did not believe the Democrats were anywhere near perfect either. But their message of equal treatment and rights for all, transparency, a preference of hope over fear and staunch adherence to the separation of state and church reached both her heart and her mind. The attributes the Democratic party supported were the tenets the democratic "experiment" espoused when the United States was founded, (with the exception of that era's racist and misogynistic norms). The Republicans, she perceived, would have no issue reverting back to 16th Century Europe, so long as they were the landed and royal classes.

At the current moment in America, the fear machine was going into high gear. Defense contractors were reportedly tripling their lobbying expenditures and contributions to "super PACS" to "deflect Armageddon from descending on the U.S. after the next election," according to a Politico.com interview with a leader of the NDIA (National Defense Industry Association). Heidi was utterly baffled by the rationale behind that statement. If Armageddon were to hit the rest of the world, from whom would the U.S. need to defend itself?

Other notable contributors to the election (from what could be discovered given the opaque disclosure laws of the Citizens United decision) included financial services from banks, insurance companies and hedge funds, the Luxury Car Manufacturers Association, the Private Jet Manufacturers Association, the Personal Yacht Builders Association, DeBeers and the Association of Coal Producers and Generators. Heidi was entranced by how the hopes and fears of the Republican base in the Midwestern and Southern states aligned with the concerns of these corporations and interest groups.

By far, however, she was the most enraged by the oil lobby, which was the largest backer of the Perry/Bachman GOP ticket. There couldn't be

---

[179]   http://fortune.com/2015/08/14/f-35-joint-strike-fighter/; http://www.upworthy.com/america-spent-15- trillion-on-a-jet-that-doesnt-work-how-many-schools-is-that-do-you-think

a more perfect alignment. Perry and Bachman had made their careers capitalizing on the dependency on this natural resource, and both had vowed to "fight to the finish" to defend its use and propagation domestically and internationally. Perry's initial reaction to the news of ISIS's strategy was that America should "simply lob a couple of nukes at ol' Anbar province. Then they'll know we mean business" (the double entendre seemed to evade him). While this galvanized the base of fear in the States—"He's got balls!"—it unleashed such international outrage that pundits named him "The Cold Warrior." Perry relished this moniker, for he believed *cold* diplomacy was an incontrovertible sign of *warrior* strength. When his foreign policy advisors explained to Perry that extolling the nuking of people was a serious threat to his campaign image, he begrudgingly slithered out of his faux pas, stating "figuratively speaking of course."

Perry's job growth platform was built on infrastructure expansion, pipelines to be specific. He had 12 planned, which he predicted would add hundreds of thousands of permanent, high wage jobs to the economy. He would re-invigorate the "new middle class," without the need for unions. When asked by a CNN reporter what he deemed more valuable, oil or people, his response would probably have made more than a few of his business school professors proud, "People are a much riskier investment, as they require much more maintenance to keep functioning, even at sub-par levels of performance. The value of oil can be quantified, projected and protected by derivatives, with exponentially less need for upkeep, producing a much higher and risk-reduced return."

Bachman also did her part to feed the fright apparatus. A nationally televised ad campaign pictured her standing on a wooded trail on the North Dakota/Canadian border, high-powered rifle with scope in hand after reports (sources unknown) surfaced of ISIS fighters crossing into America on the very path she was guarding. The voiceover (same voice as Dick's commercials) went into great detail about Sarah's devotion to national security, extolling her stolid support and involvement with the N.R.A., "The last bastion and protector of freedoms in the United States."

The trail was actually a coyote/deer run. Sarah seemed to know it well; it was conjectured this was the way she snuck in beer. Though nobody was located decked out in black, hooded outfits carrying Kalashnikovs (save some terrified men on ATVs with shotguns out for a weekend hunting trip), the closing line of the commercial, set against rousing star-spangled cymbals, made a lasting impression on all those fearful enough to believe it: "Sarah Bachman, defending the American way of life."

The election was five months away and the race was too close to call. Organizations with (unintentionally) satirical names such as Americans for Equality and Citizens for a United America funded attack ads that deluged the senses with content ranging from out-of-context to out-of-control to out-of-touch. Conservatives portrayed Democrats as Socialists and Nazis, dope-smokers and druids, peace mongers and science believers. The Democrats were up against forces who would win at whatever cost.

Heidi wasn't sure what to do. On the one hand, dosing Mr. Perry would be an absolute gas. She imagined his ever-tanned smiling face on national TV during a debate, stunning his base by drawling out proclamations about curbing gun control, domestic violence and climate disruption, with a special emphasis on curtailing carbon-based sources of energy, allowing women the right to choose, parting church and state and treating immigrants as people versus aliens. Her instincts, however, told her he was merely a puppet for a vilely more intelligent organization lurking behind the dark blue curtains of his press conferences.

She also thought about dosing Mrs. Bachman, but dismissed her as a target for three reasons: 1) She'd been too effectively brainwashed by the religious-Republican black hole to escape; 2) VP candidates of her ilk were just window-dressing; as long as she kept smiling and endured, she'd be voted in by default; and 3) Unbelievably, she was a woman, though Heidi also knew that sociopathy has no gender bias.

No, Heidi realized as she weighed her options, Dick and Sarah were not the ones. It was those with the money who could handily influence the rules…and in this case, it was the Koch brothers who had the greatest amount of leverage. She would have to get to them…and she had just the ticket.

# 34

## The Fanaticism of Faith

From the vantage point of many voters in Iowa, ISIS was a lot like the Japanese during World War II. Different looking people, a non-Christian religion (though Islam is Abrahamic), a bizarre culture lacking local John Deere distributors, inhabiting a distant land across waves of grain and some ocean, who would gladly kill themselves in the name of honor and glory, all for some God-like entity. Even if they were born and raised in the States and didn't speak their ancestral language, ordinary Muslims were viewed not as "fellow immigrants," but "agents of the enemy." This perception manifested in various treatments, ranging from ostracizing at social events, to a bevy of hate crimes, to being registered, tracked and barred from entering the country. If you even *looked* like a member of this *other* group, you'd need the U.S. flag on your arm to minimize police visits and meddling by "concerned citizens."[180]

This was to be expected, for who in Iowa would want to understand

---

[180] Per my father's personal experience during WWII

the 1,500+ years of history behind these lesser-developed cultures, and thus species, when Advanced Placement courses in U.S. History were being dismembered by doubts of their veracity by certain *other* states?[181]

To be fair, what ISIS was doing, from any perspective including those of most Muslims—Shia or Sunni—should be considered outside the parameters of any civilized and acceptable way of treating others. Mass beheadings of innocents, rape, forced "marriage"/sexual slavery and indisputable elements of genocide, all driven by a fervent belief in an interpretation of words drafted before the Renaissance, Enlightenment, Industrial, Post-Industrial and Internet ages. It sounded a lot like the Crusades (except then Christians were killing Muslims). When the President pointed this out, it triggered calls for impeachment from the GOP on the grounds he lacked the religious morals needed to run the country.[182]

From Heidi's perspective, it was precisely these "morals," more specifically their biochemical roots, that had pushed the world to its current state. A good part of history's ills traced back to the degree of maternal love received in childhood (think Putin), within or outside of the confines of religious-inspired norms (think the Mosou). The more softening and guidance of testosterone's urges, the lower the probability of vices running amok in gene pools that could easily be seduced by the raw power of muscular strength, athletic ability, idiotic daring, video game dominance, and pecking order participation. All it takes is one or two such vessels of de-estrogened hormones and before you know it, there's an armada outside banging on your walls and women.

In this context, Heidi was both fascinated and disturbed by research showing that, when facing the loss of love, men are three to four times more likely to commit suicide than women, who simply become depressed.[183] She could imagine men, lacking maternal softness and (consequently?) jilted by unrequited advances, coming up with fanciful tales to condone sexual subjugation, incest, eyes for eyes and eventual endings of the world. Someone needed to show these bitches who was boss, and if you don't please us on our terms, through sheer strength and aggression, we can and will ruin your existence. Throw in a Divine Being to manifest ultimate recourse without accountability, a really bad guy to

---

181 http://nymag.com/daily/intelligencer/2015/02/why-oklahoma-lawmakers-want-to-ban-ap-us-history.html

182 http://www.newyorker.com/news/daily-comment/obama-crusaders

183 Dr. Louann Brizendine, Ibid., p. 75.

misdirect man's innate testosterone tendencies, and kick the whole thing off by positioning women as the genesis of evil because men can't always get what they want and *voila:* the basis of Western Civilization.

Of equal distress was the observation that all "faiths" (save Buddhism), despite how peace loving they might have started out, had born groups on the fanatical fringes who took the word of God "too far," or "too literally." What was *purportedly* created to maintain order and create harmony invariably slid down the slippery slope of Machiavellian machinations, emerging in divisive political, economic, social and military guises. Religion's marketed intent was its demise.

In this context, Heidi would argue, the basis of ISIS, like most "terrorist" groups, was centuries of male-derived religious norms overpowering maternal socialization. Given that control came from men's physical strength, it was historically impossible for women's influence to prevail enough to turn the testy tides.

Over the last 100 years however, other sources of control (like finance, scaled manufacturing, exchange rates, scientific and technology prowess, the inevitable rise of women's rights, and mobile apps) started to compete with military might, and had accelerated economic growth, specifically in countries with a pronounced separation of church and state. *Of all the divides plaguing the world,* Heidi thought, *it's the speed of female emancipation that will make, or break, global prosperity, and survival.*

As it turned out, ISIS, or at least a commanding faction of its leadership, did not like to see its power challenged. It was a classic endocrine-based reaction to someone else's authority, in this case, modernity. They yearned for, and were actively trying to, return to the good old days of the 7th century when men were solidly in control, slavery of all sorts was cool, and women were merely second-class objects there to do all biddings no questions contemplated. This was why ISIS replaced the local ordinances and legal platforms in all areas they controlled with the strictest version of Sharia law imaginable. This murderous nostalgia for the past was also reflected in their barbaric execution style, the breadth of their killings (which went pretty much round the clock) and their current list of targets (which included 200 million heretical Shiite brothers and sisters as well as the leaders of all Muslim countries for not doing their jobs.)[184] Heidi imagined ISIS's leader, Abu Bakr al-Baghdadi—the self-nominated Caliph, successor to Muhammad and leader of all Muslims—on trial for

---

[184] http://www.theatlantic.com/features/archive/2015/02/what-isis-really-wants/384980/

war and humanitarian crimes, calmly claiming he was merely following the rules of his religion.

Objectively, the odds were against them. The lure of a more equal, more just (read: more feminine), and consequently more advanced standard of living (as depicted in global entertainment media accessible from satellites to thumb drives) would eventually prevail over their utopian Islamic fantasy. And they knew it. They might have made it to their Ark in time, however they knew the deluge would never stop. In fact, it would only become more pervasive and insidious over time.

But ISIS's notion of time differed from ours, for their days (and the world's days) were gleefully numbered, as preordained by their scriptures. The countdown to the apocalypse would start when an army "from Rome" was defeated at Dabiq, Syria.[185] And per ISIS's marketing consultants, the most alluring draw to the converts pouring in from around the globe was the purported potency of their capability to control the destiny of the world. It was all about control after all.

This capacity was dramatically boosted when, in April, a video was released of black-turbaned men triumphantly hoisting above their heads what appeared to be a slightly disfigured replica of R2D2, one of the main droids from Star Wars, prone on a stretcher. The hoisters were surrounded by other men wielding all sorts of weaponry, from assault rifles to pistols to scimitars, eerily dancing and yelling in jubilation as if the droid had just scored the winning point in the final seconds of the global Game of Life championships. In a deep and resonant voice that sounded like a premeditated rebuttal (albeit with British overtones) to Dick Perry and Sarah Bachman's "We're Here for You" ads, the following message was broadcast in both Arabic and English:

> My fellow brothers. God is great! God is merciful! As you know, Muhammad our prophet has foreseen the end of days and as you are surely aware those days are upon us. We have been graced by the amazing fortune and blessing of Allah with the means to accelerate and deliver this gift on the hypocrites, the infidels, who have corrupted the ways and laws of your faith. Join us and be part of the assembly who, with the guidance of the revered Caliph, will ensure your place in the history

---

[185] Ibid.

of the world and guarantee the satisfactions promised in the next life. God is great! God is merciful!"

The clip ended with the standard mushroom-shaped cloud billowing up from the detonation of an atomic device, the sound dramatically enhanced to reverberate from speakers to spinal columns, imparting ISIS's power to decide the expiration of non-believers.

It was unknown whether or not ISIS actually had a bomb, a supposition that immediately received top priority in all intelligence organizations around the world. But the hint spurred those who were hesitating to convert, queueing them up like lemmings marching toward their final cliff dive. The world was at war with an enemy who welcomed it for it justified their existence. A war that would provide the means to everyone's conceptual finale. It was a testosterone Carnival.

"Delightful," Heidi verbally remarked to herself after reviewing ISIS's advertorial, sarcasm unclouded. "Just delightful...And I was going to send Baghdadi a subscription to *Martha Stewart Living* in recognition of his Caliph status. This is going to require some serious work."

# 35

## Bath Time

Heidi loved baths. No matter how bad or brutal the day had been, when she slipped into the steaming, scented waters of her ceramic cocoon she briefly transcended the world of future obligations to a place of benign indifference.[186] Her right brain, released by the warmth of the water, ran free. She experienced some of her greatest breakthroughs—from products, to politics to personal relationships—within this temperate confine. In fact, she answered one of her Wharton admission essays on "What inspires you?" with a story about baths; she was inspired by the pure release of creativity (often with a glass of something at her side).

Heidi had been taking many baths over the past few months, ever since The Dick and Sarah Show came to market in April. They were gaining in the polls with PR support from the GOP fear machine, which was running amok with reports of "gay, Russian-backed, ISIS fighters

---

[186]  Albert Camus, *The Stranger*

purportedly seen beheading teddy bears in the Mall of America."

She had had a pivotal insight as to how to deal with the election, and was making plans accordingly. But this initiative was overwhelmed by the news coming out of the Middle East, where things had become simply ugly. ISIS was expanding; Saudi Arabia was on the brink of civil war or revolution; Syria was still an utter mess; Iraq was being held together by a combination of Kurdish forces and Boy Scouts trained by the U.S.; and all the planet's free nations, or at least those that needed oil, were diplomatically jockeying to get boots back on the ground to defend The House of Saud from their progeny—just as long as those fighting didn't come from their country.

To be fair, these nations, the U.S. in particular, had become so war-weary, so tired of seeing veterans returning without legs and, even worse, without sanity, that most were against full-scale ground operations, even when it came to battling the barbarians. To compound matters, the U.S. Congress, controlled by Republicans, was in a frenzied knot as to how to deal with this situation. Tea Party Libertarians wanted nothing to do with this foreign fratricidal fracas. *Their mess*, they said, *let them deal with it*. Then there were the ignorant boors, echoing Dick and Sarah's oil-centric sentiments, whose jabbered rhetoric was a thinly veiled excuse for colonization of the entire peninsula, including Qatar, the United Arab Emirates and Yemen, and Oman by default. These wrong-wing hawks were adamant about expressing America's military dominance, including beefing up the Coast Guard as a last line of defense against the imminent ISIS invasion.

At the end of the day, it really didn't matter. Domestic oil and defense contractor's fortunes would be considerably augmented in either scenario. Less supply (in case of ISIS victory) or control (in case of annexation) of oil meant higher prices and the sheer instability of these options would require armaments of epic proportions. "How ironic," Heidi observed, "how a substance that took millions of years to form[187]— (somehow on a planet that was divinely created 10,000 years ago according to Abrahamic dogma)—was the main funding source of so much global hatred and the backbone of the religious wrong?" If oil could only be out of the picture, what a wonderful, safer and cleaner world it would be.

And while the politicians yammered, people were dying or becoming refugees as the ISIS stain spread through most of Syria and Iraq, and

---

[187] http://en.wikipedia.org/wiki/Fossil_fuel

had dripped its way to the Saudi Arabian border, where 200,000 heavily armed men, aspiring to recreate an Islamic utopia circa 800 AD, were poised to invade and destroy the apostates.

Across the border lay the Saudi armed forces, who'd been on high alert since the Royal Family's world-shattering decrees. The army was not ill equipped, as it spent the highest percentage of GDP in the world, 10%, on defense, the U.S., Great Britain and France being its largest suppliers. The key question in Heidi's mind was "When they attack, what will the Saudi forces do?" Given her knowledge of the state of the regime, enhanced by an occasional text chat with bin Nayef, the threat of an ISIS intrusion, while potentially unifying, also created an immaculate opportunity for classic, behind-the-scenes pseudo-Caesar power plays.

Tonight's bath was particularly hot, reminiscent of *ofuro* sessions in Japan, where one would emerge as red as a lobster and as squishy as over-cooked udon. It was just 28 days until the U.S. elections and what happened in the Middle East could very well dictate the outcome.

The Saudis' decision to come out of the Middle Ages closet was fully supported by the U.S. President. However, the situation on the ground in both countries was making support extremely difficult. Given the Congressional dissension, getting any kind of approval for practical intervention was impossible. To combat this deadlock, the President wisely played his Executive Order card as a roundabout maneuver to force decisions, which triggered yet another lawsuit from the Speaker of the House on grounds the President was trying to make stuff happen.[188]

The situation in the sands of Saudi-land was equally complex. The lights in Langley had been burning round the clock trying to determine what could happen next and whom the U.S. and its allies should support. Historically, its track record covertly or overtly backing regimes had not been stellar; in fact, it was so bad that many leading pundits, within and outside the government, were wary of full-scale commitment to a specific faction.

To an educated, engaged and unbiased U.S. voting population, making sense of it all would be fraught with overall misery in filtering through the flak, especially given the relentless pummeling of the President and his hopeful successors, who were being portrayed as "four more years, but worse." This particular bath necessitated a chilled half bottle of Sonoma Chardonnay.

---

[188] Props to Andy Borowitz of *The New Yorker* for having a similar thought.

Heidi instinctively tested the water's temperature with a soft caress, as if stroking the back of a loving pet, knowing full well it was precisely 104 degrees, the level she'd requested of George when initiating her nightly ritual. She slipped out of her robe and gingerly, yet confidently, entered the tub, as the initial sting quickly gave way to blissful and existential escape.

She lay there for a while, eyes closed, simply enjoying the moment, her breaths lackadaisically slowing and becoming deeper. She sipped some wine...and then some more, and then refilled her glass. Just as her left-brain's tentacles were releasing their grip on her consciousness, a burst of sensual humming interrupted her transition. It came from a small black object nestled conveniently on a perch overlooking the tub.

"What is the message?" she wearily asked George, the relaxation of heat dissipating her voice.

"Why Heidi, it is a message from Ms. Qin. Shall I read it to you?"

"Yes please," she replied, leaning forward a few inches to ensure the message was clearly heard.

"OK. Here it goes...'You are probably reacting the same way as I am to the ISIS threat. They must be stopped. As you know, my country has many critical interests in that region and my government is frankly terrified of what could happen. I wanted to let you know I've volunteered to meet with Baghdadi in person to try and negotiate a deal. This will be an incredibly covert mission, as not even his second in command will know about it. It would destroy his credibility if he were seen doing deals on the side with sovereign governments like mine. I'll be leaving in two days and all I know about the location of our meeting is that it won't be Raqqah (the city in Syria that serves as ISIS headquarters). It will probably take place somewhere in between there and the Saudi border. Let me know if there's anything I can do. Won't be able to take a LoveBomb with me, though I'll have my MoPhone so you can track me. By the way, your elections are scaring me more than ISIS. I can't wait to see you again. Qin'"

"Thank you George," Heidi said. "Very much."

"Whatever you need, consider it done."

Heidi rested her back once again against the tub, her hands slowly moving in S movements as if channeling some unseen power in the liquid toward her feet. Even before Qin's message had ended, Heidi knew what had to be done. Trouble was, Qin was right. The U.S. elections were more troubling than whatever threats ISIS was making. From Heidi's perspective, conservative Christianity and radical Islam were very similar: two fearful and denial-bound faiths feeding on each other's ignorance, like a pair of serpents simultaneously swallowing each other by the tail. No, she had to focus on the conference. There were simply no other events that afforded a similar opportunity...in time. She would once again need to call on the strength and courage of her women. This time would be by far the most dangerous assignment imaginable, other than launching a fictitious movie about assassinating a North Korean dictator.

"George?" she inquired.

"Yes, Ma'am?"

"I need you to take a message and send it to TM7."

"OK, hit me with your best shot..."

Heidi took a deep breath, locked her lashes, and slowly started to speak.

"Ladies of The Magnificent Seven..."

# 36

## And Now for Something Completely Different...

Once her real targets had become apparent, Heidi immediately envisioned the perfect venue to mask her assault on the Koch brothers. Every summer, Allen & Company, a media-focused investment bank, held a conference in Sun Valley, Idaho. Attendees were a novel blend of content and technology moguls from Los Angeles, Silicon Valley, New York City, Seattle and upstarts from random suburban tracts whose videos seemed to dominate the new viral marketplace. Heidi had been asked to present on the power of digital distribution as an equalizing force in geopolitics. As randomness would have it, the Koch brothers had also been summoned to present on the latest trends in "super PAC" campaign advertising. Allen & Co. wanted to appeal to all flavors of balding white men, as their fees, when received, were indistinguishable in Allen's accounts.

The conference traditionally occurred in July. However, this year,

Sun Valley found itself aptly named, as a drought of unprecedented proportion descended upon the tony resort town. Wildfires, empowered by the desiccation, seemingly started with the flap of a hawk's wing though the numbers of these majestic birds had decreased dramatically as their prey, ravaged by the lack of moisture, had either died or migrated elsewhere. Fire was a huge risk, especially considering the number of cigars enjoyed by both bankers and "the biz" at this event. So the conference was rescheduled to early October, when the fall storms would be making cameos, wetting things down, and the chances for self-immolation had declined to acceptable levels.

...

Bill Koch's Gulf Stream G650 was getting ready to close its door at Martha's Vineyard Airport, when a demur knock on the plane's exterior by a petite woman with shining pewter hair and luminescent blue eyes stopped the process. She had the same youthful exuberance and fashion style as the 20-something models in Banana Republic catalogues.

"Excuse me, are you by any chance going to Sun Valley?" she inquired to the lone occupant with a knowing smile. "My plane won't start, they don't know how long it will take to fix the problem and I have dinner with some guy named Zuckerberg tonight."

"You must be Heidi Delisle," the man replied, gracefully rising from his tasteful leather seat to humbly shake her hand. His full head of white hair was set against a face weathered by wind and water. When she looked into his eyes, she was startled to see not a demigod of libertarian self-righteousness, but a man whose real love lay outside the landlocked realm of politics, whose passion, she intuited, was the sea. "I had heard you were on the island and I see you are doing a little number at the Allen gig," Heidi said, motioning to some brochures on a granite tabletop.

"Yes, I have a little place in Osterville and this is the closest airport that can handle my plane, so I sail to and from the terminal," he said with a chuckle. "And, well, so long as you don't try to liberate me," he continued with a playful grin, "sure thing, hop aboard. You must have some baggage…all women have baggage."

Heidi was surprised by both his nature and her reaction to it; she wasn't offended by his quip about her gender and the double entendre. And yes, she did have baggage, a rather large case containing some very special items.

"Why yes, William—"

"Please, call me Bill."

"OK Bill. Yes, I have a case that will need to accompany me. It should fit in the belly just fine," she said, waving to her pilot who scurried over with a sturdy-looking crate and a bright blue leather purse large enough to hold a sizable laptop or tablet.

"Oh, let me help," Bill exclaimed, leaping down the stairs to do his manly strength thing for the distressed damsel. After securing the case, he returned and with a degree of smiling pride declared, "That wasn't as heavy as it looked."

It was then that Heidi realized her internal detector, which had been softly going off in the background, was piping up: he was flirting with her. Well, he had been married three times prior…and it was hard for zebras to lose their stripes.

"Heidi," Bill shared as he closed the door from the inside. "We'll need to make a quick stop in New York to pick up my brother, Dave. If you like me, you're going to love him." He laughed.

He was indeed flirting with her. This could be fun.

A bottle of a Napa white was festively opened during the brief jaunt to La Guardia. Bill decided not to tell his brother about the "stowaway," but to let him be surprised—which he most certainly was when his polar opposite glowingly greeted him at the door. This Koch's eyes, embedded in a somber visage obviously on-edge, told a different story. They reminded Heidi of Putin's, lifeless and soulless. They spoke of an entitled and ravenous need for power and control, at whatever cost, with no regard for rules, on a scale few could have the hubris to imagine. For a moment, she wondered if Dave had the same father as Bill, as their differences were strikingly profound. Without saying a word to her, Dave stiffly motioned his brother outside.

"Bill, what the *FUCK* are you doing letting *her* on *our* plane?"

"What harm can she be? Mellow out Dave. It isn't like we're going to be sharing secrets," Bill responded with a light-hearted laugh and a wink, though there was a slightly perceptible edge to both. Watching them from inside the plane, Heidi could tell Dave had been the historic winner, evidenced by the fact that his net worth was valued at almost ten times that of Bill's paltry four billion.

Heidi imagined them as kids, growing up, Dave coming down on Bill for no good (or bad) reason, and poor Bill being constantly bullied. She could easily imagine Bill succumbing to a life in his brother's looming shadow, his brother's dominance psychically, and more than likely physically, beaten into him. *Figures he's a Republican,* she reflected. But her instincts told her, in spite of his environment, Bill had a conscience.

Dave relented and huffed onto the plane, fleetingly introducing himself with a somewhat brusque handshake before sequestering himself into the furthest chair away from where she was sitting, as if her cooties would give him Ebola or, worse, the truth. Bill, delighted with his victory, gaily sprung back up the stairs and plopped down next to Heidi with a smile equal in scale to the fading Manhattan skyline.

As Dave became conveniently distracted by the latest edition of *Reason* (Free Minds and Free Markets) and a vodka martini drier than their Chardonnay, Bill and Heidi started to bond. Life stories flowed as fluidly as the wine sluiced in their glasses. Stories of triumph and of failure, of revelations that could only come from an unclothed testing of will, of the starkest distillation of what was most important. Of love and loss.

Heidi was amazed at how quickly Bill opened up. Even with his charm mode on, his self-awareness and humility felt rare. That said, Heidi sensed something else was at play in the background. Her intuition was both confirmed and interrupted by his brother who, having milked the magazine for every last word, started mixing another libation and shifted his beady focus on them.

"Bill, what are you talking about?" Dave said with palpable condescension. "Why must you always share that story? Have you no shame?"

Bill's instinctive reaction, Heidi noticed, was to take the blame hit and cower metaphorically until the black cloud was attracted to another defenseless hill upon which it could rain freely…or reign, as it were. This time though, Bill had an ally, a comrade-in-arms he intuitively knew could shield him from this current sphere of influence.

"Oh Dave, would you please stop," Bill replied without turning either his head or gaze, grinning with the confidence of inebriated fellowship. "Really, what does it matter?"

This flagrant usurping of the alpha dog's power only incensed its hormonal reaction. Dave's face turned red.

"What does it matter?" he sniped. "You have no idea what this woman is capable of. I mean, she could have some newfangled technology with her that is recording everything you are saying! Can you imagine what the Communist media would do with these tapes?"

*You aren't far off Dave*, Heidi reflected, envisioning the LoveBomb, packed about a foot beneath his seat, that was yearning to start ticking. *Though my technology will do a little more than cause an ephemeral flood of Twitter posts.*

Bill, who was relishing his newfound freedom, stood firm and continued as if his dark shadow was being flash bombed. "Then there was the time when I caught Dave wearing his wife's bra…"

Heidi was pretty sure that if they were 20 years younger, Dave would have Bill in a headlock in about six seconds, even in her presence… much like her father had dealt with her brother growing up for similarly insignificant infractions. Dave however, used a different tactic. He glowered, took a deep slug of his drink, and played the wealth/power card.

"Bill, do I need to remind you who has the most to lose here? And what I am doing for you…and our family right now?" Dave glanced at his watch, abruptly reached for a remote on the granite table and turned on a plasma TV mounted on the wall, near what looked like a private chamber of sorts, replete with a thick, sound proofed, smoked glass door.

Fox News predictably appeared with Bill O' Reilly, in his best vaudeville voice, breathlessly comparing ISIS's invasion of Saudi Arabia to his experiences in the Falkland War.[189]

"About an hour ago, an estimated 100,000 ISIS fighters started to swarm across the border of Saudi Arabia from Iraq in three distinct lines around Highway 80. They've been met with sporadic resistance. However, it seems that the Saudi army is in a state of disarray as some regiments are letting the jihadists blow right by them, and are actually cheering them on as they pass." Heidi watched as the program cut to video of soldiers fist-pumping the black clad fighters.

"This is *unthinkable*. How can a country that is a supposed friend of the United States allow these mongrels to march across their border unimpeded? This is an indictment of the weakness of our President and his utter lack of foreign policy. And if they have a nuclear weapon with them," the video cut to the April propaganda video, "well, we may be watching massive history in the making."

With this news, Dave's expression came somewhat close to a… smile. In contrast, Bill's demeanor suddenly shifted from a warm and perceptible smugness to a cold and sullen stare at the TV, as if he were

---

[189] http://www.motherjones.com/politics/2015/02/bill-oreilly-falklands-video-cbs

somehow responsible for what was happening.

As if he were somehow responsible...

Something started screaming inside Heidi's inner mental sanctum. Something was wrong, very wrong, and it wasn't just the fact ISIS was apparently waltzing into the largest oil supplier on earth without needing to check their weapons at the border.

Heidi gasped internally as her interpretation of reality took a quantum hit that would have undoubtedly killed Schrodinger's cat.[190] These brothers really did think they could rule the world, or at least Dave did, with Bill bludgeoned into inferior submission. Not only did they wield tremendous influence on the U.S. Presidential and Congressional races (and by extension, depending on who won, the Supreme Court), but they were involved somehow in the ISIS uprising as well. How exactly she didn't know, however the mere fact that the link existed portended to some rather upsetting potential scenarios, including funding the acquisition of a nuclear device.

(As it would turn out, the bomb had been smuggled from Pakistan, whose historical religious relationship with Saudi Arabia had afforded it the funds to build the monstrosity; in penultimate irony, the House of Saud funded the means to its own literal destruction. The illicit shipment had been facilitated by shell organizations funded by charities established by The Koch Family Foundation to promote their version of world peace.)

It made *so* much sense, especially if you were a sociopath. Visions of her bath time extrapolations about potential Saudi end games seared her consciousness. Either way—destruction or annexation—the impact on the price of oil would make the Koch family come out smelling like hundred-billion dollar roses. And if their candidates won the election, they *would* rule the world. They would become master kingmakers with the most powerful military on the planet by a factor of ten at their beck and call.

What men!

She sat back in her seat, took a mousy sip of wine, and kept her eyes glued to the TV, trying her best to blend into the masterfully crafted teak paneling behind her. She knew there was a good chance Dave may have realized his slip and she absolutely could not let him know she now understood the driving force behind the ISIS invasion. Collecting the

---

[190] https://en.wikipedia.org/wiki/Schrödinger%27s_cat

Koch brothers' blood could literally save the world, but who knew what Dave would do to her if his paranoia overcame his suspicions?

Dave, evidently recognizing the grave damage his reference to "what he is doing for the family right now" combined with the Fox news footage could cause himself (and by extension, his candidates), beckoned his brother as indifferently as possible into the adjoining room, nonchalantly making sure the door firmly slid shut. Heidi could well imagine the spirit of the muffled conversation, starting with a holier-than-the-world Dave disappointingly pinning his stupidity on his brother's decision to let "that female liberal bitch" accompany them. She hoped Bill had the conviction to stand up to his brother, especially in her absence, for at that defining point in time, she only had one overriding task on which to focus: filling two syringes with blood. Little could she imagine that while fulfilling her mission, she was becoming attracted to the enemy.

She easily located the pouches in a special refrigerator situated behind a teak and mahogany inlaid door, just like the three-dimensional plan of the plane's interior holograming from her MoPhone.

Note specific donor. Peel back label. Unsheathe needle. Push needle. Withdraw blood. Reseal label. Match donor with marked vial. Push blood into vial. Re-sheathe needle.

The whole process took less than a minute. One down, Heidi thought. One to go. Again she went through her checklist: note specific donor; peel back label; unsheathe needle; push needle.

A raised voice and movement caused her to look up.

The shape of a hand showing through the frosted glass door appeared to be looking for a handle. Heidi froze. She hadn't prepared for being caught (literally) red-handed. And while her ability to think on her feet had become second nature, a necessity for the cross-examinations by male investors, male analysts and male lovers, what she was doing at that moment would require either a tale taller than their current altitude (conveniently displayed in the upper right corner of the massive TV screen) or an act of utter randomness. And again, who knew what Dave might do to her? For a moment, she imagined the altimeter might actually serve one of its purposes and let her know how far she would fall.

Fortunately, the hand stopped its quest, a different voice (probably Bill's) parried, and the figure moved away from the door. Heidi slowly exhaled, in part to diffuse her tension and in other part to make sure the needle stayed in its place. As her chest gently collapsed, she looked down and realized that during the interruption, her hands had tensed, forcing a small stream of blood out of the needle and onto the exterior of the bag, where it was queuing up the gravitational courage to dive onto her lap. She deterred it with a napkin from the table, fortuitously within reach. Without checking on the door status, she deftly filled the syringe, filled the vial, and firmly pressed the label back into place. The vials were quickly buried in the bowels of her purse and the refrigerator door had been shut for no less than seven seconds when the door abruptly slid open. Bill emerged, ad looking apologetic yet surprisingly victorious. Dave was nowhere to be seen behind him, though the view from Heidi's line of sight wasn't clear.

"Ms. Delisle," he calmly greeted her. "As you are aware by now," he said with an impish grin, "my brother has…reservations, shall we say, about your presence on this plane. So I suggested he either go play outside," Bill laughed childishly, "or simply not interact with you. He has chosen the latter and will probably sleep in the back the rest of the flight. You might not have the pleasure of interacting with him, ever again."

*Well, there is one interaction with Dave that will be unavoidable*, Heidi thought with a genuine smile. *And, given his plan, I will dose him if it is the last thing I do.* Though Bill apparently was aware of some involvement in the ISIS invasion, her gut told her he didn't know the whole story. She wanted to believe he had good in him.

"Which means…where did we leave off?" he inquired with resounding confidence, snuggling into a leather seat adjacent to Heidi, a fresh bottle of wine materializing from behind his back.

It could have been completely the wine's fault. And if not completely, it certainly aided and abetted Bill's entreaties…though in wine there is truth. She didn't know why they connected, but despite their political differences, their naked humanity brought them together.

Neither noticed they had landed until the plane stopped and the pilot emerged, somewhat taken aback that his announcement to "belt up" had been ignored. He quickly sensed his services were no longer needed and with no further ado, quietly disappeared into the innards of the hangar.

No sooner had he gone than Lexie pulled up in a Tesla SUV, which she parked about five yards from the Koch's plane. She hopped out, and with quick steps, scampered over and up the stairs.

"Hello," she started "Heidi?"

She just about swallowed her tongue when she was greeted with the sight of one of the Koch brothers locking eyes with Heidi as he semi-salaciously leaned toward her. Not only this, Lexie realized that he seemed to have the absurd intention of trading saliva with Heidi. And wait, Heidi appeared to be actually enjoying this attention. Knowing her boss as she did, Lexie thought Heidi seemed to *want* it. Lexie instinctively gave the plane's interior a "number of consumed bottles" scan and quickly concluded Heidi had a few too many. Though she heard Lexie arrive, Heidi allowed the drama to carry on one moment longer than what was comfortable (at least to Lexie). She then severed the bonding gaze and said, in a weirdly subdued voice, "Bill, this is Lexie. She's my right hand."

Bill's gaze, more inebriated by desire than the two empty bottles of wine, was still affixed on Heidi as she turned to introduce Lexie. In a similarly unconventional tone he burbled, "Hi Lexie, great to meet you."

"Good to meet you as well," Lexie automatically replied, though her instinct sensors were shrieking that something was definitely not right with this scene. She knew Heidi would do anything not to leave empty-handed, though she wasn't sure how far "anything" could be stretched. She decided to take control.

"OK Heidi, we must get you ready for dinner. Bill, was it? Thanks again for the lift."

"Yes, thank you Bill," Heidi echoed with a sultry slur, eyes returning to lock one final time with his blue horizon-like irises. "I look forward to seeing you at the conference."

"Yes, me too," came his quick reply.

Lexie led Heidi out of the plane, gently placing the LoveBomb, unloaded and waiting, into the trunk. She knew from experience to make sure Heidi got in the car without slipping on the floor mat, banging her head on the ceiling, or trying to buckle her seat belt into the driver's side latch.

"Heidi!" Lexie sternly started as soon as the plane was blurring in the rear view mirror, "WHAT was that all about?"

Heidi, who seemed almost as stunned as Lexie as to what had just transpired, just sat there in her seat, looking through the whizzing forest, vainly hoping to catch a patch of river or lake water to remind her of Bill.

"I don't know Lexie," she replied with a dichotomous mix of serious playfulness. "I don't know…"

# 37

## Keeping Up with Delisle

Lucy was beside herself. She was convinced beyond the reflection of a doubt that Heidi and crew were at the center of the good, the bad and the ugly of what was happening around the world. She was beside herself because she didn't know what to do.

On the one hand, she respected Heidi to a degree that some might conjecture she had an altar set up in her house to pay daily homage to Heidi's spirit. She was enamored with everything for which Heidi effortlessly stood: equality, justice, nurturing and, above all, peace. She'd pored through Illumina's Annual Reports, financial analyst write ups, the firestorm of online fodder, and profiles ranging from *The Economist* to *The New Yorker* to *Vanity Fair* and *Rolling Stone*. If Lucy ever had a baby, regardless of its gender, she hoped it would be like Heidi.

On the other hand, the disruptions Heidi had potentially caused were not inconsequential. And though Lucy realized many of the downstream impacts couldn't have been foreseen, Heidi's interference was pushing the world in some very needed directions. That said, Heidi's work also threatened America's interests. Or at least that was how her boss viewed it.

She had seen Carl sitting morosely in his leather seat, scotch in hand, staring out his window with a look of utter resignation on his face. He wasn't ready for what lay ahead for the States and the rest of World and, deep down inside, he was scared. His control, and U.S. control, of world events was slipping away faster than whoever was dominating the global pop music charts. Reading his expression, Lucy imagined him yearning for the days of the Cold War because at least then he knew who he was fighting, and actions followed a predictable script. The world Heidi and her crew had unleashed actually clarified, from her perspective, who the current good and bad guys were. But now the predictability factor had been removed faster than his daughter's prom dress probably had been on that special night. He was terrified.

Lucy set up a meeting with Carl to share her findings. She would have to give him an update on the bottle manufacturers and distribution channels, which had brought her to a dead end. She would also give him an overview of the cast of characters she had (accurately) linked to Heidi, including Qin, with histories, files and recent travels, at least those that could be tracked. She also prepared an analysis of people she believed had been "influenced" by Heidi and crew, with vague predictions about their future behaviors which, as time sped on, turned out to be fairly spot on. Lucy had simply asked herself, "What would Heidi have done if faced with XYZ situation?" Surprisingly (at least to her), she realized asking herself the same question would deliver roughly the same answer.

The more Lucy understood, the more it all made sense. The only thing that truly baffled her was how exactly Heidi could be directing these men to be sane. It was almost as if she'd infiltrated their minds, though Lucy knew Carl's knee-jerk reaction was born out of too many viewings of the Manchurian Candidate rather than an objective view of the facts.

Lucy presented her findings to Carl, who actively listened, didn't interrupt and actually thanked her for doing a great job. Lucy, sensing a shifting of direction, asked for a little more time and some resources to "explore" Heidi, which Carl authorized on the spot. As she elatedly left his office, she surmised that Heidi's influence may have actually, unknowingly, through some serendipitous, circuitous route, reached Carl as well…and she wasn't going to question it. *Challenging times call for challenging actions*, she thought. And who knows, perhaps his field of vision had been so shaken, exhausted and proven to be inadequate in the current global landscape, he would grasp at any alternate reality that might provide him a degree of understanding and refuge.

Whatever the reason, Lucy was enthused. This was her time to shine. After all, from her perspective, it was the cracked ones who let the light through, and she was happily cracked.[191]

[191] Evan Schultz

# 38

## Simple

At a high level, the plan was simple. While Heidi and Lexie would dose the Kochs in Jackson Hole, whoever from TM7 could make it and was willing to put their life on the line would land in Amman, Jordan within the next 24 hours. Gilat would travel there by car. From there, they would track Qin by her MoPhone. Baghdadi would probably have guards, but not enough to arouse suspicion in those around him that the leader of the end of the world was cheerfully enjoying coffee in their presence. And his meeting with Qin, given its super sensitive nature, would more than likely happen alone. Qin was to signal "the time," at which point Baghdadi would be sedated, kidnapped (possibly in reverse order) and sequestered for 25 hours or until his stem cells had been produced and consumed. At this point, he would wake up (someplace?) and it was Heidi's belief there was no way he would ever share a word of what happened for fear of losing face and credibility. He was, after all, the divine representative for the entire Islamic faith. It was a very simple plan.

A few small details came up that would merit attention, discussion and planning once they convened at the Cham Palace Hotel in Amman. Trivial things like the fact that none of them had ever done anything like this before, though Gilat's military service and background were certainly welcome and made her the de facto leader of this endeavor. She was also the only one with a weapon, a 9mm Glock which she casually tossed on her bed as if it were a hotel's TV remote, much to the shock of all present. Shalala's forehead instinctively crinkled a bit upon seeing this grim extension of phallic control. While Divine, Shalala and Elena had grown up around firearms, they had never cared for, nor wanted to use, them. Gilat sensed the discomfort and empathetically offered, "Just in case we need to show him we mean business, gals. I don't like them either. They can do horrible things to your hearing."

Two other big unknowns: "How will Qin let us know when the time is right?" and "Once we have him, where will we go with him for 25 hours?" It would stand to reason that, should the most wanted man in the world go missing for more than 30 minutes, his followers would stop at nothing to locate him. Not to mention what would happen if a U.S. or other nation's intelligence services got a glimpse of him through a satellite, drone, or random visual contact. A concerted missile strike would follow, which would not accommodate the women's plans. They needed Baghdadi alive and in control of his minions. 25 hours would require some extraordinary hiding techniques…and a good dose of luck. As to the first question, it was agreed that Qin's ingenuity and resourcefulness would prevail, and Elena reminded the group that the MoPhones could pick up any cell network, so Illumina's trusty technology should illuminate both the time and location of the snag.

From Elena's perspective, the more pressing issue was how they would get close enough to Baghdadi without attracting attention. She surmised his rock star, most wanted status meant there was a good chance his movements, and availability, would occur at night. Gilat agreed and promptly rented two ordinary-looking SUVs, both with Jordanian plates, tinted windows and functioning high beams.

"We'll need to think, drive and act by the seat of our pants," Gilat pragmatically observed, taking a jolly quaff of a glass of red. "Remember, they won't be on the lookout for us specifically. So long as we remember this fact, we'll be able to move around with relative freedom." The last two words were uttered with a tired tone that echoed the state of women's liberties in that particular part of the world, and possibly the state of Palestinian women whose treatment by their countrymen had recently made global news.[192]

A question deemed less important but worthy of contemplation was, "If Baghdadi is knocked out, how will he be moved physically, and by whom?" Divine shared a hypothesis that he might smell rather badly, being on the move so often and wearing all those robes, a concern to which Shalala, who'd flown in from the States, responded by happily pulling out of her suitcase a full package of Costco-brand baby wipes. "I don't leave home without them," she grinned.

Shalala and Gilat's easygoing humor, which Elena and Divine convivially shared, masked an undercurrent of seriousness visibly triggered with the soft thud of Gilat's jet-black gun hitting the creamy 600-thread Egyptian cotton comforter. ISIS's mass martyrdom, and its impacts on international relations and financial systems, were too prolific for any of them to contemplate too deeply, for fear of a stress-induced breakdown. Better to just know this undertaking could avert some really big, bad shit from happening, But the scale of the stakes at play was underscored when a random channel surf stopped on a sound bite of Dick Perry's Texas-tanned countenance good-naturedly mentioning, "I believe we'd all feel a whole lot better if all Muslims in the States were to visit special facilities until this whole ISIS thing winds down."

The final question that leapt ahead of the many "what's ifs" that occupied the women was more personal. Almost in unison, they chorused, "What about Qin?"

What would happen to her once Baghdadi had been captured, and presumably returned? How would she deal with his ISIS handlers? What would she report…could she report to her government? As these questions quickly filtered through the group's collective psyche, it became apparent that Qin might have knowingly signed up for a mission from which there was potentially little chance of returning, career-wise and life-wise. Gilat tried to reach Heidi on her MoPhone, but all she got was George's deep and husky voice politely requesting the caller to "Leave a message or send smoke signals so I can inform my lady of your wishes." She asked George in a surprisingly dignified tone to have Heidi call her back ASAP.

---

[192] http://www.un.org/ga/search/view_doc.asp?symbol=E/CN.6/2015/5&referer=http://www.cnsnews.com/blog/penny-starr/un-condemns-israel-mistreatment-palestinian-women&Lang=E

And then they were off, driving east toward Syria…

…

Qin smiled as she sat under the watchful eye of a swarthy, head-scarfed man cradling a Kalashnikov in a nondescript room, in a nondescript house, on a nondescript road, in a nondescript town, in a nondescript desert near the Jordanian-Syrian border. She was dressed in local garb so as to not attract attention, and to put her negotiating partner at ease. There was no visible reason for the smile. There was no art on the walls, no TV to watch, no Wi-Fi, and all she had with her was a dark brown, slightly scuffed leather attaché case and a light green roll-on suitcase that looked uncomfortably out of place in this setting.

To someone who knew about her overt mission, Qin could have been reassuringly imagining the positive end results of her discussions. Or she could have been psychologically counteracting the tremendous pressure she felt acting on behalf of her government. All of this was of course compounded by the fact that if things went very wrong or if Baghdadi had lied, she could become a ransom item that undoubtedly would be beheaded, as China, like the States, did not deal with terrorists. This stark irony could have also been the source of her smile, however it was not.

No, this smile had been coming for a lifetime, buried far away under the tens of thousands of false ones she had had to practice in mirrors, starting with her trip to the countryside as a child, to keep herself fed, alive and climbing the steps of the Forbidden City. It was an ebullient smile, a smile of a life mission actualized, a smile emanating from the realization she'd been able to rise above all the petty condescension, belittling, disregard and ignorance she had endured her entire life. All the societal attempts to crush her, her spirit, her *chi*, had failed and were behind her. She now had a chance not to make things right—she wasn't out for vengeance—but to make things good. And regardless of what would happen in the next 48 hours, she would have her chance to make a massive, yet anonymous, mark on the planet. It was a smile of happiness, of purpose, of peace.

Her reverie was cracked by the metallic chirping of a Taylor Swift ringtone chirping from her escort's crossed bandoliers. He deftly plucked a phone out of its pouch, flipped it open and grunted, "*Allah Akbar.*"

Ten minutes later, a small, nondescript car containing only a driver revved to a stop outside the nondescript house and a nondescript Qin was motioned into the nondescript car by the muzzle of a very descriptive assault rifle. She tried to abscond with her suitcase, an act brusquely rebuffed, again with the muzzle. She calmly smiled at her head-scarfed babysitter and with her briefcase firmly in tow, closed the creaky door behind her. The car started sputtering away from the setting sun, east, towards Syria…into the chasm of the night.

...

They drove for about 40 minutes in complete silence. Qin had tried to get a look at the driver when she got in the car, but he too was wearing a headscarf and she could not see much of his face. She had caught glimpses of his eyes in the rearview mirror, emblazoned by the unfettered rays of the fading light, though these eyes did not return her gaze. Rather, they kept looking ahead with the reticence of a man whose ambitions in life had been crushed into an existence of transporting other people on behalf of someone else.

Qin was very used to these eyes. She'd seen them in countless people as they transformed China. They were men and women, but mostly men, whose lives had been reduced to a dispassionate, disengaged function, each redundant day repeating itself until death interrupted the cycle. She decided to focus on the nondescript landscape as it quickly blackened, details agglomerating into blobs, then seceding into the darkness, split by the horizon and pronounced by stars above it.

She had almost started to doze, lulled by the rhythms of the engine and the monotony of the road, when the driver spoke in flawless, British English.

"Qin, so nice to meet you."

Accumulating shards of sleep shattered in a beat of her heart.

"Do I know you?" she politely responded, with an uncharacteristic hint of surprise in her voice.

"I am the man you wanted to meet," the driver casually responded, still looking straight ahead as if he was answering a common question tourists ask.

"And I am wondering what your true motives might be," he said with as much defensiveness as the car's decrepit paint had to protect it from the desert's squalls.

"What do you mean?" Qin replied with a voice recomposed, though faintly terrified.

"I know you come on behalf of your government, however I have intelligence that says you have another agenda...exactly *what* it is I do not know."

*Oh my Mao!* Qin thought, her almond-shaped eyes momentarily becoming macadamias. *How on earth could he know about TM7?* Her mind started to accelerate with the torque of a Formula E race car, overtaking slower possibilities as it neared the finish line of fact.

*Heidi was right*, she thought. *The source must be the C.I.A....And if I've been identified, the others probably have been as well. They must be warned.*

"What do you mean?" Qin ignorantly responded, trying to give her brain even a few bursts of time and space to develop a plan. She slowly snaked her hand into an internal pocket within her briefcase, preparing her MoPhone to alert her comrades that she needed help of some sort. "I am here on behalf of the People's Republic of China to ensure that our interests are aligned."

"Come now, Ms. Liu," Baghdadi casually chided her. "U.S. intelligence services, as bumbling as they may be, are usually right, at least on the surface...I mean, they were able, somehow, to know you and I are meeting."

*Right about what?* Qin thought. She tried to game out the scenarios. What if she was discovered? Could she initiate a successful attack, and what would be the consequences of doing so? Predictably, no avenue was clearly marked and she made the spontaneous decision to simply go with the flow. There were too many variables at play here. Paralysis by analysis could be deadly in this case.

"You are part of an organization comprised only of women, it seems, that is having tremendous effects on the world," Baghdadi returned with a surprisingly perceptible degree of respect (they were women after all). "From some accounts, you may have triggered what is about to happen in Riyadh..."

Why must men always have the last explosion?

"For my understanding, why would the C.I.A. inform you of such a plot?" Qin demurely inquired, though she already knew the reason. Well, at least part of it.

"Good question," Baghdadi said. "Without us, and people like us, they would have nothing to do. It is all about petty preservation of power and self-interests. The amount of money spent by the U.S., and in fact the world, on defense—be it armed forces, "Homeland Security" or intelligence services—is in itself more than many countries' GNPs. And

I must say, it is coincidental," he paused, seemingly wary of exposing the depth of his connection to the C.I.A., "that should we realize our end, an American presidential candidate and party will profit tremendously from our actions."

Qin peered in the rearview mirror again as if to reach into his brain and extract his knowledge. She also wanted to see if there were any lights trailing the car. Not that it mattered… She'd still need to do what she had to do. It was more a question of dealing with what might happen next. A quote from her childhood popped in her head, "To know your enemy, you must become your enemy."[193]

"So," she continued with as much naïve passivity as possible, wanting to redirect the conversation away from her personal agenda, "why are you interested in establishing an ongoing trade for oil via Saudi Arabia with my country? If your end game happens, won't that cause increased friction between the U.S. and China? I mean, I don't believe the U.S. would take too kindly to China having a supply contract with your organization."

"Yes, and that is exactly my hope," Baghdadi replied with a tone so relaxed it seemed as if he was out for a Sunday drive. "Your country needs oil, and lots of it, if it is to continue to grow, even modestly. The world needs oil, and China must protect its interests. You belong to a nation—one of only a handful—that can withstand the almost certain U.S. retaliatory actions that will occur when our deal is done…and discovered."

He paused for a moment, perhaps realizing he had just shown his hand in the Syrian Hold-em flip they seemed to be playing. However, he also knew Qin was no dummy and she was aware of the power her country wielded long before setting foot in this objectively nondescript desert. He continued the tour of his foreign policy strategy. "I, frankly, would love to see relations break down between not only the U.S. and China, but all nations of infidels and the states they support. The more distress in the world, the more unhappiness with your so-called civilization, the more poverty and fear, the more people will become enlightened to the brutal wisdom of the Word of Allah. It is inevitable…We are merely accelerating it."

Another flashback, filed deep in her memory's "to be forgotten" folder, rose to the surface. It was of Mao's voice on the radio, saying

---

[193] Sun Tzu, *The Art of War.*

pretty much the same thing as Baghdadi, except the source of Mao's supremacy was his little red book in lieu of the Qu'ran. Books written by men, for men, to vainly try to control men.

Qin momentarily wondered why her childhood was making such a scene in this most unusual and delicate situation. Maybe this was what happened to you before you died? She couldn't dwell on this slightly irrational hypothesis at the present moment however. She had to remain focused on the tasks at hand. Nonchalantly, she glanced down at her lap with a tired and slightly defeated body posture meant to convey she understood and saw potential in Baghdadi's plan for global domination. Actually, she wanted to make sure she pressed the correct button on her MoPhone that sent a quick, pre-typed message to TM7 that read, "I'm ready. Approach with caution." In case her attempt failed, she didn't want the rest of her troupe arriving with metaphorical bells on only to be slaughtered.

...

Approximately 13 thousand miles away, at a plenary session, two devices softly purred and two women decorously made their way outside the hall. They had both received an important message to review.

...

"So," Qin inquired, taking a diplomatic tact and showing no signs of fear, though the question she was about to ask was key to *when* and *what* would happen next, "will we be stopping somewhere or shall we start discussing the terms of our deal now?"

"We can start discussing them now, if you'd like," Baghdadi replied, his emotionless countenance cagily caching his plan, "However, I'd also like to understand what else you are up to…"

"Ok," Qin said, matter-of-factly plucking a pad of paper from her case and rummaging for a pen. "I'd like to start by understanding how many barrels you believe you'll be able to safely produce over the next five years." Halfway through the question, the pen could be heard softly hitting the floor mat of the car. Qin bent over, found it after a little searching in the dark, picked it up and rose with it in her left hand and her right shoe in her right hand. The shoe looked like nothing more than a ballet flat, except, if one looked hard enough and knew what to look for, they'd see a thin layer of color-matched steel between the sole and the bottom of the shoe. Though it wouldn't make it through airport security, it easily evaded the wand test she'd gone through while waiting, and smiling, for the introduction to Baghdadi.

There was a specific part of the back of the head, directly under the skull cap, which was particularly vulnerable to blows, at least if you wanted to knock someone out, which was Qin's intent. She knew it was a risky move. If she didn't succeed with the first blow, subsequent attempts would be considerably more difficult as her target would probably have a hint he was under attack. And if she was successful, depending on how his body might crumple, their current speed and direction could both be issues.

These risks understood, she had the gift of surprise on her side. Though the C.I.A., and thus Baghdadi, knew about TM7, they didn't seem to know how TM7 was pulling levers behind global curtains. In addition, there had been no outright physical violence thus far, and Qin had given Baghdadi no indication she was plotting to commit such a male act.

And it came, with a force that made Qin's bra tremble. Though she had often imagined striking or slapping men for being men, she had never actually done so until now. The release of pent-up frustration, accumulated over decades of daily incidents, was powerful and unexpectedly pleasing. Feeling the butt of her ballet flat connect first with his flesh and then with the hardness of his bone sent a reverberation through her gripped fingers, up her arm, to her brain, which thoroughly enjoyed the experience. Women have testosterone in them as well. She hit him a second time, though more so for the sheer pleasure of it, as his frame was already collapsing onto the steering wheel and the horn, which kept bleating until the car rolled to a stop. His right foot fortunately fell off the gas pedal. She reached over, pushed him aside, and guided the car as it was heading for a rather menacing cluster of wind-sharpened rocks. Other than the fact she had little idea where she was, had no clue if Baghdadi had a check-in plan, and could only hope her back-up team (and LoveBomb) were on their way, her mission thus far was an unqualified success.

After exiting the car and fist pumping the sky (like a Will Smith movie character on reflection), with adrenaline-infused effort, she was able to drag Baghdadi's unconscious form to the back of the car, tie his hands behind his back with her head scarf and, as gently as possible, hoist him into the trunk. She also searched him and the trunk for weapons, and removed a fairly hardcore-looking pistol and an Illumina phone from under his robes. She placed the pistol under her briefcase which she moved to the passenger seat, in case it could come in handy. And (taking a cue from Breaking Bad), she buried his phone amidst the jumble of rocks she'd just deftly avoided. *When they come looking for him, every minute of time they spend chasing down his phone will mean time not spent chasing me*, she thought.

Her final act was to take his blood, which she drew with methodological precision from the ball of his foot where the skin heals relatively quickly. Better to do this right now, while he was out. If he noticed any discomfort, it was probably from the small but aquiline piece of rock conveniently placed in his sandal.

Qin then plopped into the driver's seat and, with her adrenaline slowly descending back to Earth, peeled out heading east until she was on the pavement for a good couple hundred yards to lose whatever dirt the wheels had collected. At this point she performed a three point turn, being careful not to leave any marks off the road, and accelerated to a high rate of speed going west, toward her comrades, vainly trying to catch up with the faint glow on the horizon. *That should also buy us some time.*

At that moment she realized, for the first time in her life, she was beholden to no man.

"I have met the enemy and he is ours," she grinned, whispering into her MoPhone, which dutifully pushed the message to the group. "Where are you gals? Call me."

# 39

## Jerking Back and Forth

## (The Terrorism of Love)

Heidi's excitement at hearing Baghdadi was in Qin's control was almost matched by the explosion of chemicals racking her system since the unexpected spark on Bill's plane. Monoamines, neurotransmitters—dopamine, norepinephrine (also known as adrenaline)—and serotonin had been blasting her reality in ways she couldn't recall ever having experienced. Maybe with Tony, her first love, but never since, at least to her recollection. While she understood this reaction very well, per her research centering on E4 production, she realized she was relatively clueless in understanding "the why" behind the tumultuous cascades of emotions instructing her to walk into walls, much to Lexie's chagrin.

"Heidi, WHAT is going on with you?" Lexie pointedly inquired, pulling Heidi aside after she nearly fell down a flight of stairs while rambling around aimlessly in a euphoric stupor. "DO NOT tell me you are falling IN LOVE with that CRETAN! Remember, he and his brother are the primary money behind the Dick and Sarah show...THE SAME PEOPLE WE NEED TO BEAT TO SAVE THE WORLD!"

All Heidi could stammer was, "Bill is not at fault. It's his brother who is a sociopathic bully."

"WHAT DO YOU MEAN IT'S NOT HIS FAULT? DOES DAVE FORCE BILL TO FUND SUPER PACS? REALLY? HEIDI...ARE YOU EVEN LISTENING TO ME?"

...

Bill and Heidi flitted around the Allen & Co. conference this way for 36 hours, humans replicating the biological rituals of sparrows, stingrays and sixteen-year-old high schoolers. A purposeful glance here, a wanton look there, a rather jealous (in a protective way) stare when Heidi became engrossed in conversation with a much younger and dapper man (a reaction Heidi actually enjoyed.) Heidi's presentation was scheduled for the morning of the second day and she, per Lexie's tweet, "grocked it," generating a standing ovation, with Bill front and center in the audience. Lexie half imagined a bouquet of long-stemmed roses sheepishly presented by the now awake-and-alive Koch, his brother's lock on him dismantled by Heidi's attentive support and philosophical perspective. Behind every wannabe man, there is a great woman, after all.

The whole time, whenever Dave was in the vicinity and picked up the cues, he entered either a state of (greater) denial or condescendingly glared at them, which coincidentally reflected the content of his presentation titled "SUPER PACS: Sorry if you can't fund more than one." As his animosity accrued, so did Bill's blatant longing for Heidi to such a pronounced point that Lexie wondered if Bill's interest in Heidi was driven more by his desire to diss his brother than a sincere affection for her. She was familiar with his type: the world revolves around their bank accounts. Lexie knew it would take a cyclopean force to take priority over Bill's money. Lexie also knew it was futile to confront Heidi with this reality. It would only elicit the, now familiar, vapid stare. At least she succeeded in quietly snagging the vials from Heidi's bag to get them in process. Lexie would be damned if the brothers weren't dosed.

It was in this state, basking in the afterglow of her fervently received oration, that Heidi did the unthinkable, at least from the perspective of her logic-driven friends, who conveniently weren't around.

"Bill," she started with a coquettish smile, "I have a bottle of wine in my room. I'd like to relax and celebrate after being on stage. Care to join me?"

Bill's anguished excitement almost trumped his ability to speak. "Yes, I'd love that…" he plashed.

As they walked toward her room, the anticipation, the charge of the attraction pushed by the chemicals wafting in and out of respective glands was *so* intense looking back, Heidi couldn't even remember climbing the stairs, crossing a bridge, walking down two long hallways or fumbling for her room key. All she could recall was getting so wet she was afraid it would soak through her panties and be misconstrued as a leaky bladder.

The lock turned green, the door opened, and four feet proceeded three steps, just enough so it could close. But before she could even turn around, she felt Bill's hands, strong and slightly calloused from a lifetime of pulling in lines to trim sails, grip her waist from behind and slowly bring her body, quivering from his touch, against his. He was obviously having a similar reaction to the invite, albeit the male response. She turned her head to look at him and found her lips instinctively wanting to touch his, though she was nervous as it had been so long since she had kissed a lover. She worried she may have forgotten how. They had little choice however, as Bill's mouth softly engaged hers, tongues gracefully intertwining with the same ease and attachment as their fingers below.

Time, world peace, ideology, all stopped in the ensuing slow blur. Heidi was pleasantly surprised by Bill's steady and restrained maneuvers. He didn't want to rush and he seemed to want her to enjoy the moments just as much as he clearly was. He turned her body to face his with the confident guidance of a dancer accustomed to leading.

His tongue tenderly made its way first to her ear (which she had fortunately cleaned that morning) and then, with the speed of slightly warm honey, made its way down her neck, following the pull of gravity and the drop of her blouse. An expert hand unfastened her bra with the twiddle of a thumb and forefinger, which she deftly wiggled out of, making way for his wetness to unhurriedly circle her breasts and then, just when she was ready, gently poke, and then suck each poised nipple. Heidi was now certain a spot was peeking through the crotch of her jeans.

Bill continued his run, following the fall line of the contours of her abdomen as her hands clutched whatever protrusions from his head they could find: hair, ears, cheekbones, chin. He unbuckled her belt, unbuttoned her jeans and with startling strength, placed her on the bed where they worked together to wriggle them off, along with her final garment. She leaned back to enjoy, eyes opening and closing in seeming cadence with his brushstrokes, her hand matted in his hair, the other gripping the comforter. There was a chandelier made from random bones and leather straps hanging in the center of this room. She didn't once reflect on who made it and how they treated the opposite sex.

His licks now became intertwined with peckish kisses, down the gullies of her groin, around her bush, up the inside sections of her thighs to that irresistible corner where the arc of the thigh meets the pelvis. He paused here momentarily to ever-so-gently gnaw on this delightful bend until, sensing Heidi was more than ready, he made his final approach. His tongue encircled her with precise care and then, finally, ever so gingerly connected with her core with slow, repetitive, caressing licks. Heidi came more quickly than she had ever imagined possible, and then again, on top of him, in unison, as he let her undulating body command where his mast would best please her inner swirling winds.

Their synchronous disappearance from the conference activities went unnoticed, save for Dave, whose demeanor spiked from subdued pouty to palpably pissy when he noted the two vacant seats at lunch. Lexie also noticed. She was beside herself, arms wrapped tightly around her body as if trying to keep her body parts from dismantling. As lunch wrapped up, they traded a glare that implicitly blamed the "other side" for the respective absence though they both knew what was happening was beyond their control.

. . .

Qin was existentially ecstatic. Whatever was to happen didn't matter to her. Baghdadi could detonate a craftily hidden nuke from the trunk; or her Beijing bosses could send her back to the countryside and possibly prison; or the car could be taken out by a turban-seeking missile. She had finally tasted a freedom she'd been yearning for her entire life and it was even more delicious, expansive and powerful than her wildest abstractions. She imagined details of a life that might have unfolded had she joined the Tiananmen Square protests. But she had no regrets. If she'd joined those efforts, she wouldn't be where she was right then, playing a pivotal part in the future of the world and all its species. For at that moment, the only rules that applied to her were of her making.

She had made a life-changing choice, fully realizing she probably couldn't ever return to her prior life plan without going insane. Her sails were full with the winds of her will.

Her reverie was broken by the electronic dance hit, "I've Got the Power," which Elena had mischievously programmed to identify a call from a TM7 member.

"Answer," she instructed with blissful authority.

"Hello? Qinnie?" It was Elena.

"Yes, Elena… SO good to hear your voice. I have Baghdadi. Where are you?"

"We've been tracking you for a while. We're about 15 minutes away… and closing fast. And my, you are moving!"

"Splendid. Thank you! And, yes, I am moving… I AM MOVING!" Qin gleefully echoed, glancing at the speedometer, which read 140 km, her zeal for what was taking place matched by her newfound, liberated existence. "THIS IS AMAZING!" she said, and though the meaning of "THIS" was vague, perhaps purposefully, all who could hear the call empathized with her feelings.

"Qin, this is Shalala." She apparently had the *message if there is a call happening* function turned on. "One quick question. Does he smell badly? I just want to be prepared…"

Laughter was heard on all phones. "No, I don't think so, though to be honest, I didn't take a close sniff," Qin replied.

It was at this point another voice entered the call.

"Qin. This is Heidi. FANTASTIC JOB!" she said in as hushed a voice of exhilaration. "You're an inspiration to all of us…"

Qin's rare smile was easily imagined by all on the call.

"Thank you, Heidi, for everything. I am so honored to know you," Qin responded, veneration in her voice.

"Qin, and everyone, it is you I need to thank, and honor…preferably alive and in person! Let's get Baghdadi dosed and get you all out of there. Divine, your plan is brilliant. Make it happen. I'll be in touch."

"Heidi, one quick thing," Qin quickly interjected, with a visceral change in tone. "Baghdadi got information from the C.I.A. about us. I don't know the precise channel. He knows I'm involved and, to some degree, what we're up to, though I don't believe he knows how. They may know about *all* of us. I'll discuss this further with him when he wakes," she finished with a stern, diplomatic air.

Heidi's tone didn't mutate all that much, however her usual spritely response time was notably bedeviled as her brain tried to process Qin's discovery. "Ok…got it. Thank you. Everyone, watch out. This could get ugly. Call me if you need anything. Bye."

…

The moment she met Lucy and got a sense for her emotional intelligence, Heidi knew TM7's days of obscurity were numbered. The fact that ISIS had been made aware of them and their scheming (albeit vaguely) was another matter completely. Her mind started racing down the trails of "what's in it for who?" There were many possible players, though most eventually led back to the U.S. military-policy-oil complex. Plus the election was in three weeks.

Which led her back to the two brothers, one of whom she had just slept with 30 minutes prior.

Lexie immediately responded to Heidi's text and joined her at a coffee bar in the hotel. She'd had also been on the call. She watched as Heidi sat forward in an oversized leather chair, eyes fluttering in thought, and then morosely slumped back into its recesses with a look of utter sadness riveting her face. Sluices of tears appeared on her cheeks. The degree of despondency that suddenly overtook Heidi reminded Lexie of when she had discovered Rory had been cheating on her. She quickly surmised there may be a link between the C.I.A. and Bill.

"Oh Heidi, I'm so sorry," Lexie instinctively soothed. "What can I do?"

Heidi stayed still, her diverging emotions wreaking havoc on her thought processes, and sanity. "If it's true, if there is a link, I want his balls flambéed and fed to pigs," Heidi sulkily responded, semi-curling into a half-ball.

"Oh Heidi. I'm so sorry," Lexie repeated. She came over, picked Heidi up and gave her a massive, empathetic embrace.

"How could my read of him been so wrong?" Heidi querulously wondered out loud, wiping a gushing nose with a tissue from her purse. "I was so sure, so sure, he had good in him."

A part of Lexie wanted to say, *well, he has been married three times.* But she knew that wasn't the right point to make at that moment.

"Well, your read on people is usually spot on and—I can't believe I'm actually saying this—he may not know. Maybe it IS all his brother's doing. That's a possibility…"

"Thank you, Lexie. Yes, you are right. I must do my due diligence. I know what to do and I must proceed with extreme delicacy. I cannot and will not sacrifice TM7 for my own personal interests." The fiery Heidi was returning, with an up-to-now unknown degree of vengeance. "I will set something up."

"Ok, great," Lexie echoed. "Let me know if you need anything at all, and Heidi," she said, pulling two signature metal bottles out of her pocket, one marked 'Bill' and the other marked 'Dave.' "Here you go."

. . .

Divine's plan was born out of a movie she had loved growing up, *Lawrence of Arabia*, whose plot line slightly resembled their current situation. Surrounded by enemy forces and earnestly attempting to *do the right thing*," the main character goes into the land of sand to stage a coup. Divine figured that once Baghdadi's absence was noticed, the search would start in local towns within a certain perimeter of his phone and there were plenty of towns, and buildings within them, to keep his men busy for a good while, possibly even the necessary 25 hours. She highly doubted they would search the open desert. Who would ever think of going into that barren and dangerous wasteland with the leader of the non-free world in tow, *especially* if his men had the intel his captors were women?

So, that was precisely Divine's plan. Using Google maps, she had identified five spots, depending on where Baghdadi might be bagged, that looked like perfect places to camp out, and made the appropriate preparations. Sand-colored swathes of canvas and netting with poles, ropes and stakes to create camouflaged shade for both humans and vehicles, 20 gallons of water, local food of various flavors that wouldn't perish quickly, three fashion/gossip magazines, the latest New Yorker and Atlantic issues to hit Jordan, and two newspapers purchased from the hotel's concession stand, two decks of cards, a couple of medical journals for her giggles, speakers for her MoPhone, a case of white wine in a mini-fridge, some "extras," and a solar-powered generator to provide juice for computing/communications, cooling, and a special cooking device innocuously sitting on top of everything in its moderately scuffed crate. Like an explorer—caught halfway down a cliff between a tribe of hungry cannibals above, and an equally ravenous tiger patiently prowling below—who decides to relish his last moments of life enjoying a clump of wild strawberries, if this was to be their end, they might as well go out in style.

All these provisions fit meticulously into the back sections of the slightly battered SUVs. Shalala, who had learned to drive in London and loved it, courageously tried to keep up with the self-proclaimed "Trouble Twins," Gilat and Elena in the lead vehicle. Elena's eyes were glued to her MoPhone, tracking Qin's meteoric approach, while Gilat, accustomed to desert driving, casually hit 160 km on the straightaways. She drove barefoot and unflappably stuck a foot out of the driver side window, apparently trying to exfoliate it with the blowing sand.

Like the turbaned fighters on horseback thundering across dunes in *Lawrence of Arabia*, so did the three vehicles of women in headscarves converge. Before Elena could direct her, Gilat already had a visual fix on a car coming at them at a very high rate of speed. Gilat tapped her brakes once to let Shalala know she'd be stopping and then slowly started to pull off the road, retracting her foot from the window to work the clutch. Shalala followed. In ten seconds, Qin, brake rotors suddenly pushed to their limits, stopped. The billows of dust overtaking Qin's imaginary roadster kept the women in their cars until they cleared. They hopped out of their vehicles and came together for an impassioned and loud group embrace with Qin at the center, this being the first time since Hong Kong they had been together. "YEAH BABY!" Qin cried to the skies.

Then she got down to the business.

"Where is it?" she excitedly asked the group, with a glance toward her trunk that conveyed its occupant could be awake and listening.

Divine motioned her over to her SUV and opened a rear door, where the LoveBomb was good-naturedly waiting.

"The honor is yours," Divine whispered with a grin, flipping up the crate's lid. With her MoPhone she illuminated the innards of the machine. Qin neatly produced the vials and 30 seconds later the countdown began. "Booyah!" Elena satirically cried, raising a fist in the air as if she were in a locker room full of guys who'd just digested their final motivational diatribe before bursting onto the field with all their might. "Booyah!" the other members boomed in unison, the release reverberating off nothingness in the night. They laughed at their utter silliness.

"OK gals, let's get the fuck outta' here," Gilat softly commanded. "We don't know how much lead time we have, and I'd like to get the tents and nets up before dawn, just in case anyone happens to be looking…"

The C.I.A.'s intel on them, which had been conveyed to Baghdadi, was obviously on her mind. Her preoccupation abruptly burst when she blurted, "The C.I.A. could give ISIS guidance as to where we are! Divine, where are we going?"

Fortunately, the sky was cloudless that night with a waxing Gibbous moon and the munificent Milky Way providing ample light for the three-vehicle caravan to backtrack toward Jordan about twenty minutes on the highway (with their lights on), and then about 40 minutes south toward Saudi Arabia, slowly winding their way with Elena's guidance (and their lights off). Eventually, they arrived at a fairly good-sized ravine that ran east-west for at least a half mile. They parked on the south side where daytime shadows would assist in their cover.

By this time, noises were coming out of Qin's trunk (Qin would later admit she hadn't minded when her car encountered some rather rough bumps during the off-road part of the trip). The women paid no heed to what sounded like curse-laden *fatwahs*. They had less than four hours to set up. Baghdadi would see the light of day when it came.

...

Heidi needed a composure break to prepare for her chat with Bill. Normally, she would have gone to her room and relaxed in bed, maybe meditated a bit. However she couldn't, knowing what had happened there, the faint traces of his smell, the jumbled sculpture of sheets and pillows. In fact, she politely called the front desk and requested a new room as there was just something she found she didn't like about her current one. "No, there was nothing wrong," she said. "It's just more of a bad feeling. Yes, please move everything, as I am busy at the conference. Thank you so much and please let me know who gets the glorious job of packing my stuff up so I can duly take care of them…"

She decided to go for a walk, to momentarily get lost in a forest which, given the hordes of press and curious onlookers, would be difficult but not impossible. She left through the service entrance in the back of the hotel, stopping briefly to snag a small cardboard crate of strawberries. In five minutes she found herself in a throng of pines, under a sun-laden sky, though down the valley a storm front appeared to be churning in her general direction. It, like her potentially dark conversation with Bill, would be upon her soon. There was no escaping it; it was better to focus on the present. She popped the berries one by one in her mouth, as her lungs enjoyed hearty gulps of the invigorating rocky mountain air between bites.

She was a veteran of difficult conversations with managers, colleagues, board members, the media, business partners, etc. But the mental framework of this chat was markedly different and it was this difference—the engagement of emotions unstirred for decades—that concerned her. The usual triggers she'd learned to identify and then nimbly discount or avoid would be hidden this time, neatly fitting into a panoply of sexual attraction she had all but renounced. She couldn't disclose her involvement with TM7…unless he mentioned it. And if he did, she would come out, guns blazing, ready to mentally waterboard the fucker. And once thoroughly dosed, she would collapse into the welcoming recesses of an unlit room, drapes drawn, with two bottles of red to scrupulously inebriate her soul. She was ready. She pulled out her MoPhone, donned her imaginary trust hat, and sent him a message.

> Hello. Are you free? I'd like to see you again. Something I'd like to share with you. A storm seems to be coming though I feel like taking a walk. Meet me next to the lake near Old Dollar Road in 10?

His response came quicker than that of a virgin teenage boy.

> Sounds great! See you there!!

Heidi made sure to be there first. She wanted to be able to see the man who'd been inside her a few hours prior, who had brought her holistic ecstasy… while possibly harboring knowledge that would shatter her trust and exploit her vulnerabilities, all for his own self-centered ends.

He arrived in seven minutes, with a look of blissful enthusiasm glowing from his tanned face, eyes sparkling with the hormones of attraction. Heidi had told herself to ignore both his looks and whatever might come out of the mouth that had sensually broken her self-imposed carnal exile. Her senses had to focus on how he responded: his facial expressions, vocal intonations, timing and placement of pauses and, perhaps most importantly, his eyes. She couldn't be too cold up front; if he was aware, if he was the slightest bit suspicious of her knowledge and intent, he could prepare his responses with just enough decorum to pass her tests. She decided to simply stand there with a wry smile on her face as he, and the storm clouds, approached.

"Heidi, is everything ok?" he inquired with seemingly authentic interest. "You and Lexie left that last session looking distracted and disappeared for," he paused to glance at his watch, "an hour and 12 minutes." They started to leisurely circle the lake.

"Thanks for your concerns Bill. Everything's OK. There's just a lot going on in the world these days. A lot of surprises…a lot of change," she replied with a tone of fatigue and seriousness, surreptitiously starting to set a trap.

"Yes, there certainly is," he confirmed authoritatively though with a touch of empathy. "Too much…and way too many unknowns relative to even just a year ago. What's happening out there, particularly in the Middle East, is just plain nuts."

"Agreed," Heidi said and, after a brief pause, followed with "What is happening with ISIS is truly scary. I'd imagine that, given your interests, you're tracking that situation closely…"

"Yes, I am. That Baghdadi character is a real wing nut, let me tell you. Jim Jones all over again, only this time on a massive scale…with a nuclear weapon." He shook his head in disbelief. So far, Heidi hadn't detected anything suspicious. She decided to try a different, juicier lure. "You know, there've been so many unimaginable changes—Russia, Israel, India, Turkey, Mexico—it almost seems like something is happening behind the scenes, something we don't know about." She softly lobbed a glance at his face to gauge his reaction, looking for any sign that he knew *something*: a winnowing of eyelids, a minute flaring of nostrils, an unconscious raising or furrowing of eyebrows. Nothing.

The windy prelude to precipitation started to make its appearance.

"Well, if something is happening and we don't know about it," he said with a sanguine chuckle, "it must be very well-hidden." On the surface, this comment made complete sense. With his access to and influence on the highest levels of politics, and her involvement in the technologies of global communication, it would be difficult to slip something by them. This observation broke down quickly however, for it presumed Heidi was working with the NSA or had special code in her chips that governments could access remotely to monitor communications, actions she was steadfastly against. *Better not bring this up now however*, she thought. She needed to keep the conversation flowing.

"Haha. Yes, I suppose you are right. Say, the rain is coming sooner than I had expected. I believe there is a bar at the Sun Valley Lodge. How about a drink on me?" she inquired, with a degree of frivolity that masked both her intent and the intense emotional dissonance which, even after this brief five-minute conversation, was starting to wear on her.

"That sounds fantastic," Bill amicably replied, his ego immediately imagining another session as a follow-on to the drink. As he steered them away from the lake, Heidi felt odd. Her right brain's emotional intelligence sensed something wasn't right. Something he said…What was it?

"So Bill, what did I miss from the session?" she inquired with feigned interest. She needed time to think.

"Well, when you left, the speaker started talking about…"

Heidi nodded her head every so often, but heard only half of what he said. Upon entering the Duchin Lounge it hit her. "If something is happening and we don't know about it, it must be very well hidden," he had said. This statement could imply he was aware of TM7 and her involvement, and his light-hearted laugh could have been meant as a compliment of a job well done—you fooled most of the world—but not us. The problem was Heidi's fraying nerves were simply unable to focus on how she could test this hypothesis. The rain started to fall in sheets.

She wanted to believe her instincts were correct. Very, very badly. She had just given this man the gift of her emotional vulnerability, a prize she'd previously protected so vigorously. She had thought of it as belonging only to her or "until death did they part." Her instincts still said she had been right about Bill; her analytical side said "maybe" she'd been off. A large part of her psyche resoundingly wanted to show all her cards, but the stakes were too high and the risks too huge. Then she realized that there was no need to come to closure on this issue, right then and there. In fact, it might be better for TM7, and for her, not to know just yet. There was still a reasonable possibility that Bill was ignorant. Time would tell, and regardless of what Bill did or didn't know, time would be on her side starting in a few minutes.

"I'll have an Oban, neat," Bill merrily requested to a young waitress after they were seated in a slightly secluded high backed settee facing a fireplace, his desires only partially hidden. "Make that two," Heidi followed with a markedly relaxed demeanor. "I just love Scotland…Have you ever been to the Island of Mull…?"

The wetness of the rain melded with the physiological relaxation of alcohol. After roughly five minutes of flirty chit chat, Bill apologetically left for a visit to the loo. Heidi seized the opportunity, deftly removing the dispensation from her pants pocket and, after a quick glance around to ensure no one was approaching, added a little spritz to his drink.

Bill retuned to find a lipstick kiss and a handwritten note on a cocktail napkin bearing the establishment's logo that simply read:

*Had to go. Until next time! XO*

Heidi was quite sure he would keep the napkin. And finish that drink.

...

Baggy, or Big Daddy, as Elena jovially called Baghdadi, squinted hard and long when the trunk opened and the sun greeted his face. He narrowed his eyes, trying to identify the faces of the chorus of female voices he'd been hearing for the past few hours. He recognized Qin but that was all.

"*Buenos dias*, Senior Big Daddy!" Elena said with more welcoming warmth than the beams of the rising sun. She helped him swing his legs over the back of the trunk so his torso could be pulled up and out. Baghdadi, whose shrieking had not ceased since regaining consciousness, abruptly (and thankfully) stopped when confronted by his environs, which looked somewhat like a fanciful setting for a video of "Tea in the Sahara" by The Police. Gauzy white filament hung down from the tents to keep the sun and wind at bay. Inside, a few large and comfy pillows of Syrian embroidery were placed strategically at the corner of an expansive but thin, ivory-colored blanket on which a tall black woman and a shorter Indian-looking woman were doing some fairly exotic yoga poses in form-fitting outfits. He saw a small refrigerator with an opened bottle of wine on top, a pack of cigarettes (Divine had snagged them just for effect), a platter of fruit, a low table flanked with pillows, laptops with satellite feeds and what looked like a radar monitor. And, of course, tea. He also observed a grey-haired woman and Qin with handguns in their waistbands. Qin's looked like his, which he noticed had been missing for the last few hours. They seemed to be discussing something important. Like how to further desecrate his mind.

"What's wrong, amigo? Cat got your tongue?" Elena playfully chided. "You are surprised by our get-ups? What were you expecting? Who do you think we are, a cult of terrorists?" She laughed and led him, still bound, over to the pillows where she comfortably sat him down and politely (almost to the point of sarcasm) asked him if he wanted something to drink…or eat. He didn't answer, but just sat there glaring at the moral abominations surrounding him, which he could not escape. At least not easily. Qin and the grey-haired woman stopped speaking and they approached him.

"Good morning," Qin started with a smile. "Apologies, I don't believe you slept too well last night." He kept glaring straight ahead, though his eyes did briefly search the grey-haired women's face. "Who are you? You appear to be a Jew."

"My name is Gilat and yes, I am of Jewish descent, though I consider myself to be first and foremost, a human being," Gilat replied calmly. "And though I disdain violence, I have no qualms about using this," she said, deftly pulling the Glock out of her waistband and pretending to aim at some bad guy (for some reason they are always guys) lurking outside the confines of their enclosure to show him she was no stranger to using weapons. If you have one, she felt, you had to be ready and willing to use it. "And if I miss, Qinnie can always hit you with a shoe," she continued with cherubic irony, drawing on the Islamic version of the raised middle finger. Qin did her best Vanna White impersonation, gracefully demonstrating to her studio audience (of one) how the metal infused feature of her footwear could impact the back of the head. Baghdadi got it, and grimaced a bit.

"Qin, whatever you and your women friends are up to," he began with a cocky, patronizing and pugnacious emphasis on the word "women," "it won't work. I estimate you all have less than three hours to live before my bodyguards track you down, rape you all many times over and then, following the judgment and word of the Qu'ran, behead you."

While he seemed to believe this series of events was preordained, his hubris was notably distracted by Divine, who was effortlessly extending the range of her thigh stretches beyond what was seemingly possible. The curves and lines of her beauty rippled through the molded fabric, clearly revealing that she was sans undies.

In an attempt to regain his composure, he continued, "And Qin, doesn't your government wonder where you are?"

Qin laughed and responded with the zeal of a convert, "My government has no idea where I am right now…and I happily don't care."

"So, what are you going to do to me before I am rescued and you all are killed?" Baghdadi insolently asked, as if he was temporarily in school with women who were kicking his ass scholastically, but knew that once their school days had passed, he would be in managerial and financial control.

"Oh," Elena responded cheekily, "nothing much. We would just like some information from you and then we'll merrily wait," spreading her legs a little wider to brace for an impending explosion, "for the apocalypse." She finished with dramatic bravado, to which all the women, even Divine and Shalala, giggled. "By the way Divine, good wine choice," she added, setting an empty glass down next to a laptop.

Baghdadi cringed a bit but then his impudent poise quickly returned. "By the time you get information from me, you will all be in Hell," he gruffly stated as if that would end the conversation.

"Really?" Gilat countered, doing her best Scarlet O'Hara impression. "Oh Baggy, we think differently." She then produced a video camera already attached to a tripod, and positioned it so that the entire tent, with Baghdadi smack dab in the middle of everything, was visible in the viewfinder. She rotated it 180 degrees to let him have a look at the screen in case he wanted to comb out his beard before taping. "You know what this is yes?" The question was uttered with a twinge of restrained sorrow and anger, as they all had seen films of executions by ISIS, presumably at Baghdadi's command. The mood immediately became poignantly more solemn.

"If you don't tell us what we want to know, all I have to do is push this," she said, tapping her finger on a larger green button, "and in five minutes, the entire world, especially your Islamic brothers, will see you partying with five female infidels. It won't matter if you live or die beyond that point in time. Your Caliph credibility will have been burned to a crisp."

Meanwhile, Divine and Shalala entered into what appeared to be a couples' tantric yoga routine: seated facing each other, legs spread apart as wide as possible, feet touching, holding hands, one leaning back pulling the other forward until their mouth neared the other's crotch and then slowly reversing the pull, both emitting sensual purring sounds from the depths of their abdomens…and possibly deeper. To say it wasn't slightly lesbian erotic was like saying the sky wasn't blue. Baghdadi, and all his parts, couldn't help but notice; the perking up of a particular fold of cloth being immediately observed, and captured, by the attentive Gilat on memory stick. Baghdadi's face turned red as his mind wrestled with possible scenarios as to how he could deal with the PR fallout of getting turned on by an act of homosexuality which, per his book, was punishable by death.

"OK!" he abruptly barked with a degree of defeat, realizing his creed couldn't control his chromosomes. "What do you want to know?" In the same breath, he hissed with vitriol, "If that video is uploaded, I will personally sever your heads and then crucify your bodies…as it is written."

"You see ladies," Gilat semi-seriously reported, "preservation of personal power *is* the best form of logic." She said it as if she was concluding a group discussion begun prior to Baghdadi's release from his car. Divine and Shalala, with a slightly intimate trade of smiles, stopped their exercising and turned to listen.

"All we want to know," Qin said, sitting down in front of Baghdadi to give him her patented look of indifference, "is how and why you got information from the C.I.A. about us." She'd used this technique before, perhaps a few hundred times, with significant degrees of success.

Big Daddy apparently wasn't all that put off by the women's victory kidnapping; his innately male and Allah-granted arrogance rapidly re-ascended. He glared at them. Maybe he did feel a bit threatened by these women, who had, per his sources, caused some downright radical transformations around the world. Which was why he needed to try and overload them with the depth and breadth of his power base, names included. Regardless of reason, it was obvious, given his imperious tone that bordered on demeaning, that he was proud to be in the center ring of global events. His name would have meaning for generations to come…

"China is not alone in having an interest in what happens here," he began. "Many other powers have interests, and the U.S. is at the top of the list…militarily, economically, internationally. You may be surprised to learn that many in the highest levels of U.S. government and corporate circles were very unhappy with the Saudi family's decision to renounce Salafism." He scanned the women's faces, attempting to pick up reactions that could confirm or deny, their involvement in that mind-blowing chain of events. Nothing registered (the women had prepared themselves for this story). Though he was perturbed he couldn't elicit a reaction, he continued in professorial tone.

"For you see, there are elements in the U.S. who *like* conflict, who *like* fear, who *like* to keep its citizens ignorant as to what is truly happening outside its borders. They like it because it gives them control, and they can profit from it." The women stayed silent and unmoved, patiently waiting for the lesson to continue.

"How do you think we were able to acquire a nuclear weapon? Don't you think the timing was beyond coincidental with the U.S. elections?" his flummoxing ego puffed up his chest. "You have no idea what is happening behind the scenes, and no idea who you are dealing with. No clue who the real enemy is…"

"Who is the real enemy?" Qin asked with the perfected veil of ignorance of a student, vainly trying to learn from a master. She knew, at that point, the odds were likely she could get him to say whatever she wanted to know.

"Well, on the surface, Dick Perry and Sarah Bachman, of course," he chortled. "How they can get the American public to vote for them is a true feat of brilliance." He smiled deferentially.

"You say, on the surface?" Qin continued, playing up her subservient demeanor, hoping for another crumb of information.

"Yes, well, you always have to ask yourselves, who stands to gain the most from what happens? You can figure this out by looking at *who* contributes the most—in this case, the defense lobby, the Christian lobby, the finance lobby and, of course, the oil lobby…the Koch brothers specifically. They funded the acquisition of our bomb," he added as if it were a fluttering afterthought that, if it weren't for the strips of cloth hanging from the sides of the tents, might get lackadaisically lost in the sea of sands outside.

Though the women were ready for pretty much anything, this revelation chilled them to the bone. It was a naked exposition of the self-serving nature of men—not women—and the potential for vast death and destruction at the hands of one of the (supposedly) most developed countries in the world. Qin decided to change tactics.

"Yes, yes, the Koch brothers," she said, with a slightly tired voice. "I know all about them. Tell me something I don't know." While the women picked up on Qin's new plan and played along accordingly, Big Daddy was caught off guard by Qin's impudence. He not only took the bait, he tried his best to swallow it.

"Well, I'll bet you didn't know I received the intelligence about what you were up to directly from the Director of the C.I.A.," he offered smugly.

"Really?" Qin parried with just the right amount of ignorant incredulity.

"Yes, he called me," Baghdadi replied with the excited smile of a lottery winner with inside information, whose pleasure was being derived not from winning, but from knowing his scheme had worked, and that he was more intelligent than all the other stupid people who had foolishly participated.

"No way," Qin said, leaning back a bit with an air of utter disbelief, testing his claim and giving him one more chance to come clean.

"Yes, way," Baghdadi impishly retorted, leaning back with the relief that comes with victory.

Qin paused a moment, reflected, and admitted, "You're right. I was not aware of this information."

"And what's more, I know how you are causing all this havoc," he continued, having regained his position at the top of the knowledge-is-power food chain.

"Really? How are we doing it?" Qin inquired, her breath baited with the possibility that he could know something, but more so with a desire to know how corrupt the U.S. intelligence services really were.

"Well, the C.I.A. believes it has something to do with spray bottles," he said. Qin's razor thin eyebrows pulsed but did not move. "And mind control." She hoped her face didn't react to this news. "And," he continued, "my experiences here right now have confirmed my suspicions."

"Which are?" Qin asked with the innocence and vulnerability of a baby doe lost in a forest.

"You are using your sexual powers to blackmail leaders to do your bidding!" he declared emphatically, with the haughty look of a Jeopardy winner embedded in faintly frantic eyes.

Qin didn't respond, but merely swiveled her head, surveying her four colleagues who, in unison, started to laugh uproariously. Divine and Shalala started rolling on the blanket, holding their midsections as if they might lose the wine in their stomachs.

"Darn, you figured us out," she observed demurely.

Baghdadi just sat there, soaking up the merriment in a dazed and confused state, until his senses alerted him to the fact he'd been played… and played masterfully. At this point, he sat back on the pillows in a marginally defeated posture. He tried to keep his eyes closed for the rest of the day as TM7, aided by the speakers, laptops and wine, proceeded to do karaoke without back-up, dance alone and with each other, compare experiences related to a *Cosmopolitan* article on "The 10 Best Positions for Mutual Orgasms," and, finally, entered into a heated debate over the best shellfish recipe of all time.

Occasionally, he would command them to stop, reviving the threat of certain dismemberment and death upon discovery, but his entreaties were duly ignored by the frolicking femmes.

Eventually, the combination of heat, alcohol and exertion collided, causing the clutch to collapse, save Gilat, who maintained an eye on the radar monitor and another on Baghdadi. She was eventually replaced by the others in time.

Eventually, when his predictions of liberation did not materialize, he accepted tea, water, dates and finally, as the sun started to wane, some roasted chicken.

Eventually, at around 10:40 that night, he consumed some water and promptly entered the much-anticipated escape of slumber, aided by a good dose of sedatives, with an extra special LoveTail kicker.

The next morning, he groggily awoke to find himself in the backseat of his car, windows rolled down, completely unharmed, the camp and women nothing more than a faint memory he would try his hardest to forget. His gun was next to him on the floorboards, a marked map on the front seat showed him how to get back to the highway, and a note had been stuck in the mouth of an empty wine bottle tucked under his arm. He removed the note and looked at it. There was a lipstick kiss next to some pretty handwritten cursive:

*Had to go. Until next time. XO*

He growled, scowled, and as he moved outside the car from the back seat to the front, stuffed the message back into the bottle, and threw it as far as his bony arm could muster. It didn't break, but bounced off earth containing just enough stone to make the telltale ringing noise of a still intact vessel.

Hurling *fatwahs* at a darkening sky, as a storm was quickly approaching, he tracked down the bottle, removed his 45, aimed with one eye shut, and pulled the trigger, face and body preemptively recoiling from the sizable power the gun wielded. He had fired it before, but not many times. Nothing happened. Frustration teemed from every perceptible feature on his face and body. Presuming it was a faulty round that had abated his god-impelled duty to destroy the only vestige of his time with those female dogs, he pulled back the hammer, rotating the cylinder another 60 degrees. Again, face and body instinctively flinched as he pulled the trigger, expecting to see and hear the immensely satisfying impact of metal on glass.

The mechanism worked, the hammer dropped, but the predicted reaction was replaced by an unusually muffled "thud" of steel hitting fabric. Abjectly annoyed, Big Daddy flung open the cylinder to see what the Shia was going on. To his utter horror, the packets of death had been replaced by compact tampons whose strings, having been advanced twice, had become wrapped around the locking bolt to such a degree, that more than a bit of calm focus would be required to disentangle the strings and remove the cotton. Enraged to the point of no return, with an infuriated shriek of *"Allah Akbar,"* he flung the pistol at the immobile bottle. And missed.

He rushed to the defenseless piece of glass, picked it up by its neck and heaved it again, this time, point blank into a small wall of rock. It shattered and the note sprang free. Joyfully liberated and dancing in the coiled gusts of wind and sand (much like the bodies in motion the day prior), it too scampered off to parts unknown.

Finally, and definitively able to declare himself victor in that battle of epic proportions, he hastily returned to his car, leaving his weapon to be assuredly buried in the ensuing sand storm. He glanced in the rearview mirror to make sure there wasn't anything else inexplicable showing (for a moment he imagined himself sporting bright red lipstick and, disconcertedly, was not all that put off by this vision). He started the engine, punched the accelerator and hurriedly disappeared into the palace of the swirling winds. He would have some explaining to do.

# 40

## Real Time with Bill Maher

"Good evening everyone. Well, in just under ten days and counting…what's happening? Oh yeah, a few billionaires go up against the common Joes and Josephines to see who wins the election. And, for some reason other than the $2.5 billion that's been raised by Republican backers, the race is too close to call."

"With me tonight, I have **Arianna Huffington**, founder of the *Huffington Post* and **Mark Thiessen**, former speech writer for George W. Bush and Donald Rumsfeld and author of *Courting Disaster: How the C.I.A. Kept America Safe and How Barack Obama Is Inviting the Next Attack*.[194] I should note that many of the claims made in this book, particularly the notion that the torture techniques used by the Bush Administration were effective and morally just, have been refuted by the subsequent

---

[194] http://en.wikipedia.org/wiki/Marc_Thiessen

Congressional investigations."[195]

Mark: "I disagree with that entirely, Bill."

Bill: "I know, I know, Mark. I'm just stating the facts. But, we aren't here to discuss what has happened, or failings of prior administrations to uphold laws and Supreme Court decisions.[196] We are here, and you are here as an expert on the Jihadi mindset, to discuss what is happening over in ISIS-land and how that is impacting the elections here."

Mark: "Well Bill, I'm not sure I'm an expert on Jihadi mindsets, but I do recognize a threat when I see one."

Bill: "So what is the threat? Is it Baghdadi blowing all 5,000 members of the Saudi family sky high with an A-bomb? Is it ISIS controlling the largest supply of oil in the world? Is it getting Dick Perry and Sarah Bachman into office to deal with these folks in the same way Bush and Cheney did… a.k.a. attack first and think later?"

Mark: "Bill, the threat is one of U.S. hegemony. We must maintain our control of the world, or our standard of living, the standard of everyone watching this show, will disappear."

Bill: "Damn, I thought we had at least one member from the 1% who watched us…"

Arianna: "I am not convinced the standard of living for most of our citizens is at an acceptable level now. Incomes for 90% of the population have stayed relatively flat for decades, approximately 50 million people are living in poverty,[197] white police officers are still shooting minorities in the back[198] and climate disruptions, be they droughts, floods, hurricanes, or snow storms, are putting everyone at risk."

---

[195] http://www.nationaljournal.com/congress/senate-releases-historic-cia-torture-report-con-demning-bush-era-detainee-treatment-20141209

[196] http://ccrjustice.org/learn-more/faqs/factsheet-boumediene

[197] http://www.nclej.org/poverty-in-the-us.php

[198] http://abcnews.go.com/GMA/video/video-shows-moment-south-carolina-cop-shot-driv-er-30142768

Bill: "So how is all this linked together? And why is the election simply too close to call? The latest polls, from Rasmussen to CNN to Marist... hell, even the stat nerds at FiveThirtyEight are coming up with margins of error that overlap predictions."

Mark: "Well Bill, the American public isn't stupid."

Bill (to the audience): "Should I mention the correlation between low education levels and test scores and living in a red state?"[199]

Mark: "Bill! Let me make my point."

Bill: "Apologies, the floor is yours."

Mark: "The American public is not stupid. They are aware of, even if they don't understand them, the very complex nuts and bolts of foreign policy, oil supply and military intervention. The current president *and* the Democratic candidate are ill-equipped to deal with foreign situations such as ISIS. So ordinary Americans are scared. They deserve a president who will take bold and decisive actions to maintain U.S. safety and dominance."

Bill: "And what sort of bold and decisive actions might Dicky and Sarah take?"

Mark: "I can't speak for them directly, however I would imagine they'd have no issue with ordering a tactical military strike, like our invasion of Iraq, in order to secure our interests. ISIS is not going away. It needs to be permanently dismantled."

Bill: "You mean *killed*, don't you? And when you say another Iraq, are you saying we should unload another two to three trillion dollars using money we don't have? Just to make sure some hypocrites stay in power? In any case, it may be too late. I believe we all are aware of reports predicting Riyadh will be surrounded by ISIS fighters in the next week, and Baghdadi is personally on his way down there to push the button."

---

[199] http://levileb.blogspot.com/2010/04/final-project.html

Arianna: "You know, I actually agree with Mark's assertion that the American public isn't stupid. They aren't stupid. They're just ignorant, and ignorance needs some sort of panacea—political dogma, social distinctions, organized religion—to support and comfortably fill the void. And fear—fear of things they don't understand and can't control—only highlights and exacerbates the void."

Bill: "Arianna, you are spot-on in my opinion. Coincidentally, let's have a look at this TV/Internet campaign, funded by a Republican 'super PAC' with big dollars behind it, that just rolled out last night and it is taking over every available screen in the country."

The ad starts with a middle-aged, Caucasian mother watching her two kids frolic at an upscale suburban park with a look of unadulterated terror on her face. The female voiceover starts as the camera follows the kids.

"Do you want your children, and their children, to be raised in an equal and just society, just like you were? Do you want them to grow up with the same opportunities you had? Do you want them to worry about terrorists with the means to destroy their way of life?"

The kids simultaneously stop playing and look up over the tree line to see a signature mushroom cloud rumbling on the horizon and what looks like ISIS fighters wearing black hoods running directly towards them, assault rifles glaringly visible in black-gloved hands.

The voice returns with "America, the choice is simple and yours to make. Dick Perry is the ONLY one who can save us. Vote on November 8th and God bless America."

The ad ended with the rapidly stated legal requirement, "This advertisement was funded by the Preserve America Coalition."

Bill: "I can't think of a better example of fear-based marketing than this piece."

Mark: "It could happen."

Bill: "Really? ISIS fighters are going to parachute into Kansas City, go nuclear, and then come looking for *your* kids? I mean, maybe if they were wearing 'Kiss me I'm Shiite' T-shirts that would give them a little guidance."

Mark: "It is a metaphor."

Bill: "However, I have to say, using the woman is genius. The GOP needs the female vote to win."

Arianna: "Both sides need the female vote to win. Women, of whatever ethnic background, can decide this election if they vote."

Bill: "Right on, Arianna."

Arianna: "I would really like to know how ISIS got a hold of this nuclear weapon. I mean, it isn't as if you can just go to a bazaar someplace and ask for a medium megaton device."

Mark: "If we could have used the effective interrogation techniques that I still maintain are ethically justified and within the limits of both U.S. and international conventions, we wouldn't be in this situation right now."

Bill: "I'm going to ignore that comment. I'm with you Arianna. I'd also like to know how those cats got a hold of The Bomb. If they have one, I'll need one as well, and possibly two, just to keep them in line…One thing is for certain however, investors, and Dick and Sarah personally, are loving this crisis. Oil futures, which have been absolutely crushed for the past 18 months, and defense sector equities that have been in the doldrums for years, are going through the roof."

Arianna: "Such is the nature of capitalism. Whatever happens out there, someone is always bound to make a profit, even at the expense of potentially millions of lives."

Bill: "Mark, why are you sitting there with that big shit-eating grin on your face? Let me guess, you own shares in Halliburton and oil index funds, am I right?"

Mark: "I make informed investment decisions."

Bill: "I really do wonder where your information comes from…Well, thank you both for your inputs on my show tonight. That brings us to a close, folks. There will be one more show before the real show on November 8th. Whatever you do, Vote! Good night."

# 41

## Crossing Signals

The women made their way, posthaste, west to Jordan. They figured they had at least a five-hour head start on Baghdadi and his minions, which would put them safely across the border. Though they wanted to share their success and information with Heidi, for some reason their MoPhones weren't working.

There was a brief bump in the plans when, around daybreak, the convoy (of two) was stopped by a group of ten weapon-toting men. Qin immediately disappeared underneath the folded white rug and pillows, just in case she was a 'person of interest.' Gilat handled the men with sturdy aplomb; she'd dealt with delicately dangerous situations her whole life. The men told her they were on the hunt for a particular woman of Asian descent (no mention of an entourage of female heretics meant Baghdadi hadn't surfaced yet). Fortunately, Gilat's story—they were part of an international aid organization—worked. Why else would four women be traveling through one of the most absurd theaters of violence in the world?

No sooner could they see the outskirts of Amman than Qin's government-issued phone went berserk with a revived cell signal. She received five voicemails and eight text messages in rapid succession. Qin contemplatively replied to one of the texts. When she finished, she reported to Divine and Shalala, "Well, my government was about ready to launch an 'investigation' into my disappearance. It will be interesting to see what Baghdadi shares with my bosses about our rendezvous." She continued, "However, no matter what he does or doesn't say, I can't go back. I need to speak with Heidi."

"Understood," Divine replied empathetically. "Let's get to our hotel and then we'll call." Twenty-five minutes later, the five women pulled into the driveway of the Cham Palace. Somewhat bleary eyed from their night escapade, the troupe tumbled out of their extraordinarily dusty vehicles, went upstairs and, once inside Gilat's room, crowded around her MoPhone to call Heidi.

They caught her in the air with Lexie, heading back from Sun Valley to San Francisco. Heidi and Lexie were exuberant to hear from them and, most importantly, to learn that everyone was safe. They listened, entranced, to the whole story. Heidi was ecstatic. "MAGNIFICENT job, gals. Absolutely MAGNIFICENT!"

Qin shared her work predicament and Heidi stopped her. "Qin, I foresaw this happening and already developed a plan to get you out of there, permanently, if you'd like. I can't share details presently. Just let your bosses know you're OK and then turn off your cell phone."

"Will do, Heidi!" Qin said, radiating energy like a Chinese steel plant.

"I'd like you all to come back to San Francisco as soon as possible. The elections are in nine days, and I'd like you all here for them, if you can make it."

Gilat did a quick survey of the women in the room. No dissenters. "We'll be there in under 24 hours," she assured Heidi and Lexi.

"Great!" Heidi beamed.

"What happened at Sun Valley?" Elena interjected. "Were you able to dose the Kochs?" she finished with a deliberate mispronunciation of their name.

"Well we got one, Bill. However, the other one, Dave, was just unreachable," Heidi reported, trying to keep her composure to avoid delving into the gory emotional details. "We tried everything. He is pronouncedly paranoid."

"Well, we got one!" Elena replied. "And before we forget, Big Daddy shared with us, under threat of pleasure, that the Director of the C.I.A. spoke to him directly about us. Though they have no clue as to our *modus operandi*." The group began to giggle, as the scene was still fresh in their minds.

And then Elena matter-of-factly finished her report with "And the Kochs are behind ISIS getting the bomb."

Though Heidi's composure was unwavering, something inside her, something immeasurably deep, disintegrated upon hearing this news. The blood drained from her face as her spirit visibly withered, leaving a frail and fragile frame upon which muscle and skin merely hung. Lexie sat back and covered her mouth with both hands.

Heidi grimly grappled with this explosive information. After an unnervingly drawn-out pause, her mouth slowly started to form words. "Elena, this is very important. What exactly did Baghdadi say? Did he say they were both involved? Or just one?"

"He just said the Koch brothers," Elena replied. Noting the seriousness of Heidi's reaction she followed with, "He wasn't specific... Heidi, are you OK?"

"Yes, I'm fine," Heidi said, though the look in her and Lexie's eyes told a voluminously different story. "We'll download when we see you all. Again my magnificent femmes, fantastic work. Stick together. And don't take any chances. I don't care if the C.I.A. knows about us. It's the fact that the Director spoke with Baghdadi, and the fact that the Koch's are behind the bomb, that have me on high alert. There are too many hearts of male darkness in positions of power out there. Can't wait to see you all! Bye."

. . .

Heidi asked the pilot to stay in the air for an additional 30 minutes. She needed more time in her world to mentally and emotionally unpack the news, to figure out what parts she wanted to (or needed to) compartmentalize and then to develop next steps. She had shared most of the details of her Bill-thing with Lexie, who was still having difficulties understanding the whole scene. And while her history with Rory gave her ample content with which to spar, she was also somewhat able to put herself in Heidi's pumps, to sympathize with the insane rush of attraction that had been dormant by design for decades. She could still remember when it happened to her.

Twenty-five minutes and a healthy, basil syrup-infused martini later, Heidi had developed an outline of a plan that would hopefully save her sanity *and* the election (and by extension, the world). Somewhat to assuage Lexie and to mark the upcoming compilation of all their efforts, they decided to name this scheme "The Final Fling." The first step required Heidi to present to the rest of TM7 what exactly had happened over the last few days, from Vineyard to Valley. She had to disclose the facts, her feelings and the potential fallout. And to ask each member for her forgiveness.

The step after that was to have a little chat with Bill.

. . .

Bill knew he was on Dave's shit list. In fact, he knew he was never off it; it was more a question of his relative position on the list. From the moment Dave saw Heidi on their plane, Bill knew he'd risen at least five spots, possibly overtaking the Sierra Club, and by the time they landed in Ketchum, Idaho, he was pretty sure he had eclipsed the National Resource Defense Council. As the conference had gotten underway and Dave had noticed Bill and Heidi's flirtation, Bill estimated he had overtaken the Senate minority leader on the list. And when Dave observed two coincidentally vacant seats at the lunch after Heidi's presentation, Bill was certain he and the President were on equal footing.

From precedent (which Bill reminded himself did not predict future performance, though breaking with his brother could arguably be more difficult than foretelling the markets), he knew he'd rolled his rock to the top of the mountain when Dave simply stopped speaking to him. Actually, communicating in general. Dave blew right by him in hallways with the same degree of recognition he might have given to a potted plant.

And communication, at that point in time, was absolutely key. The election was under seven days away and their golden boy was currently running second in a race with one winner. Dave, for his part, hated losing, especially when roughly $1.2 billion of his own money was in the game. Not to mention the hundreds of millions he lost on the last Presidential election. The stakes this time, however, were the highest they had ever been, and the potential control and gargantuan sums of money to be made, were unquestionably worth the risk. To be king of the world for at least four years…who wouldn't go all in for that kind of prize?

Feeds of data, primarily from swing states, were pouring in day and night, dousing the three or four plasma TV screens that followed Dave wherever he went. Poll surveys and metadata from Internet exposures were constantly updated by county and state. These changes drove spending by his "super PACs" which, in customary megalomaniac fashion, he preferred to direct himself.

In the midst of all of these data flows, one part of one screen was constantly following ISIS, their advancements, their proclamations, the blatant "Fear of a Different World" they were able to effectively instill in the voting heartlands of America. Just wait until the nuke really goes off, Dave told himself with a gleefully cold grin. If that doesn't scare enough religiously-faithful, tax-paying citizens to vote their conscience and clinch this election, nothing would. The fact that his mindless and weak brother was clueless as to the full depths of their involvement— Bill was only aware of the oil deal they'd struck with Baghdadi should Saudi Arabia be "reclaimed"—was one of a raft of secrets floating on the mixture of oil and ocean water that both characterized and separated the brothers. Given the laws of fluid dynamics, it was a combination inevitably prone to fail.

While intense public feuding with his brother had occurred once before,[200] Dave was confident it wouldn't happen in this scenario. If his conservative calculations were correct, Bill's net worth would be boosted by another $3 billion for merely doing nothing at all, a pursuit for which he was well-suited. Dave was sure the windfall would keep Bill in line. After all, rising tides lifted all boats, except for the 80% of Americans whose inflation-adjusted incomes had only increased marginally over the last 50 years.[201] It sucked to be them.

He had been minutely concerned when, a few days prior, he heard from a source at the C.I.A. that the agency was gravely concerned with some cockamamie mind control plot to explain the bizarre global events of the last 18 months, the fortuitous, potential dethroning of Saudi Arabian royalty being a prime example. Dave glanced at a FedEx envelope sitting under a pile of reports that contained details of this plot (it was better not to use email). He would get to it in time.

---

[200] http://www.nytimes.com/1998/04/28/business/brother-versus-brother-koch-family-s-long-legal-feud-is-headed-for-a-jury.html?pagewanted=all

[201] http://globaleconomicanalysis.blogspot.com/2013/02/reader-asks-me-to-prove-inflation.html

...

TM7 met at Heidi's pad, a modest residence tucked into a very quiet ravine in the wooded folds of Portola Valley, California. Lexie had a place a few doors down the hill, arranged in part by Heidi when she heard about Lexie's college-era dream of living there. The women arrived in the late afternoon and, after mighty hugs all around, sat down to a sumptuous meal prepared by Heidi herself, after which they contentedly retired for the night. Sleeping on a comfortable memory foam bed after their Syrian exploits was very welcome, and they awoke to the smell of freshly ground coffee and omelets made by Lexie.

It was over breakfast, as they were all lounging in their PJs, that Heidi solemnly shared her rollercoaster ride with Bill. The women were initially flabbergasted, stunned into silence by the absurd irrationality of the chain of events. However, they, like Lexie, also understood Heidi was human, and it was her humanity, with all its idiosyncrasies and talents, that had sought them out, brought them together and taken them to this point in time. They knew that behind the lack of logic lay a field of intuition, a limbic ability with extraordinary powers. They had entrusted Heidi with their lives, and had no reason to stop now. Heidi wasn't even able to finish asking them to accept her apology, before Gilat interrupted her and simply said, "Heidi, I believe I speak for all of us when I say, 'No need to apologize for anything at all.' Regardless of what happens, we love you, we trust you and we are here for you, just as you've been everywhere for us."

Heidi simply sat there sobbing. She whispered, "Thank you" and hugged each woman individually.

It was Qin who observed the obvious. "And you know Heidi, if your gut is correct, if Bill isn't as involved as you think he is, if you believe he has good in him, he could be a very valuable ally, especially since he's been dosed."

Heidi, whose vitality was refilling at a rate faster than the Pentagon could spend money, sensibly replied, "Qin, you are absolutely right. And there is only one way to find out. Let's give him a call, shall we?"

...

"Hello? Heidi?" Bill answered with pleasant surprise.

"Yes Bill. It's me," she said, smiling. "How are you? And where are you?" she said, reacting to a din of voices of many sources, some near him, others coming in via speakerphones, all set against the banal blare of Fox News in the background.

"Oh, I'm at my brother's election headquarters in DC. Let me see if I can find somewhere quiet…" Heidi heard sounds of movement as he got to his feet, started walking and then seemed to close a door. "OK, there we go, is that better?"

"Yes, much. Thanks. Sorry I couldn't stay longer in Sun Valley by the way. I had an urgent matter—"

"No problem at all Heidi. I'm also sorry you couldn't stay longer," he said, politely cloaking his desires. "I suppose we'll need to wait to catch up in person until after this whole election mess thing is decided again, yes?"

"Yes, I suppose so. Let's just hope the Florida chads behave themselves," she said with a laugh.

"Haha. Yes. Let's hope," Bill echoed, that hint of anticipation demurely moistening his lips.

"Bill, I need to be open with you about something," she said, evolving the tone of the conversation from flirty to formal.

"Yes, what is it Heidi?" Bill followed, with an abundance of sincerity.

"Well, I've come into information from a very reliable source that says you and/or Dave are involved with what is happening presently in Saudi Arabia—that you helped provide ISIS with their nuclear weapon in an effort to win this election." Her vulnerability reverberated in her voice like a canary in a coal mine; all she wanted was the truth.

"WHAT?!" Bill responded, with empathetic veracity. "That's *preposterous. Completely preposterous.* I have no idea how Baghdadi got his hands on his bomb." He paused for a moment to give his synapses time to fire. "Are you saying *I* would back efforts that could kill hundreds of thousands of people, just for an election? *That is twisted.* Heidi, your source is dead wrong…though," he hesitated, trying to think through the ramifications of letting her know about his family's deal with Baghdadi. Everything…except the ramification of being honest with her.

"Yes, Bill?" Heidi inquired inoffensively.

He decided to pass. "Er…nothing. Nothing at all… "

Heidi, and the rest of TM7 listening in, immediately knew he was lying. Though they believed he was ignorant of his family's involvement in acquiring the nuke, he was hiding something. Something big, revealing and damaging. Looks of earnest disappointment made the rounds.

Heidi, who actually felt relieved to various degrees because he'd passed the first test, didn't lose it and she didn't want to broach the ownership of the Saudi Arabian issue with him then. Better to let him stew on his decision. So, she masterfully pulled off the classic "plant the seed of doubt" head trip, which piggybacked on the rubric of *I know you're lying, you know you're lying, if you'd like this relationship to have a chance in hell you'd better be open with me.*

"You sure Bill?" she said, and without waiting for a response, closed the conversation with, "Well, OK. If anything springs to mind, please give me a call. Until the winner is announced, take care…Bye." She ended the call.

Two thousand miles away, in one of the many faceless buildings on K Street, a man was heard cursing vehemently in a storage closet.

. . .

The speed of ISIS's invasion of Saudi Arabia was reminiscent of the German Blitzkrieg of World War II, though with much less armor and air support. Recognizing these disadvantages, ISIS commanders, who were veterans of many other conflicts, used the pitch of the desert night to cover their advances, blowing through the Iraqi-Saudi border in a matter of a few gunshots. Emboldened by this success, their forces roared down Interstate 80 to Sakaka, the only township of any scale before hitting Interstate 65, which would take them southeast, straight to Riyadh. It was at Buraydah on 65, roughly two-thirds of the way to the capital, where they encountered stiff resistance from Saudi tanks, infantry and planes, which slowed down their progress substantially. This was until the ISIS fighters simply went off-road, circumventing these settlements, and deftly showing up the next morning, having encircled the urban area. Any inhabitants and defense forces still there had dug in. The waiting game started, only interrupted by Saudi tanks who broke through the rings to retreat, lest they be sitting ducks for ISIS artillery.

Probably the most powerful weapon the ISIS fighters had on their side was *fear*. Fear of what would happen to those captured who wouldn't comply with their archaic beliefs. Fear of losing the Saudi way of life. And most pressingly, fear of a nuclear device the ISIS fighters only had to mention via bullhorns mounted on pickup trucks to shrink opponents into the shadows as they passed.

It was when ISIS reached Unayzah, Buraydah's sister city a little more than five miles north of Riyadh, that women, silenced for centuries and recently liberated, made their stand. For they weren't afraid of what would happen to them—it had already been done for generations. They weren't afraid of losing their way of life—they never really had one until earlier that year. They didn't fear a nuke—they had tasted freedom and would do anything, even at risk of rape or death, to uphold it. They had everything to lose and nothing to hold them back. In any case, their men weren't doing the job.

The women self-organized into pods of 15 to 20, fanning out to all major intersections where they would form a human wall, interlocking arms, to thwart ISIS's advance. It wouldn't have mattered if the R2D2 bomb-droid had made a flash appearance. The women would not yield without resisting. The act was more symbolic than effective, as the invaders, quickly tiring of their games yet apparently understanding the PR liabilities of outright shooting them, simply tied them up. The pictures and video that quickly made the global rounds were of immense inspiration to women from Mexico to Missouri to Mozambique to Malaysia, sparking global demonstrations in support of their Saudi sisters.

Heidi and TM7 looked on dumbfounded at the raw courage these women displayed, regardless of age or ethnic descent. Human Rights Watch, the U.N., the E.U., and the Global Fund for Women all appealed for proper treatment of the women, many of whom were being beaten as their numbers swelled due to the media coverage and the realization that they *could* make a difference. Although the women knew ISIS would likely reach Riyadh, it wouldn't be without some really brave acts of resistance.

Over the course of the next three days, the closer ISIS got to Riyadh, the stronger Dick and Sarah's polling numbers became.

. . .

There was something about his conversation with Heidi that really started to trouble Bill. Call it abusing brotherly trust, call it his myopia, call it simply being fooled by a master. Could his brother really be behind the provisioning of a nuclear weapon to make his "super PAC"-funded ad a reality 6,500 miles away from American shores?

Yes, Dave was a prick. Yes, he would stop at nothing to win. Yes, he had kept things from Bill in the past, some very important things. But this, this was a whole new level of sickness, of obsession, of madness at play. Doing a covert oil deal was one thing. Aiding and abetting the downright murder of a whole city just to feed his coffers and lust for dominance was something completely different.

Bill knew if he asked Dave point blank he'd get a vague or obtuse reply riddled with pomposity. The strange thing was that Dave seemed relatively relaxed, even though the elections were four days away and Dick and Sarah were neck and neck with their opponent. It was as if Dave knew something the world didn't, something not yet released that could tip the fear factor unequivocally in their favor.

Bill decided to start quietly digging, with a focus on his family's nonprofit efforts, most of which were thinly veiled efforts to spread Christian-centered libertarianism around the world. He realized his probing could raise flags of different colors. Needing to access particular documents could require passwords, or reaching out to people who ran associated organizations and legal firms, people who were very loyal to Dave, as he had hired most of them and paid them generously. Finally, the timing of his inquisition would seem a bit odd. Your family is a billion plus dollars into this election, there is less than a week to go, shouldn't you be focused on those efforts? Why are you suddenly interested in mucking around in these tangential activities?

Nonetheless, something inside Bill was starting to ache for attention. Nothing physical, purely mental at this point, though his gut told him it could eventually cross the great mind/body divide if left untreated. And a part of him didn't want to treat it for, although the feeling was vaguely pleasurable, he quickly realized he'd experienced it someplace prior, perhaps way back in his childhood, and its reappearance was disquieting in a very loud way. Was it a special kind of love that had burned him, before Heidi had been able to rekindle it from long dormant ashes? Regardless, the mere act of deciding to confirm or deny her intelligence relieved a psychic pressure that had been dammed up for decades. Whatever the outcome, he realized undertaking this investigation would make him happy. He smiled, made a quick list, and picked up his phone.

...

Baghdadi made it back to his base with marginal difficulty. He immediately resumed control of his empire after concocting a somewhat believable story about where he'd been: after his meeting he had accidentally veered off the road and hit his head on the steering wheel, knocking himself out. Though he was secretly anguished that his deal with China wasn't going to happen—as he had hoped to return to the Koch bargaining table with the assets of China on his side—he had a much bigger camel to cook.

October 31, All Saint's Eve or Halloween to Christians in the West. The time of the liturgical year dedicated to remembering the dead, including faithful believers and martyrs,[202] was less than a week away and his forces had a good deal of ground to cover if he was to take Riyadh and extract his believers before detonating the largest exploding pumpkin display the world had ever seen. He knew there was little chance any of the Saudi Royals would stick around to welcome him, but this was only window dressing for the real plan.

"I want the American public to be so scared by the time night falls in the States, the only *kids* trick-or-treating will be of the *goat* variety," David Koch's voice shrilly rang in Baghdadi's ears. It was a devilish plan, as folks would already be on edge because of the torrent of atom bomb that had been streamed to every screen in the country…and then, only eight days prior to the presidential election, kaboom.

There'd be no deal without Dick Perry's guarantee that, when elected President, he would recognize ISIS as the lawful owners of the Saudi Arabian Peninsula (*implying* the UAE, Qatar, Bahrain, Oman and Yemen were part of the deal) and would extend all rights and privileges of foreign powers thereto. The only condition Dave insisted on (albeit obliquely), was that ISIS cease all future expansions, with the exception of their madrasas because "the folks who come out of those programs are exactly what the C.I.A., Pentagon and Department of Homeland Security need to stay in business." Dave obviously understood the link between terror and control.

Baghdadi was so close to embedding his name into the stone of global history, joining the most powerful military figures of the last two millennia: Alexander the Great, Genghis Khan, Muhammad, Napoleon, Hitler… His name would never die. It was only a matter of time.

---

[202] http://en.wikipedia.org/wiki/Halloween

# 42

## God Is Great

Dave Koch was momentarily ecstatic, literally jumping out of his seat with excitement. It wasn't because his billion-dollar bet appeared to be paying off in some key states. It wasn't because his Congressionally-funded efforts to curtail U.S. military involvement in Saudi Arabia continued to hold fast.

It was because Megyn Kelley's challenging of conventional wisdom had come true per her saucy, late-breaking story: The "idiotic" attempts of Saudi women and the morale-less Saudi militia to quell ISIS's advances had fallen apart. ISIS forces had neatly surrounded Riyadh, home to four million people. A message telling "all inhabitants who believe in the true and merciful word of Allah to leave the city at once" had been distributed via Twitter posts and radio waves. These Wahabbi-wannabees had to depart in 48 hours, by 6 p.m., October 30th. Perhaps a little early, but it never hurt to be prepared, Dave mused. He needed to make sure the news outlets had adequate time to set up their cameras.

He was tangentially troubled, more annoyed really, by an email forwarded a few days ago from the CEO of one of his nonprofit organizations, an entity established to teach English to "the world's poor and downtrodden." The CEO told Dave that his brother had suddenly taken an interest in the firm's Middle Eastern strategies and finances. Bill had apparently requested bank and income statements for the last year. He was on the board of the nonprofit, so the organization to comply. Odds were the request was a coincidence, and Dave hadn't heard anything else since. In fact, come to think of it, he hadn't even seen his slothful sibling during the last two days. Anyway, he couldn't be bothered by something so banal at this precise point in time. He was days away from ruling the world.

That night, as he made his way to his apartment in Georgetown, he sent a text to a new number in his contacts. His first attempt failed, and he hurriedly checked his phone for an email to make sure he had entered the new number correctly. How Baghdadi could lose his phone was beyond him. His second attempt, with the change of one number, slid through effortlessly, bouncing off the local coordinate and forwarding to a series of digits that, if ever viewed, would be almost indecipherable unless you had spent time in the Middle East. After the space of two minutes had passed, his phone graciously served up a response.

12 a.m., our time. Confirmed. Allah Akbar.

"Yes, God is great," Dave repeated to himself with a half-smirk. "God is great... and so very profitable..."

...

Bill glanced at his watch and noted it was ten past three a.m. He'd been working literally around the clock for the last few days, tediously gathering data, some of which he printed out and scotch taped to a horizontal 4' x 8' whiteboard in the Four Seasons penthouse where he had recently taken up residence. His brother was so focused on aligning money with mayhem that he hadn't even noticed Bill had left their campaign digs. And Bill didn't mind a bit.

The printouts were affixed to a dizzying diagram of ovals kludged together with lines of various weights, some dotted, others uninterrupted, all creakily supporting a vague pyramid-shaped organizational structure with "Family Foundation" at the top. Beneath the superstructure lay a multifarious map of Koch supported entities. It was so complex that at times during its construction it almost made Bill, who would rather be on water than land, want to order up some Dramamine from room service.

What was fascinating about the whole exercise, he reflected, was the degree of unabashed engagement he experienced as he politely phoned Foundation contacts, requested documents, followed up on his requests, and pored through annual reports, financials, tax filings, vendor receipts and purchase orders. It wasn't a chore, or a bore. It was something that should have been done a long time ago. It was a question of accountability, of being honest, above board and transparent about your dealings with yourself, your employees, your constituents, your government and the world. Of actually doing what you say you're trying to do, rather than serving as retail storefronts, pretty and consumer-friendly on the outside, with duplicitous and self-serving inventories in the storeroom out back.

This was precisely how he was feeling about himself: the happy, carefree exterior shell of a billionaire with a newly discovered and spiritually pervasive sense of guilt, anguish and despair rollicking around his insides over why and how he was spending his time and money. And as his research (and awareness) rapidly progressed, he noticed that his transformation and his desire to right the wrongs increased as well. And there were *many* wrongs to right.

The Foundation funded English-teaching programs, but only if sponsored by brazenly evangelical Christian organizations, with all the spurious Abrahamic trappings of the role of women and earth-beginnings and endings. Bibles were being "shipped" (and smuggled, depending on the locale) along with "humanitarian aid," which consisted of a smattering of very used items and processed food collected from Koch Industry facilities—the weight ratio of books to the piles of tattered kids clothes and dented cans of Spam being equal. And then there was Koch Industries itself, whose oil-based profit-making means, that had provided him with wealth beyond compare, were mysteriously starting to chill his bones to the molecular core of their marrow.

All this discovered, Bill still wasn't able to confirm or deny the information Heidi had proffered. The roots coming out of the bottom of a particular beneficiary were more intertwined than the fabled Gordian knot. He had to keep digging and time seemed to be moving faster than sound…

...

Captain Chavez peered through his binoculars again to get another look. He had to be extra certain that what he was reporting was accurate... there was a lot riding on this stakeout. His pulse perked up when he learned the name of the suspect. It was not every day you were assigned a multi-billionaire to explore, especially one with the reputation of Heidi Delisle. He'd heard stories, filtering through the law enforcement circles, of parties gone wild at her place (at least as wild as technology parties could get). There were other elements however, that made the file fatter. Like how she personally intervened to secure one of his cousins a work permit. Like how she invested in making sure all fellow Latinos and, more recently, other immigrant populations she employed, could read, write and speak English at a professional level. Like how she treated all people with dignity and respect. A big part of him did not want to find anything outside of legally ordinary.

The reason for the stake was sketchy and a bit odd. "To monitor all communications and actions for signs of conspiratorial activities." Why the FBI was involved was beyond him, however he had orders to follow. And besides, hanging out in Portola Valley sure beat tracking the idiots in Oakland.

He and his squad had been engaged in visual surveillance for the past three days and as far as they could tell, it looked like Heidi was hosting a "colors of the world" sleepover. Six other women, from various ethnic backgrounds, had been seen, photographed, and images sent back to HQ for processing. The youngest one was an American named Lexie Seekay, who was easily cross-referenced in the U.S. databases. The other easy ID was Shalala of the Nobel Prize fame. Given his impressions of Heidi, it made sense she would be hosting Shalala; nothing conspiratorial there. Immigration Services were taking their sweet time identifying the others.

What he could see via his long-range lens was that the women seemed to be obsessed with two news stories, evidenced by the huge screen in the entertainment room: the elections and the ISIS threat. Frankly, they were on everyone's minds, so no evidence of conspiracies yet. The women were obviously concerned about both, their anxiety rising as the respective days of reckoning neared. At one point he observed Heidi examining a small machine which he could not identify. It didn't look all that menacing and, given Heidi's profession, he passed it off as yet another piece of newfangled technology, the workings of which his kids would need to explain to him when it showed up on a wish list for $400. He took a couple pictures and tagged them as "unidentified device."

There was a celebration for the Asian woman when Heidi shared some news that, by reading her lips, could best be interpreted as "Kwin is now an Illumina colleague." The ensuing drink fest made him wonder how many square feet her wine cellar occupied.

It was now the morning of Halloween and the news channels were buzzing with the emerging story in Riyadh. Per reports from Fionnuala Sweeney, a CNN international correspondent, an estimated three quarters of Riyadh population—3 million people—had stayed rather than pledge allegiance to the Islamic fundamentalists who had occupied their city. Thousands of women were "confiscated" and threatened with rape on camera if they kept up their nonviolent protests.

"Jesus Christ," he thought to himself. "What the fuck?" At least in his religion, women weren't gang raped on video.

The call came in at 11:30 a.m., just as he was imagining making the neighborhood rounds later that evening with his son, who was going to be a character from the video game League of Legends.

"Captain Chavez, we have received a confirmation that all seven women need to be brought in for questioning immediately. Proceed with caution."

Apparently, either Immigration had come through with some hits or some other information had been discovered. Whatever it was, he had a job to do.

"OK, HQ. Ladies and gentlemen, you know the drill...Frank, you have the back hill, Annie, you cover the ravine. Tom, follow me."

Three minutes later, two bulletproof-vested agents materialized at Heidi's front door. One rang the doorbell and then took a step back so as not to panic those inside.

There was a clamor of boots, followed by a brief pause, and then the door swung wide open. The two agents were greeted by seven women, decked out in cowboy outfits, complete with hats and bandanas, though no weapons were visible in their holsters, "to avoid any chance of being inadvertently shot for being brown," a rather saucy Latina explained.

"Hello!" greeted Heidi, who wore a silver star on her suede vest that read, Sheriff. "We've been waiting for you. Come on in."

Captain Chavez and Tom were taken aback, to say the least. Stunned would have been a better depiction.

"Ms. Delisle, I have been asked by my superiors to take you," he started, surveying the six *deputies*, "and the other women in for questioning immediately."

"Well," Heidi replied, playing along with a bit of cowboy cockiness, "so long as you lock us up, I'm sure we're all amenable."

Six ten-gallon hats nodded gleefully.

"But before you cuff us all," she said without missing a beat, "why don't you, and Tom, Annie and Frank come in and join us for some drinks and entertainment. It must be wretchedly boring out there. Besides, we have something we want to show you. It could be considered 'evidence'."

"Well, Ms. Delisle, we're all on company time right now," Chavez replied, with a discernible crack of uncertainty in his voice, his amity for Heidi making a cameo.

"Oh hogwash," Heidi countered. "Come on in, please." And then, as if she was repeating to a choir, "Do you really think you can dilemma us prisoners?" referring to the classic interrogation technique.

Chavez knew in his gut that whatever questions would be asked would be non-startlingly wastes of time. He made the on-the-spot call to explore. He wanted to believe she was innocent and whatever 'evidence' she was offering could provide him with cause.

"Ok, we'll hear you out." And in two minutes, with a few dried pine needles in their hair, Frank and Annie joined them at the door and were joyfully ushered inside by the perhaps soon-to-be captives.

"Are you sure we can't tempt you with some drinks?" a slightly-sloshed Elena asked the captain with a hint of flirtatiousness.

"Or some food?" Gilat inquired with her best professional hostess demeanor.

"Well, if you force us...yes on the food," Chavez acquiesced, much to the surprised delight of his squad. "I mean, how dangerous can you all be?"

The entire troupe made their way to the entertainment room, where glasses were poured and plates were filled.

"So," Frank asked, making conversation though with a glint of professional data-gathering in his voice, "you're all costumed up a bit early...When does the party start? I presume it's a cowboy theme?"

Heidi replied with a smile. "Oh, I believe the party will start in under an hour...though no one else has been invited. In regards to our costumes, we are The Magnificent Seven." She deftly hit a button on a console and The Clash song by the same name started playing in the background, the infectious beat sparking dance moves in Shalala and Divine, similar to those recently done in the Iraqi desert. This was the most unusual call for questioning the FBI agents had ever experienced.

"So, Captain," Heidi started with an unbroken smile, "I'll bet you're here because someone up top thinks we've developed a way to control men's minds." She sat down next to Chavez and Annie. Chavez liked having Annie's intuition with him. Meanwhile, Tom and Frank did a cursory inspection of the house. "Why, yes," he replied, with surprise, though the fact that Heidi knew all their names before they showed at her door indicated she had information. "How did you know that?"

"Captain, we have our ways," Heidi respectfully replied. "Let's just say we also have little electronic birdies…"

Given her industry, Heidi thought, this shouldn't be a major revelation, though for a moment she imagined the petrified look of shock on Chavez's slightly flabby face if he knew the information came from C.I.A. high command via Baghdadi.

She continued, "Well, I can assure you we have no potions, do we girls?"

Six cowboy hats slightly and sassily shook their heads.

"The things men can dream up."

Annie interjected with a faintly practiced laugh to put all at ease, "Haha, yes Ms. Delisle, men," she said with emphasis on the last word, "can think up some pretty crazy things. That said, there've been rather odd happenings around the world recently. Israel and Palestine are peaceful, Iran has backed away from the brink, China is behaving itself and even Russia is playing along. What's your take on these, shall we say, unorthodox events?"

Heidi replied with deference, "Annie, I am so glad to know you are aware of these issues and developments. I have been tracking them quite closely myself and all I can say is that it seems the world is finally undergoing some much-needed doses of sanity, the current elections and what's happening with ISIS being notable exceptions."

At which point Divine turned a knob on a remote console, softening the music, while she motioned to the TV on the wall. A BBC reporter was sharing a late-breaking update on the ISIS situation. It had been over 24 hours since the deadline had passed, and there hadn't been a word, though there were unconfirmed reports that both Baghdadi and the bomb had been seen on the outskirts of the city. Apparently, a cryptic tweet had just gone out that read "Soon it will be over. Prepare your cameras." Given the context, the correspondent nervously reported, this could be a signal that something was going to happen.

"It seems an end is near," Heidi remarked, her charismatic jauntiness being replaced with a somber soberness that immediately pervaded the room.

"Let's see what happens next."

. . .

On the surface, he knew he hadn't changed. In fact, he knew he couldn't change. He was the Caliph, the human incantation of God, the unifier of all real Muslims, the deliverer of history, after all.

These facts notwithstanding, Baghdadi knew he was changing. In fact, he knew he was changing at a rapid pace. *How* he was changing was harder to pin down, though he realized it must have started with his kidnapping by the female infidels. Could these strange feelings, spirits he couldn't shake that were only growing stronger as the days passed, have been brought on merely by his interactions with those heathens? This must have been why Allah so presciently determined women should be covered in cloth, anonymous in public and subjugated whenever possible.

Regardless, Baghdadi had to keep secret what was roaming through his mind. What started as a trickle of thoughts soon became a rampant flood of inner voices, sniping, whining and then outright screaming at him to not only stop his invasion but, he recognized with abject horror, to renounce the foundations of his beliefs.

As his forces easily overran the border, and made their way south to Buraydah and finally to Riyadh, his internal dissonance worsened, eventually rising to a fevered pitch that prevented him from sleeping. He became glassy-eyed during his daily meetings with his military officers. His only respite was when, upon learning of the Saudi women's nonviolent protests, he blurted out the order not to harm them, but to merely threaten the usual punishments for disobeying. He was in purgatory, caught between a newfound heaven for which he was not ready and recently identified hell, without a Virgil within 1,000 miles to guide him.

And he had these deals to keep with Dave Koch, who had supplied him with the means to achieve his destiny, and Dick Perry, the presumed next President of the United States of America, who had promised him the peninsula. He couldn't back out of those commitments, or the plethora of Allah-inspired promises he'd made to his faithful troops. What would Dave and Dick do if Dick won the election without him playing his part? He would face certain eternal ignominy, probable death and the unrelenting power of America's military might that would most certainly rain down on his lands and people. There was no graceful or even brusque exit. He was fucked.

As the day of reckoning quickly approached, he started to withdraw. He needed to distance himself from the coterie of commanders that typically enveloped him. He needed time and space, to reflect on his life, to boldly probe his innermost fears and regrets, to pray, and to weep.

He had responded to Dave's text, confirming the time of "the spectacle that would dwarf all others." He had personally inspected the bomb, making some final, critical adjustments to its triggers. He had summoned the entire cadre of ISIS leadership to review the device, pose for big grinning group shots and selfies with it center frame for posterity and social media-feeding post-event. And most importantly, to be present, to be part of history when he pushed the button on the mobile phone.

Night fell and the countdown began.

He called his wife and children.

# 43

## Kaboom

It was a classic atomic detonation. A blinding flash hotter than the sun, as the uranium-235, triggered by a chemical explosion, started releasing the force of 325,000 tons of dynamite. Then, the shock wave, visible by the roll of dirt and debris concentrically expanding from ground zero, flattening and burning most everything in its path. Finally, the trademarked upsurge of the radioactive cloud, eventually plateauing many miles above the earth's surface, spreading outward, like grotesque flower petals from a deranged Dr. Seuss book, ready to drift wherever the winds of misfortune might blow. Man's deadliest invention yet, at least to quickly kill as many of your enemies, or at least their citizens, as possible.

These were the images that appeared on screens around the world, at precisely 10 p.m., Greenwich Standard Time, 5 p.m., Eastern Standard Time, 2 p.m. Pacific Standard Time and 6 a.m. Tokyo Standard Time. Bar patrons carousing in London, Boston parents getting their kids ready to go trick-or- treating, West Coast workers catching a quick TV or internet fix, a family outside Osaka getting up to face the day. A band of seven already-costumed cavorting women accompanied by four FBI agents in a living room in Northern California. And a man with a slightly perverted smile in a nondescript office building on K Street.

The world held its collective, horrified breath.

# 44

## The E Ticket

T hen a face very few would recognize appeared on the screens of all global channels. He was obviously shattered; makeup could only cover up so much, though he really didn't seem to care. When he started speaking, slowly and directly to his audience however, his face lit up with the confidence of fact, the power of purpose, and the integrity of doing the right thing.

"Hello. My name is William Koch, though you can call me Bill, and I thank you for your attention this evening. This film is what my brother, David, wanted to actually happen tonight in Riyadh, Saudi Arabia, at this precise moment, as a means to secure the election of Dick Perry and Sarah Bachman as President and Vice President of the United States of America." He briefly paused for breath, and then calmly resumed.

"I know this because I have acquired incontrovertible evidence," he continued, brandishing some papers, "that my brother used funds from our family foundation to aid ISIS leader, Abu Bakr al-Baghdadi, in acquiring the device in question from the military forces of Pakistan."

The world gasped in collective oneness.

"Further, I'm aware of a deal with Baghdadi, brokered by my brother which, in conjunction with promises from candidate Dick Perry, would give ISIS control of the Saudi Arabian peninsula in perpetuity, so long as ISIS worked in conjunction with other key players to control the price of oil."

"While I understand I personally may be open to due legal process stemming from this disclosure, I believe it is my obligation, as a very concerned global citizen and fellow human being, to make the world aware of these facts so that all those involved may be brought to justice."

Dave and Heidi's facial expressions, separated by 2,851 miles, momentarily became one of utter shock and awe.

"The stakes of humanity's future are on the line. On November 8th, I implore my fellow Americans to think of casting your ballots not merely as a civic duty, but as a moral obligation to *every* living inhabitant of our world, and the world as well. Millions of people have died to give you this right. It is a right more than one billion of your fellow humans still don't have."

"And finally, if a new friend of mine is any gauge of the kind of person we need to lead the country, and the world, away from self-interested darkness, and into the hope of communal light, I beseech you to vote for women who have been liberated from the clutches of the past, in whatever contest they may be listed. For I believe it is only through their intrinsically peaceful and empathic nature at the helm that we have a chance of surviving ourselves. Thank you for your attention this evening. Good night."

...

As it turned out, the E4 (and possibly the lingering memories of TM7 antics) was able to liberate Baghdadi from his hormonal and dogmatic shackles. He saw redemption, and realized he had but one option to make it out of the tunnel of shadow, a choice that could save not only the 3 million people who would have been incinerated/radiated by the blast, but perhaps the entire planet given the collective stakes at play.

There *was* an explosion in Riyadh at midnight, but it was merely the chemical detonators needed to trigger the actual nuclear reaction. They had been reconfigured by Baghdadi during his final review. The bomb's potency was permanently neutered, rendering it a useless piece of metal containing a random lump of radioactive material, which was immediately snagged by U.S. special forces for safekeeping.

The detonation also killed Baghdadi, and all of ISIS's top leadership. It seemed Baghdadi had informed them the firework was scheduled for 1:00 a.m. and just as they were leaving to get out of harm's way, the blast occurred. ISIS would try to regroup from this dramatic setback, however, given the Caliph's death, and his plot to collude with the enemy had been unearthed (and broadcast globally), their moral high ground became a disenfranchised flood zone of empty rhetoric. ISIS quickly joined the litany of groups that failed to create a utopia based on interpretations of millennia-old words originally passing between the mouths of men.

...

Heidi and crew had known what was coming. Or at least they had a good idea. Heidi had predicted, based on her intuition and a strong belief in the power and prior performance of her invention, what would happen to both Baghdadi and Bill. She knew Baghdadi was a man of principals and this steadfast conviction, with a little nudge, would inevitably turn his transcendent tides. Though she was sad to learn of his death, she understood precisely why he did it. Given the same set of circumstances, she would have done the same thing.

She also instinctively felt Bill had a conscience and, once freed from his fraternal foe, would do the right thing. Her only concern was whether he had adequate time before his public announcement to disinter the labyrinthine money trail his brother had constructed.

Making more zeroes, losing many zeroes, having more zeroes than the other guys on the *Forbes* list didn't matter to Bill. Fame didn't matter, and detonating the nuclear Koch family didn't matter. Even the probable indictment, trial, some form of punishment and media mash-up surrounding the proceedings didn't matter. What would matter to Bill was finally having his time for comeuppance, to wave his proud and very righteous middle finger in his brother's cragged face and say, "I am right. You are so wrong. I win." All Heidi had to do was provide him the reason—saving the world.

She had also prepared herself, albeit briefly, to deal with similar challenges—personal financial losses, potential legal actions, falling from fame's grace, etc.—though they all paled inconsequentially when compared to the happiness she experienced of making a positive impact on the world.

OK. Maybe, per Bill's opaque reference to Heidi, there was something else at play behind Bill's efforts. Maybe his decision to go public had an additional reason. Something money can't buy, something that can elude most of us for most of our lives, something that, as our days dwindle, can become all-consuming.

Given the same circumstances, Heidi would have done the same thing.

...

Once Bill's mea culpa had sunk in, the ashen-faced agents, Captain Sensible Chavez, Tom, Frank and Annie, promptly left, convinced that the only threat these women posed was to whomever they might hook up with later that evening.

...

Bill's broadcast (which he made at considerable expense, at least considerable if you aren't a billionaire), subsequent appearances on every major news show and eventual, peaceful arrest by the FBI, were more than the GOP spin mavens could handle. Even Dave's furious retort claiming his brother had fallen under some "spooky mind control power initiated by a bunch of feminist Communists," wasn't able to appease enough of the Republican base who, as exit polls revealed, believed Bill's story. A significant percentage, especially women, reported needing to reevaluate their involvement with the party given "its underlying philosophy, its stance on human rights, and its philosophical effects on Supreme Court choices."

Dave's initial efforts to avoid arrest included propping mattresses up against the windows in his Upper East Side NYC penthouse to keep the flurry of news and FBI helicopters at bay. A viral video of him looking like Jack Nicholson in *The Shining*, taken by one of his staff, probably didn't help either. He was brought into custody, with significantly fanfare. Word was he would be tried for treason.

Dick Perry, who was also indicted, and Sarah Bachman, who, upon learning of her running mate's fortunes immediately declared "The Lord's will being done, I will solemnly and earnestly fill the void," handily lost the election. The two of them joined the ignominious cast who failed to arrogate power using the fear emanating from extrapolated interpretations of fictions written millennia prior.

The vast majority of the world breathed a sustained sigh of relief. The crisis had passed and their future was most definitively brighter. While America was overwhelmingly respected as an icon for the kind of pluralistic, open and advanced society for which they all yearned, they didn't want to be bound to its power. People like freedom.

...

The new U.S. Commander-in-Chief immediately issued a bold statement outlining the philosophical underpinnings of her new foreign policy strategy that echoed another powerful female head of state's prescient remarks when asked what to do about the Russian conflict in the Ukraine: "I understand the debate but I believe that more weapons will not lead to the progress Ukraine needs. I really doubt that."[203]

> "Looking back over the course of our political, economic, and military hegemony, there are a few undeniable facts: we have lost many more wars than we have won, the scale of our military spending in times of peace and war has had significantly deleterious effects on our national debt and could be put to much more productive uses. And when we independently take sides in regional conflicts, there is a high probability that the people we are trying to defend will one-day end up using our weapons against us...

> Thus, my administration's policy toward these kinds of engagements will be based on the notion of 'caring arms instead of military arms.' We will actively support whatever refugee efforts are needed to ensure the safety of those innocents, particularly the women, children and elderly caught in the wrong place at the wrong time. We will not support regimes with whom we do not share a common set of human rights, specifically those of women and whatever minorities, of whatever background, who might exist within their borders. I look to the U.N., recently

---

[203] Angela Merkel, Chancellor of Germany. http://www.reuters.com/article/2015/02/07/us-ukraine-crisis-idUSKBN0LB0IA20150207

untrammeled by politics and self-interests, to take on the main responsibility of dealing with crises of all sorts in a collective and collaborative fashion. Again, too many lives and trillions of dollars have been spent playing kingmaker when, inevitably, it is the people of these countries who will decide their future, and whose well-being should be our primary focus.

Henceforth, whenever I say human rights, I am also including the rights of the environment, as each and every person on this planet deserves to live in a healthy, sustainable, and non-threatening location and climate. And while this may require some dramatic shifts in our collective national and international priorities and expenditures, I hold these needs to be self-evident, as we are all created equal. These rights, then, must be included in the same breath as the pursuit of life, liberty and happiness…We must tend to our own gardens first.[204]

Finally, following the lead of my German peer in her efforts to bring Russia back from military pariah to economic participant,[205] the United States will embark on progressive initiatives to establish free trade zones around the world, and while this may require us to retool our domestic economy, we have done it many times before, and we can, and will, do it again."

. . .

The next few years were trying, as testosterone-pumped men made gallant attempts to regain control. Most notable were outbreaks of right-wing conservative groups, many with religious backgrounds that saw their archaic power base eroding with the now-flowing waters of justice, common sense, compromise and equality. And while not all rivers streamed with the same degree of fluidity and transparency, the laws of nature eventually prevailed.

---

[204] Voltaire, *Candide*

[205] http://rt.com/business/250909-merkel-russia-trade-zone/

Over time, and faster than she had ever imagined, the world Heidi had hoped for started to emerge in the stock ticker data encircling her desk. Armed conflicts dwindled. Nuclear weapons and related delivery systems, including submarines, were decommissioned faster than depots could handle them. Military spending was superseded by economic development, infrastructure, health care, R&D investment, debt reduction and education expenditures, which was reflected in drops in the number of refugees, deaths due to starvation, hunger, orphans and people living in different castes of poverty.

These factors, combined with steadier international capital markets, kicked off the virtuous cycle of growth in output…and happiness. Global initiatives to dramatically and rapidly reduce emissions were undertaken with impacts observed from pole to pole. Family planning became a household concept around the world. Rapes and domestic abuse cases tumbled as enforcement became transparent and commonplace. Nationalism was supplanted by regional openness and cooperation. Divisive dogma diminished and democracies of all flavors flourished. Finally, female representation, and wages, in all levels of business, government, universities, and non-profits (including respective boards) accelerated, which only increased the speed of the flywheel's revolutions.

All because of a few tipped gorillas.

# 45

## Epilogue

TM7 didn't dissolve outright. Given their shared experiences, disbanding was unthinkable, and group texting never stopped buzzing for various reasons—Gilat and Elena trading fragrant barbs, Lexie's latest fashion finds, ranting about people who could use a good dose, leadership guidance, relationship advice, etc. The last thing Heidi wanted to happen, however, was to see TM7 follow in the footsteps of other powerful organizations that believe they could control the world. Not that any of her Magnificents would ever think in these terms; they had way too much estrogen to even ponder, much less play, being God. But she was mindful that their power didn't slip into harmful hands. To this end, she had all LoveBombs returned to her residence for safekeeping. Not decommissioned or destroyed. Just stored in case some random wing nut really started to cause a ruckus.

TM7 was able to leverage the new world order quite nicely. Without any coordinated planning—just following their personal stars—they were able to go on and achieve some notable accomplishments.

...

Shalala married a Brit ("We met drinking Cosmopolitans after all!") and birthed three hooligans, who grew to be happy and confident tax-paying citizens. Shalala also ended up leading UNESCO, the United Nations Educational, Scientific and Cultural Organization, which she steered with grace and aplomb. In ten years, with a revitalized U.N., world education levels, particularly amongst women, lifted dramatically, with the predictable effects on economic growth. Global social dialogues, freedom of expression, the recognition of fundamental human and animal rights, and sharing of a breadbasket of incredibly useful data all blossomed under the watchful eye of the diminutive, brown-skinned, black-haired embodiment of Athena.

...

Divine developed a long-term relationship with a man of Japanese descent, born in San Francisco, hatching two delightful and surreally attractive daughters who, while obviously coming from similar chromosomal backgrounds, were utterly unique. With Heidi's blessing and funding, she eventually started her own biotech firm, Lovebirds LLC, which created a new category of therapeutics focused on personalized hormone balancing to optimally harness the positive effects of endocrinology, based on one's specific genome and age. In her later years, she would return to her homeland and run it.

...

After some fiery relationship crashes, Elena settled down with a Brazilian cowboy she met while touring a sustainable/organic cattle ranch, eventually adopting four children over the course of time because, per a group message, "his sperm are scared of my eggs." She wound up running the Global Climate and Ocean Group at the Gates Foundation, which focused on both policy and investments to synchronously combat our environmental "SNAFU"[206] as she would lovingly describe the global

---

[206] Acronym for Situation Normal. All Fucked Up.

state of ecological abomination. And while reveries of lashing herself to forests never quit, she found the resources and clout of a $40+ billion foundation were handy in making scaled change possible.

...

Gilat woke up one morning in Haifa to find her husband patiently waiting for her outside her building. He was brandishing flowers. "I don't know how it happened," he confessed, all military authority and self-importance astonishingly gone. "The world is at peace...and it is so much better than being at war. I realized I had become so addicted to that mindset of justifying everything as another reason to kill my adversaries, I couldn't imagine the kind of happiness peace brings. I am so sorry for everything I have said and done to you. It was completely misguided, and my fault. And now the ONLY thing I want is for there to be peace between us as well." He told her he had retired from military service, and over the course of the last year, he had been willingly broken and rebuilt by a psychiatrist to prepare for that morning, and whatever days lay ahead. In time, Gilat let him back in. They sold their place in Tel Aviv and bought a slightly larger place in Haifa with a similar view of the sea, where they would toast their fortune, cherish the memories of their sons and love each other as equals whenever Gilat wasn't speaking, blogging or doing book tours.

...

Heidi didn't like playing 'hardball,' though the term made her chuckle given the technology she had pioneered. She wasn't bad at playing though. Given that a substantial portion of China's burgeoning middle and upper classes were enjoying Illumina devices, she discretely "hired" Qin away. Qin would eventually run all Chinese operations for Illumina and, no longer obediently bound to her government, carefully yet openly took on a female partner, and quietly pushed agendas for the entire LGBT community in China. It seemed she had harbored feelings for Heidi for some time however, once freed, the universe of opportunities opened like a giant scallop shell from which her Venus was birthed. Heidi admitted she had wondered if Qin was gay as it was the only conceivable explanation for the odd undertones that kept chiming throughout their adventures to date. The two women, having happily talked things through, became even closer, joined-at-the-hip friends. Heidi would go on to enjoy many a night out in Shanghai with Qin and her partner in the years that followed.

...

It was inevitable that Lexie would bump into Rory as their social circles revolved with a high degree of overlap. It happened at the Jamba Juice near Stanford in Palo Alto, where he took her order. She was a bit surprised to note how seeing him, in lieu of waking buried memories, didn't elicit even a spadesful of dirt. It turned out he'd been caught with the wife of a general partner of one of Silicon Valley's top venture capital firms, and had been summarily (and figuratively) blackballed from that industry. Given the money flow from Sand Hill to all major tech hubs around the world, his future prospects weren't the peachiest. Lexie knew a good bargain when she saw one...and her feminine instincts told her to give him a second chance, at least at employment. She introduced him to Illumina's Big Ideas Group where he flourished, collaboratively developing a line of products based on two words uttered by Socrates that he had ignored during his studies but recently took to heart: "Know thyself." Her college vision of a Portola Valley life, already mostly realized by her own doing, eventually became everything she had always hoped for. Lexie would one day, with unanimous Board approval, run Illumina.

...

Heidi followed the Koch brothers' trials with intense interest. First, she wanted to see how Dave would try to "technicality himself" out of jail and possibly a death sentence, in both U.S. federal courts and the International Court of Justice out of The Hague. Even with his cases being fast-tracked through respective systems, factoring in the predictable appeals, he would be in litigation, in prison, and unable to take part in any activities outside his defense until he died of natural causes.

"Another immensely powerful sociopath brought down by his own doing," Heidi happily observed.

But it was Bill's trial that really caught her attention. She watched each session with rapt concentration on his body movements, facial expressions and of course, every word he said. Then she rewound and watched him again. Lexie, taking note, surprised Heidi with a file of her favorite clips.

Predictably, he was a treasure trove of glittering information about his brother and family's illicit dealings. And though he publicly stated he didn't necessarily want one, at the insistence of his attorneys he accepted a plea deal that reduced his jail time in exchange for bringing his brother, and Dick Perry, down. He was sentenced to five years in a medium-security prison, located coincidentally in Leavenworth, Kansas, approximately 200 miles from Koch Industries' headquarters. Orange was his new pinstriped blue.

...

At TM7's stolid suggestion, Heidi joined and faithfully followed a 12-step program.

...

He wasn't expecting any visitors that day. His aloof gaze out a dust-dirtied window was intended for what he presumed was another reporter or book author wanting to monetize his experiences. He was fine with this, as it helped him pass the time, though he had finished the cycles of purging his past a while ago, at least as much as was feasibly possible. Besides, *all* he had was time.

The visitor's footsteps slowly approached, softly clacking off the linoleum floor, with a perceptible mix of apprehension and anticipation. This was nothing new; people still perceived him as "that billionaire who heroically saved the world" instead of Bill, the human, who was just doing his biochemical job. His wearied stare remained while the visitor got settled.

"Hello Bill," the visitor started with a calm familiarity. "You look well."

Bill froze. The only reaction the voice elicited was a slow closing of azure eyes and a tsunami of a smile rushing to the surface of his now-bearded face.

"I knew you'd come," he replied, in a tone of liberation that transcended the three electrified, 20-foot barbed wire-encrusted fences surrounding them. He opened his eyes and turned to face her. "I knew it."

"I am exceedingly proud of you," the visitor continued with an unabashed grin, a slight jolt of emotion cracking her words.

The next 25 minutes seemed to sail by with a wind of 35 knots blowing behind the clock's arms, spinnaker out. They didn't know where to start and, perhaps unconsciously, where they wanted to end. So they tacked and jibed from one topic to another, vainly trying to collapse the space of time between marks. Heidi shared whatever she could: TM7, LoveBombs, the G20, Baghdadi. Not only did she feel she owed it to him, she wanted him to know, with the full understanding that she could not stop him from sharing every last unbelievable detail with the next reporter who showed at the prison's gate.

For she desired, above all else, to thank him for having the courage to follow his convictions and for doing what he instinctually knew was right. The knowledge of truth was the only currency she could provide him in his current situation. It was all he needed. He thanked her with grace, humility and respect, again off-handedly downplaying his involvement as something anyone in the same circumstances would have done.

Their time was nearly up. He asked, with a look a thousand fathoms deep, if she was seeing anyone. She smiled, shook her head, and then reached into her purse and extracted a slightly wrinkled, white, embossed cocktail napkin with a few handwritten words on it.

"I didn't know if I was going to give you this when I showed up today...and I have no idea where it might take us...but I want you to have this."

She kissed it, placed it on the table and, with a final smile said, "I left mine and kept yours." Then she stood up, turned on her toe, and left with a slightly faster cadence of footfalls that echoed more anticipation than caution.

Bill picked up what she had left, eyes voraciously soaking up the imprint and inscription, as if he was reading the mainsail of his life, looking for a heading draft of wind to help redirect and recharge his bearings before the sunset doldrums inevitably kicked in. He beamed, as if, after 50 years of futile and fruitless efforts, he had finally won The America's Cup. On reflection though, he realized he'd been given a prize extraordinarily more valuable than whatever his once-blustery imagination could conjure.

He would add it to his collection.

# Help Rock the Boat!

Dear Reader,

Thank you for finishing The E Ticket! I hope you found it enjoyable, memorable, thought-provoking and, most of all, inspirational. YOU can make a difference, from how you treat others, what you buy and eat, for whom you vote, to how you dedicate the time of your life.

If you share my conviction that we need more women, liberated from the clutches of the past, in power, I humbly ask you to consider taking any or all of the following actions:

Wherever you are, check out www.emilyslist.org for encouragement and to potentially get involved in some way. If you are outside of the States, organizations promoting women's rights and empowerment abound. Get involved.

VOTE!

Make hiring, compensation, and promotion decisions based on competencies, potential and the ability to make teams work and grow.

Plug the book, wherever you'd like. Online reviews (Amazon, iBook, etc.), blog about it, tweet it, harass your book club to read it, and gift it to whomever you think could use a good dose of E4!

Visit www.TheETicket.com, sign up to join the crew and keep your eyes open; I may be in your area and would be delighted to make any appearance to push this agenda.

Finally, I strongly recommend two reads I have found invaluable to living a human life: *Leadership and Self-Deception* by The Arbinger Group and *The Happiness Advantage*, by Shawn Achor. Both have great Tedx talks on line as well.

My sincere thanks for the gift of your time!
Be well and stay in trouble,

Lawler

May 21, 2016

Made in the USA
San Bernardino, CA
26 July 2016